Praise for
The Unbroken Horizon

"A dual timeline narrative, Jenny Brav's *The Unbroken Horizon* is a searing work of historical fiction that chronicles the trials and tribulations of two seemingly disparate female characters. Through powerfully evoking both the past and the present, Brav presents a poignant and atmospheric portrayal of two lives touched by great tragedy and awe-inspiring triumph. An emotional and sometimes shocking story that combines finely crafted fiction and carefully researched facts which render it both entertaining and informative."

– Erin Britton, San Francisco Book Review

"Author Jenny Brav has crafted a highly emotive story of human connections, survivalism, and the strength we find within ourselves to live through trauma. ... Overall, *The Unbroken Horizon* is a poignant and moving tale of triumph, connection, loss, and hope that readers of accomplished dramatic works are sure to adore."

– Reader's Favorite ★★★★★

"The scope of *The Unbroken Horizon* itself is admirable. The novel spans 100 years between the two women's lifetimes, covering many historical events as well as Maggie and Sarah's personal experiences during those events ... It would be easy to become lost in such a wide-ranging and historical story, however, Brav elucidates the connections between Maggie and Sarah's timeframes with precision and clarity. ... Brav's is a unique style of voice, one that can grip the reader, draw them in, and hold them even after the last page."

– Independent Book Review

"*The Unbroken Horizon* is rich in detail and emotion, making it easy for readers to become invested in the characters' lives. Brav's vivid storytelling and authentic portrayal of emotions evoke deep empathy ... In addition to its captivating plot, the book features an array of well-developed secondary characters, each contributing to the story's depth and complexity. The novel explores themes such as love, loss, friendship, and the importance of self-discovery. [It] is a must-read for fans of historical fiction. Jenny Brav's masterful storytelling and unforgettable characters will leave a lasting impact on readers' hearts and minds."

– Maria Yinks, LA Book Review ★★★★★

"Brav skillfully alternates between Sarah's path to healing and Maggie's courageous journey, offering an immersive exploration of the human spirit. The novel delves into the historical struggles faced by the black community as they fought against racism, showcasing the strength and determination of its predominantly female characters. I wholeheartedly recommend *The Unbroken Horizon* to anyone who relishes stories infused with historical elements or narratives that deftly intertwine parallel characters. Jenny Brav has masterfully crafted a captivating tale that enlightens readers on various historical and social perspectives while simultaneously offering a richly layered reading experience.

– Literary Titan ★★★★★

The Unbroken Horizon

Jenny Brav

atmosphere press

© 2023 Jenny Brav

Published by Atmosphere Press

ISBN (paperback): 978-1-63988-766-8
ISBN (hardcover): 978-1-63988-806-1
ISBN (ebook): 978-1-63988-807-8

Library of Congress Control Number: 2023904114

Cover design by Kevin Stone

No part of this book may be reproduced without permission from the author except in brief quotations and in reviews. This is a work of fiction. Names, characters, places, and incidents are either the product of the author's imagination or, if real, used fictitiously.

Atmospherepress.com

To Dad. I'm grateful to have experienced the purity of your great big heart for the short time we had together. May your thwarted dreams of becoming a writer take flight through me.

Content Advisory

The novel contains descriptions of sudden death, lynching and other forms of racial violence, sexual violence, and mental health struggles. It also contains historically accurate words used for Black people in the early twentieth century (until the late 1910s, Colored, and starting in the late 1910s/early 1920s, Negro) which are not used in modern times. I did consider modernizing the language but upon consultation decided against it, in part due to the large number of news headlines and broadcast quotes, organization names, and the New Negro anthology title (which my fictional character, Maggie, worked on) that used one term or the other.

Chapter One
South Sudan, April 2011

The Rainy Season

Sarah

I woke to a pounding down the sides of my canvas tent, causing its foundation to tremble and shake all around me. The first thought in my sleep-addled, half-Californian brain was "Earthquake!"

When my mind finally caught up with my racing heart and I remembered where I was, recognition pushed my thin lips open in a rare smile of elation.

Rain.

After five months of relentless heat and dust. So *much* dust, everywhere. It clung to our patients like plastic wrap. They arrived with chapped skin and lips, as parched as the land around them. At night, no amount of brushing off and shaking of sheets could eliminate the thin layer of grit that inevitably coated my bed. Dust caked the insides of my laptop until one day it just stopped working, and Okot—my nurse-friend, Hiba's husband and the compound's wizard logistician—had to rescue it from the dead with his magical touch.

I heard peals of joyful laughter breaking through the thunderous sound of the rain. I put on a thin bathrobe over my flimsy nightdress (most nights it was so hot I wanted to sleep naked) and lifted the side of my tent to see Mariol and two of his sisters dancing and splashing in the rapidly forming mud puddles.

The nurse in me cringed—knowing all too intimately that mud is host to a cesspool of disease-carrying bacteria—and wanted to shout at them to go home. A dormant child part of me longed to join in. To be that carefree.

In the moment, I did neither, only tied the flap to the side of the tent and dragged my wicker chair to the entrance so I could enjoy their frolicking and still be somewhat sheltered. The wind was blowing the other direction, so thankfully very little rain was entering the tent.

Mariol grabbed the younger of his two sisters by the wrists and started twirling her. She giggled with glee as her legs flapped like flags in the wind. He threw his head back and howled at the rain as though he were a wolf serenading the moon. His dark skin glistened, and his soaked red shorts clung to his thin frame.

I felt my heart soften, as it always did around Mariol, and the habitual bracing in my stomach relaxed a little. I closed my eyes, remembering the first time I met him, six months before. The small, matchbook plane that had taken me on a cramped and bumpy ride from Juba had just spit me out onto the tarmac. I was tired and crabby from thirty-six sleepless hours of travel. As I teetered unsteadily on my legs, Mariol came up to me and held his hand out, giggling at his own formality.

He tried to keep a straight face as he said in clipped but proper English, "My name's Mariol. Welcome to South Sudan."

I shook his hand and smiled. "So pleased to meet you, Mariol. I'm Sarah," I said, before spotting a sign behind him that had my name, Sarah Baum, written in large, block letters.

After that day, Mariol and I became the unlikeliest of

friends, thanks to his persistence and unflappable nature.

He and his family lived very close to the plane landing strip (and hence to the bush hospital where I worked, since they were 600 feet apart). His father, Chol, came from a long line of Dinka cattle herders who'd lived on that land for generations, originally drawn to the river that ran through the area.

When the bush hospital had set up camp five years earlier, Chol had taken it in stride. In fact, thanks to his father, then four-year-old Mariol was among the therapeutic feeding center's first patients, and after that, the boy became a regular fixture on the compound. He learned English from the various international workers who came and went, and because of that his accent and expressions were a motley blend of different cultures.

Mariol's mother, Aluel, had had a harder time adjusting to the planes and the comings and goings of the staff. Mariol said his mother's family came from a village nine hours away by foot, and he knew she missed them, along with the relative quiet there. They went back to visit as often as they could.

Soon after my arrival, Mariol discovered my habit of an early morning run and often followed me part of the way, mimicking my short, clopped strides. Although laughing at myself was never my forte, I found that I missed him on days he didn't show up.

Over time, my normally steel-clad defense mechanisms eroded, and I started seeking out his company on my days off almost as often as he did mine. I learned to identify each of his family's six cattle by sight—no mean feat for a city girl. I sensed that I needed the joy he brought to my life much more than he needed the entertainment and novelty I brought to his.

*

Small but strong fingers wrapped around mine, pulling me out of my reverie and out of my chair. "Sarah, dance," Mariol instructed, pumping my arms up and down, as though trying to infuse joy and life into my stiff limbs. "Have fun! You need to get more loose!"

I laughed, thinking I could take that many different ways. But it wasn't the first time I'd been encouraged to loosen up. While others' observations felt like judgments and only served to further activate my bristliness, Mariol's unbridled enthusiasm was contagious.

In many ways, he was my alter-ego. His nine years to my thirty-four. His sunniness to my snarkiness. My childhood had been as replete with every creature comfort I could want as it was bereft of any emotional warmth and connection, especially after my father died when I was twelve. A fleet of sullen babysitters raised me, and as an only child, I was perpetually lonely. Mariol's childhood was the opposite. His family had few material possessions by the subjective standards I was accustomed to, but even without knowing their language, I could tell how much love and care they had for each other.

I shook my head to clear the cloud of childhood memories that had suddenly darkened my mind, and as I did, hundreds of droplets flicked from the tips of my long, black hair. Mariol and his sisters laughed and started doing the same. Their joy was catching. Without thinking, I flung my head back and extended my legs and arms out in an X shape, welcoming the drops pelting down on my face and body as they attempted to cleanse me of the stress of the last five months.

A moment later, however, the myriad tasks requiring my attention came tumbling back into my mind, and I felt the tension return to my shoulders and stomach. I waved goodbye to the children and ducked back into my tent to prepare for the day.

*

Seemingly overnight, blades of grass grew out of the dry earth, and yellow flowers appeared out of nowhere. However, the rains brought their own set of challenges. As the skies continuously poured buckets of water down on us, the whole area became a big, wet marsh.

"That's why they sometimes call this part of Sudan the world's biggest swamp," Hiba informed me with a smile, and I automatically beamed back at her. I liked all the Sudanese nurses I worked with, but Hiba was my favorite due to her gentle nature and calming presence, as well as our mutual love of Mariol. She came from the same Dinka tribe as he did and was close friends with his mother. In fact, she had been the one to encourage Aluel to bring her oldest son to the bush hospital's therapeutic program.

A few days later, we were saying reluctant goodbyes to Mariol, who was traveling with his mother to visit her family. Knowing how excited he was and how much Aluel missed her village, I tried to hide my sadness behind forced enthusiasm. The compound wouldn't be the same without my friend, but the knowledge he was returning the next week cheered me.

As it turned out, we had little time to notice his absence, because we were soon responding to the first malaria outbreak of the season. Jean-Claude, the Belgian head doctor, called the nurses and logistics staff into the large admin office at 7:00 a.m. to inform us of our malaria strategy. I would say "discuss," but that wasn't Jean-Claude's style. He had more of an authoritarian bent with a very low tolerance for dissenting opinions. Not usually one to mince words, I clashed with him a few times early on before I learned that biting my tongue was the best way of avoiding his ire.

He stood in front of a map of the region, which had clearly been hung by someone much shorter than his six-foot, two-inch frame, and he had to stoop as he pointed to a village that was a nine-hour walk away since the mud had rendered the unpaved road impassable by car.

"We received a report that there has been a death in this village. You will start with the villages closest to us and slowly make your way out to this one." I strained to hear his low, accented voice over the whir of the generator and the pitter-patter of the rain.

"That's Mariol's mother's village! She's currently there with her children!" the usually quiet Hiba exclaimed, referring to the outermost village Jean-Claude was pointing to.

"It will take us at least three days to get there if we do all the other villages first! Who knows how many people will have died by then? Shouldn't we go there first?" I was thinking of Mariol's beaming face when I said goodbye to him the week before, and the words slipped out before I could stop them.

Jean-Claude approached the long table where Hiba, the other nurses, and I were sitting and stopped in front of me. He fixed me with his cold, pale-blue eyes and drew up to his full height. His sparse, sandy hair seemed to be standing on end along with the rest of him.

"You're letting your emotions get the best of your professional sense, Sarah. For all your flaws, I didn't think that was one of them. We need to be systematic about how we do this. If we go to that village first, by the time we finish the internal radius, the malaria may have spread and caused more deaths. We need to manage and contain it in as many places as we can before we spend an entire day going anywhere."

He's right, it's not safe to be too soft, a familiar voice in my head chided me.

I felt a flush creeping into my cheeks and nodded, not quite able to meet Jean-Claude's stare face-on.

"Three of the drivers will be accompanying you on foot,"

Jean-Claude continued, seemingly satisfied with my reaction, "to carry the medical equipment and tents since the cars are useless right now. I need one of the nurses here to help me, so Kamal will stay back."

This time, I had no trouble hearing him. His tone had a finality that allowed no space for discussion and reminded me of my mother's impenetrability. *No wonder he rubs me the wrong way*, I thought, not for the first time. Old feelings of powerlessness and impending doom rose to the surface, and soon my insides were roiling. When the meeting was over, I rushed to the outdoor latrine and retched.

"You look pale, are you okay?" Hiba asked an hour later, as we got our bikes ready for the trip. Jean-Claude gave us the choice of walking or biking (maybe to give us the illusion we had a say in something?), and we both decided to risk the tires getting stuck in the mud for the chance of moving a little faster.

"I must be blue, then, because you don't get much paler than I already am," I joked, mostly to avoid answering her. Vomiting was a rare occurrence for me unless I was very sick. Or extremely stressed. Neither of which I had time for right now.

"How are *you*, Hiba? Are you worried about Aluel and Mariol? I'm sorry Jean-Claude ignored you completely this morning. That man has the warmth of a jellyfish."

"What do you have against jellyfish?" Hiba joked back, mimicking my American accent.

Hiba had quickly caught on to my particular brand of sarcasm after my first few jokes at Jean-Claude's expense and now often one-upped me in that department. She and Mariol kept me on my toes and laughing, which was a blessing.

"Worrying doesn't help, although praying might." She winked, knowing I was an atheist. "I'm just hoping we get done with the other villages quickly."

Her tone was light, but her usually bright eyes looked tired. I watched as she unconsciously clenched and unclenched her jaw. I squeezed her hand to let her know I knew how she felt. All we could do was our job and hope for the best.

I ended up carrying my old, rusted Schwinn almost as much as I rode it since the tires kept getting stuck in the red, squishy mud. Hiba fared a little better than I did, being used to navigating the rainy season and having eagle eyes for the firmer patches of land. By the time I got to the closest village, she and the other three Sudanese nurses had already checked a fifth of the villagers. There were only a few mild cases of malaria, and the unease I'd been feeling since that morning started to dissipate.

We arrived at Aluel's village three days later, and when she spotted us, she grabbed Hiba's arm and pulled her in the direction of one of the huts.

"Mariol has malaria and is very sick," Hiba shouted back at me before running after her friend, with me at her heels. Her words dropped like stones in my stomach.

When I saw the usually energetic boy lying listlessly on a blanket, sweat beading at his brow, the dread I'd been fighting for the past three days gripped my heart like a vise.

I took his temperature—104°F—and checked his eyes and tongue while Hiba listened to his heart and took his pulse. We looked at each other, the same fear mirrored in both of our eyes.

"Severe anemia," we said in unison. My heart sank. The only chance of saving him was a blood transfusion, which we could only do back at the bush hospital.

I radioed the compound and was relieved when Okot answered instead of Jean-Claude: the Belgian doctor was the last person I wanted to talk to. I explained the situation to Okot.

"In addition to prepping for a blood transfusion, please ask Jean-Claude whether two of the water carriers can meet us halfway to relieve the drivers, who will be carrying Mariol on a stretcher."

"Okay. Good luck. Tell Hiba I'm thinking of her," Okot said.

The nine-hour walk back was a somber, silent affair, save for the occasional racking sobs coming from Aluel and Hiba's low, reassuring voice. We took as few breaks for pee, food, and rest as our bodies allowed. It hadn't rained in a day, and the bikes were rollable, if not rideable, which was lucky since we had the equipment and the tents strapped to them to free up the drivers to carry Mariol. For a while, I had both the bikes so Hiba could walk arm in arm with her friend, her other hand alternating between holding Mariol's hand and mopping his beading brow.

One of the drivers, on a break from his rotation carrying Mariol, relieved me of the extra bike. I caught up with the stretcher and checked Mariol's forehead. The heat from his sweat almost sizzled my hand. Both his whimpers and his silence worried me. I felt dread mounting with each step, and the "what ifs" short-circuited my thoughts into a frenzied fear loop.

What if we don't have the right blood type for the transfusion?
What if we don't get there in time?
What if I'd convinced JC to go to their village first?

Fearing a full-blown panic attack, which I knew wouldn't help anyone, I tried to get my thinking under control.

"You're letting your emotions get the best of you," I heard Jean-Claude's words echoing in my mind. Remembering a trick I often used to relax anxious patients, I counted backward and forward in my mind to try to stay calm.

*

Back at the compound, Jean-Claude instructed Hiba and me to stay with Aluel while he tended to Mariol with Kamal, who was much fresher than the rest of us. Hiba held Aluel's hand and reassured her in Dinka, while I paced in front of the medical tent, trying to catch either snippets of conversation or a glimpse of Mariol. Patience had never been one of my strong suits.

When Kamal came out a few hours later, he shook his head. The haunted look in his eyes and haggard slump of his shoulders made him look ten years older than when he'd entered the tent. "I'm so sorry, there was nothing we could do," he said to Aluel. Hiba translated as her friend collapsed in her arms and started wailing.

I stared at him, my brain unwilling to grasp the finality of his words. I shook my head either to clear it, or to resist reality, but this time there were no cleansing raindrops. No laughter. Only the sharp pain of grief. I wanted to rewind the reel and have Kamal come back out and tell us that Mariol was going to be okay.

He couldn't be gone. He was nine. He had his whole life ahead of him. My mind kept skipping over Kamal's words. Not wanting to accept that Mariol would never again dance in the rain. Never know intimate love. Or heartbreak. That I would never hear the sound of his laughter again. "Never" was an eternity too big to compute in my brain.

"Hiba, JC wants to talk to you when you're ready," Kamal said gently.

After she'd gone, I turned towards Aluel. She was rocking back and forth, as she moaned in agony. The sobs racking her body seemed to come from the very core of her being. I hesitated for a moment, knowing that there was nothing I could do to alleviate her pain, before gently taking one of her hands. She gripped mine back so tightly that her nails dug into my skin. I welcomed the distraction from the nausea in the pit of my stomach. Tears streamed down both our faces.

When Hiba came back out a few minutes later she took Aluel's other hand and we silently sandwiched the grieving mother, trying to transmit whatever solace we could through the warmth and touch of our bodies.

"JC said I should take at least a week off to grieve and help Aluel and her family."

"I'm glad you'll have time away, Hiba, and that you can be there for Aluel. I'm so sorry for both of you," I said, my voice thin and wavering from crying.

"JC wants to see you, too, Sarah." I nodded in acknowledgment, but I needed to say something to Mariol's mother first.

"Aluel, I'm so sorry we couldn't save Mariol. He was more full of life and light than anyone I've ever met. It's so unfair." My voice cracked as I struggled to put into words what I felt, while Hiba interpreted for me. Aluel, still too overcome by grief to speak, clutched my hand to her heart in response, before releasing it so I could go.

I was trying to fight my tears back when I went inside. Jean-Claude stared at me with stony eyes.

"You will have to cover for Hiba for the next week, so pull yourself together," he said, in French, presumably so Kamal, who was taking care of Mariol's body, wouldn't understand.

When I first arrived, the nurse I took over from had told me Jean-Claude was a little kinder to French speakers, but he hadn't responded to any of my attempts to speak to him in his mother language. I hadn't even known he'd heard me until now. But somehow, I found him even more chilling in his native tongue.

"This is their life, but it's not yours. You and I choose to be here, so it's our job to be able to make the hard decisions, to not get attached, so we can keep doing it over and over again. How have you been able to survive so many years of doing this without knowing that?" he asked, with a mixture of curiosity and scorn.

His words slapped me in the face. It took every ounce of my energy to swallow my tears and subdue the grief.

For the next week, I switched to autopilot mode in order to keep my feelings at bay.

Jean-Claude is right, my inner nemesis berated me. *It's your fault you're in pain. You should know better than to get close to anyone. It always leads to heartbreak.*

"I just need to make it until Hiba comes back, then everything will be fine," I told myself at night before getting into my cot, to try to counter the negative voice. My last thought was a fervent hope that I wouldn't have any nightmares. Especially not *the* nightmare. The one that seemed to hijack my unconscious mind every time something bad happened.

Where I was a Black girl, alone in the forest, in the dead of night. Surrounded by white hoods and torches. Barely breathing, hoping they wouldn't find me.

Chapter Two

The Nightmare

Sarah

I'm crouching in tall grass behind rows of cotton. Terror is a leaden weight in my stomach. I can't move. Someone is after me, although I can't quite remember who. In my left hand, I have a bundle of something I keep touching for reassurance. There's a sliver of a moon above me. I'm grateful that it isn't full enough to reveal my hideout, but is visible enough to comfort me. Trees surround me. They are both familiar—I sense I've been here many times—and not. As the sky darkens to a midnight blue, the leaves become indistinct orbs swaying in the wind.

A sharp noise rouses me. *I must have dozed off,* I think, panicked. There are voices and footsteps in the distance. My body's stiff and cold. My legs are numb, and I have to feel them with my hands to make sure they're still attached to the rest of me. My heart's beating so loudly I'm sure it will give me away.

The cotton's long stalks obscure my vision, but the men's voices grow nearer, and the flickering of the torches twirls with the shadows of the trees. They're too far to find me, though, and I breathe a sigh of relief.

Until I hear a low voice I recognize. Dad? I can't make out

what he says, but the response is loud and angry. Then there's fist on flesh and a grunt of pain.

Holding my breath, I slowly and carefully straighten my torso to peer above the billowy balls of cotton. I gasp, and quickly cover my mouth with my hand, when I see pointed white hoods—six or seven of them, carrying torches and sticks. One man has several long ropes. I can't see him, but I know him by the shape of his body: He's the man who's after me. I also see the huddled figures of two other men I seem to recognize. My father? My brother?

The rest is a blur. The men move away from me, but a dim light from the torches remains. One of them shouts to another to toss him the rope. Frightened, knowing there is nothing I can do, I bury my face in the earth and cover my ears with my hands. I count to one hundred and back, but I jump with every noise and crackle and have to start all over again.

Finally, I'm shrouded in silence.

I make myself count a few more times before getting up, to make sure they are gone and because I'm not sure my limbs are still working. My right leg has fallen asleep and nearly collapses under the weight of my body. I shake it to get the blood flowing again.

As I approach the trees where I heard the men's voices, my heart pounds in my chest, and my stomach flutters in fear. Something moves in the tree in front of me, and I freeze in my tracks. I see the rope flashing in the thin moonlight and spot a body dangling from it. The head bobs up, and I scream. I know it's my dad, although his skin is as dark as Okot's. He didn't die of a heart attack! He was murdered, I think.

I run over to the second body, whom I recognize as my brother, although when I look up, he has Mariol's face. I tug at the bundle I've been carrying, and the contents scatter. I find a knife and clamber up on the tree's knobby base. Hanging on with one arm, I try frantically to hack through the rope with the other, but the fibrous strands only tighten around his neck. I can hardly see what I'm doing through my sobs.

My brain is numb, and I can't think clearly, but somewhere the thought comes that I can't help them and that I need to get out of here before the same thing happens to me.

A raven swoops close to my head, its loud cawing somehow breaking the grip of fear that's been keeping me pinned in place. Glancing behind me to make sure nobody is coming, I crouch down and gather my scattered belongings.

Before I know it, my legs are carrying me as far and as fast as they can.

When I woke up, I was drenched in sweat and could barely breathe. Mariol and the other man's face swam in and out of my field of vision. I felt a throbbing pain above my left eyebrow and turned my flashlight on to glance at my watch. 3:47 a.m. I took two Advil, hoping to relieve the pain. While the pills took some of the edge off the sharpness, the throbbing remained. I tossed and turned, trying to get back to sleep, but couldn't.

I finally gave up around 6:00 a.m., feeling groggy and disoriented. I took two more Advil, hoping to dull the migraine a little more. I wrote down what I could remember of the dream, both to give me something to do and because I knew Patrick, my therapist, would ask me about it when I returned home.

I considered telling Jean-Claude I was sick, but I remembered how cold his eyes were when he told me to pull it together. And with Hiba gone, the clinic was understaffed. I glanced at the weekly schedule Okot handed out every Monday. I had to think hard to remember what day it was. Wednesday. I checked my morning round: the maternity ward. My favorite. My heart lightened a little at the sight.

"Just two more days until Hiba comes back. And then

everything will be fine. I can survive two days. I can always take a nap at lunch if I need to," I whispered, trying to rally myself into feeling better.

When I got to the maternity tent, I saw Jean-Claude examining a woman who was panting and heaving, supported by a man and a young girl. I gasped at the brightness of the naked bulb in the tent and suppressed an urge to cover my ears at the loudness of the woman's moans. Taking a deep breath, I steadied myself against the side of a cot.

"Piath went into labor at home, but after hours of pushing, nothing was happening, and she was losing blood so rapidly they carried her here. Jean-Claude says the baby's breech and she needs a C-section," Kamal informed me.

This was bad news. We weren't equipped to do any kind of surgery, and the risk of infection was too high. In these cases, our best chance was to get the patient airlifted to a surgical hospital in Lokichoggio, on the Kenyan border.

"Quick, Sarah, contact the UN and see if they can send the plane over!" Jean-Claude barked.

I nodded, careful not to move my head too much. I slowly made my way to the administrative tent, hoping that my migraine would pass so I could think more clearly.

Once there, I found I couldn't focus above the pitter-patter of the rain and the wheezing of the old stuttering generator that lived just outside. I made a mental note to ask Okot if we could get a newer model. The sound was even louder than usual, and I figured it had to be on its last legs.

I had sealed the tent flaps securely upon entry as was our protocol to protect the computers from humidity during the rainy season and dust during the dry season. I suddenly found it hard to breathe in the tightly enclosed space. I decided to ignore the clutching sensation in my throat, trying to concentrate on the task at hand, knowing that a woman's life depended on me.

I picked up the satellite phone, hoping its weight might steady me. Instead, the screen kept swimming in and out of focus, and I couldn't see the numbers I needed to dial.

The migraine that had started that morning as a throbbing pain above my left eyebrow had now invaded my entire forehead, its pounding rhythm shattering any semblance of coherent thinking. I gasped for air.

I'm hyperventilating was my last thought before I blacked out.

When I came to, I was in a cot in the infirmary, and Hiba was by my side.

"Hiba, what are you doing here?"

"Shhh," she quieted me, taking my hand in hers. "Jean-Claude contacted me on the emergency phone, and I came home early. You've been out for a day."

"A day? How is that possible? How is Piath?" I asked, remembering what had happened before I fainted. "I hope she's okay! Did someone call the UN?"

"Yes, she's okay. By the time Okot found you, it was too late to have her airlifted, so Jean-Claude had to perform an emergency C-section. The baby was already dead, but he was able to save Piath. He was pretty amazing, I was told."

"I'm so relieved! I feel terrible. I put her life in more danger. And I'm sorry you had to come back early. Jean-Claude is going to kill me. Is he livid?"

She looked at me, and I could tell she was debating what to answer. Her hesitation made me wonder if I even wanted to know.

"Don't worry about that now," Hiba finally answered. "You need to rest."

*

Jean-Claude was surprisingly calm when he came to talk to me in the infirmary. His face was inscrutable.

"I clearly miscalculated the impact the child's death would have on you, Sarah. I want you to take a five-day break and do whatever is necessary to come back refreshed and ready to tackle all the work we have."

What have you done, Sarah?! I thought, berating myself for breaking down, endangering a woman's life, and putting myself in this position.

"I'm so sorry about what happened—and for Piath. I made an unforgivable mistake. I appreciate the break and the second chance. I promise I'll come back ready."

Jean-Claude scanned my face, as though searching for a breech in my sincerity. But I meant every word. I *had* to be ready.

"Tell me, Sarah, do you like being a humanitarian nurse?"

My throat tightened at the question, terrified of what he was getting at.

"Of course! I love it. It's my whole life."

In fact, I didn't have anything else to show for my life. No husband or boyfriend. No kids. No close friends, at least none that lasted more than a year after my last mission ended. My relationship with my mother was strained, to put it mildly, and I had no other close family members. I found it hard to breathe just thinking about not having the one thing that brought meaning to my life, so I brought my attention back to Jean-Claude.

"Then remember: It's your job to care just enough to want to keep doing the work, but not so much it clouds your judgment. We need to be able to be here for every patient, not just one or two. When you first came, I thought you had a healthy shell, but it seems that boy made you soft."

I had to agree. The events of the last week left me feeling like a deflated punching bag, absorbing each hit life sent my way.

Toughen up, Sarah!

"If I don't think you're fit to work when you come back, I'll have to send you home. I'll let headquarters know, so they'll have a replacement on standby if need be. With malaria season and potential cholera outbreaks, I can't be down a nurse."

I went on break, vowing to close the emotional door my friendship with Mariol had opened and to keep the feelings of grief and loss that were crowding my heart and mind at bay. I needed to find that hard professional veneer Jean-Claude valued, to prove to him and to myself that I could still do the job.

Hiba came to see me before I left.

"Don't take what JC says too seriously, Sarah. He might think you're like him, but you're not. You need to cry and let your feelings out. I know how much you loved Mariol." She took my hand in hers.

I knew that if I started crying, I might never stop. And if I fell apart, Jean-Claude would send me home. I'd spent my entire life running away from my emotions. I'd even made a career out of it. Surely, I could do it again.

Holed up in a hotel room in the capital of South Sudan, I spent hours zoning out on my laptop, watching episode after episode of *Scrubs*, willing myself not to feel. I took a Benadryl before bed to knock myself out.

"I'm back on track!" I thought after nine hours of dreamless sleep.

The next night, however, my nightmares caught up with a vengeance.

Mariol was sick and needed my help, but I couldn't get to him in time. The mystery men were after me, shadows more than form, and I had to choose between saving him and saving myself.

I started to run, but roots came up from the ground and

grabbed my ankles, tripping me and pinning me to the earth until my face was submerged in dirt. I couldn't take in any air, and I was sure I was going to choke.

The next thing I knew, I was in a room, tied to a chair, with my mother looming over me. "You're such a disappointment, Sarah," she said, her voice stern. Her face morphed into that of Jean-Claude's.

"Pull yourself together!"

I woke in a cold sweat, a paralyzing migraine gripping the left side of my head.

I couldn't even look at any of my screens, and that night I got three hours of sleep. In my agitated, groggy state, I considered trying to set up an emergency Skype meeting with Patrick. But I knew he would ask me how I was feeling, and I didn't want to unravel more than I already had. I kept on telling myself to "pull it together," as if it was a magic mantra that would help everything else go away.

When I returned to the compound, Jean-Claude took one look at me and shook his head.

"I'm going to recommend you be put on probationary leave for three months. Go home and get the necessary mental health treatment you need," he said, his voice dripping with disdain.

I didn't even have the energy to resist.

It's your fault, my inner nemesis whispered. For the most part, I agreed.

Chapter Three
May 2011

Return to Berkeley

Sarah

I usually loved flying. Everything about it, really. All the things others hated. The anonymity. The overpriced junk food. The endless hallways. The honesty of the harsh neon lights that revealed every little blemish. As I waited in the long security lines, I made up stories about my fellow travelers. Where they were coming from. What was waiting for them at the other end of their voyage.

More than anything, I loved being suspended in mid-air. Watching secret cloud worlds unfurl before me (I always got a window seat, no matter how long the flight). My dad used to say that while I had yellow-green cat eyes, I had the soul of a bird. I loved knowing that when the plane landed, I'd either be beginning a new adventure or getting a well-deserved rest until the next one.

This time, however, the trip home felt like a flight of shame. I didn't know what I dreaded more: the long hours stretching ahead of me with nothing to do but reflect on everything I'd lost (Mariol. My job. All self-respect); or what waited for me when I landed.

What was I going to do for three months at home in

the Bay Area? And how was I going to avoid my mother (or Amanda, as I had sometimes started calling her when I left home at eighteen as a way to mark my maturation)?

I huddled miserably in my seat as the blasting AC did its best to freeze the migraine out of my temples. I wondered if the plane was much colder than usual as I wrapped my scarf over my head. I glanced over at my seatmate, a stout young man clad in a T-shirt and shorts. He was as spread-eagled as one can be in such a tight space and showed no indication of being cold. Could my body temperature have dropped?

Are you surprised with everything that's happened? You're a mess!

In ordinary times, I carefully regimented my life, every moment accounted for. Nine to twelve months on mission, as it was called. Two weeks to relax and recover on a beach somewhere. Then two weeks at home to do laundry, get my annual medical and dental checkups, and have a check-in with Patrick. My mother's job as the head of the Alta Bates surgery department kept her so busy, I generally only saw her in passing while I was home. It was better for both of us that way. When I started this work seven years ago, I had had my own apartment, but it didn't make sense to keep getting subletters for the majority of the year and kick them out for the few weeks I was between missions. And this way I could also save some money. My income wasn't very high, but my expenses were also minimal.

Panic gripped my stomach as I thought of three months of unstructured time stretching out in front of me, with nothing to do but reflect on my life choices.

I have to see Patrick ASAP. I need to fix these nightmares, migraines, and insomnia so I can go back.

Seeing that the Wi-Fi was enabled on the flight, I shot Patrick a quick email:

"Things went terribly wrong, and I was sent home early.

When's the soonest opening you have? I hope you have a weekly slot open for me because it's going to be more than a one-off this time."

And to my mother, so she wouldn't think I was an intruder on the off chance she was there when I arrived:

"Will be home tomorrow around 9 a.m."

With any luck, she wouldn't be there, so I'd have time to settle into my misery. Hopefully, she'd have forgotten that I wasn't due back until September and assumed this visit was normal. The last thing I needed right now was her judging stare. Or, even worse, her indifference.

Luck was not on my side, of course. As soon as I exited the taxi, I spotted my mother on the front porch, watering her perennials.

"Good morning," I said warily, as I hefted my suitcase up the five stairs that led to the landing.

"Sarah? I thought you weren't due back for a few months," she said, her sharp hazel eyes scanning over my body. Her wavy, once black hair had more gray in it than I remembered. She gave me the quick pat on the shoulder that passed for a hug in my family.

"Yeah, I guess you didn't get my email that I was arriving today. Long story." And one I had no desire to subject to her scrutiny. "Shouldn't you be at the hospital?" I asked, struggling to maintain the thread of this conversation when all I wanted to do was curl up in my bed.

"It's Sunday, Sarah. You look terrible. So pale. Have you lost weight? You can ill afford it, what with your slim frame." I could feel myself getting smaller as she spoke, as though her words and the coolness of her tone could shrink me back into the helplessness of my childhood.

"I'm just tired. Long flights. I never sleep on planes. I'm

going to lie down now," I said, more defeated than prickly, feeling the weight of the fatigue and the past weeks crashing down on me.

I need to get out of here as quickly as possible was my last thought before drifting into a deep, thankfully nightmare-free sleep.

"Hi, Sarah, welcome back. It's good to see you," Patrick greeted me a few days later, shaking my hand. I was five-foot-seven, and he was at most an inch or two taller, so we were almost eye level with each other. The equality in our heights was somehow comforting, as was his welcoming tone of voice. A nice antidote to Jean-Claude. I felt my stomach unclench ever so slightly.

Stepping into his office was like walking into a time warp. When I had first decided to become a humanitarian nurse seven years ago, I'd had a few panic attacks, which led me to seek out a therapist. He came highly recommended by a colleague of my mother's—one of the few I knew and trusted.

Ever since then, his office had become my landing pad between missions, the place I went to regroup, reflect, and recharge before heading off to the next destination. He was one of the few constants in my life—besides my mother, who was more like a constant irritant.

This time, however, being here felt different. I'd never been sent home early before, and I felt so embarrassed. I looked around in an attempt to anchor myself. But the familiar surroundings—with the carefully arranged plants, the soothing photo of the waterfall, and the collection of rocks and crystals—clashed so radically with my internal turmoil and the setting I had just left that I felt even more disoriented than before.

Five days ago, I was living in a tent in South Sudan. A few

weeks ago, Mariol was still alive. Now I was here. Nothing made sense.

"It feels strange to be back," was all I could muster to say.

Patrick nodded, his light brown eyes patient. Compassionate.

"Take your time, Sarah. Do you want to tell me what happened, or is there something else you're needing right now?"

"Honestly, Patrick, the last thing I want to do is tell you what happened. But I know I must. I *have* to get better so I can go back."

That was the only thing that felt clear right now. I took a deep breath, not sure where to start.

"I became friends with Mariol, a young Sudanese boy who lived near the bush hospital where I worked. He was so full of life. Always laughing and getting into some mischief." I smiled automatically, remembering. And then pain gripped my heart, as I remembered further. I fought against the tears gathering around my eyes. I picked up one of Patrick's stones to steady myself. I could still hear Jean-Claude telling me to pull myself together.

"He died of malaria. We might've been able to save him if we'd gotten to his village sooner, but Jean-Claude, the head doctor, had his own priorities," I said, forcing the words out. How I wished I could swallow them back. Reverse time. Grief clutched at my throat, threatening to break the dam of my self-control.

"What are you feeling, Sarah?" Patrick asked, sensing something in my face. I shook my head no. I forced myself to take deep breaths until I could swallow without the risk of choking.

"I'm not ready to feel. Or to talk more about Mariol," I said at last.

"That's okay, we can go at your pace."

"After that, I had the nightmare again—the same one I

had in Sierra Leone. Along with the migraines and insomnia. Because of them, I blacked out when I should've been calling backup, and a pregnant woman almost died—" My voice broke at the end, and I cleared my throat before continuing.

"So, I'm now on probation for three months. You have to help me get better, Patrick." I could hear the pleading in my own voice and resented myself for it.

"That sounds hard, Sarah. I'm glad you reached out right away. Can I ask you about the nightmare?"

I nodded yes. Right now, that felt safer than thinking about Mariol. Or feeling my emotions.

"It always starts in the forest with trees towering above me. Sometimes, I wake up there. Other times, I hear noise and loud footsteps, and I can feel the terror rising within me."

I clasped and unclasped my fingers, trying to divert my attention from the torrent of images and emotions threatening to overtake me. Holding my gaze on the chipped nail of my right thumb, I continued.

"In the dream, I see white, pointed hoods and the glowing light of torches. I'm always a young Black girl. Sometimes I can see myself like I'm watching a movie. Other times, I'm seeing through her eyes. I wake up drenched in sweat and shivering at the same time. When I go to the bathroom to rinse off, for a second the face staring back at me from the mirror doesn't look like mine ... It's hard to describe."

I closed my eyes, remembering this feeling that defied words. I thought of the first time I went to Africa, on a study-abroad program in Tanzania my junior year in college. That was the only time in my life I'd felt something similar.

After I'd finished my program, I volunteered to teach English in a remote village of Eastern Tanzania for a month. I didn't see another white person—or a mirror—for weeks. One day, a government official came to the village, driving a fancy black car. The children crowded around it the way they often did around me, curious and reaching out but not quite touching. A third of the villagers owned bicycles. A lucky handful, motorcycles. Nobody owned a car.

The official invited the woman running the school and me to have lunch with him. When I got in, I caught sight of my face in the rearview mirror. I looked so pale, as though the vibrancy of the colors surrounding me might swallow me up. My light green eyes were too big for my face, my straight dark hair only accentuating the oddness of my ghostly skin tone. No wonder the villagers all stared at me, I thought as I gazed at this face that did not seem my own.

I opened my eyes to see Patrick watching me, waiting patiently.

"Lost in memory?" he asked gently.

I nodded, not offering an explanation, and he didn't press me. I resumed my description of the nightmare.

"This time, I saw two Black men hanging from ropes. Dead. One of them seemed to be my father, though he wasn't my actual father. The other I knew to be my brother, but when I went to him, he had Mariol's face. And of course, I don't have a brother."

"That's not uncommon in dreams. When's the first time you had the nightmare, Sarah? As I recall, you were a teenager?"

"I was probably thirteen—it was after my dad died and we'd moved to Paris. Then I had it again the first time I went to Tanzania. It was the night after a woman died in childbirth at the clinic where I was doing my service project. Her obvious agony and the fact we couldn't save her really shook me. The insomnia and migraines didn't start until I was in Sierra Leone, though."

"Did anything change then? Anything that might have triggered the insomnia?"

I sighed. "It was after a girl I'd been helping treat for cholera died of complications in my arms. I had really thought we could save her, and I was devastated. That night, I had the nightmare, and for the next few days, I could only sleep in two-hour chunks and had a debilitating migraine. I stayed in bed, rested, drank lots of electrolyte-infused water, and after a few days, I was okay.

"But this time, when I went on R&R, the insomnia and migraines got worse rather than better. When I came back from break, I was so sleep-deprived, I was almost delirious. That's when Jean-Claude sent me home," I said, feeling my heart drop as the reality of my situation sunk in even more.

"Patrick, do you think I'm having a nervous breakdown?" I asked, my voice shaking a little.

"What you describe sounds more like you might have PTSD, or post-traumatic stress disorder, especially since the nightmares seem to be triggered by death. After so many years working in conflict zones, I'm not surprised."

I nodded, feeling a little reassured by his words.

"Sarah, I know that in the past you haven't wanted to try some of the trauma healing modalities I'm trained in, and since you were only in town for a session or two, it didn't make that much sense anyway. Under the current circumstances, I highly recommend we try one of them, EMDR, at least once or twice, to see how you respond."

"EMD ... what?" I asked, raising a skeptical eyebrow.

"R. It stands for Eye Movement Desensitization and Reprocessing. I'll ask you to describe a difficult or traumatic memory while you follow the side-to-side movement of my fingers with your eyes. It's a way of releasing the emotional charge from the past so you can feel freer in the present. Of course, it's your choice, but I think you might be surprised at the results." He leaned forward, as though his body were willing me to take a risk. Try something new.

Oh God, no, was my first thought. *Don't make me feel.* But right now, I was ready to try anything so I could return to work.

"Okay, we can try it next time I see you," I agreed reluctantly and thought I saw relief flash across his face before it was replaced by his usual amiable but somewhat neutral expression.

"I'll give you some information so you can read up about it if you're interested. I suggest starting with the memory of your father's death, both so you get used to the technique and because it sounds like his death might have been the original catalyst for your nightmares."

My father's death, really? I thought, raising an eyebrow, but didn't say anything. It seemed a little facile to pin all my issues on that. My nomadic lifestyle, my fear of commitment, my chosen career, now my nightmares and migraines … However, thinking of Dad's heart attack twenty-two years ago felt much less emotionally charged than talking about Mariol, Piath, or Jean-Claude, so I nodded again. Patrick smiled at my expression before continuing.

"My second suggestion is for you to do some automatic writing about your nightmare, to get it out of your subconscious and into your conscious memory."

"What does that mean?"

"You would write down a question for your dream self, for example, 'Who are you?' And then write whatever comes to you. I'll jot down a few more questions you could ask. If nothing comes, it's fine. But I think it might help get your nightmares out of your mind and give you some distance, as well as more clarity." He paused for a moment, his brows coming together slightly, as though in thought.

"As I recall, you like to journal, right?"

I nodded, pleased that he remembered. There was something about having a witness to my story that was comforting, especially given how transient the other aspects of my life were.

"This is a similar process to journaling, and that's part of why I think it might be helpful."

"Okay," I said, ignoring the part of me that didn't want to do any of this.

After my session, I decided to take BART to San Francisco. Both trains and water had a calming effect on my nervous system, and I liked the view of the Bay from the other side of the bridge.

It was 1:23 p.m., and the train car wasn't too crowded. I made my way to two empty seats in the back, putting my bag in the seat next to me to discourage anyone from sitting there. I felt my body relax as the train started moving, and I closed my eyes.

I woke with a start as the automated voice was announcing "Embarcadero." Heart racing, I made a mad dash for the doors and squeezed out just in time.

At the Ferry Building, I made a beeline for Peet's Coffee. I had dreamed of a chai latte when I was in South Sudan and had woken up with the taste of cinnamon in my mouth.

I ordered one to go (generously sprinkling it with cinnamon) and found a bench outside. It was one of those perfect May days that gave newcomers to San Francisco the false promise of a warm, sunny summer. Locals knew enough to take advantage of the warmth before the fog and cold rolled in.

Three gulls circled overhead, squawking. I wondered if they had spotted something in the water. A man sat down at the other end of the bench. I stifled a groan. I hoped he wasn't a cheery Californian looking for any excuse to start a conversation. I relaxed when he pulled out a newspaper. I pretended to be watching the line of loud tourists waiting to take the ferry to Sausalito as I glanced over at him. He was probably in his sixties with a slight stoop to his shoulders.

The migraine I had woken up with had dulled into a mild ache thanks to the pills I'd taken earlier. Remembering Patrick's suggestion of automatic writing, I took out my notebook and pen.

I stared at the blank page, then at the Bay, and back at the page. I took out my dream journal and flipped through the latest entries. And suddenly, it started coming back. The darkness of the forest, the fear. The ache in my head sharpened, and the images vanished again.

I took a deep breath, willing myself to stay with it. I glanced at the questions Patrick had written down for me.

Feeling a bit silly, I closed my eyes and asked my dream self: "Who are you? What is your name?"

I paused, waiting. As I slowed down, my sensory perceptions came into sharp and clear focus: the subtle breeze tousling loose strands of my hair. The reddish-orange of the sunlight filtering in through my closed eyelids. The fluttering of the gulls' wings splashing against the water as they took flight. With each breath, I felt like I was starting to tune into a different frequency. And then, I heard it—

"Maggie Burke," came the answer, seemingly out of nowhere. I say "heard," but it was more like a sensing or a knowing than an actual voice.

I opened my eyes, stunned. I hadn't really expected an answer. Outside, everything looked more or less the same. The gulls had landed on the pier and were squabbling over a piece of bread. The last of the tourists were boarding the ferry. The older man was reading the sports page intently.

I closed my eyes, repeating the same slowing-down process to see if anything more would come.

"The trouble started because of my breasts," came from that same place. I waited to see if anything else would come. Rather than words, I suddenly had a feeling in my body of someone grabbing me … trying to force themselves on me.

My eyes flew open. My bench companion was gone, and I was all alone, except for the nausea gripping my stomach and spreading to my esophagus. I took slow, deep breaths while staring at the water to calm myself.

When I closed my eyes again to access Maggie, all I felt was darkness. As though whatever connection I'd opened up had shut down.

Chapter Four
September 1914

My Breasts

Maggie

The trouble started because of my breasts. I told them not to grow, but there was nothing I could do about it. They sprouted up last fall—like small, soft cotton balls pushing out of my skin—and kept on growing until they looked more like little apples.

They pushed against the fabric of my worn work dress in a way that drew the eyes of the white men, like moths to a candle. My shoulders pulled inward, as though they could hide the protruding bumps. My breasts made my face all but disappear, and I resented them for that.

Not that any of the white men paid me much mind before that, except to give me orders or to wish I wasn't in my mother's skirts so they could have more time with her. I saw how Mr. Tanner looked at Mama, and I felt sick to my stomach every time he did. I couldn't forget that day, eight years ago, when I'd been helping Mama in the big house.

I was maybe six, and she had me scrubbing the floorboards. They looked sad as they stared back at me, gleaming but lifeless. We made a sorry pair. I thought they must long for their days as trees, much as my legs yearned to be running outside. I didn't notice Mr. Tanner come in or hear what he said to Mama. But I felt her breath catch, and my heart started racing. I glanced up and saw her standing as she had been, but she seemed frozen. Her eyes looked far away. Mr. Tanner had opened the door of the bedroom and seemed expectant.

"Maggie, go outside," she said, her voice low and almost gruff. I was confused, but dropped the rag, knowing better than to argue. I turned before going and saw her following Mr. Tanner to the room, shoulders slumped.

The next day, Mr. Tanner sent me to the school for Colored children that they built in town after slavery ended a few decades ago. Ended on paper anyway. My oldest brother, Andre, said in reality it made no difference. That we were only free sharecroppers in name.

From that moment on, my life changed. Learning to read and write opened the door to worlds I hadn't known existed, made me want something I couldn't name. At school, I could be anyone I wanted to be, and I would daydream I was my teacher, Mrs. Bell. She came from somewhere up North, had gone to college, and didn't speak like any other Colored person I knew. Every day, I practiced talking like her until the sounds started flowing naturally from my tongue, crisper and less round than the ones I was used to.

When the other tenant farm children teased that I was putting on airs as we worked the fields together, I pretended I didn't hear them, holding my breath until I could go back to the classroom. Andre, overhearing them, beamed as though it were a compliment, saying, "tha's 'cause she go to school!"

Andre, older than me by ten years, often acted like a second father to us all, but to me in particular. Arthur, younger by two years, was a spitfire, and by far the most outgoing and good-humored of all of us. He often got into capers he was quickly forgiven for. Mama had two miscarriages following Arthur. Roy—four years younger than Arthur and four years older than me—never seemed to know where he fit in and was sullen and angry more often than not. Two years before I was born, Mama had had a girl, Gracie, who died when she was a few weeks old. This was one of the reasons Andre—who'd been eight at the time and was heartbroken when his baby sister died—was very protective of me. That was probably what irked Roy the most, since he idolized his oldest brother and was often seeking his attention.

Roy was the only one of the boys who went to school for any length of time, but he was kicked out for making trouble. I tried to teach Andre as much as I could. But I realized that it was hard for him, after a long day's work, to try to tease sense out of the strange shapes I showed him. He was good with numbers, though. And just as proud as Mama and Papa when I came home with the best marks. Especially in English. I loved how words made everything else vanish.

There were plenty of reasons for me to want to disappear around here. Especially when the gossiping tongues started wagging. They thought I didn't hear them when they talked about how light my skin was—shades lighter than Mama's mahogany skin. Sandalwood to Papa's charcoal face and arms. When he washed in the tub Mama filled for us once a week, I saw that the parts that had never felt the sun's scorching glare were lighter than the rest, but they were nothing like mine.

I heard them, but I drowned their words in that place that was as quiet as the bottom of the pond behind the shack Mr. Tanner built for us. Papa was my papa no matter what they said. When I was little and too tired to walk, it was his shoulders that carried me as my hands burrowed in the lamb's wool of his hair.

I should have stayed with Mama and helped her with the cleaning. She asked me to, but I didn't want to. The air was so stale and dead in that house that I couldn't breathe, and it was haunted by the image of Mama's hollow eyes as she followed Mr. Tanner into the room. I wanted to be with Papa and my brothers in the fields. As hard as the work was, I loved being outside. Although my back ached and my fingers stung where the cotton furrowed into the skin, I could look up whenever the overseer wasn't watching. The sky stretched out as far as my eye could see, showing me the way out. No matter how stiflingly hot the air got, I could breathe better there than cooped up in the airless house.

The day the troubles began, Mr. Tanner decided to send Sammy, his youngest son, to supervise the work. I hadn't seen Sammy in over a year, not since he went to boarding school. Mama told me his daddy sent him away for misbehaving with a girl in school. The other day, I had overheard the foreman say Mr. Tanner was keeping him home this year to train him to take over the work in the fields and to keep him out of trouble.

When we were little, Sammy sometimes played with Roy when Mama was minding Sammy for Mrs. Tanner. Andre and Arthur were already off working with Papa in the fields. Sammy was one year older than Roy and the boss's son, and he used both to his advantage. His favorite game was tying Roy to a chair while he poked and prodded him. Once, he tipped the chair so far back the leg slipped out and Roy fell on his head. My brother was furious. When Mama was tending to his wound, I heard him ask why she let Sammy do that.

"I can punch 'im, Mama. I know I can."

"Hush, Roy. I know you angry an' hurtin', but you can't win this fight. Bes' leave it be," Mama said in her soothing voice.

Roy was maybe six at the time, and his eyes seemed to

harden when she said that, as though part of him disappeared into the dark of his eyes, to a place only he knew about. After that, he started getting into fights with the children of the other tenant farmers.

Sammy never noticed me, however. It was as if the three years that separated us, my girl-ness, and the color of my skin made me invisible. Not even worth a glance unless he got bored with bullying Roy and was looking for someone to tease. Both his indifference and his casual cruelty rankled deep inside me.

I wished I could be invisible now.

"Hey, Maggie, look at you, all grown up!" Sammy drawled when he arrived in the field and caught sight of me. He was also much taller than I remembered. His eyes scanned my body and stopped at my breasts. His smile widened, but there was no warmth in it.

I felt hot and uncomfortable and ducked behind a cotton shrub. I could feel his eyes boring into me. Fear writhed up from my belly to my throat before curling up in a tight ball inside my ribcage. But after a while, Sammy seemed to lose interest and went to talk to the men.

I went back to picking and soon got into that rhythm where everything else—time, hunger—faded away. Thoughts slid off me as my body led me into a silent dance. It was the same place I went when I read a poem in my tattered textbook at school.

The other day, I discovered John Keats's "To Autumn," and the walls of the tiny classroom dissolved into "mists and mellow fruitfulness." I could see Autumn and his friend the maturing sun as they bent together to conspire on "how to load" the fruit onto the vines wrapped around the thatched houses.

*

Right now, although the noonday sun was still attempting to burn through my scalp between my braids, a playful breeze took the edge off the heat. It ruffled the stillness of the leaves and whispered that fall was on its way. Eventually, my bladder pulled me out of my reverie, and I walked away from the others to find a private place to pee. I was still in a bit of a daze as I watched the urine create a little rivulet in the earth.

A sharp noise startled me into realizing I wasn't alone, and I scrambled to pull my undergarments up. Too late. Sammy lunged toward me, pinning me down with the weight of his body with one hand on my mouth, the other fumbling for his trousers. I struggled to free myself from his grip.

I caught him off balance and managed to slide out from under him, but he grabbed my ankle. He pulled me down as I yelped for help. He shoved my face into the earth. His panting seemed deafening to my ears, his legs held my hips tight, and I couldn't move as he yanked my dress up. I felt something hot and hard at my backside.

And then, I couldn't feel his heaviness or hardness anymore. I felt like a rabbit miraculously freed from a trap, and my spirits lifted until I saw Andre straddling Sammy, pounding his stomach.

"Stop!" I screamed, pulling my torn dress down as best I could. Rage had twisted my brother's face so that I barely recognized him.

"Not my sistah!" he shouted. "I cain't do nothin' about what your daddy did to my mama, but you ain't gonna touch Maggie! You hear? Ain't she s'posed to be your half sistah?" he grunted in between punches. His words almost knocked my breath out of me since they'd never been uttered out loud before. But I was scared he was going to kill Sammy, so I made myself turn to go get Papa. That's when I saw him running toward us, Sammy's men not far behind.

"Maggie, run! Go tell Mama!" Papa shouted at me.

I took off toward our shack. I turned back once, and the last thing I saw was Papa pulling Andre off Sammy, and Sammy's men surrounding both of them.

"You gotta git, Maggie. It ain't safe here," Mama said after I told her what happened. I held onto her as I did when I was a child, but she gently pried my fingers loose. She took out her most prized possession, a purple shawl that had belonged to her mama, and bundled a few things for me. Two slices of bread, the last of our soap, her gourd, the butt of a candle, some matchsticks, and a small knife.

Her hands trembled as she tied the ends of the shawl and placed it into my hand. Her eyes were threatening to spill over, and I could see the terror deep inside of them. But also the determination.

"Hide in de tall grass by de cotton 'til dark. They be lookin' fo' you. Keep goin' North, an' don' stop 'til you know you safe."

I clung to her harder, shaking my head. She held me for an instant before giving me a firm but loving push.

"I know, chile. But you was never for this life, anyways. God have bigger plans fo' you. I think you gon' find yo'self out there, who you be when nobody lordin' over you. Now git."

I did what she said. I hid in the tall grass by the cotton until we were bathed in darkness. And that's when I saw what they did to Papa and Andre in the dead of the night. With only the trees, the moon, and me as witnesses.

Chapter Five

That Day

Sarah

"Did you still want to do the EMDR session on your dad's death?" Patrick asked.

"I do, if you think it will help fix my nightmares and insomnia. I slept terribly again last night. But do we have time to talk about the automatic writing? I tried it, and I'm still kind of tripping out about what came up." My head felt heavy from the lack of sleep, and my words seemed to be coming from far away.

"Of course. We scheduled two hours for this session, so we have plenty of time for both. I was planning on checking in with you about it anyway. What happened?" The concern in his eyes was such a departure from Jean-Claude's coldness. I felt my body relaxing, ever so slightly.

"To be honest, I assumed it was woo-woo and wouldn't work, so I really just asked the question to humor you … but after a minute or two, I sensed a presence answering me, saying her name was Maggie Burke! It was the strangest sensation. I felt like I was on drugs or something. What does it mean?"

"What do you think it means, Sarah?" His voice was gentle as he handed my question back to me.

"I have no idea! If I did, I wouldn't ask you!" I said, exasperated despite his kindness. "Please don't therapize me right now and just be straight with me, Patrick. The whole thing kind of freaked me out. I didn't get much beyond 'the trouble started because of my breasts,' but I got the feeling something bad happened. Some kind of sexual assault. I felt nauseated, and then everything shut down. Who is she?"

"We'd have to explore that more to know, Sarah. And with the subconscious, the answer is often less linear and factual than the cognitive mind would like. My suggestion, for now, is to keep tracking your dreams. You can also continue the automatic writing if you want, but stop if it gets too overwhelming."

"Okay. I think I'm ready to do the rapid eye thingy now," I said, feeling suddenly antsy and wanting to change gears, even though my shoulders tensed as soon as I'd said the words.

Come on, let's do this. We have to get better. And then we never have to think of any of this again, I pleaded with the part of me that was dragging its feet.

"We don't need to do this right now if you don't want to, Sarah," Patrick said, sensing my resistance. His ability to guess what I was feeling was both unnerving and reassuring.

"I want to," I said through clenched teeth.

"How about we start with a happy memory of your father." It was more of a statement than a question.

"Honestly, I don't remember much of him. He was a civil rights lawyer, and he worked *all* the time. Both my parents did. Although he was definitely more fun to be around than my mother the rare times he wasn't working."

I closed my eyes, combing the sparse Dad files in my memory bank, surprised to find more happy ones than I had thought I would. I must have buried those deep down.

"I was seven or eight. It was my winter break, and my mother was busier than ever with a spike in surgery cases due to an icy month. Dad had some unexpected free time—I think he had a case that fell through or settled at the last minute or something—so he took me to a beginner's ski resort in Western Maryland and taught me to ski. I have terrible foot-eye coordination and totally sucked, but we laughed so hard every time I fell, it didn't matter. We ended up spending more time making snow angels than skiing. And at night, we sat by the fire, sipped hot cocoa, and played Scrabble. He had an old magnetic travel set his mother had given him …"

I stopped, fighting back the urge to fidget, except for curling and flexing my toes in my running shoes. My heart ached. I felt a longing I hadn't allowed myself to experience in a long time. Remembering the good was almost more painful than the memory of his death.

"Can we go to that day, Patrick? I want to get it over with."

"Yes. Let's take a few breaths first, though, to help transition from one memory to the other." After we'd done that, he continued:

"You can describe the day of his death in as much or as little detail as you want. I may interrupt you with a question, and at times, I'll wave my fingers back and forth and ask you to follow them."

I nodded and closed my eyes. This memory was readily available, having split my childhood in two. Even after twenty-two years, I remembered every minute as though it were yesterday.

"It was June 14, 1989. I was twelve years old. The night before, the three of us had had an early dinner at my mother's favorite French restaurant before taking her to the airport. She had a surgeon's conference in Boston, I think. I mostly remember exchanging shy smiles with the boy at the table next to ours.

"The next morning, I woke to the wailing of my dad's alarm clock. I was both annoyed and surprised. He almost always woke long before it went off, heading out for his morning run before reviewing the day's cases. I asked him once why he set the alarm at all. I think his answer was 'just in case.'

"Anyway, I shouted at him to turn it off and was getting ready to barge into his room and give him a piece of my mind when it finally stopped. I think I'd just gone back to sleep when it went off again. I yelled at him: 'Hey, Dad, are you in the shower? I'm trying to sleep here! Some of us are on summer break!'

"It didn't stop, so I stormed into the bedroom, figuring he'd left and forgotten to turn it off. When I saw he was still in bed, I froze. I'd never seen him sleep in, not even on weekends. I said something like 'Dad, you have to get up, it's late,' but he didn't respond. The sheet was covering his face, so I couldn't see him."

"Sarah, what are you feeling right now?" Patrick asked, startling me. I'd almost forgotten there was someone else in the room with me.

"I feel sick to my stomach. It's hard to breathe. I'm anxious and want to make sure Dad's okay, but at the same time, I don't want to touch him or go anywhere near him."

"Sarah, open your eyes and follow the movement of my fingers."

After a few minutes, my breathing was less labored, and I felt calmer. I continued:

"I approached him on tiptoe, grabbed the sheet with two fingers, and jumped back. His eyes were closed, but his face looked pasty. He still didn't respond when I shouted his name. At that point, I ran into his office and called 911. I was shaking so hard it took several tries before I could dial it properly. 'It's my dad, he's not moving,' I told them, barely able to get the words out.

"When the medics arrived, they said he'd had a massive

heart attack. They pronounced him 'deceased.' One of them, a young woman, squeezed my shoulder. 'I'm sorry, sweetie,' I remember her saying. She was the only one who was kind to me that day …"

I stopped to let out a breath.

"Sarah, what are you noticing in your body?" Patrick's voice cut through the fog of the memory.

I had told this story countless times, but I had never allowed myself to actually feel it. It was as though my mouth and voice were doing the retelling, disconnected from my heart and from the rest of my body.

"I don't know. I feel numb. Frozen. I can't move. I can't feel anything," I said, following Patrick's fingers with my eyes. Slowly, I started noticing a heavy weight in my chest, making it difficult for me to breathe.

The movement of the fingers stopped. For a moment, I felt myself stop breathing too, and I gasped for air. Then I felt a subtle shift. Like a big boulder, lodged in my heart, starting to budge just a little. My breath came out jagged and uneven.

"Take slow, deep breaths, and just allow what you're feeling to come up," Patrick instructed.

Without any forewarning, tears started streaming down my face. I wrapped my arms around myself and rocked back and forth, sobbing. When the tears finally subsided, I felt exhausted. But also, a little lighter.

"Sarah, is that enough for today, or do you want to continue?"

I wiped the residual tears from my face.

"Oh, I want to continue. I don't want to have to revisit that day again."

To gather myself, I gazed behind Patrick at the framed photo of the waterfall crashing into sparkling turquoise waters surrounded by lush green trees. Although the picture looked professionally shot, I knew Patrick had taken it, and I imagined him kneeling to capture the perfect image.

I sighed, bringing myself back to the present.

"After telling me my dad was dead, the medics asked me for a relative they could call, since I was a minor and couldn't stay alone. I had no idea which hotel my mother was staying at and couldn't remember the name of her conference, so they went through the list of people I might be able to call. They were able to reach my Grandma Belle, my mother's mother.

"She arrived forty-five minutes later, lips pressed together. I only saw her once a year, at most, and she and my mother had a frosty relationship, but I remember desperately wanting her to hug me and tell me it was going to be okay.

"Instead, she patted me awkwardly on the arm and said, 'Your father always worked too hard. I'm not surprised it came to this. Maybe your mother will learn from this, or she will be next, I'm sure.' And then she went off to make phone calls to try to locate Mom at her conference.

"Her words felt like a slap in the face. I barely slept that night, but when I did, I dreamt that Mom had died too, and Grandma Belle was sitting there stonily, saying, 'I told you so. Now it's just the two of us, kid.'

"My mother arrived the next afternoon. I couldn't wait for her to come. I just wanted her to hug me and reassure me, even though that wasn't her way any more than it was her mother's. She did hug me, which was unlike her. And she was sobbing. I'd never seen her cry before, and it felt like my whole world collapsed."

Although I said the words, I had gone numb again.

"Allow yourself to feel things collapsing, Sarah. It's okay. You're safe now." Patrick said, and for a split second, I believed him.

I felt the boulder shudder and dissolve a little, but then it lodged in my throat.

"Sarah, what are you believing about the world and yourself right now?"

"I don't know. I guess that I'm alone. That I can't trust that things will be okay."

"What new belief would you like to replace that one with?"

"I have no idea. I'd love to believe that I'm not alone and that everything will be okay, but even now I don't. Not for a second. After all, I was just asked to leave South Sudan because I wasn't okay."

Patrick continued guiding me to feel my feelings, follow his fingers, and describe what I was sensing. By the end, it felt like there was a little more space. Some of the boulder was still in my heart, but some of it had shifted to form ground under me.

When I got home, I drew a bubble bath and wept for an hour into the soapy water. I went to bed at 8:00 p.m., feeling completely spent, and fell into a deep sleep.

Chapter Six

The Long Walk

Maggie

They say death is the end, but for me, it was the beginning. My rebirth into a world as fickle as it was steadfast, as cruel as it was beautiful. I didn't know how long or how far I ran, deep into the heart of the forest. The faint moonshine weaved in and out of leaves to show me the way.

Finally, I couldn't go any farther and collapsed on the ground. When my breath was less jagged and my heart was no longer pounding in my ears, I opened Mama's bundle. I took out one of the slices of bread and started nibbling on it. The tiny morsels barely made a difference to the hunger clawing at my belly, but not knowing how long I needed the food to last, I didn't want to eat it all.

Holding the rest of the bundle in my lap, I buried my face in Mama's shawl. The smell transported me to cold winter days when we huddled around our fire pit after a long day's work, and I leaned into the warmth of her body with her shawl wrapped around both of us. I felt a deep longing for her in the pit of my chest.

"Mama, what am I gonna do?" I whispered into the night. I wrapped the shawl around me and lay down in a fetal position with the treasures from home in the crook of my arms. I was exhausted and my whole body ached, but sleep eluded me. Every hoot, howl, and crackle in the night sent fear through my veins. I longed for the bed I shared with my brothers, with Mama and Papa's hushed voices lulling me into fitful slumber.

When I woke at the first light of dawn, grief had me in its grip and wouldn't let go. Every time I got up, the image of Papa and Andre's bodies hanging limply from the tree swam in front of my eyes and knocked me to my knees as I sobbed uncontrollably.

"How can I go on with them gone?" I hollered into the void, getting nothing in return except the sounds of the forest drowning out my voice. I felt frozen. I couldn't go back—that much was clear—but every step forward would take me away from everything I knew and loved, would somehow confirm that my brother and father were truly dead.

The next morning, weak from crying and hunger, I realized I had to find a way to keep going, or I would die as well. I willed my mind to go blank, to stop thinking of Andre and Papa. Mama's voice rang in my ears: "You gon' find yo'self out dere."

"No, Mama," I said out loud, shaking my head. That seemed like wanting too much. "Just let me survive and get to safety. And I promise I won't ask for anything more." I bargained with the wind, the trees, and anything out there that might be listening.

With that promise, I started walking in the direction I thought was north until I couldn't see anymore, and exhaustion lured me into agitated bouts of sleep. This time, the sounds of the forest seemed much less fearsome than the demons within that I was determined to ignore. The trill of a cricket helped pull me back into a fitful but dreamless sleep. When I woke up, I realized it was people that I was frightened of, and I vowed to stay as far from them as I could.

My days turned into a hunt for survival. Senses heightened. Eyes and nose became feelers for food. My fingers were claws, coaxing berries from their bushes and ferreting roots from their hideout in the earth. I thought I heard my ancestors whispering secrets gleaned from the earth of their homeland, showing me which plants were edible and which to steer clear of. The sun was my compass. She rode over my right shoulder in the morning, and over my left in the evening, sharing equal time between the two. Mama had told me to "keep goin' North," and it was the only direction I had.

I had never felt both so alone and so free. Not beholden to anyone or anything but my own survival. Freedom was my lover, and I was both intoxicated and frightened by his touch.

As I walked, the poem "To a Skylark" sprang to mind. When we'd read it in school, I'd been mesmerized by Shelley's descriptions of the songbird's joy, in contrast to human suffering and pain.

I felt the pull of the skylark now, inviting me to soar with her far above my earthly sorrows. The sounds of the forest became my song, the hymn that kept me going and gave me hope.

I didn't know how many days had passed when my belly rebelled. In short, stabbing pangs, it screamed that it wanted more than roots and berries. I had finished the water from the last stream I passed. Despair began to nip at my ankles, dragging my feet down. All I wanted to do was curl up and sleep.

Just then, a raven cawed overhead.

"Go away," I told him, but he was insistent. He swooped as close to my head as he dared. He told me to follow him, I knew in the way one knows in the wild. Reluctantly, I complied and took off in the same direction.

I heard it before I saw it. A brook gurgling happily over rocks. The sky was still fanning out over a little clearing. For days, I had spotted it only in intermittent patches of blue peeking out from between the trees and only now realized how much I missed seeing its vastness.

Dipping my head into the icy water, I drank greedily, as though the brook might change its mind and stop flowing midway. I filled my gourd and started taking my clothes off. When I got to my undergarments, my breath caught in my throat as the image of Sammy pinning me to the ground crowded my vision.

Looking around furtively, I reassured myself that the only one looking was a frog, and he seemed more wary of me than I was of him. Finally stripping naked, I slowly lowered myself into the water, waiting for each part to adjust to the cold, washing the grime off with a little of the soap Mama gave me.

The water sang to me softly and told me to rest. That I didn't need to fight so hard. I allowed myself to float on my back. The feeling of being carried was so unexpected and comforting, tears started streaming down my cheeks. The warmth of home, of being held, seemed a little less far away. The brook received my tears without hesitation. Sorrow, release, and joy all mingled as one. I was still careful not to think too long or hard of my father and brother, but I felt lighter, nonetheless.

When I looked up, I saw a doe standing in the clearing, looking at me.

"Trust your heart," she seemed to be saying. I begged silently for her to stay and keep me company, but she turned around and bounded away.

After a while, realizing she wasn't coming back, I got a piece of netting I'd found along the way and started dragging it slowly in the water. I prayed to the raven to lead the fish to me. I stood there until my feet had lost all feeling. Hope—my elusive and fickle friend—started seeping away.

Just then, I felt a tug.

A trout!

That night, I struck a match against the underbrush and made a small fire to roast my catch. I was far enough from humans to feel safe. I woke up every few hours in the night to fan the fire—both to keep me warm and to discourage any animal that might mistake me for prey.

I went on like this for weeks. How many I didn't know. Time had lost all meaning. One day, I managed to catch a rabbit, but the look of terror in its eyes as I prepared to wring its neck was so familiar, I let it go. I regretted my decision when I awoke the next morning with a gnawing ache in my belly. At night, the frost bit through Mama's shawl and nipped at my ankles and ears.

The fish had gone into hiding, and the earth had swallowed her berries. Hunger hollowed out my insides and blocked all other thought. Sadness filled my heart as the cold and the lack of food finally drove me out of the forest.

"I won't forget you," I whispered into the wind as a goodbye. "I found a home among your trees and learned the lark doesn't need anybody's say-so to fly."

I climbed the highest tree I found and spotted smoke to the east. As the trees gave way to stumps and the songs of the birds and insects gave way to the grinding of metal against wood, I felt heavyhearted. Fear slid back into the pit of my stomach, but I knew I must go on. I had promised myself I would survive and find safety, and that was no longer possible in the woods.

I found a Colored encampment near a big field. Their huts were far from the landowner's house. I watched the people for a few hours, spotting a woman whose weary smile reminded me of Mama's, although she was as short and stout as Mama was lean and tall. Adeline, I learned later, was her name.

"Heavens, chile, yuh done scared me!" she exclaimed when I came out of hiding. But one look at my weary eyes, tattered clothes, and twigs matted into my hair, and she asked me no questions. She helped me wash up, and that night, I ate with her and her family. I didn't know what she told them, but none of them asked me any questions.

"It's too dangerous fo' us if yuh stay more'n a night, or da head tenant might fin' out," she said, looking worriedly toward the big house. She told me that their shack belonged to the landlord, and he didn't want visitors. But she gave me a set of clothes her son had outgrown and cut my hair.

"Yuh be safer as a boy," she told me. "Yuh can say yo' name is Matthew, like in the Bible."

She tied a cloth around my chest underneath the big work shirt. There was hardly a need for that. After weeks of near starvation, my breasts had gone back to hiding in my chest, so that only a tiny crest was peeking out.

"Times be hard, but they says it's gettin' bettah. Try to keep yo' mouth shut. Yo' voice is soft and deep enough to be a boy's, but it's bettah to be silent. They like 'at bettah anyhow. But it's almost November, an' winter's comin', so don't try to go farther north 'til you see flowers blooming on the trees. You gon' freeze to death oth'wise."

She slipped an apple into my shawl, along with a few matches to replace those I had used. When I left Adeline and her family, I felt lighter. Like I had gotten a little piece of my human self back. I'd been wild for so many weeks now, I wasn't sure I would remember how.

Chapter Seven

Paris

Sarah

I woke to sun streaming through the slats of my blinds as my alarm blinked 8:07 a.m. For an instant, I felt disoriented, unsure of what day it was or why I had slept so late. Then the day before came flooding back. The EMDR session with Patrick. I must have slept for twelve hours. When was the last time I'd done that? Not even when I was sick.

I considered going for a run, but my legs felt heavy. Lazy, even, which was in sharp contrast to their usual baseline tension, the feeling of a tight coil ready to spring into action at any moment. Instead, I felt the pull of my childhood memories, as though the session had awakened all of my unhealed younger selves, who were now clamoring for my attention.

Right then, however, the growling of my stomach was louder. I went to the kitchen to grab a bowl of granola and yogurt.

"Good morning, Sarah." My mother's voice startled me. She was sitting in our breakfast nook, half-hidden from view by our Ficus tree—which seemed to have doubled in size since I was last home. My mother was sipping a cappuccino from a purple mug I had made her in a high school ceramics class. A light green bathrobe was wrapped loosely around her waist, and she looked smaller than I remembered. She had a sudoku puzzle book propped open next to her.

"Oh, hi, Mom, I didn't see you in the corner." It took me a second to remember it was Saturday. I kept losing track of days now that I wasn't working.

When I was a teenager, it had seemed strange that my workaholic uptight mother slept in on weekends. Nowadays, I was grateful that my mother had some way to recover from her frenetic schedule.

"You're up late. Aren't you usually back from your run at this time?" My mother asked. I was a little surprised she knew my routine. Our paths didn't cross much when I was home, and I'd only seen her once in passing since the morning of my arrival.

"That's true, but I slept in today. I've been pretty exhausted."

"Yes, you don't look any better than when you landed," she remarked. I bristled for a second, assuming a judgment, and then took a deep breath. I remembered Jean-Claude's admonishment.

Pull it together, Sarah.

"I'm working on it. I'll be better soon," I said as I heated water for tea and poured granola into a bowl.

We looked at each other awkwardly, not knowing what to say. My mother picked up her pencil and looked down at her sudoku book, signaling the end of the conversation. I muttered, "Good luck with the puzzle," and took my breakfast tray back to my room. I had my younger selves to attend to anyway.

I looked around the room that had been mine since I was fourteen. On one side, the wallpaper was a light shade of lavender, and on the other side, my mother had put up a sheet of cork, so I could pin my photos and paintings without damaging the wall. I hadn't bothered to take anything down since I was so rarely home. I looked at the photos as though for the first time.

Age fourteen. Frizzy hair (I had permed it to try to give body to my straight black hair and had instead ended up looking like a poodle) and pink eye shadow which *Seventeen Magazine* had promised would highlight the jade green of my eyes.

Age seventeen. High school graduation. I had one arm around Betsy Meyers, my best friend at the time, and was throwing my cap with the other, smiling broadly. I couldn't remember feeling as happy as I looked in the photo.

But right now, it was my twelve-year-old self—not featured on the wall—who was clamoring the loudest. The one whose father had just died and whose mother thought it was a good idea to cart her to another country two months later. I had been furious. I had overheard my mother and father arguing about a possible move to France just weeks before his heart attack. Amanda had been granted a year-long fellowship as a visiting surgeon in the American Hospital in Paris and thought it was an opportunity she couldn't pass up, especially since she was due for a sabbatical.

My dad, Saul, who had worked so hard to gain recognition as a respected human rights lawyer in the highly competitive DC scene, was angry that his wife seemed to want him to throw it all away to go to Paris for a year.

"This is an extravagant whim, which is really unlike you, Amanda!" Eventually, my mother had relented and turned the offer down. After my father's death, she had contacted the hospital and learned the fellowship was still available.

Crouching down, I dug under the bed and unearthed a cardboard box marked "Journals. NOBODY BUT SARAH CAN OPEN." I hadn't thought of my journals in years, and I had to brush off quite a few cobwebs. I found a little notebook labeled "1989. Paris." I rifled through it to jog my memory.

August 12
Mom called me into the kitchen last night and told me we're moving to France. I'm so mad! How could she! She doesn't know I heard her and Dad fighting about it. And she tried to make it like it was for me. As if! When was the last time she put my needs first? And how is leaving all my friends going to help me right now?? I told her she was just waiting for Dad to die so she could go to her stupid Paris. She didn't even bother responding.

September 8
I still can't believe this is happening! I wish I could run away! I didn't talk to Mom the whole flight over, and I don't think she even noticed. Her nose was in her French books the whole time. It's so unfair! I'm never going to forgive her. And I'm never going to let her do this to me again!

September 19
I HATE THIS SCHOOL! I HATE FRENCH. How can so many vowels strung together make only one sound? It's so hard! And the kids are such snobs. One girl's dad is the ambassador to Finland, and she thinks she's all that and a bag of chips. They would've eaten her alive in DC, that's for sure.

I rested the journal against my leg and closed my eyes, remembering those first few months in Paris. I had never felt so lonely, so lost. My mother enrolled me in an international school, and they placed me in an "adaptation" class with other students who didn't speak French. We had two hours of language class a day on top of all the other classes. I had one year of Spanish under my belt and couldn't get my throat and lips around the strange nasal and guttural sounds French was composed of. Eventually, however, I was able to tease some sense out of it. Find the patterns in the madness. I opened my eyes, looking for that entry.

October 15
I did it! I ordered a meal in French all by myself. "Je voudrais une assiette de crudités pour commencer, et puis un boeuf bourguignon avec des frites. Et des profiteroles pour le dessert." The waiter was super cute and he winked at me. Which doesn't mean anything because French guys are such flirts. But still!

And there's a new girl who just came from Senegal, Fatou. I think we might become friends. She's in my gym class, and we tied for first place in a race. She's so fast! She's also an only child. Her mom found out her husband was cheating on her. One week later, she and Fatou were on a plane to stay with Fatou's aunt in Paris, even though the school year had already started.

October 29
Fatou and I went to the Pompidou museum yesterday. It's so weird, with all the inner plumbing tubes on the outside. An inside-out building. It looks how I feel! I saw some Matisses and Picassos we studied in art class in DC, and then we had some Nutella crêpes. Nutella is the best! It was warm enough to eat them outside.

There was a Japanese busker singing "Hotel California" who stumbled over all the words! I almost spit out my crêpe trying not to laugh. Fatou showed me some water sculptures out back. Mom says they're inspired by Stravinsky's Rite of Spring. Whatever. Way to ruin everything, Mom. But they are fun and colorful.

I'm starting to like Paris. DON'T TELL MOM! And I love the Metro—it's better than the DC one. And my French has improved so much with Fatou helping me. My head teacher says I'll be able to move out of adaptation classes into regular ones soon. I can't wait. Then Fatou and I will have more than just gym class together!

November 18
Will it ever stop raining?! Nobody warned me about the winters. It can't even get properly cold and snow. At least that's fun. And sunny. Here it's just gray and miserable. Even Fatou is grumpy! I'm sorry I ever teased her about being overly cheerful.

"City of lights indeed! More like city of lightlessness! I miss the sun!!" Fatou keeps complaining. She's clearly homesick. The other day we went to the African quarter near Barbés-Rochechouart to browse the shops. She said it reminded her of the Marché HLM in Dakar where she'd go every weekend with her friends. I've never seen such bright colors and patterns as the fabrics she showed me.

I wonder if I'm homesick. Not exactly. I do miss my friends and the free Smithsonian museums (it's so expensive to go to a museum here!). I miss living in a big house. I miss Dad. At least when he was around, he was nice. Unlike some people!

December 20
Yay! School is out, and I won't be alone for the holidays! Mom said I could go with Fatou and her family to the South of France for Christmas since she will be working and we don't celebrate anyway. She says it's because she's an atheist and Dad was Jewish, but really, I think she just can't be bothered.

And I did really well on all my exams! I'm so happy. The teacher said I'd be moving into the regular class after the Christmas break.

January 3
Happy New Year! I loved the vacation with Fatou's family. Her mom is really nice. And we stayed with her extended family. Aunts, uncles, cousins. I had no idea you could have so many relatives who actually enjoy each other's company. And the food is so good! I never want to eat another TV dinner. Lamb Yassa is my favorite! It's so peanuty and lemony and spicy.

They're Muslims and don't celebrate Christmas either, so I didn't feel too weird. Fatou introduced me to her favorite Senegalese singer, Ismaël Lô, who she said made his first guitar himself using fishing wire for strings. We're so spoiled in the US!

His music is so haunting and soulful. Of course, I can't understand a word of it since it's in Wolof. I still like it. Maybe that's even why. I feel the music more when I can't understand it.

February 28
I HATE HER! How could she? Just when I was liking Paris and making friends! Of course.

Last night, the witch sat me down and said: "I got a position as head of the surgical department in Berkeley. It's quite an honor. We're going to sell the house and move to the Bay Area. You'll see, you'll love it. It's warm and sunny, and people are so much more laid-back than in DC." She's the worst mother in the world! I will never forgive her. All she cares about is her fucking job.

I closed the journal, feeling a tight ache in my heart, reliving both the powerlessness and the rage. My mother loved structure and precision, hence her career as a surgeon. She couldn't stand the messiness of emotions. Teenage drama especially got her hackles up, so I had had to swallow my indignation and go along with whatever decision she made, all the while fuming inside. I didn't think my mother had ever been an adolescent. I imagined her born with a scalpel in her hand and a string of obsequious interns hanging on her every word.

Leaning into that time in my life and remembering my session with Patrick, I wondered what my younger self was learning then. I reopened the journals and reread the last entry.

"Thirteen-year-old Sarah. What are you learning?" I asked, and closed my eyes.

After a second or two, the words started coming. Opening my eyes again, I grabbed my current diary, and started writing what came to me without thinking too much:

"I can't trust anything."

"I will lose the people I love. There's no point in getting too attached."

"I have to forget the past and keep moving forward, no matter the cost."

I paused, noticing a tight lump in my chest. My breathing was shallow, and with great effort, I attempted to slow it down.

"You still live your life that way," I berated myself. From my work with Patrick, I was starting to see the ripple effect of that belief into the next twenty-plus years of my life.

I felt overwhelmed. Could I really heal that pattern? It felt so deeply ingrained. And if I did, who would I be?

Next to the February 28 entry, I wrote a possible new belief for myself.

"What if it's safe to trust?"

I put my hands on my heart and whispered to my thirteen-year-old self: "That's what I want for you."

"Yeah, right, as if!" I imagined my teenager retorting.

My legs were feeling antsy and tight again, so I decided to go for the run I'd skipped earlier. When I came back, I felt a little lighter and calmer, but needing a break from my childhood.

The name and the voice I'd heard at the pier kept on echoing through my mind. I tried to forget the image and nausea that had swept over me after that. On a whim, I Googled "Maggie Burke." I found an actress ... a lawyer ... an accountant. I added "1920s," guessing at the era. Nothing.

So, I picked up the notebook where I had started the automatic writing.

"Maggie, what happened next?" I asked, and waited for an answer. Nothing came. I'd almost given up when a blurry image of parallel and perpendicular lines appeared in my vision. Blocks? Tracks? It was hard to tell, and it disappeared as quickly as it came, as though my inner sight had shuttered down again. I tried to concentrate harder, but the hint of a headache started nudging my temples.

Too much, I thought, deciding to take a bubble bath instead. Might as well enjoy creature comforts while I had access to them. With any luck, I'd be back in the field in a few months.

Chapter Eight

Working on the Railway

Maggie (Matthew)

I learned that each town had a street where men and boys went in the hopes of being picked for day labor. The wait was the worst. Feet shuffling nervously, elbows jostling to get closer to the street. The dank smell of desperation. Then the sound of the cart coming. The men came out, eyeing us the way they might inspect a mule. Checking us for size, strength, health. We all hoped for the jobs that lasted weeks. The moment before they decided who would be chosen, there was a hush, as though all of us were holding our breath. And then it was over in an instant. There was the thrill of being selected, even though we knew we would be treated like dogs and kicked around if we were too slow, our bodies protesting against tasks that bled our fingers and broke our backs. But still, it was work. When we found ourselves alone, standing in the dust of the departing horse cart, there was the sinking of despair in the pit of our stomachs, the gnawing of hunger. There would be no food today.

    I was small and wiry from my years helping in the fields. When they needed big, strong men for tough physical labor, their eyes skimmed right over me as though I wasn't even there, but I was almost always chosen for jobs that required dexterity and speed. Picking fruits and vegetables. Working in garment factories. Shoveling, cleaning, carrying light loads. I stood out with my short, curly hair, smooth golden skin, and big eyes. But I discovered that being mistaken for a Native Indian or a Spaniard (I learned we were fairly recently at war with Spain) wasn't always much better than being Colored. I said little, kept them guessing about my origin, and eventually, they lost interest and left me alone. I found most people would rather talk about themselves, anyway.

In those first few months, I couldn't count the number of jobs I worked. "I just need to survive and get somewhere safe" was the refrain I kept repeating to myself, over and over, especially when every muscle in my body screamed to stop. The worst was coal mining. My soul suffocated in the dark, airless tunnels, and my lungs choked and gasped for air. I couldn't sing the song of the skylark without the sky, although there were many men who did, their deep voices echoing in the tunnels. I was grateful to them, for their song was a lifeline I hung onto.

My body grew stronger and leaner, and many days, it forgot it was ever a girl. My main daily concern was how to urinate without being found out. I drank as little as possible. When working out in the fields, I hung back and waited until the others were out of sight to relieve myself. One day, I found a thin rubber tube that had been tossed aside. I washed it out and kept it in the pocket of my overalls. When I needed to pee, I unzipped my trousers, and slipped it in, holding the end to my genitals. After a few messy tries, I was able to pee standing up. Bathing was harder as I had to avoid the communal taps, but being clean was a luxury, and we had all gotten used to being smelly. I carried a cloth for the rare times when there was an indoor latrine where I could steal some water and sponge myself off. I washed my head with some soap when I could, although I found the lice loved my warm scalp and tightly curled hair. I had to shave it off several times. I stopped bleeding when I was in the wild, and even now, I'd only get the occasional spotting of blood, which I stanched with an old cloth. I ate enough to stay alive and have the energy to work, but not enough for my curves or the monthly bleeding to return. They were both curses anyway.

At first, I was grateful for the onset of winter, as it allowed for more layers and fewer baths and made it easier to drink less. But then I discovered that the days I was chosen were far fewer than those I was not, for in the winter they mostly needed people to carry heavy loads. It was too cold to sleep outside, and the few coins I'd saved were rapidly dwindling to pay for food and the crowded room I shared with nine other seasonal workers. Desperate and lost, I stumbled to a nearby hotel and rummaged through the bin looking for leftover scraps to fill my belly.

"What are you doing?!" A short, thin man asked. He was puffing on a cigarette, half hidden in the doorway. Startled, I dropped the piece of chicken I was holding and prepared to run.

"Wait, don't go," the man said. "I'm Jimmy. I can see if we've got work washing dishes. You look like you could use the money."

I worked there for a few weeks, and even though the owner was bad-tempered and made us work long hours without extra pay, I was grateful not to have to look for something new every day.

One evening, after I caught a mistake on the menu, Jimmy looked at me funny.

"Matthew, you know your letters?" he asked, surprised. I nodded.

"Then why you wastin' time in this hellhole? You should go to the post office. I have a buddy who works there, and I know they could use someone good."

Taking his advice, I went to the small postal office located inside the railroad station. When they found out I could read and write better than most of them, I filed, wrote, and read letters for those who couldn't. They wanted me to stay, but the nightmares had returned, and I knew I had to keep moving or I would get swallowed up by my past. Staying anywhere too long made my heart ache for my family so much I felt ill.

"I just need to survive and get somewhere safe," I reminded myself.

One day, when the edge was starting to thaw off the cold, and I'd seen the first magnolias budding on a tree, I heard a man outside the post office shouting "Get a job with the railway, get a job on the railway!" I looked up and saw a line forming behind him. I went out on my lunch break to see what they were offering. They told me that we would be working our way north, and after asking me a few questions, they said the job was mine if I wanted.

Working on the railroad, "Where are you from?" was a question seldom asked. Every man I met had a story etched on his face. Rumors drifted on the wind whenever someone turned his back. Mac killed a man and dug his way out of prison. Flavio's family kicked him out when they found him in bed with another man. Hank's girl was as sweet as white corn, and every night, he moaned in his sleep as he dreamt of holding her in his arms once more. Pepe hadn't seen his family in three years, not since he left Mexico, and some said his wife took another husband. Our lives were like the tracks we helped build, a long, steely line snaking behind us. Fixed and immutable. Heavy with secrets and the weight of actions and choices we couldn't change. Lies. Mistakes. The grief of loss and betrayal. Loads far heavier than what they asked us to carry every day. Monsters best left buried.

Men were tighter lipped here than anywhere else I had been in my young life, and it suited me just fine. I felt the spell cast by a force far greater than any of us could fathom. Strands of a web from this life and all those that came before us. The unsung sorrows of our ancestors came to haunt us in the dead of night when all else was quiet but for the trill of the crickets. The future stretched out in front of us, as yet unwritten. The beauty of the unbroken horizon. We placed our hopes in each track we laid down, as though we could brand the earth with our dreams and make her keep her promise of redemption.

I shared quarters in the caboose with Pepe, a gentle giant of a Mexican who spoke with a heavy accent, and Hank, a small but brawny white man from the Ozarks. I liked Pepe. He was quiet and worked surprisingly fast for his size. He could make and repair anything. He wired a light bulb in our caboose so we could see at night. He could build a fire out of three twigs and some brambles.

At night, "Where are you from?" was a song that played in my mind when the alternating sound of Hank moaning and Pepe snoring cut through my sleep like a hacksaw. I came from cotton and wheat. From the sweet taste of sugar cane juice dripping down my lips and coating my chin with its sticky residue. I came from love so deep it defied the white man's wrath at every turn. I came from sorrow that knew no bounds until it grew wings and soared above its captors with immeasurable joy. I came from the rich red soil of Africa, from slave ships where my people were piled on top of each other like cattle. I came from the desire to own and conquer, from lust and violence. I was the lark and the caged dove, the vulture that circled over its prey until it was too weak to protest. I was as wild as the wolf and as meek as a rabbit whose throat was about to be slit.

One day, I found a stone so perfect I wanted to cry. The river had polished it until it was as smooth as a baby's bottom. The cream color of its surface shimmered with gold and silver.

One side was streaked with a thin sliver of cobalt blue. I kept the stone close to my body at night, like a good luck charm. If nothing else, its weight against my chest brought me comfort.

Pepe saw me holding my stone one day and nodded. He noticed much more than he said. The week before, he'd built a collapsible shed so we could bathe in privacy wherever we stopped.

"We no do that in México," he'd said to Hank, who liked to bathe stark naked outside our shelter, even when it was brutally cold.

I wondered if this was true or if he'd seen my discomfort. Pepe hauled water for us once a week so we could clean. At night, we stared at the fire in silent companionship.

I was learning more about the world of men than I ever had from my brothers and father. How they talked about women among themselves. Especially Hank. There seemed to be little else on his mind, except perhaps eating. But when he thought nobody was looking, I saw the slump of his shoulders. The doubt. The frustration. The desire for something else. He had a sharp mind for numbers. He could remember any number he saw.

"Fat lot o' good it does here," he said.

I often caught him looking at me, his brow creased in thought, and each time he did, my insides squirmed uneasily. The look reminded me of Sammy. I made sure he was gone before I bathed. I slept in my clothes, which was easy since I didn't have any others. I was relieved Pepe was also in the caboose with us. From him, I learned reliability. Steadiness. Although he was fast, he was never in a hurry. I knew he had a wife, three children, and aging parents he sent money to in Mexico, but he rarely talked about them. I saw him staring at the stars at night, as though he could follow their spattered trail back home. I knew that look.

One night, I had strange, disturbing dreams. I was a rabbit running through a meadow, chasing a squirrel up a tree, when all of a sudden, I was snatched up by a pair of hands that held me too tightly. In the next instant, I was a woman, naked, interlaced with a man in fervent lovemaking.

I woke up with a start, disoriented and confused, and it took me a moment to realize that someone was behind me, holding me tightly, rubbing himself slowly against my back while he moaned softly in my ear. His hand fumbled at my belly, trying to get under my shirt. His touch was startlingly gentle, almost tender. I opened my mouth to scream and felt a hand cover my mouth.

This time, though, I was no longer the scared rabbit. I'd been in the wild too long for that. The hunter, once awakened, did not easily lie back down. I felt anger snake from my belly to my hands, ready to strike if need be. I lay still, waiting for him to relax his hold. And then, quick as a fox, I elbowed him in the groin and slid out to the other side of the caboose. I turned to face Hank, claws out, ready to attack first. In an instant, Pepe's lumbering body was between us, and he had Hank in a stranglehold.

"Leave heem alone!" Pepe hollered in a thunderous voice. When he let go, Hank sputtered to the floor.

"I wasn't doing nothin'—just havin' a little fun," he blurted out when he caught his breath. "How do we even know Matt's a boy? Have you ever seen him naked? Even if he is, he's purty enough to have some fun with. He was enjoying it, too, until he woke up!"

This time, Pepe's voice was so quiet it was even more menacing.

"Leave. Heem. Alone," he said with finality. Hank whimpered and shuffled off to the far corner, and for the rest of the night, Pepe slept near me. I didn't think I could go back to sleep, but I must have, for when I woke up, sun was streaming in through the little window, and Hank was gone. We never saw him again.

"Thank you," I said to Pepe as we prepared to go to work.

"I no help you, I help heem. If I no go between, you kill heem," he said, looking serious for an instant, then breaking into a grin. I laughed too. His smile faded, and he looked closely at my face, as though he could see inside.

"It no matter to me. Who you are. We all have story. Some things we no can fix. Even Pepe. You must let 'em break. Start again. *Un nuevo comienzo, si?*"

Relief washed over me. I felt the veil of secrecy lift ever so slightly. There were many days when I did not know myself. Sometimes, I believed the lies I told others. Home and girlhood felt like a distant memory.

And yet I was always guarded, a sentinel standing watch over my secret, careful not to let anyone in. Now, at last, I had a friend. Someone who saw me. Saw through me. Protected me. The bond between us was stronger than ever, although the words that passed between us were even fewer than before.

A few days later, Leo took Hank's place. He was seventeen, two years older than I was. Tall and lanky, as ebony as my father. He had dark, fathomless eyes and cheekbones that reminded me of a warrior. His nose was flat. He looked a little like my brothers, and yet the feeling inside me was entirely new.

Suddenly, my body had become a being in its own right, over which I had little control. And it had no doubt it was a girl. My skin burned and my belly fluttered whenever Leo was nearby. My hands longed to brush against his skin. I worked alongside him whenever I could. I saw him once, naked, and I could not avert my eyes.

Pepe saw me looking at Leo, and he started sending him away on errands as often as he could. When Pepe and I were alone, he shook his head at me.

"No. It's too dangerous. Remember Hank," he conveyed without words. There were many more like Hank around here. I knew, although my body rebelled. Slowly, I let go. I only addressed Leo when necessary. I turned away from him. Pretended I did not see him. That I did not care. But inside of me, something shriveled up. A little piece of hope slipped away.

Chapter Nine

Puzzle Pieces

Sarah

"My migraines are better, and I'm grateful for that," I said to Patrick.

"But ever since our EMDR session, I've been on such an emotional roller coaster. Reading my old journals opened up a floodgate of memories all wanting my attention. There are moments when I feel calmer and more at peace than I have in years. And other times I feel so agitated and grief-stricken, the smallest thing makes me cry."

Patrick nodded but didn't say anything, so I continued.

"I have no desire to do any of the things that usually bring me pleasure. It's hard to get up in the morning, I haven't run in a few days, and I have no appetite. All I do is mope around and navel-gaze, which is not like me. I need action," I said, a hint of desperation creeping into my voice.

"Patrick, are you sure this is helping me? I feel like a patient lying on an operating table with my guts spilling out, but I have no idea what the plan is for sewing me back up!"

Patrick smiled empathetically.

"Sarah, I can understand that this is overwhelming. Your coping strategy for so long has been to block off your feelings and just keep forging ahead. But at some point, the old strategies stop working and everything you've been running away from catches up to you." I nodded at his words, since that was how I'd been feeling.

"It's not as clear-cut as sewing a patient back up, I'm afraid. In some ways, it's more like a puzzle with many missing pieces. It's our job to find those pieces and fit them back where they belong. Right now, we're at the part where the jigsaw is just a jumbled mess on the floor."

"Okay, I'll bite, but what are the pieces, and how do I find them?" I asked. Both my jaw and stomach clenched at how messy and open-ended the process seemed. I jammed my feet in my shoes to stop them from shuffling. I was glad I wasn't wearing sandals.

"The pieces represent wounds, old beliefs, and protective mechanisms that are stuck in time. They need to be healed and released in order for you to start feeling more whole. To know that you have more options than running away, shutting down, or fighting." He paused, seeming to scan my face for how this was landing.

"Yeah, that makes sense, I think."

"How did you feel working with the memory of your father's death?"

"I have to say, I've always thought all that inner-child talk was hippie psychobabble, but I could really feel in my body how the grief and shock got lodged in me."

"Exactly. Some therapists refer to it as a trauma capsule, a part of you that gets trapped in a traumatic event and isn't aware that it's no longer happening. This is because the limbic system, which governs your fight-or-flight response, has no sense of time."

Watching Patrick get animated as he spoke, I had a momentary vision of him giving a lecture to a large audience. I wondered if he engaged in small talk at parties or jumped right into talking about dysregulated nervous systems.

"What about the trauma from my time in South Sudan and other missions? The recent stuff feels much more urgent, especially since I'd like to get back to the work when the three months are up."

"I understand. And in my experience, the core wounding happens early on, and later events only serve to compound and reinforce existing beliefs and coping strategies. We can do a little of both if needed. But if we unravel the childhood wounds first, by the time we get to the current ones, they should be less intractable."

"I'm not sure I get it, but I trust you," I said. And I found that, despite my default skepticism, part of me meant it. Another part of me was probably huddling in fear.

"Thank you. And we can always revise our strategy as needed. So, one part of the puzzle is your early wounding and beliefs. Another part is your nightmares. You've had them off and on for decades, so I'm guessing they're trying to reveal something important."

"I haven't really been able to connect with my dream self, Maggie, since that first time. When I tried again, I got a blurry image of what looked like train tracks, but then everything went dark. It felt like too much for my system right now."

"I know it can be a lot. And it's great that you are in touch with your limits. For now, my recommendation is to take a break from actively trying to connect to her. However, if anything does come up spontaneously, especially in your dreams, write it down. Does that feel manageable?"

I nodded, although I could feel my temples start to throb.

"Third, and most importantly for you right now, is for you to learn ways to regulate your nervous system, which is stuck in survival mode. As such, it's constantly vacillating between hyper- and hypo-arousal, with very little chance to reset."

"I think I know what you mean. I often feel like I'm either

wired or tired. I rarely, if ever, feel rested. But I don't know how to change that," I said, with a hint of frustration.

"What are you feeling in your body right now?"

"I feel maxed out. It's hard to describe what I'm feeling. My body feels jangly and ragged. I have to focus hard to process what you're saying, as though the words are coming in garbled, and I have to unscramble them to understand."

"Yes, that's exactly what I'm inviting you to notice. Let's slow things down. I'm going to show you a few easy breathing and concentration exercises that might help."

By the end of the session, I felt both more settled and also a little agitated.

"I think the part of myself that's hypervigilant, as you say, is so used to being one step ahead, it's having a hard time staying in the present moment, Patrick," I said, but at least I could smile about it now.

"The fact that you're aware of that is huge. Before our next session, Sarah, I would like you to go to one meditation group and one yoga class. I know it's not typically your thing, but I think it would be helpful to try both at least a few times to see how your body responds. If you don't like either one, you can try something else."

"Yoga and meditation, huh?" I asked, with a cocked eyebrow. "Okay, I'll try. But for me, running is my meditation. It's what clears my head and gets me the most in my body."

"That's great, and I'm definitely not asking you to stop running. But when you do, I also invite you to be mindful of *how* you are running. Are you in the flow and feeling at peace? Is there a frenetic quality to your gait? Are you pounding the ground?"

"Whoa, that's a lot, but I'll try to notice without getting too much in my head about it."

"Perfect. You may find that sitting in meditation is a different kind of practice than running, which I think might benefit you, especially *because* it's challenging," he said with a small smile. I sighed. Just what I needed. More challenges.

"When I say stillness, what comes to mind for you, Sarah?"

"Being trapped. Dying," I answered without thinking. There was something about stillness and silence that terrified me, as though they might ensnare me in their steely grip and slowly suffocate me.

I thrived on movement, stimulation, change. After I reached the one-year benchmark in any given country, I started to feel a thin veil of lethargy clouding my mind and hooding my thinking. Numbness and complacency set in. That's when I knew it was time to move on.

"Exactly. And it's that feeling of being trapped that's wanting healing, which isn't possible if you keep avoiding it. Right now, you have time and space you usually don't have. I know it's uncomfortable, but it's the perfect time for you to allow yourself to feel what comes up for you when there's nowhere to run."

I felt wound up after the session and our talk about stillness. I changed into my running clothes as soon as I got home and went for a quick sprint in my neighborhood—feet pounding against the pavement, as though I could pulverize it back to earth. I was definitely not running with my body, and I really didn't care.

I have to get out of here, I thought for the umpteenth time. I would take cholera and patients oozing with pus over grueling soul-searching any day.

That night, I dreamt that Maggie and I were hauling something very heavy and dropping it to the ground. Sweat was dripping from every pore in my body, and I finally collapsed in exhaustion. "Does it ever end?" I asked, but Maggie was too far in front of me to hear.

Chapter Ten
New York, May 1915

The End of the Road

Maggie

When we laid the last track in New York, I knew I had arrived. There was a different kind of wilderness here. So many houses weaving their way along meandering roads. One right next to the other, so that there was no room for them to breathe. The sky looked cramped sitting on top of all these houses instead of sprawling across the never-ending spread of land.

The marketplace was a-bustle with people, motorcars, buggies, bicycles, food carts ... There were more people than I had ever seen before, and when I walked down the street, there were no curious stares. Only indifference. The stones whispered that I had survived and was finally safe. Nobody cared who I was here.

"I made it," I said out loud and had a sudden thought of Mama. I wondered how she was. What she'd think if she saw me here. Tears caught in my throat. I thought I was going to choke.

I'm not there yet, I reminded myself and reluctantly pushed the thought of home out of my mind again.

I didn't say anything to Pepe, but he knew. It was time for me to stay and for him to move on. We had been working together for six months. Leo had left us a few weeks ago. He met a girl in Pennsylvania and stayed behind. I pretended I didn't notice, although the first few nights, my sleep was pinched short by the ache in my heart.

I had to find work. I heard from the men on the railroad that there was an employment office. But first, I had to become a girl again. At fifteen, almost a woman. This was something I *could* fix. Or at least mend. The tattered rags of my identity. I didn't want to build my future on a lie.

But I was grateful for the days spent as a boy for they had helped me discover parts of me I had previously been forced to file away. My courage. My will. My "no." The boundaries of what was possible had expanded considerably. I hoped I'd be able to hold on to those when I reclaimed my girlhood.

I went to a clothing store downtown with some of the savings I had stashed away in Mama's shawl. Although the pay was a pittance, I had few expenses and had kept almost all I earned. "I'm looking for a dress. For my sister. Nothing too fancy," I told the clerk.

"Her size?"

"About like me."

He came out with a plain yellow frock and matching scarf I liked instantly. The color made me think of daffodils. And spring.

"*Un nuevo comenzio*," as Pepe would say.

I went back to the caboose one last time to change. Pepe was there. As soon as he saw the package I was holding, he went out to give me privacy. I peeled off the shirt and trousers that had been my shield for all these months, like a snake shedding its skin. Then, the wrapping that had bound my breasts. I looked down at them for the first time in what seemed like years. Even when I bathed, I chose to ignore them. As though looking would make them real and bring home my lie.

They were so small from months of near-starvation. Barely visible. Raw from the bindings. They did not know what to do with this newfound freedom. I came out wearing the dress and scarf and saw the hint of a smile playing around Pepe's lips and eyes. I smiled back, thanking him silently for all he had taught me. He nodded ever so slightly. I left without a word. We had no need for long goodbyes. I knew he would be with me wherever I went, like the polished stone I still slept with every night.

I walked into the employment office—one cramped, dingy room at the end of a street. A Colored man sat behind a desk, smartly dressed in a suit, with small, round eyeglasses perched on his nose. There were a few men in line ahead of me.

When my turn came, the bespectacled man glanced up at my dress, my flat chest, the scarf hiding my short hair, and then back down to the paper in front of him. I stood there, watching him, the way I had learned from Pepe. My body was straight, tall, still. I gazed at him until he looked up again. This time at my face.

"Hi, sistah. This ain't no place for a pretty girl like you. What you doin' here?"

"Looking for work, just like everybody else here. Isn't this an employment office? That's what it says on the door, anyway," I said softly yet firmly, looking straight at him until he looked away.

" Course," he answered, a little gruffly. "What can you do?"

"What I can't do might be quicker. I can pick, haul, mine. I can sew and cook some. I can read, write, and count."

"Sure you can. And my brother's the president. But I might have just the thing for you. The Jones family is looking for a girl to clean, cook, and take care of Josie, their six-year-old daughter. They just arrived from Alabama. They're important folk. He's a doctor. Colored. They have a small room you can stay in. They'll want to meet you first, though. Go to this address and ask for the missus."

The house was away from the main bustle and surrounded by trees. I had to walk a while and ask a number of people before I found it. It was bigger even than the Tanners' house. Regal. Three stories high, it gleamed white—shiny and proud. It made me think of what an eagle's nest might look like if it were a house. I felt nervous. A slim young woman opened the door. She was tall with mahogany skin that reminded me of Mama and was wearing a pretty blue dress. From another room, I heard a child cry out.

"I'm coming, Josie," the woman called out. For a moment, I was confused.

Had the Joneses already found someone? I almost turned around and went back from where I came, but then I remembered I had nowhere to go back to, so I summoned my courage.

"I'm looking for Missus Jones," I stuttered.

"I am Mrs. Jones," the woman said, not unkindly.

"Of course, I'm sorry," I said, trying to recover from my mistake. I had somehow been expecting a doctor's wife and mother to be older. More worn out. Rounder. Like Mama.

"Did the employment office send you?" she asked. I nodded mutely.

"Can you cook? Clean?"

I nodded again, then said, "I helped my mama at the Tanners' house," finally regaining the use of my tongue. I did not say that was in another life—before I was a boy. And that I wasn't sure I remembered how.

"Have you ever worked with children?"

I shook my head no. Sammy was the Tanners' only child, and he was older than I was.

"Well, you look more alert than some girls they have sent. We can try for a week and see how it goes. You want to go get your things and come back?"

I shook my head no again. I had no things to get. I was wearing Mama's shawl, and I gave Pepe the boy's clothes to give to someone who might need them, as well as Mama's gourd. I was holding the stone tightly in my right hand, for luck.

Mrs. Jones ("Call me Edna," she said, although I knew I wouldn't) showed me the house. They'd moved there one month ago and had just finished furnishing it. I also met Josie. She was small and thin, with big black eyes that followed me around. She did not utter a word, but I could tell, like Pepe, she was watching everything.

"The move was hard on her. She doesn't say much, but once you get to know her, she is a sweet, talkative girl," said Mrs. Jones, looking uncomfortable for the first time since I arrived.

That night, I found myself staring at the ceiling, unable to sleep. It had been so long since I'd slept in a room, and I'd never had my own. The bed was soft, and the room was too quiet. I tossed and turned, but sleep eluded me. The ceiling stared back at me. Cold and unforgiving. It wondered how long I could make it. So did I.

I suddenly wished I were sleeping outside. The wind nipping at my face, trying to bite my cheeks as I burrowed farther into Mama's shawl. The cadence of the cicadas carrying me to sleep. I even missed the caboose. Pepe's soft snoring rising and falling like the tide. The silence seemed unnatural. It made me think of death.

And then, I heard something. It sounded like a whimper. I tried to ignore it, but the sound got louder, more insistent.

I followed its thread down to Josie's room, opening the door gently. She was thrashing in her bed and shaking her head.

"No, no," she cried out. "Don't hurt him!"

I gently shook her awake. "Josie, it's okay. You're just having a bad dream," I tried to explain.

She clung to my arm. I started stroking her hair. I felt a stirring inside, and before I knew it, I was singing the words to "The Gospel Train's A-comin'," a song Mama used to sing when I was scared:

> *I hear it just at hand*
> *I hear the car wheel rumblin'*
> *And rollin' thro' the land*
> *Get on board little children*
> *Get on board little children*
> *Get on board little children*
> *There's room for many more*

Josie's grip slowly started relaxing. When her breathing evened out, I started moving ever so gently away. She woke and grabbed my leg.

"Don't leave. Please," she begged, hugging me so tight I could barely breathe. Eventually, I stretched out next to her, her soft body nestled against mine. I felt something warm and soft move inside me. A memory of the rabbit I couldn't kill flashed before my eyes.

When I woke, the sun was streaming into the room, and Mrs. Jones was standing over me, looking startled.

"Maggie," she snapped, "what are you doing, sleeping in Josie's bed?"

Josie stirred next to me, her hands still clutching my arm. She opened her eyes and blinked at her mother a few times.

"I had the dream again, Mama. I was scared. Please let her stay, Mama."

Mrs. Jones looked from Josie to me and back. I could see the fatigue in her eyes and little lines of tension creasing at her forehead. Her face softened.

"I'm sorry I didn't hear you. I must be more tired than I think. You okay, honey?"

Josie nodded.

"Maggie, I need your help in the kitchen. We are hosting many of the prominent Coloreds in New York tomorrow evening. I need the house to be spotless, and we have lots of cooking to do."

"Yes, ma'am," I answered, relieved. For the first time since I ran from home, I could feel my muscles unwinding just a little. I sent silent thanks for getting this far and prayed that nothing went wrong.

Chapter Eleven

Yoga and Meditation

Sarah

"Relax into your downward dog," the svelte yoga instructor said in a mellifluous voice.

Yeah, right, I thought. I had somehow managed to escape what some would call the yoga fad for the past two decades. There was nothing that seemed natural about it to me. Not the cushiony rubber mats. Not the eternal good humor of those teaching it. And definitely not postures that required me to twist into a pretzel. My muscles were wiry and tightly coiled, which was the opposite of stretching and flexibility.

My wrists strained to hold up the weight of my body. My hamstrings protested against my straight legs and wanted to buckle at my knees. My heels felt miles away from the floor. I silently cursed Patrick for sending me here.

Next time I want to settle my nervous system, I'll go running. Thank you very much.

But as I pushed my way up into cobra pose—my lower body reaching down toward the floor just as my upper body arched up—I felt a slight opening in my chronically stooped shoulders. For a nanosecond, my mind was clear and free from any thought.

After class, my body felt both achy and a little looser than usual. The sun had burned through the morning fog, and after shedding my extra layers, the heat felt soothing to my well-worked muscles. I had no desire to hunch over my laptop or my journals. As I biked through downtown Berkeley, I decided to stop and explore some of my old haunts from high school and college. I wasn't usually one for reminiscing—walks down memory lane just made me sad—but between the EMDR session with Patrick and reading my old journals, I felt a desire to remember.

Walking through the gourmet ghetto, the smell of melting cheese wafting from the Cheeseboard tempted me. Between the deliciously gooey pizzas and live music, that place had been a favorite refuge of mine during my UC Berkeley years.

Yet I found myself drawn to the game store instead. I couldn't remember the last time I'd been inside. Probably not since my fifteen-year-old Dungeons and Dragons phase. I didn't know what I was looking for. I saw a Scrabble set and thought of my dad. But it looked too bright and commercial, nothing like the musty travel set we had both loved.

I wonder what happened to that set? I thought idly as I continued browsing the aisles. I found myself in the puzzle section. I stared at them, transfixed and confused by my own enchantment.

Puzzles had never been my thing, although I remembered that Grandma Belle had been a big fan. Probably because she loved creating order out of chaos. I thought of what Patrick said to me about finding the missing pieces and wondered if that was what had drawn me here.

Doing an actual puzzle might not be a bad idea.

And maybe by the time I was done with the last piece, I would be ready to leave. I picked out a puzzle representation of Monet's *Water Lilies*. I had loved that painting ever since I first saw the original in the Orsay Museum. I had a momentary thought of Paris, but it quickly faded.

As I was turning to leave with the puzzle, however, bright colors on the bottom shelf caught my eye. Pulling the box out, I saw hundreds of colorful hot-air balloons, some on the ground waiting for liftoff, the rest soaring in the blue sky. The image reminded me of my missing parts returning to me. Not to mention that with all the different colors, I thought this puzzle would be easier than the more monochromatic lilies.

I didn't realize until I got the box home that it contained 1,500 pieces. Even my grandmother, who was an expert puzzler, stuck to 1,000. Daunted, I decided to listen to relaxing music instead.

The next evening, I went to an introductory meditation class recommended by Patrick. I just wanted to get my "homework" over with. The event was led by the daughter of a famous mindfulness guru from the 1960s, and the room was packed. The chairs were all taken, but there was an empty cushion on the far left side.

The teacher was fairly young, with long, red hair that flowed halfway down her back. With her aquiline nose and sharp eyes, she reminded me of an eagle. A red-haired eagle. She rang the bell and gave brief instructions on how to sit with the tailbone raised up slightly so the spine and head were stacked and straight. I shifted uncomfortably on the yellow, crescent-shaped pillow, my body straining to find a comfortable position. I had to fight the urge to slouch.

I was reminded of when I was five or six, and Grandma Belle's Catholic sister took me to church, dolled up in a stiff, uncomfortable dress. I had fidgeted and squirmed the whole time, my gaze fixed on my brand-new Minnie Mouse watch until I was released to run and play outside.

The first ten minutes of meditating were excruciating.

So much for the limbering effects of yoga, I thought. If anything, I felt even stiffer than usual. My lower back ached, and my left foot went numb as it started to fall asleep. My muscles tensed with the desire to move, and my mind buzzed with worried thoughts about how much longer I had to stay still.

And then something shifted ever so slightly. My body started easing into the silence. As my breath deepened, my thoughts began to slide off my shoulders, the way they did when I got into my running groove. I felt an expansion in my chest as some of my habitual tension melted away. Unfortunately, the feeling lasted all of a minute (at most) before the fidgetiness returned. I resorted to counting my breaths until the bell rang. I lost track around eighty-five.

I considered leaving at the break but decided to stay to listen to the talk. The topic was on the ways resistance might appear when starting a meditation practice.

"The resistance could manifest as physical pain, or it might show up as thoughts trying to pull you out of the now. The key is to allow the feeling to be there without either pushing it away or collapsing into it. Remember, resistance is not your enemy. It's trying to protect you from pain or from losing a sense of control. Fighting it is like arguing with a toddler throwing a temper tantrum. It's utterly futile." A few people laughed. Parents, I figured.

"The only thing that will calm the resistance is presence. Compassion. Self-love."

I felt my skin crawl at the last two words.

Wouldn't self-love just lead to a proliferation of narcissists in the world? What we really needed was a little more self-control. I mean, what was the point of meditation if it wasn't to manage one's thoughts and emotions?

Back home, I found my inner fourteen-year-old wanting attention. I wondered if the foray into the game store had roused her from my memory graveyard. Or perhaps it was the evening's talk.

"It figures," I said out loud. "That girl could write a thesis on resistance."

Chapter Twelve

The Joneses

Maggie

The days started blurring into each other as I settled into a rhythm. A week had come and gone, and there seemed to be a silent agreement that I got to stay. I was too scared to ask Mrs. Jones outright for fear that she would change her mind. Josie was gone half the day at school. I took her there and went to get her, even though she could easily walk the fifteen minutes on her own. I relished those walks, and I sensed she did too, although many times we said little to one another. We took a shortcut through a big park, and on our way back, we often stopped to watch butterflies land on wildflowers or insects burrow into the earth.

    Back at the Joneses', I cleaned and cooked. The house had started warming to me and no longer resisted me when I went to polish the floorboards. As I did, I tried not to think of cleaning the floor in the Tanners' house when I was six and seeing Mama's frozen look as she followed Mr. Tanner into the room. Now that my survival was no longer a constant concern, it was harder to keep thoughts of home at bay, and the ache in my heart became part of my daily life.

    Mrs. Jones sometimes accompanied her husband on his rounds. He was also tall and slender, and he reminded me of an elm tree. He sported a thin mustache and small, round glasses perched on his nose. He had not said a word to me except for "hello" when Mrs. Jones introduced me to him the first day.

Every morning, I got up at 4:00 a.m. and made dozens of baked treats that Mrs. Jones brought to the patients and their families. There was another Colored doctor in town, but I heard he was about to retire, and that was why Mr. Jones was asked to come.

Other times, Mrs. Jones was home. Once a week, her husband invited the prominent Colored men in town to get together. They talked in hushed tones in his office, which was also his library. Mrs. Jones often took the opportunity to invite their wives for lunch to get to know them better. Although she was always moving or doing something, she had a quality of stillness that reminded me of a mountain. Or a tree. Or, simply, the earth. Pliable, yet steady.

At night, we all sat together at the dining room table. At first, I was uncomfortable sitting with them, like I was part of their family, and it only made me miss my own even more. But they insisted, and eventually, I came to cherish this time. When pangs of guilt gripped my heart, I told myself Mama would be happy to see me so well taken care of.

Back home, we didn't have a kitchen table. Not a proper one. Just a small work table that had belonged to the Tanners before it got so worn they couldn't use it anymore. There was rarely time to sit anyway—since we were up from sunup to sundown in the fields or in the Tanners' house, all with different chores.

Mama prepared food for us at the little wood stove, but the rare times we did all sit together, we felt cramped, with my brothers sitting on the bed, Mama and Papa on chairs, and me on the floor. Sometimes the boys argued, and Mama hushed them. Other times, we sat in comfortable silence, too bone-weary to talk. That tiredness that blankets the whole body and makes the brain feel like it's full of ants as you fight to stay awake when all you want is to slump into a deep sleep.

The Joneses' table—made of sturdy oak and with an extra leaf that could be slid in to make room for more guests—came with them all the way from Alabama. I'd never seen anything like it. One of the legs had a little gouge in it, and I imagined the workers struggling against its weight as they hoisted the table onto the extra wagon the Joneses had hired to transport their things.

This table had seen *many* dinners! With Mrs. Jones asking Mr. Jones about Mrs. M's rheumatoid fever or Mr. H's hemorrhoids. Sometimes, Mrs. Jones took one look at the puffiness in her husband's face and the dullness in his eyes, and she didn't ask a thing. She focused on Josie's table manners instead, or filled the room with bright, cheerful chatter that didn't require a response or even much attention.

I wondered what this table would say if it could talk. I imagined its life as a tree, standing tall and proud with roots meandering to the center of the earth. I could relate. I hadn't been a skylark in a while and had forgotten what freedom tasted like. Fallen back into old habits of serving others.

In part, I tried to stay as busy as possible so I wouldn't think about Papa and Andre … or wonder what happened to Mama and my other brothers. I was worried that if I did, I would never be able to stop my tears. And I had promised myself that I would survive. Although I felt safe for now, I couldn't ward off the feeling that danger was just around the bend.

There was plenty to keep me occupied. I was particularly curious about the gatherings in Dr. Jones' library. Sometimes I overheard them when I was cleaning, their anger carrying their voices across the closed door.

"This has got to stop! At some point, we need to stand up

for ourselves. Say no. Now they want to close our schools!"

During the day, the library was empty and often called to me. I had never seen so many books in one place. Not even in the little school I attended back home. I tried not to pay attention as I dusted the bookshelves, but their titles beckoned to me. Not the big medical textbooks with all the diagrams. I couldn't make sense of those. But the poetry. And Shakespeare's collected works. Mr. Jones had a book with all of Keats's poems that my hands were drawn to. Soon, my fingers were caressing its spine.

"Just one page," I told myself, as I settled into Mr. Jones' armchair. I was mesmerized by the words. Transfixed. Time stopped. I was in the sea, in the middle of its "eternal whisperings," when Mrs. Jones flung open the door.

"Maggie, there you are, didn't you hear—" She stopped mid-sentence, staring at me. I'd been caught red-handed sitting in her husband's chair, the book lying open and naked like a lover in front of me.

She walked over slowly, turned over the book, and stared at me. I looked down, my cheeks on fire. I felt so ashamed of myself. I had nowhere to go. I couldn't afford to make this kind of mistake. And yet, I knew that if I had to do it over, I would probably do the exact same thing.

"I'm really sorry, Missus Jones. I was dusting it, and I was curious to see inside," I said when I couldn't stand the silence anymore.

Still, she stared. Fear quivered miserably in my belly.

"It won't happen again, I promise. Please give me another chance."

"You can read, Maggie?" is all she said when she finally broke the silence.

"Well, yes ..." I stammered.

"And you like Keats?"

"Oh, yes ma'am, we read 'Ode to Autumn' in school, and

I loved it. I love the words. There's nothing more beautiful. They make everything else melt away …"

Mrs. Jones looked at me thoughtfully, like it was the first time she was seeing me.

"You know, we have been having trouble with Josie at school. She seems to have no interest in learning to read. She just stares out the window. I don't know what to do. But she seems to like you. She trusts you. You have similar ways. Quiet, watching, but under the surface, at the bottom of your eyes … There is a whole world down there." She paused as she looked closely at my face.

"Maggie, would you like to try teaching Josie to read?"

I looked at her, and I could feel a smile starting in my eyes until it pushed at the corners of my mouth.

"Oh yes, I would!"

"Good. We will try it for a few weeks. You will go with her to school and study with the older children, and at night, you will help her with her reading."

The next day, Mrs. Jones hired another girl to help with the cooking and cleaning, "just for a few weeks, then we'll see." I accompanied Josie to school. Since my work was less, my pay was cut in half, which was fine by me. Mrs. Jones gave me her old clothes to wear, and I was fed and housed, so there wasn't much more I needed.

From that day on, my life was never the same.

Chapter Thirteen

The Bay Area

Sarah

I sifted through the box of old journals until I found what I was looking for. The diary had a plush teal cover and was labeled: "1990. Fucking Foggy Bay Area!!!"

"Okay, fourteen-year-old self, let's see what puzzle piece you hold and how we can fix you so you stop freaking out," I said out loud. "I know you want to get the hell out of here as much as I do!"

Looking out the window, I saw my mother's car in the driveway, meaning she'd probably carpooled to work and her car was up for grabs. My legs suddenly felt twitchy, wanting to move.

"Let's go to the redwoods," I said, sensing the trees calling me. The Oakland redwoods had been the first ones to make me feel welcome in my new home, and when I'd learned to drive, I spent many afternoons there. It seemed like the perfect place to connect to my sullen teen self who'd just been carted back across the Atlantic to the other end of the country.

I parked the car in the shade and walked half a mile along a wide trail that bordered what should have been a stream, although it was more of a trickle due to lack of rain. There was a picnic table next to a grove of redwoods called Old Church.

Taking out the journal, I opened it with a surprising feeling of tenderness.

August 12, 1990
Sunny California, my ass! It's freezing cold, foggy, and 60°F. I could kill Mom. She promised me warmth and sun!
 And why do random strangers smile at me? I'm sure they're high on something! Oh, and I'm going to punch the next person who asks for my astrological sign. I have never been anywhere so fake. I can't wait to be 18 so Mom can never do this to me again. I miss Fatou.

September 5
The kids in my school are weird. Between the piercings, the colored and/or shaved hair, and tattoos, I feel like I'm watching a freak show. What's the point of making friends anyway, since who knows where Mom will go next? At least there's a decent library. And my English teacher is nice. He's said we could write short stories for extra credit. That'll keep me busy.

October 22
Today's my 14th birthday. Mom got me a card and another journal. She probably thinks I should be grateful she thought of it. I wish Dad were here. Maybe we'd play Scrabble. He might even take me to a restaurant. At least I like to think he would. I'm starting to forget what he looked like, and I'm not sure what's the truth of him and what's my imagination.

February 9, 1991
I haven't written in a while. I still don't have any friends, but who needs them? On another note, it's freezing in

August here, but the fucking magnolia trees are blooming in February. Even the trees are messed up. I'm trying not to feel too lonely. Fatou wrote me a letter, and I bawled my eyes out. What a crybaby! I'm glad nobody saw.

I sighed, remembering those days. I had felt so friendless and shut down. As ironic as it was for someone who moved around as much as I did, I had clearly never done well with transitions.

I got up and walked a few feet until I was inside the closest grove of redwoods. I lowered my body to sit against one of them, and I felt the knobby yet surprisingly smooth roots supporting the curve of my tailbone, a blanket of needles at my feet. My shoulder blades rested against the rough bark. When I looked up, the geometry of the circular spokes of the trunks meeting the shimmering canopy of leaves reminded me of Notre Dame's rose window. I took a deep breath, feeling my whole being shudder with the magnitude of the beauty surrounding me. Remembering the yoga/meditation class, I thought maybe Patrick was onto something. I could see how learning to calm and control my inner demons would help me keep it together when I was finally able to go back to work.

When I returned to my journal, I felt a little lighter and better able to hold space for the younger me. I rifled through the pages until I got to my sophomore year in high school when I entered a gothic phase and dressed in long, black clothes. The pink eyeshadow was replaced by thick, black eyeliner that contrasted with my pale skin. I'd painted my nails a bright, garish green. "Thank goodness that only lasted a year," was all my mother had to say about that period in my life. It was also when I got my first boyfriend. If you could call him that.

September 8, 1991
There's a new boy, Greg. He sits behind me in English class. He's thin and awkward. He has wild blond hair—I doubt he owns a brush. I've caught him looking at me in the cafeteria and at recess. His dad just retired from the military, and Greg says he's used to moving every two years. That's even worse than me.

September 29
Greg asked me to join his Dungeons and Dragons group and I said yes. We played today with two boys from his chess club. How nerdy can you get? But I have to admit, it was also kind of fun. Greg has a car. He's sixteen. He was held back a few years ago because he'd had to change schools halfway through the year and had missed too much to catch up. He drove me home. I let him kiss me. It was really wet. And sloppy. I don't know if I like him.

October 28
We did it. Honestly, I don't know what the big deal is. We hadn't planned on it. Well, I hadn't. He had a condom in his pocket, so he might have. He took me to Point Reyes for the day on Saturday "to celebrate my fifteenth birthday," he said. It was warm and sunny. The ocean was so wild and free on the rocks. We raced back to his car. I won. We were both laughing and panting. He started kissing and touching me, and I let him. I guess it was okay. It hurt though, and I don't know what all the fuss is about.

November 3
I hate boys! Things are so awkward with Greg. He could barely look me in the eye after Point Reyes. I don't get it. And a few times I caught him snickering with other boys, looking my way. I'm never going to let another boy kiss

me! I wish I was attracted to girls. I bet it would be easier … Kate and Lucy are so in love. They look really happy. I told Kate it seemed simpler, and she said sarcastically, "Yeah, dealing with homophobic assholes is so much easier!" She has a point, I know. But still.

I closed the journal and felt a pang of embarrassment, regret, and compassion for my confused young self. I'd been so closed off from my own emotions and needs. Even now, I could feel the urge to distract myself, to not feel the ache in my heart. The shame. The longing for love and attention.

I wanted to tell my younger self that things would get better. But would they really? Wasn't I still disconnected from myself? At least I could tell her that she wouldn't live with her mother forever. She'd travel the world, help others as best she could, and have wild adventures along the way. Even if she was still at the mercy of others' whims, she'd have more freedom.

Especially if I work hard to kick these nightmares and migraines, so I can return to the one thing that makes sense in my life, I thought.

Opening my journal again, I scanned my last entries to find the missing puzzle piece. What was the belief that was taking root in my younger self's teenage mind? At first, all I could see was a jumble of teenage rantings and felt mounting frustration with myself.

I am beyond fixing, I thought.

And suddenly, I heard the words "I'm unlovable," clearly. As I searched my memory for evidence that I didn't believe this, I felt the tightness in my chest and knew it to be true.

Shit. I guess I just need to convince myself I'm lovable, then.

On my way back home, I stopped by the library. I found a book of affirmations for the inner child and another of meditations for calming the anxious mind. I also selected a few books on Maggie's era and ordered some they didn't have in stock. I hadn't tried the automatic writing again, but the dream where we were hauling something heavy had an urgency to it that made me think I should do some research. Between the puzzle and the books, that should keep me busy enough until Patrick gave me the green light to return to my life.

Chapter Fourteen

Classroom Magic

Maggie

Just as I had back home, I lost myself in the classroom. And found myself again. I felt like a sapling in the spring after a long winter freeze, soaking in the April showers. Parts that had been dormant for so long were coming to life. The soft tendrils of curiosity had grown into an insatiable need for more information. My brain burned with the desire for knowledge. Here, time stopped. Thirst, hunger, and all bodily sensations ceased to exist or to matter. I was carried to worlds beyond time and space. I learned the why behind the instinctual wisdom I gained in the wild about plants and animals.

I saw the seeds begin to grow in Josie, too, as the squiggles I showed her began to come into focus as letters and the letters as words. The journey back from school could take up to an hour now, as we wandered off our path to discover what the world had to offer. If Josie could spell five or more things we saw on our trip, I would tell her a story at night. I had found a passion for storytelling, and in Josie, an avid listener.

Nowadays, she wouldn't let anyone else tuck her into bed. "Tell me the story about the rabbit, Maggie. The one you caught but couldn't eat," and "Tell me the story about how the wolf lived through the winter." Her favorites were about animals. I avoided stories that might scare her. Her nightmares were fewer. So were mine. But sometimes, out of nowhere, I saw Andre's body dangling in front of me, and my breath stopped.

Although Josie had started talking and smiling more, every once in a while, I saw her disappear into a dark place where nobody could reach her. Like when a crow swooped overhead, cawing at her loudly, and she ducked whimpering under a bench. I stayed there with her for a long time, holding her, before she was willing to come out. Even then, her whole body was shaking. I recognized that place and knew that I could coax her out of there for a little while with my words and stories. But in the end, she would have to choose where she wanted to reside.

One day, when Mrs. Jones and I were in the kitchen preparing scones for her husband's patients, I decided to ask her, even though my heart was racing and I was afraid of offending her.

"Missus Jones, what happened to Josie? Back in Alabama?"

I watched as a shadow crossed her face, and her expression became distant and unreachable.

I cleared my throat. And without thinking, I started telling her about the memory I'd pushed away these past two years. "I know it's none of my business, but I've been there too. I watched Mr. Tanner's men hang my Papa and my brother, Andre. Andre was just trying to help me, to get Mr. Tanner's son off me. And that's why I ran away. I don't know what happened to Josie. But I know what it's like, having a secret pain sitting in your chest, waiting to burst at any time. And feeling like you got to keep it secret or it might swallow you up."

I talked quickly, looking down, the words tripping over each other, afraid that if I stopped, I'd lose the courage to continue. This was the most I'd ever said to Mrs. Jones, and

I was scared of how she might react. But I knew I had no choice, not if I wanted to help Josie.

"It's the first time I told anyone what happened. But it helps." It did. I'd been holding the words on my own so long, I felt a little lighter sharing my load with her. Even though I could also feel the pain and grief I'd held at bay for so long creeping into my chest and tightening its grip around my eyes. I took a deep breath and turned my attention back to my employer.

"And I think I can help Josie, too, if I know what happened."

When I looked up, tears were streaming down the sides of her face, and her eyes were warm and kind, taking me in.

"I'm sorry, Maggie. About your brother and father. About not telling you what happened to Josie. I keep on thinking that if I don't say anything, it will go away, but I know it just buries it further inside of her." She took my hands in hers. "I've been so afraid for her, so afraid of losing her. So afraid it is my fault."

She sighed and then continued.

"I wasn't there, so I don't know all the details. She was with the nanny, Grace, and they were going to the market. There was a Colored man in front of them who wouldn't step down from the sidewalk to let a white man by. The white man started kicking him, but he wouldn't budge. Other men started joining in the kicking. Grace tried to get Josie out of there, but Josie broke free and ran toward the first white man—screaming, punching with her tiny fists, begging him to stop. Grace said it was like she lost all reason." She paused, and I could see her struggle against her anger and sorrow.

"The man slapped Josie and started hitting her before Grace finally managed to pry her away and carry her home. Grace was beside herself and wouldn't stop crying and shaking for days. But not Josie. She just went silent. Her bruises were superficial and were gone within a week, but not the inside ones. I watched her disappear before my very eyes. My sweet, lively little girl." Mrs. Jones was sobbing now, and I stroked her hands.

"I'm so grateful to you, Maggie, for helping her. And bringing some of her old self back. But sometimes I'm so envious I want to fire you because I want to be the one holding her and helping her lick her wounds."

"I know, I know. It's all right," I crooned softly, as though she were Josie's age.

When her sobs had subsided, I went on to say:

"Thank you, Missus Jones. You helped bring me back to life. And the best I can do with that gift is give it back to Josie as best I can. That's the only way I know to thank you."

She looked up at me, her smile hesitant at first. And then, finding mine, it spread to her eyes. I felt I'd found the sister I never had.

"Call me Edna," she said, and I knew I couldn't call her anything else.

The next day, I took Josie to our favorite park. There was a tree we liked to sit by.

"Today, I'm going to tell you a story for free, because you've been such a good girl. Would you like that?"

She nodded mutely.

And so, I told Josie the story of Rabbit, who was sweet, loving, and carefree. Rabbit loved to wander and play in the fields. Her mother had warned her not to go far, and especially not near the woods, for there were many creatures there that could hurt her. One day, she was chasing Cricket through the fields and wandered further than she planned. She found herself at the edge of the forest. She heard sounds and decided to see what was going on. It was a pack of coyotes, and they had surrounded Wolf.

Rabbit liked Wolf, for she had seen him many times in

the distance, but not once had he tried to eat her. She enjoyed listening to his lonely song at night when she couldn't sleep. It was an unfair fight—ten coyotes against one wolf—and without thinking, she leaped at one of them, trying to bite him with her little teeth. The coyote turned around and snapped his teeth at her, grazing her ear, but she managed to get away.

After that day, she was afraid to go out in the fields. She stopped eating. She didn't want to tell her mother what happened because she didn't want to get into trouble for straying so far, and for attacking the coyote and getting hurt. But finally, she told her mother. Her mother loved her so much that all she did was listen and lick her wounds. And every day after that, Rabbit went with her mother into the fields, a little further every day, until she was no longer scared to go out on her own.

As I told the story, I watched Josie's face go still as she retreated into her quiet place. But then, slowly, I saw her curiosity pull her back a little. I saw a glint of recognition in her eyes, followed by a flash of pain. Then, silent tears spilled from the well of her sadness and fear.

I held her close. "I know, little one, I know. You're a good, brave girl. You did everything you could. You gave that man the sweetest gift you could. You're a fighter, and nobody can take that away from you."

Six months had passed since that conversation, and every day I watched Josie open a little more. Some days, the words just couldn't come out fast enough. As she rattled off the events of her day in rapid fire, Edna and I just listened and grinned, both of us brimming with pride. Ever since I'd shared about Papa and Andre, we'd become much closer, and she treated me more like a younger sister than her employee. I guessed she was twenty-eight or twenty-nine, just a few years older than

Andre would have been, and her care for me had a similar quality. Protective. Understanding of my quiet ways.

The reminder of what I'd lost sometimes sent my mind reeling into a panicked, frozen place, and I had to take quick, forceful breaths to bring myself back. With time, however, I found it a little easier to push the memories away. Otherwise, I feared the guilt and worry would never let me out of its grasp.

One day, Mr. Milton, the principal, called me into his office, and I felt a sudden rush of panic. I had been feeling so happy these past few months that I kept waiting for something terrible to happen.

I hadn't met with him since my first day of class, and he looked at me for a long time, as though he were studying a rare breed of animal.

"How old are you, Maggie?" He finally asked, pensively. The question startled me, and I couldn't guess where the conversation was leading us.

"Sixteen, sir."

"So young. You seem older, somehow," he said.

I nodded, still wondering what he wanted from me.

"Mrs. Dunbar says the work you have done with Josie was close to a miracle, and she's also seen you helping some of her classmates in similar fashion. Your teacher, Mrs. Avery, says that you are already at the top of your class and could easily learn much of the material on your own with books she can provide you." He paused.

I waited, unsure of what I was supposed to say.

"Mrs. Dunbar would like you to be her assistant teacher while you finish high school. We can't officially give you a salary as you aren't certified to teach, but we can give you a small stipend. And if you show the aptitude she assumes you will, once you have your diploma, she can help you study for the teaching certification. If you want, of course."

For a moment, I was speechless. I could feel the joy and panic collide in my chest. The first was the excitement over a chance I hadn't even let myself dream of. The second was the old fear that if I let too much happiness in, I would have to pay for it dearly. Or someone I loved would. With great effort, I pushed down the fear and let my eyes and my smile shine with my response.

Chapter Fifteen

Hot-Air Balloons

Sarah

I stared at the picture of the hot-air balloons, wondering what had possessed me to buy it. I didn't even like puzzles.

Maybe it'll be calming, like fishing, I thought. At least it would give me something to do, unlike sitting in silence, counting the seconds until I could get off the cushion. I wondered if Patrick would accept puzzling as an alternative to meditating. Anything that helped calm my thoughts, right? I hadn't had a nightmare in a few days, and overall, I was sleeping well, which I took to be a win.

I ripped off the plastic packaging and brought the box downstairs to the dining room adjacent to the kitchen. I couldn't remember the last time we'd used the room, and I hoped my mother either wouldn't notice or wouldn't mind because the large, oval oak table was the only one big enough to hold 1500 puzzle pieces. I ran my hand against its polished surface.

I need to find the end pieces. That was about all I could remember from the rare times Amanda had left me with her mother, usually because the babysitter had canceled last minute. That and color coordinating the pieces, a task which usually fell to my young eyes and nimble fingers.

I turned on the radio to a jazz station and sifted through the pieces like I was panning for gold. There were so many, it wasn't that easy to find the end ones. I took out a few plastic containers so I could start sorting out like-colored pieces. Although each hot-air balloon had so many colors, it was trickier than I thought.

"Hi, Sarah."

I jumped at my mother's voice, then glanced at my watch. 8:12 p.m. Had I really been at this for hours? Not only that, but I was so engrossed in what I was doing that I didn't even hear her come in or feel her in the doorway, watching me.

"What are you doing?"

"I'm doing a puzzle." *Obviously*, I thought, but knew enough not to say. What did she think I was doing?

"Whatever for?"

I considered saying "for the same reason you like sudoku puzzles," but I didn't want to push her away. Although I wanted to be more truthful with her, it felt too vulnerable to say that I was broken and that the puzzle was a metaphor for the missing pieces I was searching for.

"My therapist has been encouraging me to do meditative things as a form of stress relief," I finally settled on.

"Your grandmother *loved* puzzles," she said, her voice dripping with disdain. Liking the same things as her mother did not bode in my favor. "I never saw the point of it, personally."

"I remember that about Grandma Belle, although I don't remember much else." Seeing a way to try to connect with my mother, I added, "I was never sure why the two of you were so distant."

"My mother is the last person I wish to discuss, Sarah. *I'm not the one in therapy.*" And with that, she turned and left.

I took a deep, shaky breath, fighting back tears. Why did she still have the power to make me feel so small, even after all these years?

Of course, when my brain thawed from the grip of my mother's icy judgment, I thought of the quick repartee I could have used instead: "Your mother doesn't have the monopoly on puzzles. Don't blame the poor puzzle for your mother's meanness."

But at least I didn't fall apart. That was something. If I could keep it together with my mother, the next "Jean-Claude" I encountered should be a piece of cake.

I heated up some leftover Chinese takeout, and after I'd wolfed it down, I returned to the puzzle. Two hours later, my shoulders and neck ached from hunching over the table, my eyes stung from staring from box to puzzle piece over and over again, and my head was starting to throb. With all of that, I had barely completed two-thirds of the outer edge. I had one container of variations on blue (for the sky) and a jumbled mess of a wide range of different colors. So much for meditative. If this was a metaphor, I wasn't sure I wanted to know what message I was getting.

Maybe I should stick to yoga.

That night, I dreamt that I was in a hot-air balloon, but it wouldn't take off. My fourteen-year-old self was in a red-and-orange balloon, and she kept circling me.

"I'm scared. Are you coming?" She asked before disappearing into the blue sky. Mine finally took flight, and I came across my dad. He was half in and half out of his, his body hanging at a strange angle.

"Dad," I screamed, but he wasn't moving. Behind me, I heard someone calling my name. I turned around and saw it was Maggie.

"Hurry," she said. "Hurry!"

I shook my head. "I can't."

Chapter Sixteen
May 1917

Electricity in the Air

Maggie

One year had passed since my conversation with Mr. Milton and two since I'd first arrived in New York. The girl I'd been then was barely recognizable. My body had blossomed into a different being. Edna hired Bessie, a cheerful girl whose family they'd known in Alabama, to do the cooking. She was from the South, and everything she made was smothered in butter that melted deliciously in my mouth. Under her care, my body had jutted out of its former state of semi-starvation. Whenever my shoulders started slumping as I tried to hide in the cavity of my chest, Edna put a gentle hand on my shoulders and drew me back out.

"Come on, Maggie, what're you hiding from?" she said with a smile in her voice, and I turned away, so she wouldn't see the tears well up in my eyes. I had pushed the thought of home so far down inside of me, it rarely came up anymore. But when Edna was kind to me like that, I felt my heart tugging for Mama.

I was so busy with Mrs. Dunbar and my studies, I had little time for the job I'd been hired to do. Shortly after beginning the assistant teaching position, I asked Edna if she'd wanted me to move out.

"Heavens, no," she'd exclaimed. "Not unless you want to, of course. As far as I'm concerned, you're like family. You've brought so much to Josie and me."

We'd agreed she'd stop paying me, and I'd get room and board in return for light housework and continuing to help Josie when I could.

Josie, now eight, continued to surprise me. She was at the top of her class and had come out of her shell completely. She'd become somewhat of a leader with the other girls. So much so that sometimes I had to rein her in. One day, when she had a new playmate over, I overheard Josie bossing the girl around.

"Mary, you gotta sit over there. I'm the teacher, and you're in trouble, so you gotta be in the corner."

I opened the door and saw her looming over poor little Mary, who was huddling in a corner.

"Well, aren't you getting big for your britches! How about the two of you come on down for some pie Bessie has prepared," I said. Secretly, my heart was celebrating her sass. It was a welcome change from her sullen quietness.

I had passed the exam and gotten my high school diploma at the beginning of the year, and Edna had hosted a small party to celebrate the event, along with my seventeenth birthday (like most other southern Colored folk I didn't know the exact date but knew it was close to January 1, 1900). The thought of how proud Mama would be punched me in the stomach with grief and guilt, and I once more had to banish any thought of home. I knew reaching out would only put Mama—and possibly myself—in harm's way. And even if, by some miracle, a letter did reach them, none of them could read.

In addition to the grief, I felt the familiar seesawing between joy at my blessings, fear that I would lose it all, and guilt that I had so much. A voice niggled in the back of my head that I had bargained for survival and safety. Happiness and fulfillment hadn't been part of the deal. I told myself that it was okay to take what was given to me as long as I wasn't the one requesting it. *Asking* for more than I already had would really be tempting fate.

I was therefore overjoyed when Mrs. Avery—who taught the fourteen-to-eighteen-year-olds—suggested I assist her so I could gain experience with older students. As much as I enjoyed helping Mrs. Dunbar, I was longing for more of a challenge and to learn more advanced teaching material. I had been trying to work up the courage to talk to Mr. Milton, but the voice kept warning me about asking for too much, so I was relieved I didn't have to. Mrs. Dunbar took the change in stride. "I will miss you, Maggie, of course, as will the little ones, but I'm happy for you. I want you to learn as much as you can."

Another piece of me fell into place with teaching. I felt as though I was bringing the freedom of the forest to the students, unlocking doors they hadn't known existed. I saw some of myself in each child, in their curiosity, their fears, their doubts. In the parts of them that were wide open and ready to soak everything up. And those that were so deeply walled in their prison of pain that they couldn't hear a word of what I was saying.

I deemed it my sacred task not only to transmit information but also to find the key that unlocked the secret gift each one possessed. Working with the older students now, I discovered I had to be more creative—and more patient—to find the key. With what they'd already experienced of the world, many of them had already built ramparts around their hearts and minds. They were also skeptical that someone their age—even younger than some of them—had anything to teach them. But this only motivated me to try harder.

As I started falling into a more natural rhythm with the

assistant teaching, I felt my attention start spreading to different shores. At night, words tugged at my mind. Stories wanting to be told. Voices needing to be heard. They were getting louder, and I knew I needed to start listening or I wouldn't be able to hear myself think over their cacophony.

I decided to buy myself a notebook. It was leather-bound, a deep chestnut red, with thick yellow pages waiting for my hand to scrawl across them. When everyone had gone to bed and the house was quiet, I strained my eyes in the dim light of the oil lamp, letters tripping over each other on the page. I wrote with my mother's voice. Full, warm, welcoming, and strong, but also a little worn around the edges. Tired. Sometimes brittle with worry. My pen seemed to be able to express the pain in a way that freed me, rather than binding me in knots of guilt and grief the way my thoughts did.

I wrote with the voice of the wild that knew no laws but its own. The trill of the cicadas, the low growl of a hungry bear on the prowl. The soft murmur of the wind that picked up into a deafening howl. I wrote with the voice of the children I was trying to teach, the inner voice that didn't show as they sat quietly, pretending to pay attention. The impudence. The inquisitiveness. The pure aliveness and the innate knowing that many had already lost, especially the older ones.

At times I wondered where *my* voice was amongst all those clamoring for my attention. I felt like my story had been drowned out, and then I realized that they were telling my tale too. Time lost all meaning when I was writing, and I often found my hand still moving across the page as the first light of dawn broke. I bought more wicks for the lamp, so Edna didn't know, although at times I noticed her staring at my tired face and the dark grooves carving their way under my eyes.

The change was not just within me. I could feel it all around. An undercurrent of tension. A shift in the air that was almost palpable, like heat that was visible on a steamy day. I felt it in the voices of the men who came to Mr. Jones' meetings. A barely perceptible tremor, like the first rumbles of an earthquake. Something big preparing to shake you up.

One day, a man I had never seen before joined Mr. Jones's group. He was a little taller than I was—small for a man but wiry, stealthy, with tightly wound energy that was so intense I could almost feel the prickles when I was near him. His voice was low and resonant. I learned his name was Mr. Grant, and he was a lawyer from Boston. He seemed to be a friend of Mr. Jones.

"Now is the time. We need to act. Momentum is building. We have to collect as much information as we can about lynching. We need dates, we need names, we need facts," I heard him say the fourth time he came to the house for a meeting. Not able to contain my curiosity, I'd asked Edna about it.

"They want to introduce legislation opposing lynching. I wish them luck, but we all know the laws are written to help the white man. Not us," she'd said, shaking her head.

I found as many excuses as I could to be near the room when they met, trying to overhear them. My ear was pressed against the cool, smooth surface of the door when all of a sudden it opened on me, and I stumbled inside. Mr. Grant was standing in front of me, a bemused smile on his face.

Mr. Jones frowned at me and got up to herd me out, but Mr. Grant motioned for him to sit down. "I thought I felt someone spying on us. What's your name?" he asked.

"Mag … Mag … Maggie," I stuttered, mortified that I'd been found out.

"Why are you listening to us? You going to rat on us?"

"No, sir, I'm just interested in this matter, that's all."

"And why is that, Miss Maggie?" he asked with a smile, his gaze both amused and scrutinizing. I looked at him, took a breath, and decided I had nothing to lose. At this point, my best defense was the truth.

"Well, it's just that they lynched my brother and father. Mr. Tanner and his men. Because of me. My brother was trying to protect me from the Tanners' son. And if a law is passed that says they can't do that, I'm interested. I teach at the school, and I know a few children who have lost family members. What you're doing is important," I said, not even pausing to breathe for fear I'd either lose my nerve or be overcome with the grief that was beneath the words I was uttering.

I had never spoken to a group of grown men before, and the quiet with which they listened was daunting. Mr. Grant's smile had vanished, and his expression seemed to be one of sadness and remorse.

"I'm sorry to hear about your family. I apologize for the lightness in my tone. None of us here have had the experience you've had. Of course, you'd be interested," he said, looking at me so long I started feeling uncomfortable. I wasn't used to being seen.

"Would you like to join the meetings, so you won't have to listen at the door?" he asked, some of his earlier humor creeping back in.

I looked at Mr. Jones first, to see what he would say, and was relieved to see him nod.

"Yes, I would, if I'm not teaching."

"Good. And maybe we can help each other. We've been looking for a note taker since we're all so busy talking we forget to do it ourselves. Is that something you'd be interested in?"

"Yes, I'd love to help," I said, thinking that if I had something to do during the meetings, I'd feel more comfortable.

"Do you know shorthand?"

I nodded, though I didn't really know what that meant. I figured if it had to do with writing, I could do it. And I wanted to be able to actively listen to their conversations without needing to do it in secret.

"Have you heard of Ida Wells?" he asked me.

I shook my head.

"Never mind. Why don't you come next week and take the meeting notes? We'll see how it goes."

The meetings took place on Sundays after church, when I wasn't assisting at school or studying for my teaching degree. Edna agreed with the plan, even though it meant I'd be helping her even less. She took me to meet her friend Angela, who was Mr. Miller's secretary and could teach me the basics of writing shorthand. Mr. Miller was a prominent Colored lawyer in town with a big, round belly and trim mustache. He'd come to one of the meetings at Mr. Jones's house but stormed out angrily, saying he did not want to "mix with rabble-rousers." Angela showed me how to shorten words so I could write what they were saying faster. It wasn't difficult, like the pictures we showed children to jog their memories about letters and words.

The men were happy with my work, and soon I was part of the meetings. At first, I sensed the men were holding back around me, speaking less vehemently than they normally might, glancing at me if they had cussed without thinking. They made an effort to include me in the conversation. Being one who likes to observe and understand before I speak up, the attention so early on made me squirm a little, and I found it hard to simultaneously take notes and participate.

Eventually, we all eased into each other's company, and sometimes I sensed they almost forgot I was there. When I spoke up to ask them to clarify something they'd just said, they looked startled, as though the wallpaper had suddenly grown a mouth.

Except for Mr. Grant. I often caught him looking at me, his dark, bottomless eyes boring into me, as though he were trying to see inside of me, understand what made me tick. The attention both excited and scared me. Where I came from, being visible was rarely a good thing. I had to keep reminding myself I was safe, though the part of me that had learned to mistrust people wasn't so sure.

Being involved made me feel a little less helpless. I was drawn to the stories they were collecting because of what I had lived through. I could also understand the difficulties the men faced in getting people to open up and trust them. The fear. I knew it well. I wasn't sure how *I'd* feel if asked to put my story in writing for others to read. So many of us had learned that to hide what we knew was the only way to survive.

One evening, after a meeting, I stayed in the room to finish the notes. Once I was finished, Mr. Jones locked them up in the safe, so I had to work quickly. He had made it clear that if anybody ever asked me, I knew nothing about the meetings.

Tonight, however, my attention was stayed by the story told by the parents of a seventeen-year-old girl from Oklahoma who was raped by two drunken white men who entered her room as she was dressing. Her brother, hearing her scream, kicked in the locked door and killed one of them. The brother escaped, so the angry mob hung Marie from a telephone pole instead.

My handwriting swam in front of my face as I heard her scream. I could taste her fear. Metallic and cold in her mouth. I felt my own, as I saw Andre and Papa's faces swinging in front of me. And the question I had been running away from since that day echoed through my mind.

"Why me?"

Marie's brother escaped, and she was hanged. Why him? Why me? Why was I allowed to live when those who tried to save me died?

I was about to lose myself to my demons when I heard a small cough. Startled, I turned to see Mr. Grant in the doorway. I didn't know how long he had been there, watching me with his piercing eyes. I felt small and vulnerable, having been caught in the darkest, most intimate of my thoughts without any hint as to what the viewer was thinking. But then I saw a softening in his eyes, as though he were allowing me in, for just a second, so I could see he understood.

"Mr. Jones is waiting for the notes," he said before he turned around and left.

A few weeks later, Mr. Jones came to talk to me, with Mr. Grant hovering like a shadow behind him.

"Maggie, we need your help. There is a thirteen-year-old from Mississippi who witnessed her uncle's murder. He was helping us collect stories about what was happening there, and we need to find out what happened to him, but the girl is too scared to speak to us. You were so good with Josie, and Mr. Milton has been singing your praises. I think if anybody can win her confidence, you can. And I have been able to convince Mr. Grant to give you a try."

I looked at Mr. Grant, but his gaze was inscrutable. For some reason, I felt irritation flare up.

"Yes, she's scared. Wouldn't you be? Is this what's best for her—or for you?" I asked before I really knew what I was saying.

Mr. Jones was taken by surprise since I had never talked to him in that way and glanced from Mr. Grant back to me, looking a little unsure.

"Well, yes, I would be," he finally said, "And I know these are painful things to bring up, possibly dangerous. But if we can pass this bill, maybe we can prevent it from happening again. That's the only reason we want to collect these stories."

"I know that, and I'm not suggesting otherwise," I said, my irritation subsiding. "I was just imagining I was in her place. I will go, but she will only talk to me if she chooses to. I'm not going to pressure her." The two men nodded in agreement.

*

The next day, Mr. Grant took me to see Asma. He was silent the whole way there, and I noticed his jaw clenching and unclenching, causing a vein to play hide-and-seek with his neck. I sensed the men were much more nervous about how this could end up than they were letting on. When Mr. Grant told me he would come to pick me up two hours later, his vocal cords were so tightly strung in his throat that they sounded a bit screechy.

Asma was sitting in a small kitchen. I gathered she was staying with distant relatives for now. She was wearing a red dress that was frayed at the seams. When I came in, she was staring intently at her clasped hands.

"Hello, Asma," I said. I sensed small talk would only make it worse, so I squatted in front of her but a little off to the side, so she could either turn toward me or away from me. "You know why I'm here, but you don't have to say anything if you don't want to. I know how hard it is. I've been there. You have every right to be scared," I told her and then I waited.

After a few minutes, I extended my hand close to hers, not touching. Letting her choose the next step. She hesitated. Her hand reached toward mine, but then pulled back before any contact. I nodded and smiled to acknowledge her, then looked away to allow her space.

When her hand finally found mine, she held on for dear life. I thought my fingers were going to go numb, she squeezed them so tightly. Her body started shaking. I just held her and stroked her hair with my free hand. We stayed in this position for what seemed like an eternity, her body racked by agonizing, tearless sobs.

Then, it all came pouring out of her. The sound of footsteps in the night. Muffled voices at the door. Her uncle going out quickly, without a fight, so they wouldn't search the house for others. Her hidden vantage point up in the attic from which she could see it all. Her uncanny attention to detail. Although the men were hooded, she was able to name each one, and I knew that was a curse she would live with her whole life. The sound of their voices and names indelibly imprinted in her memory, there to haunt her no matter what she did to erase them.

I understood all too well. I knew that when you came face to face with the darkness, there was no turning back, no pretending, no matter how hard you tried. At some point, it had to come out or it would swallow you up. I was grateful I had the leather journal to hold it all for me. At least for now. I allowed her to talk until she was spent and had fallen asleep in my arms.

I didn't know how long we'd been like this when I looked up and saw Mr. Grant, waiting near the door, eyes pointed downward as though he didn't wish to intrude, although I could tell every muscle was on alert. He looked over when I did and nodded. Again, I saw some warmth flickering behind his eyes. His jaw looked relaxed. Perhaps even relieved.

"You did fine work," he said on the way back. I was surprised by how good this unexpected praise made me feel.

After that, more people offered to talk to us. Wives. Daughters. Fathers. There were so many stories, I was drowning in them. So much pain.

Mr. Grant and I had gotten more comfortable around each other. We were both still tense and silent on the way over due to the danger of our mission and the unknowns of what we might encounter. But on the way back, we relaxed. He always asked me how I felt, and I was grateful not to have to be alone with all the feelings the stories evoked. As intent as he was on the work, he seemed keenly aware of the impact listening to the horrific tales might have on me, considering my own history. I got to witness glimpses of kindness I suspected few were allowed to see.

One day, after the man we'd been talking to had thanked me over and over again for listening, for caring, Mr. Grant remarked, "The hope can be harder to bear than the pain, sometimes, can't it?"

"What do you mean?" I asked, a little confused. I had been deep in thought, slumped against the cab door.

"Holding the weight of their hope," he explained. I nodded, too tired to talk.

When he helped me out of the cab, his hand squeezed mine and held on for a second before letting go. My fingers tingled for hours after, although his grip hadn't been very tight.

Mr. Grant was right. Because I wielded the pen, I became the keeper of people's hope. I could see it in their eyes when they confided in me. Some nights, the burden felt like a brick pressing down on my chest. At times, I thought the weight would suffocate me. But I couldn't stop. Their hope kept my hand moving late into the night.

I wrote until I was so tired that Mrs. Avery asked me if I was okay since I wasn't as attentive as I usually was to the students. But it still didn't feel like enough. The names and the dates and the facts … How could they do justice to the stories? To the sadness and anger and despair and defiance that seared my heart. Words started streaming out of me, dripping their outrage onto the page.

> *I hear the necks snap*
> *As they hang*
> *From the bridge*
> *The lamppost*
> *The tree*

They scream
For me to stop
The pain
But all I can do
Is weep
Tears
For being alive
Tears
For having ears
To hear
The tales
No ears
Should hear

One night, Mr. Grant came to gather the stories and found me weeping in the study with this half-finished poem scribbled in my notebook instead. He picked it up and read it. I looked up at him through my tears, feeling exposed, ready to rebuke him for reading without asking. I stopped when I saw his eyes.

They shone with his own tears, as though acknowledging the weight of what they'd read. And then, his hand took mine, as if of its own volition, for Mr. Grant looked a little surprised by his action too.

His hand was startlingly warm. Alive. Comforting. As though it wanted to talk to me.

"This poem—" he started to say before the words choked in his throat and died away.

I found my own hand responding to his, swaying to a rhythm I didn't know was there. My heart, which I had all but forgotten about since I left home except as an organ that kept me alive, started to ache, to long.

I looked up at Mr. Grant with searching eyes. For a second, his eyes lit up with a similar longing. And then I was startled to see what looked like a flash of fear. He dropped my hand abruptly, as if he'd been burned.

"Frank, what are you doing?" I thought I heard him mutter to himself as he rushed out of the study.

The next day, I overheard him talking to Mr. Jones agitatedly.

"I think it was a mistake to involve her. It is too much. Too personal. She is too young," he was saying. "If they ever catch her, she will break in a minute. She isn't strong enough for what we're asking of her."

"But, Frank, I don't understand. It was your idea to have her take notes in the first place, and she's the only one who's been able to make any headway. We would have nothing without her! And this is a critical time for introducing the bill. We *need* the facts. Did something happen that you aren't telling me?"

I heard the surprise and bewilderment in Mr. Jones's voice. I was furious. I had never felt so betrayed in my life. Not by one of my own, that is. I dropped the book I was carrying, so I was sure they heard me, and turned around to leave.

Chapter Seventeen

Tanzania

Sarah

"How are you, Sarah?" Patrick asked.

"Overall, I'd say I'm doing well. I tried a yoga class, and I've done it a few times at home with an online teacher. To my surprise, I'm starting to enjoy it," I chuckled. "I don't think I stretched enough before, and the yoga's actually helping reduce my post-running aches. I can't say I'm really getting the hang of meditating, but I do like the breathing exercises you sent me."

"I'm happy to hear that. I would recommend continuing to meditate a little every week, just to see if something shifts as you get used to it. And if not, that's fine. The yoga and breathing serve a similar purpose."

"I read my journals from when I was a teenager and started thinking about those puzzle pieces you talked about last time. I even got a real puzzle to have a visual of what we're doing," I admitted.

Patrick laughed. "What's the puzzle of?"

I showed him a picture I'd taken on my phone of the hot-air balloons.

"That's perfect."

"Yeah, that's what I thought too, but to be honest, at first it stressed me out a little. I haven't done a puzzle since I was a young kid, besides occasionally helping my grandmother with hers. But I think I'm slowly getting the hang of it, and it's pretty hypnotic. I can easily spend a few hours without feeling the time go by."

"Puzzles can be a calming activity. Just make sure to breathe and take breaks," he said, inviting me to do so then before he asked, "Have you been connecting with Maggie?"

"A little bit. I tried automatic writing again, but all I got was a fuzzy image of something that could have been a railroad track, and a headache from trying too hard. I did have a couple of dreams where I was with her, and I got some books out of the library on the United States' racial history in that era to get a sense of her life, but it's been hard to motivate myself to start reading them. I'm worried about opening Pandora's box and getting overwhelmed, so I've been more focused on settling my nervous system."

Patrick nodded gently in approval. "There is wisdom in listening to your body and knowing what you're ready for, Sarah."

"I know it's only been six weeks, but I feel like I'm on track for returning in a month and a half."

"Based on how you're doing now, I don't see why not. I've been wondering if you want to talk about the boy who died in Sudan, though. Mariol? It doesn't have to be now, but I think it would be helpful to do some EMDR on that memory. I know his death was traumatic for you."

At the mention of Mariol's name, I could feel my throat tighten. I shook my head no.

"I'm not ready," I said when I could speak without the threat of tears. "It's too fresh. I want to keep doing what we're doing so I can get better as quickly as possible."

Patrick looked at me pensively. "Okay, as you wish. Your job is really important to you, isn't it?"

"Of course," I answered, surprised by the question. It reminded me of Jean-Claude asking me if I liked being a humanitarian nurse, and I felt a momentary panic clutch at my heart. I took a deep breath before answering. "It's what gives my life meaning."

"What do you love about it?"

"The pace, for one. There's never a dull moment. And even though the needs always exceed our capacity, it feels like we're making a difference—like I'm part of something that matters. On a personal level, I like that we get to know each other deeply and quickly. There's no room for small talk. It feels so much more real than anything I experienced before I started doing this work." I closed my eyes, remembering. I could feel pins and needles crawl through my feet and legs—always a clear sign they wanted to move.

"Did I ever tell you about my study-abroad trip to Tanzania, Patrick? When I decided to be a nurse?"

"You've alluded to it, but never in detail. Do you want to tell me about it?"

I nodded. I'd much rather think about that than Mariol's death.

I was twenty-one, a linguistics major and English minor at UC Berkeley—much to my mother's chagrin since she had tried to encourage an early interest in biology. In truth, I still had no idea what I wanted to do, but I was good at languages and had always liked both reading and writing. Books had been my most reliable companion throughout my childhood, and journals had been my refuge in tumultuous times. I figured I'd start there and see where life took me—which irked Amanda no end.

"You're no longer a child, Sarah. You need a plan. What are you going to do, be a high school English teacher?! You were always such a good student. I'd hate to see you throw it all away."

"I can think of worse things to be than a teacher. And there's more to life than being practical, Mom! There's also such a thing as having time to enjoy your life!" I retorted, as though I didn't have a care in the world.

But in truth, my mother's comments burrowed deep into my subconscious, where they took root and grew weeds of doubt. What *was* I going to do with my life?

The linguistics department highly encouraged students to study abroad to learn or perfect another language. I knew immediately that I wanted to go as far from my current life and my mother as possible. In large part due to my time with Fatou and her family, I was drawn to studying somewhere in Africa and thought of going to Senegal to study Wolof. However, the only program that worked with my requirements was a French-language program based in the capital, Dakar. I wanted the opportunity to learn a completely new language and to live in more remote areas.

Eventually, I picked a cultural immersion and Swahili language program in Tanzania with a rural component. I had heard the language spoken a few times and loved the way it sounded simultaneously lilting and emphatic. I needed both more poetry and more confidence in my life.

"If I ever wanted to live or work in Africa, knowing French, English, and Swahili would open many doors for me," I told my mother as a way of justifying the practicality of my decision.

"What good will that do you?" Amanda asked.

"I could be a translator for the United Nations," I fired back.

She raised an eyebrow. "You'd be better off learning Arabic then. At least it's one of the five official languages of the UN." But at least she didn't actively oppose my choice.

A few months later, I was getting off a plane in Dar-Es-Salam. As I made my way through the throngs of people to the tall, mustachioed man holding a placard with my name, the warm, humid air mixed with the exhaust from the cars assaulted my senses.

We drove to the program's compound, alternatively crawling through backed-up traffic and weaving in and out of nonexistent lanes. I found myself bracing my feet against the dashboard and gasping for air until my lungs adjusted. We spent the first afternoon in the Village Museum, where the teachers showed us how to distinguish the huts of one ethnic group from another in preparation for our village stay.

As I admired the roundedness of the Sukuma's thatched hut, two teenage boys who were racing each other jostled me, one on each side. When I looked down a few minutes later, I realized that the neck wallet I had bought for safety was gone, and with it, my passport and the one hundred dollars I had changed into Tanzanian shillings the night before.

I had to stay back to report the theft, block my credit card, and start the proceedings to replace my passport. One of the language teachers stayed back to help me, while the rest of the students were sent to villages with no running water or electricity and placed in pairs with host families.

I joined them two days later. We had four hours of Swahili classes every morning, followed by classes covering the history and politics of the country. Having started out on the wrong foot and later than the other students, I found it hard to gain my bearings. The first week, I hated everything about my surroundings. I hated Heather, a fellow student and my roommate for the village stay, who had already learned full sentences in Swahili and seemed eternally happy and optimistic. The curious children who pointed at me and followed me as I attempted to find a quiet spot to pee. Above all, I hated myself, hated that I couldn't love it there. Hated that I was homesick for a home that had never been warm or welcoming.

I couldn't hate Agnes, my host mother, who was one of the kindest people I'd ever met. Her husband was getting an MBA in Dar-Es-Salam and only came back on weekends. Every morning, Agnes balanced a heavy frying pan on the stone oven (basically three slabs of stone on the clay floor with a little bonfire of twigs and logs in the middle) and heated some lard and fried plantains because she had discovered it was my favorite. I was grateful for her generosity, but couldn't make myself open up, even to her.

At the end of the first week, the village put on a dance for the students. I sat between Agnes and Heather. I had gone there sullenly, prepared to hate it as I had everything else. But I found myself transfixed by the dancers' majestic grace, and my body started swaying of its own accord to the rhythm of the drums. After a while, I felt a gaze and turned to find Agnes staring at me.

"It's the first time I see you smile since you got here," Agnes said. "You know, Sarah, in life, you can choose to laugh, or you can choose to cry. Me, I laugh, because it brings me more joy. And otherwise, I'm afraid I would flood the river with my tears. I can tell you're in pain, but I think you're making things much harder than they need to be." She gave my arm a gentle squeeze before letting go.

I looked down, startled. My cheeks smarted with shame at how I'd been acting for the past week, and I felt hot tears prickling the corners of my eyes. Yet I also felt a wave of relief deep in my chest at being treated lovingly but firmly, like an adult who had choices and was accountable for the decisions I made.

To my own surprise, that seemingly small moment of being seen was what I needed to break down my defenses. After that, I threw myself into mastering the language and intricacies of village life with a newfound passion. For the first time, I actually felt part of something. I woke early to join Agnes' oldest daughter, nine-year-old Adimu, in fetching water every morning and evening. We rose at 5:00 a.m. before we both had to be in school. We walked thirty minutes down the dirt path that led to the river, carrying empty jugs. By the end of the third week, I could balance a jug of water on my head and carry on a basic conversation in Swahili. I had also learned that being able to laugh at myself, at least a little, was critical to my emotional survival.

When I left the village at the end of the fourth week, I didn't even try to hide the tears streaming down my face as I said goodbye to Agnes.

"Dear one, you have done me proud. Just keep smiling, learning, and writing. And don't forget me!" Agnes said, wiping off a tear before turning to hug Heather goodbye.

After a few recovery days, we were sent to different parts of the country to work on service projects ranging from infrastructure to education and healthcare. I had indicated no preference for what project I worked on, so I found myself volunteering with two other students in a community hospital in the central city of Iringa. Every morning, we had an hour of Swahili and an hour of studying public health in Tanzania. After lunch, we worked three to four hours providing whatever non-medical support we could to the staff.

The conditions in the three-hundred-bed hospital were basic, and I could only imagine my mother's horror had she seen how rudimentary the equipment was. The first week, I shadowed the nurses and doctors until I got the lay of the land and knew what some of the main implements were. After that, I alternated between fetching whatever the medical staff needed, doing as much of the initial intake as I could with my rudimentary Swahili to support the overworked nurses, and following the doctors on their rounds.

The maternity ward was the most heartbreaking and heartwarming ward of the hospital. Although the medical staff worked hard for all their patients, the importance of bringing new life into the world seemed to bring out the heroes and heroines in them. I witnessed many miracles in that ward, and every lost gamble shredded my heart.

I became friends with Laurence, a French doctor in her early forties who had been there for over a decade. Though barely five feet tall with wild chestnut curls fanning out around her face, the whole staff held her in the utmost respect. She spoke fluent Swahili and spent time getting to know each of her patients by name, no matter how tired or busy she was.

Two weeks after my arrival, I watched Laurence resuscitate a seventy-two-year-old man on the brink of death with just CPR and a defibrillator, standing on a footstool for better leverage. Each of her movements as she pushed on the man's chest and released was deliberate, rhythmic, fast yet unhurried. Beads of sweat gathered at her brow, her jaw was set, and her eyes glinted with determination. Watching her win this duel with death through sheer force of will sent chills down my spine.

I decided then and there I wanted to become a humanitarian nurse. I knew I didn't have the patience to become a doctor. And even though my mother thought that nursing was "beneath her daughter's potential," she had to concede that it was, indeed, practical.

"How do you feel having recounted all of that to me, Sarah?" Patrick asked when I slipped back into the present day.

"Mixed. It feels good to remember why I got into this field in the first place. Tanzania was the first time I felt truly alive, accountable for myself and others. I also feel a little sad when I think of how lost I was before that. That's probably part of why I'm in such a hurry to get back. I don't know who I'd be otherwise." I paused, considering something else. "Patrick, is this memory a piece of the puzzle too?"

"What do you think, Sarah?"

"I don't know. Maybe. I guess it could represent my joy and aliveness."

"Is that still how you feel when you work?"

"Alive, definitely … Along with a ton of stress and pressure. Joy? I don't know. I'm often holding my breath, crossing my fingers that I don't mess up. But honestly, I don't expect joy out of life." I felt more joy with Mariol than I had in a long time, but I was afraid to bring him up again for fear Patrick would insist on working on that memory.

"I'm afraid we're out of time, Sarah. If you feel inspired, you might use 'What brings me joy?' as a writing prompt and see what you come up with. And keep doing the practices. I'll email you a meditation you might find helpful, as well as a nutritional questionnaire. I've found that the proper diet can be supportive for a calmer nervous system."

As I pedaled home, the wind streaming through my hair (I'd forgotten my bicycle helmet) and the memory of my transformative time in Tanzania still fresh in my mind, I felt renewed motivation to return to the work as soon as I could.

If I can learn to handle Amanda calmly, I'll be ready for anything, the thought came to me. I remembered our last conversation about the puzzle and bristled.

Why do I have to be the one to make things right? What about her? My petulant teen wanted to know.

It's not for her, it's for us. To prove we can pull ourselves together and not fall apart when things get tough, I argued. And then, remembering the affirmations book I'd gotten from the library, I tried a different tack. *And because you matter. You're enough,* I thought, feeling disingenuous as I did. Neither of us was fooled. I guessed it was a case of "fake it until you make it."

I decided that my mother would be the litmus test for my readiness to tackle the Jean-Claudes of the world. To strengthen my resolve, I dredged up the image of Mariol's body and willed myself not to feel. My heart tightened, but I didn't want to collapse—or vomit.

Progress, I thought.

In my room, I found old writing paper left over from my childhood (when was the last time I wrote a letter?). Daisies lined the edges, and I hoped it wouldn't be too cheesy for the note I planned to slip under my mother's door.

"Dear …" I paused. Mom? I had stopped calling her that to her face when I began to work. Amanda? Mother? Those felt more comfortable nowadays, but distancing. If I was trying to make nice with her …

Dear Mom,

I'm sorry I took over the dining room table without asking you for permission. Let me know if you want me to move the puzzle somewhere else. And I didn't mean to pry about Grandma. You can talk to me when and if you want.

Thanks for letting me stay here as long as I need to.

I paused, not knowing how to end it. "Love, Sarah" would really be over the top, since I couldn't remember the last time either of us had said "I love you" to the other. I added some *X*s and *O*s and signed my name.

Chapter Eighteen

Wildfire

Maggie

For the next week, I did not see Mr. Grant. I was dreading seeing him and simultaneously anticipating it. The anger roiling inside of me made my stomach churn, and I had very little appetite. I wondered if he'd sensed that, as he'd made himself scarce. There had been no stories this week. Mr. Jones had asked me, but I'd refused.

My body was grateful for the break, and my muscles had slowly started unclenching and uncoiling. My mind had used the extra time to chew over what I would say to Mr. Grant should we cross paths again. The desire I'd felt when he had held my hand confused me, so I chose to focus on my anger instead.

One night, I heard Mr. Grant's voice in Mr. Jones's study, though I couldn't make out what he was saying. I heard Mr. Jones's voice get louder.

"Frank, they have been coming in a steady stream, and they will only talk to her. I don't know what happened between the two of you, and I don't want to know, but you need to make this right with her. I'm warning you."

I couldn't make out what Mr. Grant responded to him, but when he knocked on my door a little while later, I was ready. I opened the door so quickly that he almost fell onto me.

"Maggie …" he started, but I didn't let him continue.

"Not strong enough, huh? You see me cry, and you immediately take it as a sign of weakness, don't you?" I said, drawing up so I was as tall as he was, unleashing the fury in my voice and eyes. My limbs shook with rage. "You pretend to be kind to me, and then you turn on me. And now you need me to come back, do you? You're the one who's weak. I'd like to see *you* talking to them. Well, you can do it on your own if you're so much better …"

"You're right, Maggie," he said, so softly it stopped me in my tracks. His contrition made him look smaller than I was used to, catching me off guard.

"I *am* the weak one. You're strong and brave. And caring. And passionate. And infuriating. You awaken feelings in me that I have not felt in a long time, and that frightens me to death. Because in some ways you're so wise to the cruel ways of the world, and in other ways, you're still such a child. I'm scared that I'll hurt you without meaning to. That I might forget what I'm here for. It's my weakness that I fear, not yours."

I looked at him stunned and speechless. My fury had subsided somewhat with this unexpected concession, although I wasn't ready to forgive him yet.

"Then why didn't you say that to Mr. Jones? Why did you make it my fault?"

"Because I was a coward, and I didn't want to admit what I was beginning to feel. It seemed easier to break things before they started. I'm sorry. I did tell him today, though. I would understand if you never wanted to see me again, but I hope you don't punish those who are coming to us for help because of my idiocy," he said, looking at me so intensely I felt my insides melting.

I paused, pondering his words. I recognized that he, indeed, wouldn't be the one to pay if I said no.

"Okay. I agree. But don't think I'm going to forget so quickly," I said, still feeling guarded and hurt by his actions.

"I understand. Thank you. Truce?" he asked.

"Truce," I said, holding my hand out. Instead of shaking it, he held it gently in his for a moment, as though I'd handed him a precious gift. His hands were even warmer than before and matched the intensity of his eyes.

"I truly am sorry," he said, his face looking pained.

"I forgive you. This time," I said, finding it difficult to stay angry with him.

Searching my face for permission and finding it in the slightest nod of my head, he brought my hand to his lips, kissing it with something akin to reverence.

He then returned my hand to me and left without a word. My knees felt like they would buckle under the trembling of my legs, so I sat. My insides were writhing like a snake whose head had been lopped off but whose body hadn't yet caught up.

That night I could not sleep. My body was burning up as though I were sick, though I knew I was not. My head was a jumble of bumblebee thoughts buzzing for my attention. My hand felt branded by Mr. Grant's kiss. I had been overwhelmed by so many emotions in my brief encounter with him, I couldn't make heads or tails of what I was feeling. I rose and lit a candle, scribbling in my notebook to try to calm the buzzing of the bees.

I woke the next morning at my small writing table, with the candle burned down to its wick, and the last words dribbling from the page. My neck protested when I moved my head from its perch on my right arm.

"You look terrible, Maggie," Josie said at the breakfast table, her lips pursed into a pout. I knew she was angry with me. And hurt. Between teaching and preparing the classes and helping the men with the stories, I'd had very little time for her, and she had asked for Bessie to take her to and from school.

"Difficult night," I said, feeling fragile. Which might be why I was more sensitive to her hurt than I had been in the past few weeks. I had been so wrapped up in others' misery, I was unable to see hers.

"I'm sorry, Josie," I said. "I know you're hurting, and I don't know how to change that right now. But I love you just as much as ever, even though I haven't been good at showing it these days."

Josie turned away from me, just as I saw tears welling up in her eyes. I put my hand on her shoulder, squeezed it gently, and let go. I had to trust this would mend in time, for I was too weary to say anymore.

That evening, I heard footsteps outside my door. I was both hoping it was Mr. Grant and also fearing it. The knock sounded loud and ominous. "Come in," I said, my voice screeching on "in." When I saw it was Mr. Jones instead, I was both relieved and disappointed beyond words.

"Maggie, we need your help. There has been trouble in East Saint Louis, Illinois. I don't have all the details, but we hear it's gotten the attention of a Republican representative from across the river in Missouri, Mr. Dyer. We need to collect those stories. Now. We have a number of people waiting to talk to you. Will you meet with them?"

I nodded my head in mute agreement.

"I will be accompanying you myself because this is becoming more dangerous. Mr. Grant left a few hours ago to go to East Saint Louis to talk to people there. He will be gone at least a few weeks." He looked at me long and hard when he uttered Mr. Grant's name. With the instinct of the tracked, I wiped my face clear of all expression, although I knew Mr. Grant had told him something.

Mr. Jones gave me instructions for the next day and bade me goodnight, leaving me to my jumble of emotions. Mr. Grant. Gone. I never would have dreamed that could leave me feeling so empty. Just as I had with Andre and Papa, I pushed the sadness down and dredged up as much resolve as I could to transmute my internal turmoil. I was as ready as I could be.

Chapter Nineteen
July 10, 2011

Independence

Sarah

I woke up to early morning sun nudging me out of bed, although my clock informed me it was 6:12 a.m. For the past week, I had been greeted every morning by a cold, oppressive fog that led me to burrow under the covers as long as possible. This early morning sun was a pleasant treat.

So, I grabbed my sweats and biked to the north end of Aquatic Park in West Berkeley. I parked my bike in front of the animal shelter, although it was too early for the volunteers to be out walking the rescued dogs—often pit bulls, I had noticed.

After stretching my calf and quad muscles, I headed toward the west end of the lake, which ran parallel to the highway, doing that part first before there were too many cars speeding off to enjoy this sunny Sunday. My feet pounded my body into full wakefulness.

I jogged past a row of cypress trees with gnarled, twisted trunks. Their leaves fanned out over the road, making a little canopy, and draped down into the water lakeside, looking like piney weeping willows.

I crossed a family of mallard ducks waddling from the

lake to the grassy patch on the other side of the path. A minute later, I passed a human family, the toddler pumping her little legs on her bright red trike as her parents ran alongside her. The Amtrak train lumbered by, honking so loudly and long you'd think it was a foghorn.

I remembered a discussion in my freshman year of college with my friend Phoebe about whether to go for a walk around Aquatic Park or a lake in Tilden Park, near campus.

"Sarah, I don't understand why you'd want to go there when we have this beautiful lake practically on our doorstep! Last time I went to Aquatic Park, I saw condoms and a used needle on the path." Phoebe had scoffed at the time, and I had never brought it up again, although I kept going on my own.

Maybe for the same reason I was drawn to working in conflict zones, I thought as I started my second lap around the two-plus-mile loop. Because it was real, messy, and in places stunningly pretty, just like life.

After I biked back home, I showered, listened to a grounding meditation Patrick had recommended, stretched, and journaled. Hunger drew me to the kitchen, where I started making a smoothie. As part of my attempt to clean up my diet, I blended mango, coconut milk, chia seeds, kale, and carrots in the Vitamix and had almost finished when my mother padded in.

My heart beat a little faster. We hadn't spoken since I'd slipped the letter under her door, and I had no idea how she'd taken it.

"Want some?" I asked at last, as I poured myself a tall glass of my concoction. Amanda glanced at it and made a face as she pressed the button on the espresso machine and went to sit at the kitchen table where she picked up *The New York*

Times. On my last visit home, I'd teased her about still getting a physical newspaper.

"Everybody reads the news online nowadays! Save some trees."

"Well, if everybody reads it online, it's not my newspaper that's going to decimate the rainforest, Sarah. Besides, I like reading the paper with my morning coffee, and somebody's got to keep *The New York Times* in business."

My mother put the paper down and went to get her coffee.

"I read that South Sudan just became an independent country," she said to me in passing. "Did you hear?"

I spun around—not because of the news (in a January referendum, over 98 percent of the population of South Sudan had voted in favor of becoming an independent nation, and we knew it was only a matter of time until it became a reality)—but more in astonishment that my mother both remembered the last country I had been in *and* showed an interest. I wondered if she paid more attention than I gave her credit for.

"No, I hadn't heard. That could potentially resolve a lot of the tension in that region." I thought of Hiba and Okot, and Mariol's family, and felt a sliver of hope. "Thanks for telling me, Mom. My therapist has asked me to go on a news fast this week to allow my nervous system to settle, so I had no idea."

"Whatever you're doing, it seems to be working. You don't look nearly as peaked and emaciated as when you first arrived," she said as we sat down at the kitchen table. I looked up, surprised she had noticed.

"I suppose you and your therapist talk all about what a terrible mother I was," she said, her voice casual—a throwaway comment for a lazy Sunday morning. My eyes widened, and my hand froze, the glass suspended inches away from my mouth. Although she acted like she had no interest in the response, the question itself showed a vulnerability that was rare—if not unheard of—for her. My mother was full of surprises this morning!

"No, it's not the 'blame it all on the mother' kind of therapy at all," I said when I'd recovered the use of my tongue. "In fact, I think that kind mostly went out of fashion in the '70s and '80s. We've been working through the trauma of Dad's death, and he's been teaching me healthier ways of coping with stress and dealing with my emotions."

I put my hand over my mother's in a spontaneous act of tenderness—and quickly removed it when I saw her wince. I felt a familiar wave of hurt and anger wash over me. But at the same time, I felt a tinge of something akin to tenderness.

"Sorry, I know we're not that kind of family," I said softly, careful to wipe out any trace of sarcasm from my voice.

She's the litmus test, I reminded myself.

Amanda looked sharply at my face, ready to lash back. Seeing my expression, however, she stopped. A big sigh shuddered through her body, visibly lowering her shoulders and leaving her looking a little deflated.

"And I'm sorry we're not that kind of family, Sarah. You were such an affectionate and sensitive child."

I was stunned for the third time in the space of ten minutes.

"What do you mean? I thought I was a 'sullen, angry' child!"

"Well, that too, but that came later," Amanda said, closing her eyes. "You were a happy baby. I remember how you'd stare at me with your big emerald eyes. And I ... I guess I was scared. It seemed like so much responsibility—much more than the decisions I made every day about people's lives. So, I turned away. By the time you were a toddler, you had stopped following me around and turned to your father instead ..."

My mother slowly opened her eyes, looking disoriented at finding herself face to face with her thirty-four-year-old daughter. She patted my shoulder awkwardly and picked up the *Times*, marking the end of our conversation.

"I think that is quite enough emotion for a Sunday morning," she said in her usual business-like tone, but this time there was also a trace of humor. "But before I forget, I did want to thank you for your note. Your puzzle is fine where it is. I'm probably not going to have a dinner party any time soon."

After swigging the last sips of my smoothie and putting my glass in the dishwasher, I went up to my room, still reeling from the conversation we had just had. Instead of spinning out about what it meant, I went to the BBC website and searched for South Sudan news. I scrolled through the article and watched a video of people shouting for joy in the streets, banging homemade drums, and jubilantly waving the South Sudanese flag.

"The South's independence follows decades of conflict with the north in which some 1.5 million people died," I read. "(Sudan's President Omar al-Bashir) stressed his country's 'readiness to work with our southern brothers and help them set up their state so that, God willing, this state will be stable and develop. The cooperation between us will be excellent, particularly when it comes to marking and preserving the border, so there is a movement of citizens and goods via this border,' he told journalists in Khartoum."

I closed my eyes and noticed a stirring in my heart. A ray of optimism that the country would be able to recover from the scars of the civil war and rebuild itself as a nation. And I felt the tight, hard cynicism of my mind. There were the ethnic tensions between the Nuer and the Dinka, for one thing, but as with many conflicts, beneath the factionalism lay disputes over natural resources—in this case, oil. While most of the oil fields were in South Sudan, Sudan controlled its exports, and I predicted fractious discussions about how to divide the oil debt and wealth.

In that moment, however, my heart won over. I opened my email account and sent Hiba a quick message.

Dear Hiba,

Congratulations on South Sudan's independence! Are you celebrating? I'm so excited for you and the country. What a time of hope and change. Do you know what that means for the clinic? I hope for you it won't be closing.

How are you? Have you seen Aluel? If so, send her my regards. I hope she's doing okay. How is JC? Is he behaving?

I miss you and think of you often. I'm sorry I haven't been in touch more often.

Your friend,
Sarah

I felt called to watch the video again and the pure elation on people's faces struck me. I felt their excitement in my body. The possibility of real change. And I hoped they wouldn't be let down by those who governed.

Suddenly, I thought of Patrick's prompt. "What brings me joy?" I shut down my laptop and opened a new journal I'd just bought since I'd finished my last one. It had a red, hard cover with the words EMBRACE THE CHAOS written in bold, white letters. Without knowing what I was going to write, I started moving my pen across the page.

Running with my hair loose. Leaning against a redwood tree. Helping a woman give birth. Holding newborn babies. Watching my patients get better. Travel. Sex?

I hesitated to write the last one. And finally added the question mark. I wanted to be honest with myself. Although it had been a while, it was true. Most of the time. Depending on whom the sex was with. The messy part came after, with the emotions.

Eating delicious food. Meeting new people. Listening to music. Especially jazz. Bubble baths. Learning a new language. Mariol's smile ...

As I wrote the boy's name, tears started streaming down my face, unbidden. I threw the journal across the room.

You're supposed to feel happy, not sad, you dimwit!

I decided to go downstairs to continue with the puzzle. I needed something where the progress was linear. After three hours, I had filled out most of the bottom with its olive-colored grass and tiny people lining up to get into the grounded hot air balloons, and I had six piles of tiles divided by color and pattern. I was tired but satisfied.

Chapter Twenty
July 2-10, 1917

Riots in East Saint Louis

Maggie

The past week had been a blur. School was out, so I could focus all my time on collecting people's accounts. Time felt thick, like molasses. I moved through it as though I was sleepwalking. My heart was splintered with fragments of stories, images of death etched in my mind, words said and unsaid.

The pieces of my fragile world had begun to crumble around me. Josie was still angry with me. Mr. Grant was gone. My heart felt empty and desolate. I was bowed down by the weight of the tales I'd become the keeper of. The burden of waiting. For what, I did not know.

Edna and I clung to each other as the shipwrecked might to a raft. In April, President Wilson declared war on Germany. And the war in Europe, which had been distant and remote, was now in our backyards. Edna's younger brother, Hector, had been selected as one of the men who would be trained to lead the Colored combat units. He was a teacher, and although he had never fought before, he got the highest score on the army's classification test. A few weeks before, he'd left to go to the training camp in Des Moines, and we expected he would be deployed shortly.

I discovered that under pressure, Edna's earth began to quake. I sensed the tiny tremors of fear shaking her being at its foundation. I did my best to be the rock for her she'd been for me, which wasn't always easy since the dark shadows and worry lines under her eyes mirrored mine as I waited for news of Mr. Grant. Public radio transmission had stopped so the government could use it for the war efforts. Edna and I scavenged every day for scraps of news we could find on the fighting in Europe as well as the riots in East Saint Louis.

"Lewis said white workers went on strike against the Aluminum Ore Company, so the company brought in close to five hundred Colored workers to take their place," Edna told me. "The whites didn't like that. They lodged a complaint with the mayor's office. That same night, they claimed one of ours robbed a white man, and after that, the white mobs were out of control. Pulling our people from trolleys and streetcars and any of them they found on the street and beating them. They called in the National Guard, although I hear the governor already let them go. Some people think it's just going to get worse."

Edna had a collection of Frances E. W. Harper's poems, and I loved the way her words transformed unbearable pain into the beauty of the lark when she sang in the dead of night. We read "Home, Sweet Home" about the civil war over and over again. It told of men who should have been brothers turning against each other in carnage. And how the thought and longing of home drew them together, if but for a short time. The words somehow brought me some peace. That we could turn human folly into a message of hope: "May mother, home and Heaven, be our watchwords evermore."

That night, I fell asleep to the image of my mother's tired but loving face watching over me, and I slept sounder than I had in weeks.

The next morning, when I thudded into the kitchen, feet

still heavy with sleep, Edna was already up and pacing the floor.

"Edna, is everything okay?" I asked blearily. I was usually up before she was.

"Lewis heard early this morning that there was violence in East Saint Louis yesterday. We don't know all the details yet, but it sounds like there was shooting in the Colored part of town. They say some houses were burned. There has been no news of Mr. Grant. Paul, who went with him, lost track of him when the violence started." Edna paused to breathe, and fear slinked to the pit of my stomach as my heart started racing.

"Lewis has gone to the NAACP in Manhattan to see if he can get more information. I thought about waking you, but decided to let you sleep until we knew more." While part of me wished I'd known when she did, another part was grateful for the rest.

"Also, if you feel up for it, we might need your help later."

"Of course."

That day, as we waited, time slowed to a crawl. Molasses moving backward. In the end, there were no stories to collect, as everyone was busy trying to gather what happened. I read Josie a book to distract my mind, even though she was now reading circles around us. Her body felt warm against mine, and I realized I'd missed her. I felt a pang of sadness at the distance that had come between us, and I silently vowed to try to patch things up between us faster than I had already planned.

Bits of information started filtering in that day and the next.

"Some white people opened fire in a Colored neighborhood ... Later, a car with a journalist and two police officers went to investigate ... A few residents opened fire on it ... My cousin George said they thought it was the same people come back to shoot them again …"

"An officer was killed … maybe two? I dunno …"

"A huge mob swarmed that part of town."

"A journalist there said the whites cut off the water supply in that neighborhood and started burning houses down … When people fled their homes, they started shooting …"

"Maybe forty dead? Maybe hundreds …"

Two days after the riots, still no news of Mr. Grant. My heart had been flip-flopping helplessly in my chest. And then we heard from Paul that Frank got beaten up by the mob. Even though they said he wasn't hurt too badly, my heart dropped like a boulder into the pit of my belly.

"Lewis says he was punched in the stomach and will have some nasty bruises, but thankfully, it's nothing that won't heal. He'll be returning in the next few days, whenever he's well enough to travel. The NAACP is outraged and has decided to organize a protest on Fifth Avenue at the end of the month. We need to start spreading the word."

We started going house to house, telling people about the march. That evening, Edna, Mr. Jones, Josie, and I went to hear Marcus Garvey speak in Harlem.

"The East Saint Louis Riot, or rather massacre, of Monday second, will go down in history as one of the bloodiest outrages against mankind for which any class of people could be held guilty," his voice resounded, washing over the gathered crowd in waves of truth.

"Hear, hear," we all echoed back.

"This is no time for fine words, but a time to lift one's voice against the savagery of a people who claim to be the dispensers of democracy."

His words stayed with me as I waited for what came next, reminding me that my worries were trifles compared to what we were up against.

*

It was days before Mr. Grant came back—and even more days before I saw him. I did not know how I would feel, how he would look, what would happen. I had replayed his kissing my hand so many times in my mind I was beginning to think it might have been a figment of my imagination. That I was making it mean so much more than it did.

And then he was here. The deaths in East Saint Louis had stirred outrage among us, and our work collecting stories had gained momentum. People were pouring in, and there was talk that Representative Dyer was going to support introducing an anti-lynching bill in Congress.

I was in the study, frantically writing up my reports so I could give them to Mr. Jones when I felt him. I turned my head, and he was standing in the doorway. As was so often the case with him, I didn't know how long he had been watching me.

He seemed smaller than I remembered. Somehow deflated, although the sharpness in his eyes as they bore into me had remained intact. There was the hint of a bruise on his left cheek. I stood as he walked toward me. His gait was uneven and strained, and I saw him wince a little. I went toward him to spare him any more movement. I reached up toward his right cheek, not quite touching it, but he still flinched involuntarily.

As I started to pull my hand back, he stayed it with both of his, his eyes a question. I caressed his other cheek with my free hand in response. I felt his body shudder, as though he were willing his wall down. A tear welled up and dripped down to my fingertip.

"Mr. Grant, I was so scared ..." I said, not quite ready to finish my sentence.

We stayed like this for a long time, both weeping silently, joined in pain and longing.

"Please, call me Frank," was all he said that night.

Chapter Twenty-One

Connections

Sarah

Ever since my conversation with my mother, I had felt a subtle shift. I hadn't realized how much I had internalized the image of myself as angry and difficult. Even as I had learned to counter her criticisms with scathing sarcasm, I had still absorbed every hurtful word she hurled my way. That I had been an affectionate and open baby was a revelation. For the first time, I believed Patrick when he said, "Your mother's inability to love you had nothing to do with you. Or your worth. It had everything to do with her and her own wounding."

"The hard, tight ball I so often feel in my chest is starting to soften. It's amazing! But at the same time, I'm feeling more vulnerable. Unprotected. I've been more agitated than I was a couple of weeks ago," I said, my vocal cords tightening. A metallic taste of fear coated my tongue. I could hear the countdown in my head. *One more month to get it together.*

I picked up a stone from Patrick's collection and rubbed my finger across its black surface.

"Sarah, you had the first real conversation you may ever have had with your mother. Of course, that's going to stir up uncomfortable feelings," he said, a kind smile on his face. "Close your eyes and allow yourself to slow down with that feeling. Where do you feel the agitation in your body?"

I turned my attention inward. I had definitely become more aware that I *had* a body since I'd started working so closely with Patrick. Seeing him weekly, and sometimes even twice a week, was a far cry from the annual sessions I had between missions.

"I feel pins and needles in my chest, while at the same time there's a heavy feeling like someone is pressing down on my heart. I feel a sense of dread."

Patrick asked me to trace the feeling back in time to see if a memory came up. As he guided me, I remembered a time when I was about five years old. I had forgotten all about it until that moment.

My parents worked late nights. I only saw them for part of the weekend, and even then, they tag-teamed on who would spend time with me while the other worked. My babysitter, a fifteen-year-old neighborhood girl named Amy, had picked me up from kindergarten and microwaved two of the TV dinners my mother had bought for us.

Outside, a May shower was beating against the windowpanes as Amy sat me down in front of the TV to eat. When she went into the kitchen to talk on the phone, I could hear snippets of conversation and guessed she was chatting with Joe, a boy in her class she couldn't stop talking about. Her voice was giggly and higher pitched than usual.

All of a sudden, jagged lightning bolts electrified the night and lit up the house. A minute later, the lights went out, and the TV went dark. I had a panicky feeling, an awareness of being completely alone. My chest was heavy, and I couldn't breathe. I screamed and threw myself on the couch, sobbing. I heard a crash in the kitchen and Amy swearing colorfully. After what seemed like an eternity, she came out with a lit candle.

"What's wrong, Sarah?" she asked.

I had no words for the fear and the hollowness I felt, and the tears kept streaming down my cheeks.

"It's just a storm, Sarah. You're such a baby! Grow up!" Amy said in disgust. She found a flashlight and went to do her homework at the dining room table. I remained frozen in fear and eventually fell asleep on the couch, my cheeks still wet from my tears.

Patrick invited me to imagine that my current self was there with my younger self, reassuring her and letting her know she wasn't alone. Although he had asked me to do something similar a few times before with other memories, this was the first time I could actually feel a connection to that younger version of me. I imagined my five-year-old self sitting in my lap with her head resting on my shoulder. By the end of the session, the agitated and heavy feeling had significantly diminished.

"Thinking back on it now, it seems like an insignificant event," I said at the close of the session. "But I remember such a strong sense of aloneness and fear. Like the darkness was going to absolutely swallow me up. That's probably when I started running away from stillness and getting angry so I wouldn't feel scared."

Patrick nodded approvingly. "That's a good thing for you to be aware of. As homework, I'm going to have you sit with the question 'How would I feel if I allowed myself to be in the here and now, completely? Without trying to run away.'"

I stopped by the grocery store on the way home. Munching on some kale chips back in my room, I reflected on the session with Patrick. I jotted some highlights in my "Embrace the Chaos" journal so I wouldn't forget.

Remembering that profound sense of aloneness, I suddenly felt a strong desire to connect, to reach out. During my missions, there was no time to waste on platitudes or small talk. Being thrown together in a struggle for survival, the friendships forged could feel very intense. Although we often knew little about each other's backstories, we were bonded together by shared experience. But for the most part, the connections dissolved when we moved on to the next job. It felt a lot like building castles in the sand. But perhaps that was just me, since I knew others who made concerted efforts to stay connected.

I opened my laptop and found a response from Hiba in my inbox.

> *Thanks so much for reaching out. Yes, it was quite the party! Okot and I were out in the street until 1:00 a.m., and the next day we were very hoarse from shouting.*
>
> *How are you, dear Sarah? I hope you're enjoying the time off. I'm almost envious, the work is so intense. Just kidding. I know it broke your heart to have to leave.*
>
> *You don't want to know about JC. He's the same as ever, and Anne, the nurse who replaced you, is now his favorite scapegoat. So, it clearly wasn't you.*
>
> *I miss you. Do you know when you'll be returning to the field? I hope they send you somewhere on the African continent.*
>
> *Take care, and come visit any time.*
> *Love, Hiba*

Reading her words, I felt an ache in my heart.

Look what you did! If you hadn't screwed up, you could be there now, my inner nemesis whispered. I hadn't heard the voice in a while, and its vehemence caught me by surprise.

It's okay. I did the best I could, I tried to counter with an affirmation, noticing how much more tentative the positive words felt than the negative.

I wished I had a friend like Hiba here. Thinking of Patrick's question, I thought that if I allowed myself to be here fully, I'd want to connect more deeply with people, rather than simply waiting to leave again.

On a whim, I went to the Facebook website. I had previously resisted the trend, not being one to look back or feel nostalgic about the past. While I was working, the internet connection was spotty at best. In my free time, I had no interest in knowing who had married whom or what my "friends" had eaten for dinner. Between missions, my priority was to recuperate and get ready to move on again, so reconnecting with old friends seemed pointless.

I had plenty of time now, however. I thought about the friends I had made at UC Berkeley and wondered if Phoebe was still in the Bay Area. I found a picture of myself from South Sudan, where I was holding a three-year-old boy we had treated for cholera. He was holding my thumb and looking at me with a smile that beamed right into my heart.

Once I'd uploaded the photo and completed my profile, I searched for Phoebe Carter, hoping that was still her name. I scrolled down quite a few names before I found her (married name Leroy). As I was searching for other friends, I saw that Phoebe had accepted my request, and a minute later, I received a message:

"OMG! Sarah, is that really you? Where the hell are you?"

"I was in South Sudan, but I'm back at my mother's place in Berkeley for the time being. Where are you?"

"I'm in Walnut Creek with my husband and two daughters. Let's get together! My schedule's a little hectic, but I'm sure we can find time. I'll send you friend suggestions of UC Berkeley friends I'm in touch with."

An hour later, I had twenty-three friends to my name. It didn't compare to the hundreds most of them were friends with, but it gave me a strange sense of accomplishment.

I then searched for Fatou, wondering where my Senegalese friend might be. We had both left Paris at around the same time and kept up a correspondence through the end of high school and the beginning of college but then lost touch. The last email I had for her was an AOL account, which bounced back when I sent a message. I scrolled through the various Fatous … and then there was my old friend; her smiling face in a white-trimmed box with a beautiful beach in the background. According to what I could see publicly, she lived in Dakar. Feeling excited, I sent her a friend request. With the time difference, even if she was as active as Phoebe, I wouldn't get a response until the next day.

I looked up from my computer, rubbing the screen fuzz from my eyes, and noticed my mother outside the window. She had her big, yellow sun hat on and was crouching by a flower bed, garden shears in her right hand, her left pulling at offending weeds. Strands of hair peeked out from under the hat—the black almost entirely invaded by gray now. I noticed that my mother held her body more gingerly than she used to, not crouching with the ease of a panther anymore.

It was strange how old age had taken up residence in the woman who had seemed so indomitable and indestructible in my youth without my noticing. While I was busy living my own life—or running away from it, as Patrick would say.

I hadn't seen my mother much since our conversation the week before, although I made a mental note to check her schedule and suggest a dinner. I reflected on how little I knew about this woman whose body had once housed me, how little I knew about her inner life and workings.

She never told me what it had felt like to lose her husband in the prime of her life and career. What it was like to sit at the table with a sullen, rebellious teenager and not know how to talk to her own daughter.

"I just hope you have children, so you know what it's like!"

she had once said in exasperation.

"What, so I can let someone else raise them? No way!" I had retorted, with as much sixteen-year-old disdain as I could muster. Eighteen years later and childless, I'd held true to my promise.

My mother never told me why she chose surgery as a career, although I always assumed it was because she loved the neatness of it, the swift incisions, the urgency that left no space for doubt or dilly-dallying. No messy emotions or conversations. Although, having spent years in makeshift bush hospitals, I now knew there was nothing neat or clear-cut about surgery. That by the time the patient needed surgery, the odds were stacked against the surgeon. That human error was one of the biggest causes of fatalities. How many had died despite her best efforts? Did they still haunt her dreams at night?

I also had no idea why my mother had never remarried. Was it by choice or out of resignation? Lovers wove their way in and out of her life and were undoubtedly more numerous than the ones I met during my brief visits home or that my mother happened to mention in passing on the phone or in an email. Like an offhanded comment about going to the opera with Joe.

"Whoa, back up, Mom, who's Joe? Have you mentioned him before?"

"Oh, I guess not. He's nobody, just a doctor I met at a gala a few weeks ago. I've seen him once or twice since then. He's just as busy as I am, so it makes things easier." A short laugh that let me know the topic was closed.

Did my mother get lonely? Did she have friends beyond the nurses who responded to her clipped commands and the interns who hung on her every word? The acquaintances who filled her social calendar with glittering events? Was it that my mother never told me or that I never asked?

It was several hours since my snack, and my stomach growled that it was time for my evening smoothie. I stopped in the garden beforehand, wanting to catch my mother while she was still there. She started when she saw me hovering over her.

"Heavens, Sarah, you scared me! You can be so quiet when you want to!"

"Sorry, I didn't mean to startle you. The garden looks great—impressive, especially with all the fog and cold we've been having."

She nodded with a small smile.

"Hey, I've been doing some thinking and realizing that I haven't really been taking advantage of this time with you. I know you have a busy schedule, but I'd like to find some time to do something together."

My mother looked tired, but pleased. "I would like that. I know you'll be gone before I know it. I'll look at my planner when I'm done here." A few hours later, we made a date to go to dinner and a concert the next Friday.

Chapter Twenty-Two
July 28, 1917, to January 1918

Hope

Maggie

It was a time of hope. My heart sang with possibilities I didn't quite dare to name. My hand wrote late into the night, as though to capture every fleeting feeling before it disappeared. Frank (oh, how good his given name felt on my tongue!) and I had hardly had a moment alone since his return, but our eyes stole furtive glances, pregnant with meaning, and our fingers brushed against each other when they could. We got caught up in the whirlwind of preparations for the march on Fifth Avenue. Time felt like a dream, and my heart raced with an anticipation I didn't quite understand.

And then the day of the march was upon us. I had never seen so many people in one place. So many Colored people. Thousands and thousands and thousands. Streaming in like an army that had no end, all in one place. And what a place. I had never been to Fifth Avenue before, and the area was as grand as we were solemn.

The lead organizer for the event, James Weldon Johnson, had asked all the women and children to wear white and the men to wear black. There was a lot of grumbling from the women that they would have to pull out their wedding dresses. At Edna's request, Bessie had made me a dress out of an old white curtain. When James instructed it be a silent march but for the drums, many of those assembled protested.

"Haven't we spent enough of our life in silence, James?"

"I want my voice to be heard!"

But the effect was breathtaking. The silence, the black and white of our attire, the beating of the drums ... I felt like I was walking down the aisle of a church. Our solemnity and reverence spread to the onlookers who had gathered around us, and they too fell silent as they witnessed our progression. Our only words were those written on the pamphlets we handed out and on the signs we carried.

Mine read, "RACE PREJUDICE IS THE OFFSPRING OF IGNORANCE AND THE MOTHER OF LYNCHING." Josie, who'd been so inspired by Marcus Garvey's speech that she insisted on coming with us, held a sign that said, "MOTHER, DO LYNCHERS GO TO HEAVEN?" Edna held her hand, and in her other was a placard with the words, "MR. PRESIDENT, WHY NOT MAKE AMERICA SAFE FOR DEMOCRACY?" In the silence, I heard all of our steps echoing together. And for the first time since I got involved in recording the stories, I truly felt the power of what we were doing. Hope stirred in my belly and heart, like the skylark taking flight. My heart opened, spread its wings, and claimed a stake in the sky. The muffled rhythm of the drums whispered that change was possible. Indeed, inevitable.

I felt the strength of the words that stared back from the pamphlets those of us without signs handed out to the curious and the indifferent:

> *We march because, by the Grace of God and the force of truth, the dangerous, hampering walls of prejudice and*

inhuman injustices must fall.

We march because we want to make impossible a repetition of Waco, Memphis, and East Saint Louis, by arousing the conscience of the country and bringing the murders of our brothers, sisters, and innocent children to justice.

We march because we deem it a crime to be silent in the face of such barbaric acts.

We march because we want our children to live in a better land and enjoy fairer conditions than have fallen to our lot.

That night, although I was bone-weary and my eyelids were drooping shut, another poem pushed its way through my pen to honor the day passed.

You Cannot Keep Us Down

We came out in droves
Because you cannot keep us down.

We came out in droves
Marching to our silent outrage
Women in white
Men in black
The persistent heartbeat of the drums
The only sound.

You can kill our brothers and sisters
Our mothers and fathers
Our sons and daughters
But you cannot keep us down
And you cannot kill our spirit
Though you try.

Your fear and your outrage
Are our bloodline.

You cannot keep us down.

We will come out in droves
Armies of life
Women in white
Men in black
To show the depth of our pain
And the color of our courage.

We will persist.
We will resist.
We will survive this, too.

You can silence our tongues
But not our hearts
Or our spirits
Or our hope.

We will come out in droves
Until we silence
Your hatred
And your fear
With our courage
And our will.

We will.

In the months since the march, life had resumed its normal course, although at times, my heart took flight and there was no stopping its soaring. Hector had been deployed to France, and every day, Edna waited for the mailman with bated breath.

Frank began courting me in earnest, taking me to the pictures and for walks in Central Park. When school resumed, he sometimes picked me up at the end of class—until the students started teasing me.

He was much more concerned with our thirteen-year age gap than I was and had not even kissed me yet, though our hands often took the place of our lips, locking together as though they wished to never part.

Representative Dyer of Missouri was interested in introducing an anti-lynching bill in Congress, and Frank went to Washington, DC to discuss the terms with him. He wrote me often with descriptions of the city and of the progress they were making. I devoured his words and sent him my poems and the thoughts that I could share with no one else.

During that time, I kept my promise to Josie and carved out special time each week to be with her. I read her stories, and she told me hers. She had become quite the storyteller, and I was secretly proud. We went on discovery walks where we explored places we had never been before. We went to Manhattan and rode the trolley. I could feel her pain at my sudden neglect start melting away, and my heart gladdened.

One day, Edna came into my room after everyone had gone to bed.

"Maggie," she said. "You know that I have come to love you as a younger sister, right?"

I nodded, but fear had gripped my stomach. She laughed at the expression on my face.

"Don't look so frightened, dear, there is just something I feel I must say. Because I want your happiness, and I worry about you. It's clear that something is developing with Frank," she said, pausing for confirmation.

I nodded again, not sure what to say.

"He is a good man, and Lewis respects him like few others. But he is also thirteen years older than you, Maggie. And you are barely out of childhood. In many ways, you are old beyond your years, and God only knows you have seen far more than anyone should have at any age. But in other ways, you are as innocent and wide-eyed as Josie. And Frank can be very closed off. Hard to read."

"Yes, I know. But you should see him when he is with me. He's so much softer. And his eyes can be so tender when he looks at me."

"I'm happy to hear. The only thing I ask is for you to get to know him better before jumping into anything. Did you know he was married before?"

I shook my head, feeling like the bottom had dropped out of my stomach.

"I don't know what happened. I think his wife is dead. But these are things you want to know about a man. These things matter, later. When all those feelings that are sweeping you up calm down."

Although I tried to dismiss her words, they planted a seed of doubt in my heart and ignited the voice warning me against too much happiness. *Remember your promise. You survived, and you are safe. You said you wouldn't ask for more*, it cautioned.

"I haven't asked for anything. It came to me. That's allowed," I pleaded with myself, hoping I could adjust the terms slightly without dire consequences.

But I couldn't settle. As soon as Frank returned from Washington, DC, I blurted out the words after a quick hug.

"Edna said you were married before. Is that true?" I asked, my voice sounding young and petulant. I saw his eyes cloud with a shadow of pain and regret.

"Yes, it is. I'm sorry I haven't told you before. Do you mind if we go to Central Park to talk about this?"

We settled on one of our favorite benches near a little

stream that was bathed in a soft fall sun. Frank took my hand and said he'd been trying to find a good time to tell me about his wife, that it was such a painful topic for him to bring up that he kept on putting it off, that he'd thought that if I knew him better when he told me, that I might not be scared off.

And with that, taking a deep breath before launching into the story, he took me down the hallways of his heart and soul. The dank, musty rooms that smelled of fear and death and the bright, glittering rooms that promised magic. He told me of his wife, Lillie, and the love that had blossomed from their childhood friendship.

"Oh, Maggie, you should have seen her when we were children. She had the brightest eyes with flecks of gold in them, and she was always laughing and playing. She had three older brothers and a younger sister, who died. Her father, who was the preacher for Colored folks in our town, doted on her." His eyes lit up as he told me.

"We were so young when we married. I was twenty-one and had just started law school, and she was eighteen. We thought all we needed was love. Nobody could make me laugh like she could. But then the trouble started." Frank stopped talking, and his eyes became glassy as he got lost in memory.

Still with that faraway look—as though he weren't really with me—he said their problems started when she got pregnant and lost the baby due to complications during the birth. And then her beloved father, a well-respected preacher, was threatened.

"He was a good man, one of the kindest I ever met. One Sunday, after having visited a nine-year-old girl who had been raped by three white men, he could not contain his rage during his sermon. Citing the book of Malachi, he preached, 'Do we not all have one father? Has not one God created us? Why do we deal treacherously each against his brother so as to profane the covenant of our fathers?' He said that God had not put us on earth so some of us could crawl while others walked all over us. The following day, three Colored men tried to go into a white restaurant. Word somehow got out that they were inspired by the minister's sermon. That night, Lillie's mother found their dog with his throat slit with a note saying, 'the preacher's next.' Her mother was able to convince her husband to leave town with her, for her sake."

"I'm so sorry, Frank, that's terrible," I said, stroking the hand I was holding. He squeezed mine before continuing.

"Lillie was heartbroken, and when I started getting involved in the anti-lynching work just after law school, she begged me not to. I wouldn't listen. I didn't take her fear seriously. I tried to reason that I was doing the work that her father had been forced to stop. And then there were the miscarriages. One after another. Three, total. I had no idea how deep her sorrow for each baby was. One day, I came home and …" his voice trembled and cracked, and he had to force himself to finish. "She'd taken her own life …"

Tears began streaming down his face, soon joined by mine. We clung to each other, our pain and our loss mingling until they bled into each other. If anything, his story deepened my love for him. My heart, finding an ally in her sorrow, felt less lonely.

When our tears had cleared, moved by what he'd shared, I told Frank what felt like my deepest secret—because, despite the gossip, Mama, Papa, and I had never talked about it. Even though I was afraid if Frank knew he might love me less.

"I think my father was Mr. Tanner. The white landowner where we were sharecroppers. That's why my skin is so light," I exhaled, my voice so thin and reedy that Frank had to lean in to hear what I was saying.

"Poor Mama. I saw her once, going into the room with him. She looked so trapped, so empty." I said, sobs drumming at my chest as though they might break open my ribcage. Frank held me gently, stroking my hair.

"Oh Maggie, I'm so sorry. For you, for your Mama, for your Papa and brother ..." For perhaps the first time since I'd left home, I allowed myself to completely surrender in another's arms.

Later that night, I whispered to myself, "I survived. I'm safe. I can have this."

A couple of months later, on our way home from a nice restaurant where Frank and I celebrated both my eighteenth birthday and my passing the teacher's examination, we shared our first kiss. And all I can say is that the sweetness and passion far surpassed my imagination.

Chapter Twenty-Three

Old Friends

Sarah

"Gimme back Elmo!"

"Mom! Tell Chloe to stop!" The girls shrieked, and one of them kicked the back of my seat.

"Girls! Cut that out," Phoebe said in a well-perfected 'don't mess with me' mom tone that was loud enough to be heard above the din of fighting without actually yelling.

"Madison, you can play a game on your iPad for ten minutes and let your sister have Elmo. Remember our talk about sharing? And, Chloe, use your words, don't just grab," Phoebe said, all the while keeping her eyes on the road. The girls settled, and the back seat was soon blissfully quiet.

"Look at you, Phoebe! Who would've thought back in the day that you'd become supermom? I'm impressed," I said, remembering some of the raucous parties she'd thrown our senior year at UC Berkeley.

"I don't know about all that. It's called survival," she said, pushing back a stray strand of blond hair that had escaped her ponytail. Except for a few more wrinkles and a couple of extra pounds from giving birth, she hadn't changed at all.

"But yeah, who would have thought? All that money spent on law school used to mediate spats between a four-

and six-year-old. And here you are, saving the world." I could hear the wistfulness creeping into her voice. "How the tables have turned," she implied, but didn't say.

When we met in an advanced French class the second semester of our freshman year, she knew exactly what she wanted to do: study environmental law and hold big corporations accountable, all the while making lots of money. I was taking a smorgasbord of liberal arts classes, hoping something would eventually inspire me enough to want to make a career out of it.

"Oh, I want to play something I brought specially for you," she said, turning on the CD player, and the Indigo Girls came on, crooning "Closer to Fine." The song saw us through many late-night study sessions.

As we sang-shouted the chorus in unison, Madison groaned in embarrassment. "Mom, please!"

Phoebe rolled her eyes, laughing. "That one is six going on sixteen," she said as she turned off the ignition.

"Okay, who's ready for the ocean?" she asked to excited cheers. The temperatures had soared over the past few days—rare for late July in the Bay Area—and Phoebe had asked me if I wanted to join the three of them at the beach.

"I have the girls all day since it's summer vacation, but at least we can catch up a little while they're playing." I'd happily said yes, and since my mother had taken her car, Phoebe had agreed to pick me up.

Even though it was a weekday, the parking lot was full, presumably with other families who'd had the same idea, and we had to walk a quarter of a mile to get to the beach. Phoebe ended up carrying a hot and cranky Chloe part of the way. We found a spot close to the water and shaded by the cliff's edge. After we'd all stripped to our various swimming wear and lathered on sunscreen, Phoebe and I caught up while Chloe made sandcastles and Madison played a game of tag with the crest of the waves, squealing when the water came higher than expected, submerging her up to her belly button.

"Not too far, Madison," Phoebe entreated her.

Once we had filled each other in on the past eight years since we had last seen each other, the conversation petered out.

"So, what's your plan now?" she asked.

"I expect to be given the green light to go back in a couple of weeks, and then I'll have to wait to see where I'm assigned." I could feel the hope and excitement mounting even as I said the words. "What about you, Phoebe? Do you plan on going back to work?"

"Maybe when Chloe starts first grade. I'll have to see. It's hard to reenter the job market after years out of it, especially as a lawyer. And I don't know that I have the fire and grit for that work anymore."

We fell into silence, and Phoebe went to help her younger daughter with her sandcastle, while I joined Madison in a three-way game of tag with the ocean, running in and out of the water, and to and from each other. By the end, we both fell onto the sand, laughing.

After a minute, Madison bounced back up and started kicking at the waves, giggling as she splashed me. Without warning, an image of Mariol laughing in the rain, head back to better feel the full effect of the drops, flashed before my eyes. I felt as though I'd been punched in the stomach and all the air had been sucked out of me.

I flopped over on my belly and put my face on my hands just before the tears started streaming down my cheeks.

"Sarah?" Madison asked, hovering hesitatingly over me.

My grief puddled in my fingers before dripping into the sand, mingling with the ocean foam. I took slow, deep breaths to calm myself.

"I know, you're playing hide-and-go-seek!" Madison exclaimed, having figured out what I must be doing, face in the sand.

"Chloe, come hide with me!" Madison called to her sister.

Feeling more settled and welcoming the distraction, I sat up and wiped my tears with the back of my hand. Keeping my eyes closed, I counted loudly to twenty.

"Ready or not, here I come!" I shouted. Phoebe, looking ready to go, pointed silently to our left. I found the girls hiding in a tiny alcove carved into the side of the cliff.

"You're good with kids," Phoebe said when we'd piled back into her SUV.

"It's the part of my job I like the best," I acknowledged, and we both smiled at each other, perhaps relieved that we still had something in common. As we said goodbye, I wondered if I would see her again before I left.

Back home, I did some yoga to counterbalance the stop-and-start sprints on the beach. As I leaned forward in pigeon pose—my right leg bent in front of me, the left leg stretched out behind me—I thought of Mariol again.

"Goodbye, my friend," I whispered into my mat, planting a tear-moistened kiss on it, imagining it was the boy's face. "I will miss you."

Straightening my legs out behind me, I sobbed until I thought I must have poured out all the pain and loss from the last few months. That night, I slept soundly for twelve straight hours.

The next evening, as I waited for my mother to get ready, I felt calmer than I had in months. Years, perhaps. She emerged in a shimmering gold-and-black dress that showcased both her angles and her curves in the best of ways and silenced any previous thoughts I'd had about her age.

"Wow, Mom, you look stunning. That dress could bring Vivaldi back from the dead!" I said without thinking. She raised an eyebrow, skepticism written all over her face. Where I once would have bristled or felt deflated, however, I found there was now enough space in my heart to have compassion for her automatic guardedness.

Although we'd originally planned to have dinner before the concert, Amanda had been delayed by a work emergency, and we had very little time to spare. Thankfully, the Bay bridge traffic to San Francisco was pretty light for a Friday night. We squeezed into the symphony hall with minutes to spare before the doors closed. Since my mother had season tickets with assigned seats, she brushed past the usher to the upper balcony, and I almost tripped over a few feet trying to keep up.

I sank into the seat with an audible sigh. My mother looked over at me and flashed me a wry smile.

"And you thought you had to go to Africa to have an adventure."

I hadn't heard my mother's dry sense of humor in a long time. I snort-chortled loudly, as I'm prone to when taken by surprise. Mortified, I clamped my hand over my mouth. Glancing over at Amanda, I saw her body shaking with silent mirth. Giggles bubbled up through my own fingers, and tears of glee were soon streaming down my face.

As the lights dimmed and the music began, my insides felt cleansed out and ready to receive the beauty as though I'd never heard the *Four Seasons* before. When we got to the part in "Spring" where the instruments crescendo in urgency like a sudden flurry of wingbeats, my heart tripped over the poignancy of its beauty. I felt an ache for something I hadn't felt in a long time. And suddenly an image of sitting in the Sainte-Chapelle in Paris with my mother flashed before my eyes. She had taken me there because she had wanted to show me what she considered to be the most beautiful church in the city.

"I think Notre Dame is overrated, especially since you can no longer get near the Gargoyles. The Sainte-Chappelle, on the other hand, is like sitting inside a jewelry box," she'd said. Not only had we arrived when the noonday sun scattered prisms of light across the floor, we had happened upon a free concert of Vivaldi's *Four Seasons*. We'd had a lovely time, and after, she'd stood in line to get me an out-of-this-world chocolate ice cream from Berthillon while I'd waited on a bench. It was such a happy memory that, until that moment, I'd completely forgotten. I wondered what else I'd distorted or deleted from my conscious mind?

At intermission, I turned toward my mother. "Mom, do you remember …" I started to say.

"That day in Sainte-Chappelle?" She completed my sentence. "Of course, Sarah. That's why I chose this concert to go to."

"Oh wow, thanks. I hadn't remembered until now." I spent the rest of the concert basking in the warm glow of our companionable silence.

"I feel ready," I said to Patrick ten days later, during our check-in. "I haven't had any nightmares, insomnia, or migraines in weeks. I have many tools under my belt to calm my nervous system, and I even find myself missing yoga when I don't do it. And my mother and I are actually getting along! Which I never would've thought possible. Not in a million years. The concert was such a success, we made plans to have dinner together tonight."

"You're definitely in a different place than you were three months ago, Sarah, and I want to acknowledge you for your commitment to your healing and the progress you and your mother have made," he said, smiling. "I did want to check in about Mariol, though. I would still recommend doing a session on his death. It was a sudden and deep loss for you, in addition to being the trigger for your nightmares and trauma response."

"I felt a big release of grief the day I went with Phoebe and her girls to the ocean. I feel so much lighter," I said.

But then I noticed a slight pinching in my heart, which I quickly pushed out of my awareness. I had tread water for three long months, time suspended as I waited to be given the green light to get out and move on with my life. Nothing was going to ruin this moment.

Patrick studied my face carefully. I smiled, beaming with the genuine excitement I felt at finally being freed from this holding pattern.

"That's great, but a release isn't necessarily the same as healing. However, you are the only one who can know if you are ready, and I trust your judgment. So, does your body give you a yes? Are you sure?"

Like you're sure about anything?! My inner nemesis mocked, and I felt my stomach clench. But I chose to ignore both. I *had* to get out of here—it felt like a matter of life and death to me. I closed my eyes and concentrated on relaxing my face and looking convincing. When I opened them, I had wiped any trace of doubt from my face.

"I've never been more sure of anything, Patrick."

"Okay then. I'll write a draft letter for your organization, and you can look it over before I send it."

"Thank you!" I exclaimed. "I can't wait to get back. I appreciate all your help."

"You're welcome, Sarah. That isn't to say there isn't deeper healing work we could be doing, but for now, I think you have what you need to be able to successfully return to work."

That afternoon, while doing a happy dance alone in my bedroom, I found myself excited at the prospect of sharing my news with my mother during our dinner together. Times had certainly changed! I sat down to finish the puzzle. All that was left was the vast expanse of sky at the top and in between the hot-air balloons.

"Ready or not, here I come," I said, as I scattered the azure, cornflower blue, grayish- and purplish-blue pieces on the table. "Time to fly."

Chapter Twenty-Four
November to December 1918

Elation

Maggie

On November 11, Germany signed the armistice, and the War in Europe ended! We had started thinking it would never end, especially after the German offensive on the Western Front in the spring. That day, we (Frank, Edna, Mr. Jones, Josie, Bessie, and I) gathered in the kitchen around the radio. Transmission had resumed as the end of the war became imminent, and when the news came, we all started shouting and hugging each other.

Edna began to sob—I think it was the first time she'd taken a deep breath since Hector left. We had received his last letter less than three weeks before, and he was alive, miraculously with all his limbs intact!

Frank picked me up and twirled me around. And as he did, he whispered, "Maggie, will you marry me?" If he hadn't been holding me then, I would have fallen.

"What?" I asked in disbelief, not trusting I had heard my ears.

"Maggie, will you marry me?" he asked again, this time so loudly that the others heard and disengaged from Edna. All of a sudden, with all the eyes on me, I felt shy, and I wanted to run away. Instead, I nodded mutely, a smile slowly spreading all over my face.

There was another round of shouts and hugs. "You just want to wring all the tears from my eyes!" Edna admonished playfully, though I could tell she was about to burst from happiness too. After Frank and I had talked, and after watching the two of us grow more in love with each other over the course of the year, she'd told me on more than one occasion that all her concerns over our union were gone.

My heart was soaring so high it felt like it would never land again. I never knew such joy was possible.

The Colors of Your Heart

*I have seen the colors
Of your heart,
Your angels
And your demons,
And I love them all.*

*I have seen the colors
Of your heart
The dark purple bruises
And the bright golden light
And I say yes
To them all.*

*I have seen the colors
Of your heart—
You have painted them
All over my body
All over my heart
All over my soul.*

> *I have seen the colors*
> *Of your heart*
> *And you have seen mine.*
> *I say yes to now*
> *I say yes to forever*
> *I say yes to never again*
> *Alone.*

I wrote this poem after he proposed and handed it to him the next day. I watched as his eyes clouded with emotion, a little smile playing on both our lips.

Since then, time had felt like a slippery fish I was trying in vain to catch up with. Representative Dyer had offered Frank a permanent position on his staff in Washington, DC, to help him with the anti-lynching bill he introduced in April.

"The NAACP hasn't endorsed his bill yet. Moorfield Storey, their president, has said the bill is unconstitutional," Frank told me that night, in an attempt to explain why we might have to leave New York imminently.

"We know we have an uphill battle, trying to impose criminal liability for mob actions on private individuals. We have been emphasizing the Fourteenth Amendment, which allows Congress to enforce equal protection and due process rights …" he paused, scanning my face for signs of understanding. I nodded, although in truth I hadn't grasped all of it.

"Anyway, I have been talking to Moorfield these past few months, and I think he's ready to come around. Which is why Dyer wants me to join his staff and work on this full time, so we will have momentum if the Republicans take over Congress—and we will do all we can to ensure that happens with next year's election." Frank paused to catch his breath before continuing.

"My dearest Maggie, I know how much you love Edna and Josie and that this is all very fast, but would you be willing to move to DC with me at the beginning of January?"

"Yes, I am," I happily agreed. As much as the Joneses had become my family and New York my home, my heart was ready for another adventure. One that was not born of death and tragedy. And since I wasn't teaching, I didn't have to worry about that commitment. Knowing we were at a critical juncture in the movement, I had wanted to devote more time to collecting the stories and had decided not to teach this school year.

And so it was that we were rushing to get married before we went, in order to have all our friends present to celebrate with us. Edna had bought some beautiful white fabric, and Bessie had been fussing over me to get my dress ready in time. Josie had been uncharacteristically shy around me, as though my becoming a wife had turned me into a different person. But she glowed with pleasure when I asked her to be my flower girl.

We were planning a quiet affair. Preacher Brown had agreed to marry us in the Joneses' garden. When we began talking about who would give me away, my heart felt heavy. Since I arrived in New York, I had tried to think of home as little as possible. But now, thoughts of Papa and Andre, unanswered questions about Mama and my other brothers, escaped from the box I kept them in. They cut into the happiness of the day that was to come, although I tried not to show it. I was grateful to Mr. Jones for saying to me, "Maggie, would you do me the honor of allowing me to walk you down the aisle? But only if you start calling me Lewis, mind you."

The day of the wedding, I was nervous. Edna had been with me all morning, reassuring me, fixing my hair, and helping me get into my dress. When Lewis came to tell us that Frank had been delayed, I felt an old familiar fear flailing in the pit of my stomach. Frank had been acting strangely preoccupied this past week, and I'd found myself thinking of Lillie, his first wife, and of Edna's warning last year. Edna must have read my mind, because she started patting my hand.

"Maggie, I know you are worried, but Frank will be here as soon as he can. I promise. And when he gets here, I'm sure all will be forgotten. He loves you very much and would do anything for you. He has really shown that this past year. I think you are making the right choice. Now don't fret yourself unnecessarily, my dear."

Finally, Bessie came in to announce Frank's arrival, and it was time for me to leave the house and go into the garden. In a daze, I walked toward Lewis.

And there, at his side, looking smaller and more fragile than I remembered, was Mama.

Chapter Twenty-Five

The Unraveling

Sarah

I slammed the book shut, feeling nauseous. I stared at the title, trying to find my ground. *At the Hands of Persons Unknown: The Lynching of Black America.* Feeling guilty that I'd been avoiding reading the books I'd gotten from the library on the United States' racial history, I'd picked one of them up and started reading it. I'd been soaring so high since I'd sent Patrick's letter, I'd somehow presumed myself to suddenly be immune to emotional turmoil.

That was genius of you to read this now when you're getting ready to leave. What were you expecting? A walk in the park? My inner critic mocked.

I sighed, for once agreeing with my nemesis. What *was* I expecting? This was such a brutal part of my country's history that still informed present-day reality. I closed my eyes; images of ripped-off fingernails and quartered limbs swam into my vision. They soon intermingled with snippets of some of the horrors I had witnessed in my own work.

A fifteen-year-old former child soldier in Sierra Leone whose stone-cold eyes sent shivers down my spine. A seven-year-old girl who was taken as a sex slave by the rebels in the Ivory Coast, whose vagina was so mangled it was beyond repair. An old man whose leg was blown off by a land mine in the West Bank as he was chasing after one of his goats.

I felt my throat close, and my stomach roiled in agitation. *Not now,* I pleaded with myself. *Not when I'm so close to my goal. I have to stay calm.*

I had spent six-plus years knee-deep in the poverty, cruelty, and injustices that humans learned to rationalize and compartmentalize. The only thing that kept the pain from swallowing me up was the hard crust of my professionalism. My role as a nurse gave me a task to focus on and kept the feelings of helplessness at bay. And, if I was honest with myself, the fact that the country I was working in wasn't my own also provided a little distance. Some part of me still believed it couldn't happen at home. On my doorstep. I felt an overwhelming sadness at the inequities embedded in the fabric of the society I'd been born into, knowing I was in part complicit just by the fact of being born white.

To distract myself and to clear my head, I went for a run in my neighborhood. My feet pummeled the concrete as though I could pulverize the injustices with my shoes.

After a shower, I checked my emails. Seeing I'd received a response from my organization's HR department, I felt anticipatory excitement.

> *Dear Ms. Baum,*
>
> *We have received Patrick Noels' evaluation, thank you. Jean-Claude Perrin, your previous supervisor, has recommended you also have an outside mental health assessment done with an independent psychologist to supplement your therapist's evaluation. I'm enclosing a list of local clinics for your convenience. Please have it completed & returned to us within the week.*
>
> *Let us know if you have any questions.*
> *Sincerely,*
> *Sandra, H.R. Coordinator*

I re-read the email, stunned. How could Jean-Claude still be ruining my life, even so far away? Why? I felt panic grip my chest. An outside mental health assessment? Did they think I was that unbalanced? I sent Patrick a text on his emergency phone. I'd only used it once in all the time I was working with him. He called me on my cell phone thirty minutes later, and I explained the situation.

"I can understand why that would sound scary, but really, they're pretty straightforward, Sarah. I think you'll be fine. Just don't forget to breathe and ground beforehand. I would guess they will evaluate you for anxiety, depression, maybe PTSD. And if you want to take more time to set it up, remember, that's okay. They say they need it in a week, but there isn't much they can do if you send it a little later than that, right?"

By the time we hung up, I felt more relaxed.

You've got this, my inner cheerleader chimed in—a nice break from my nemesis. I decided not to tell my mother about this new development until after the evaluation, both to show myself that I knew it would go well and to avoid worrying her. She'd seemed genuinely happy for me when I'd told her the news of my imminent return. A little wistful, too, which was a testament to how far we'd come.

The first two clinics didn't have openings until the next month. The last one had a slot the next day at 10:30 a.m. (due to a last-minute cancellation, I was informed, so I would appreciate my luck). I booked it, feeling a residue of optimism.

That night, I dreamt that Maggie and I were running through the woods. "Quick, we have to find the way out," she urged as she grabbed my hand. I tripped on a root and fell flat on my face.

"It's too late, you waited too long," she shouted before disappearing into the mist.

Next thing I knew, Jean-Claude was standing over me.

"Pull yourself together, Sarah! You're a disgrace," he said disdainfully.

I couldn't move.

There's no way out, I thought as somebody started shoveling dirt all over me. I choked and coughed into the earth. *They're going to bury me alive.*

I woke up in a sweat at 2:10 a.m., with a sense of déjà vu.

I did my breathing exercises and listened to some of Patrick's recommended meditations. A few hours later, I fell back into fitful slumber.

When I got up around 7:00 a.m., I felt like a train had hit me. The beginning of a migraine was encroaching on the right side of my head.

"No, no, no, not again!" I said out loud. "Pull yourself together, Sarah," I heard in Jean-Claude's voice.

I called the clinic to reschedule, but the next opening wasn't until October, so I got my bike out, trying to breathe through the flutter in my stomach as I pedaled to my appointment.

I arrived early and found my way to an empty corner of the waiting room. I breathed through my mouth to avoid taking in the sterile, lifeless smell of the hospital. Although much worse smells didn't affect me in my capacity as a nurse, for some reason I found them nauseating as a patient. Like getting motion sickness as the passenger of a car, but never as the driver. But mouth-breathing made inhaling deeply that much harder, so I tapped out a rhythmic beat with my foot to steady my heart rate.

"Sarah Baum, Sarah Baum!" a loud voice over the intercom startled me out of my seat. I followed a young man in scrubs down a maze of hallways to an empty, windowless room, with metallic white fluorescent lights.

"The doctor will be with you shortly," he said as he rushed off to his next task. I listened to his footsteps echoing through the hallway until I couldn't hear them any longer.

"Sarah Baum?" Came the voice behind me. I stood and turned, offering my hand to the woman who would be administering my test. She took it unsmilingly as she introduced herself as Dr. Findley.

She had a crew cut that suited her oval face. I almost gasped when I looked up at her eyes. They were the exact same icy blue as Jean-Claude's. In an instant, I saw an image of his sneering face.

Breathe. You can do this. Patrick said it wasn't hard. Just answer honestly, I told myself in a desperate attempt to pep talk myself into relaxation.

We sat down on opposite sides of the long but narrow plastic table.

"Over the past two weeks, have you felt nervous, anxious, or on edge?" she asked in a flat monotone.

You mean, besides right now? Snarked my inner nemesis.

"Sometimes."

"How often? Several days, half the days, every day?"

"It depends. The last two weeks have generally been good, so probably several days."

Her pen hovered over the page. She raised an eyebrow and fixed me with an intense stare, as though willing me to pick one.

"If I average it, I guess half the days," I said, trying to say it as a statement rather than a question mark.

Over the next hour, she went through the list of questions about worrying, irritability, restlessness, trouble falling or staying asleep, feeling bad about myself, nightmares about a traumatic event … As I answered some degree of yes to all of them except those on suicidality, I felt myself getting increasingly agitated.

See, there really is something wrong with you!

My attempts at slowing things down by drinking water or clearing my throat were met by either an impatient thrumming of her clipped fingernails on the tabletop or a sharp repeat of the question. Eventually, I stopped attempting to find my own pacing within the test and merely tried to keep up with her speed. An image of being on the plane to France with my mother, feeling powerless over what happened in my life, flashed through my mind.

By the end, I felt so flustered I lost track of what I was saying, focusing on getting through the questions and out of there. I mustered a thank you as I fled out of the room and managed to keep it somewhat together until I left the building. I then burst into tears, feeling young and alone.

When I had recovered enough to see the road, I biked home as quickly as I could, thankful my mother wasn't there when I arrived.

You're such a failure! I thought as I looked at myself in the mirror. My inner cheerleader was silent. She agreed too. I stayed in bed the rest of the afternoon, watching cute animal videos on YouTube so I wouldn't have to think.

Chapter Twenty-Six

Reunions and Departures

Maggie

The rest of the wedding ceremony was a blur. I must have said "I do," for I had a ring on my finger to prove it, but I had no recollection of it. I'd felt enough emotions that day to last me a lifetime! I kept on waiting to wake from this unbelievable dream in which I was getting married, and Mama was there to witness it.

After Frank and I exchanged our vows, I fell into Mama's arms, and we held each other and wept until I thought I'd wrung all the tears I could out of my body. And yet, they still kept coming. Finally—after the tearful rejoicing and devouring the feast Bessie prepared—Mama and I sat down together in the garden, while the others busied themselves in the house.

At first, without the security of the others, we were strangely silent, almost shy with each other. There was so much to say, so much that had changed for both of us. Our two worlds stood like a gaping chasm between us. I studied her face. Time had etched worry lines into her cheeks and between her brows. Strands of white had claimed territory in her hair. And there was a haunted look that crept into her eyes when her mind started wandering to some other place.

But right now, she was scanning my face too, eyes alert and curious, looking for her little girl in this young woman she had just witnessed getting married. And then—once our souls had recognized each other, and we had taken note of the changes—the words came. Slowly at first, and then tumbling over each other until there was no stopping them.

After I fled, my mother had insisted my brothers leave too. She gave them the name of a cousin she had in North Carolina, Catherine. Roy and Arthur wanted her to go with them, but she refused.

"I know is' too dangerous if we leaved together—despite de talk 'bout us being free. I also think dat if I stay, dey might not go aftah yo' brothers. But I don' tell 'em that," Mama said, with that faraway look on her face.

I moved in closer to her, and I felt my whole being melt with love for her, as I took in—perhaps for the first time—the immensity of her heart.

Mama was flogged, though she insisted that the pain wasn't as bad as it could have been.

"Mr. Tanner pro'ly tole them to go easy on me," she said, her voice breaking at "easy," betraying the bitterness I knew she felt.

Many on the plantation said he had a soft spot for Mama. But I'd seen it, and I knew there was nothing soft about his liking of her. It had poisoned all of our lives, but it might have saved hers, in the end.

I thought of her being flogged and all that transpired, and tears started flowing down my cheeks. Mama stroked my hair the way she did when I was a child.

"Now don' you worry, baby, is' all water under the bridge now. 'Bout six months after that, Arthur came back for me. They'd found Catherine and managed to find some work doing day labor. An' so I left with 'im, 'n the dead of night."

Mama was now living with Arthur and his wife, Anna,

the daughter of one of Catherine's friends. They had a little baby girl named Margaret. My eyes teared up when I heard they named her after me. Roy, my youngest brother, lived nearby and was apprenticing with a blacksmith.

I invited her to move to Washington, DC with Frank and me, but she shook her head.

"I done finished with moving, Maggie. But you mus' come visit. Your brothers'd love that."

That night, after the Joneses had gone to sleep and Mama was settled in my room, Frank carried me over the threshold of his apartment. He held me as I wept and covered me with soft kisses until I fell asleep.

We made up for the lost time in the following nights. But I would always be grateful that he gifted our wedding day and night to my reunion with Mama.

Chapter Twenty-Seven

The Inner Nemesis

Sarah

It had been four days since the mental health assessment debacle, and I'd spent most of that time in my room, emerging only to scavenge for food and go to the bathroom. I canceled both my appointment with Patrick and a dinner date with my mother via text, claiming I was sick with a virus. An ominous email entitled "postponement of return to mission" had arrived from HR, but I hadn't been able to bring myself to open it yet.

I heard a hesitant knock on my door. I decided against pretending I was asleep. I'd been avoiding my mother in part because I hadn't told her I'd been asked to do an external evaluation in the first place. I didn't want to have to explain the situation or face my shame. But I knew I couldn't keep hiding from her forever. And I didn't want to sabotage all the progress we'd made.

"Come in," I said, and a moment later she was standing in the doorway.

"Are you feeling better, Sarah?" my mother asked, her brow furrowed. Worry was a strange look on her, I decided, feeling almost shy around her concern.

"A little."

"I thought you were supposed to leave again, soon. Did I

get that wrong?"

"No, I was, but plans have changed. I'm afraid you're stuck with me a while longer," I said with a weak smile.

"Is everything okay?" she asked, and I scanned her tone and face for judgment. Not finding any, I answered somewhat truthfully.

"Not really. I messed up, and I don't know when I'll be able to go back. But I don't feel like talking about it yet. I'm going to have to do some serious soul-searching, just not right now."

"I see. I'm sorry to hear that, although for what's it worth, I'm happy to have you around a little longer. I know I'm not always the most available, but do let me know if you need anything. Now that I know you're staying, I'll stock up the fridge for you. There's some soup for you for tonight, since I knew you weren't feeling well."

The kindness and thoughtfulness of her words touched me. Caught me off guard. For the first time in days, my heart tilted ever so slightly upwards.

"Thanks, Mom. I really appreciate you checking in on me," I said, finding that I meant it.

"What am I going to do now?" I asked Patrick when I'd finally mustered the courage to set up a session. Now that I'd emerged from my self-pity cave, I was surveying the tattered remains of my goals, trying to see what I could still salvage. "I was so focused on returning to work, I have no Plan B."

"What did HR say to you, Sarah?"

"That based on the mental health assessment, they didn't think I was stable enough for the work right now. That they would check back in six months. Six months!" I said, choking on the words. I was trying hard not to feel the despair and profound sense of failure threatening to swallow me up.

"I'm so sorry, Sarah. I know how much it meant to you.

And I apologize if our work together wasn't sufficiently integrated. I truly thought you were ready, too. Do you have a sense of what happened? I know those tests can be intimidating."

I sighed. I'd been avoiding thinking about what happened, but with effort, I closed my eyes, remembering.

"I choked. I think Jean-Claude doubting your assessment and wanting a second opinion threw me for a loop. Made me start thinking 'What if there is something really wrong with me?' Then I read a book on lynching and had a terrifying nightmare the night before. When I arrived, the doctor giving me the test had eyes that looked uncannily like Jean-Claude's, with similar mannerisms, so I think I went into a bit of a freeze state." I sighed. As I remembered the perfect storm of events that had led to my unraveling, a panicky feeling gripped my throat.

"I'm such a fuck-up! Do you think I have more serious mental health issues? Should I be on meds?" I exclaimed before I could filter what I was saying.

"I think you've been through a lot and that healing the deeper core issues and not just the symptoms is more immediately necessary than I thought. But there's nothing wrong with you. Answering yes to those questions isn't failing. It's just an indicator of areas where you need greater support," he said, and I could feel the tension in my chest and throat ease up ever so slightly.

"As for medication, I can't prescribe it myself. But we can discuss the possible pros and cons as I understand them, and if you want to know more, I can give you a referral for a psychiatrist I trust."

"Okay, that sounds good. I don't think I want to explore that route quite yet ... It was mostly my fear talking," I admitted.

"I noticed you called yourself a 'fuck-up.' Do you often say that, or something similar, to yourself?"

I felt myself blush—as though he'd discovered a deep, dark secret. I shrugged.

"Yeah, maybe, though I'm usually not that harsh. I'm kind of embarrassed. It's not very self-lovey of me."

"Is that why you haven't mentioned those thoughts before?"

"I guess so. I wasn't actively trying to hide them. They just seem shameful, somehow. And I've been working on cultivating my inner cheerleader, especially with that book of affirmations for the inner child I got out of the library. The positive just feels so much less natural than the negative."

Patrick nodded knowingly. I imagined I wasn't his only client with these kinds of thoughts. "I understand, and there's nothing to be ashamed of. Bringing your self-talk to light and normalizing it can soften the impact. Would you be interested in exploring the thoughts further? I'm guessing they have something to do with why you froze."

I hesitated, not sure I wanted to give my inner critic more airtime than necessary. But I noticed that voicing my inner narrative had brought me some relief, so I nodded.

"Sarah, if you had to give these thoughts a name, what might that be?"

"My inner nemesis," I said without hesitation. "It's like a villain in a Marvel movie that's talking to me, trying to trip me up."

He made a few notes on his notepad, then asked. "What kinds of things does your inner nemesis tend to say to you?"

"It depends on the situation. 'You're doing it wrong.' 'It's your fault.' 'You suck.' 'You always mess everything up.' Things like that," I said, looking down.

"Thanks, Sarah. I know it can be hard to say these things out loud. Do you remember the first time you heard your inner nemesis?"

"No, not really. I was young. But I do know it got worse after my dad died."

"Does it sound like or remind you of the voice of someone you know?"

I thought about it. "I don't know. Maybe my mother's, but she doesn't say those things explicitly. It's always felt implied, though."

"What do you think the voice is trying to achieve for you?"

"You mean, besides crush me to smithereens?" I asked. "I don't think it's trying to do anything beyond destroy me."

"I know it feels that way, Sarah. And usually, although the methods backfire, the negative thoughts want something for us. For example, for us to do better or try harder. To avoid humiliation. To avoid disappointing others. To avoid failure, or even to avoid success, if that seems too scary."

I took a breath and mulled his suggestions over in my mind before I spoke again.

"It's so worried I'm going to mess up. I guess it wants me to succeed? And also to avoid judgment. If I'm judging myself first, nobody else's criticisms can sting as much."

Patrick nodded.

"That sounds right. I'll give you an optional worksheet to further identify your automatic negative thoughts if you choose to."

"It'll give me something to do, so right now, I'd like that." I looked at him and decided to ask the question that had been on my mind for the past week.

"Patrick, I'd also like your suggestions on anything I can do for these nightmares … and to get more in touch with Maggie. I feel like I've been skirting around them, not wanting to open Pandora's box or do anything that would ruin my chances of returning on mission. But that obviously backfired, and with that last dream, I got scared I might have somehow missed the boat."

"I'm happy to hear you ask that, Sarah. I know you didn't feel ready before. I would recommend hypnotherapy." He paused to give me time to react.

"What, you mean like in the movies, where they swing a pendulum back and forth, and then when the person wakes up he or she doesn't remember anything?"

Patrick laughed. "I'm afraid movies and TV don't give accurate depictions of hypnosis. It's simply a way of getting more deeply in touch with your subconscious and what it's telling you. Your cognitive mind remains aware of what's happening, and there is no forgetting when it's all over. I'll send you some information on the method and the website of a practitioner I think is very talented. You can look it over, and if you're interested, we can talk more about it next session."

When I left, I felt a tiny bit clearer and lighter. I might not have a Plan B yet, but at least I had a possible next step.

Chapter Twenty-Eight
Washington, DC, January 1919

Spanish Influenza

Maggie

We left for our new life on January 1, 1919. The night before, the Joneses held a small (at our insistence) party for us and to ring in the new year. As many tears were shed as alcohol was consumed, but the tears were as much of joy as of sadness. Nineteen eighteen had been a hard year, not only for the war but also for the ongoing flu epidemic that had taken so many lives.

"As if it wasn't enough that men are waging war against men, now the germs are waging a war against us too," Edna had complained to me at the start of the epidemic. We all prayed we'd left that behind us.

Frank had found us a little cottage in LeDroit Park, two blocks from Howard University. When I'd first heard of this college—for Colored people, taught by Colored professors—while I was studying in New York, I'd been amazed. I'd harbored a secret wish to go there ever since.

"The day they hire a Colored president at Howard, now *that* will be something," was Frank's response when I gushed about living so close by. He was harder to impress. But I could tell he was pleased too.

Our house was one-story high and yellow, which Frank said was auspicious, as it was the color of the dress I was wearing when we first met. We lived in back of the Brinkmans' house, whom we rented from. Benjamin Brinkman was a professor of literature at Howard University, and his wife, Sadie, was a librarian. They had a beautiful garden full of rose bushes and magnolias, which we shared with them.

I had survived and was safe. With a home of my own. How long had I yearned for this moment? Muscles tensed, breathing shallow. Waiting. A longing in every cell of my body. The hope that had allowed my legs to keep moving, even as they wanted to buckle under the weight of despair and grief. The dream of a place where I could soothe my weary feet at the end of a long day. And now I even had a husband to hang some of my worries on, so I didn't have to bear the burden of living alone.

I hoped a fresh start would erase all the old wounds, like wiping chalk from the blackboard at the end of a lesson to make space for a new one. If only it were so easy.

When I was little, I'd almost stepped on a snake thrashing around like a bee had stung it. At first, I was scared, thinking it might strike me, but I soon realized it couldn't see anything. I pointed it out to Papa, who laughed at its plight.

"Look, Maggie, it ain't shed is' skin proper. It done formed a hood round is' eyes!"

Some days I felt like that—I'd started to slough off my old life, but bits of it stayed stuck and clouded my vision. I saw everything through the veil of what had happened to me and my family and couldn't fully embrace the gifts I was being given now. My skylark, once caged, had trouble trusting the blue sky and kept waiting for it to fall.

And the world, being what it is, always seemed ready to oblige.

*

Five days after we arrived, before we had the chance to unpack all our belongings, the Brinkmans' three-year-old daughter Rose fell ill. Benjamin and Sadie rushed her to the hospital while Frank and I stayed with their five-year-old son, Thomas. Benjamin returned that night without his wife or daughter. Rose had the flu, and Sadie didn't want to leave her. Benjamin's face was ashen.

"I took her to a park last week. They said it was safe. A woman thought she was so cute and kept playing peek-a-boo with her. Her face was so close to Rose's. What if that's what made her sick?"

He was too worried to hear our reassurances that it wasn't his fault, that he couldn't have known.

Later that night, Frank told me he'd heard two of Representative Dyer's staff talking about the flu epidemic over lunch that day:

"They said Health Officer Dr. Fowler authorized the reopening of schools and churches in October, but apparently, it was against his better judgment. The churches in particular put a lot of pressure on him to do so because they were afraid of losing members by being closed for so long. Eventually, he caved, even though he warned everyone that the minute there were large groups of people gathering, the number of flu cases would rise again."

Over the next two weeks, I spent every day at home with Thomas, since the Brinkmans did not want him at school in case he got sick too. Frank and Benjamin went to work while Sadie, who'd taken sick leave from the library, stayed at Rose's bedside. Thomas brimmed with energy and curiosity. He flitted from place to place like a hummingbird, and it was impossible to get him to sit still.

Since I had strict instructions from his parents not to go out to any public place where he might be exposed to the flu, we spent hours playing hide-and-seek. I learned every nook and cranny of the house and garden. The first few days, he kept asking where his mother and sister were, but then—as children did—he got used to how things were. He had a vivid imagination, and together, we made up stories that he insisted on acting out. One day, we found a crow with a broken wing in the yard. It was shivering and weak, but still alive.

"We have to save it, Maggie!" Thomas said fervently. I had a sudden image of the raven that showed me where the brook was when I was in the forest.

"We will try, anyway," I agreed. We took it inside and made a nest of twigs we'd dug from the cold earth. Over the next few days, Thomas spent hours caring for the bird, and I discovered how loving and patient he could be.

When Benjamin got home, he sometimes agreed to let Frank go to the hospital and take over from Sadie—a white gauze mask over his face—to give them a few hours' reprieve. Frank refused to let me go, despite my protests. Knowing his grief at having lost his first wife, I didn't insist.

On Wednesday, two weeks after they went to the hospital, I heard the Brinkmans' car pulling in around noon. My whole body started shivering, and I somehow knew it was over, even before I saw Sadie and Benjamin coming out without Rosie. I shuttled Thomas up to his room before he could hear his mother's sobs or ask about his sister. When I came down, Benjamin looked up briefly and shook his head before returning his attention to his wife's pain. That night, unable to sleep, I got up and wrote this poem.

The Sound of Grief

Low and guttural,
Wrenched from that
Place
Man cannot reach
Nor bring solace.

The sound of grief—
Deafening
Yet eerily quiet.
Hollow.
Silence where noise
Should have been.

Absence
More keenly felt
Than presence.
Regret rattles mercilessly
Through the hallways
Of the mind.

The sound of grief
Pulls me
Into the bottomless well
Of my own pain.

And then presses me
To crawl back out,
To become a life raft
To another.

All the while, Frank and I were learning to find our cadence together amid the chaos that seemed to be our life. After Rose died, I continued going over to the Brinkmans' every day. I'd bring food and whatever comfort I could to Sadie. Seeing the spark I'd noticed in her when we first met be snuffed out by sorrow scared me.

It brought to mind and heart the pain I'd been pushing down for so long. At night, visions of Andre and Papa's bodies hanging lifelessly crept back into my dreams. I was reminded of my bargain in the wild and that if I asked for too much I might lose everything. Again. At the same time, witnessing Sadie, day by day, claw her way back to some sense of purpose reminded me that on the other side, there was life. Resilience.

When Sadie returned to the library ("I need something to do to keep the grief at bay," she said) I took care of Thomas during the day. Until the deaths dwindled and they felt safe sending him back to school.

While the Brinkmans accepted our generosity during Rose's illness, after Sadie returned, they insisted on paying me for the time I spent with Thomas. One of the teachers at his school got very sick with the influenza and nearly died. Her husband refused to let her return, and Benjamin asked me if I was interested in teaching there.

I felt torn. Frank was encouraging me to help him with his activism since I'd been so successful collecting stories in New York. But the heavy burden of the work weighed on me, and I was starting to sense that wasn't my calling. My heart whispered to apply for Howard.

"Don't want too much," came the knell of doom in the dead of the night.

Eventually, I said yes to the teaching position, telling myself I should be happy I even had work, considering how hard the times were. That it was good for me to be doing something I knew how to do. That there would be plenty of time for me to be challenged.

As a compromise with my heart, I enrolled in a night class in poetry and literature at Howard that Mr. Brinkman offered to working students. He was quite taken with my poems.

One evening while we were having dinner in the Brinkmans' house, he suggested I submit some of my poetry to a publisher.

Although the skylark in my heart fluttered with excitement at the possibility of my words reaching more people, another part of me was terrified. Reminded me of the danger of being too visible. Wanting too much. That night, the fear won out.

"I'm Colored and a woman. Nobody has ever heard of me. And my poems don't even rhyme. Why would they publish me?" I protested.

"What about Phyllis Wheatley? And Frances Harper?" Frank said, and I rolled my eyes because I knew he would bring them up.

"What about Alice Moore Dunbar?" Benjamin asked, and before I could try to cover up the fact that I'd never heard of her, he went on to say, "She was married to Paul Dunbar, and for a few years they lived around the block from my family. They were the talk of the neighborhood! We could hear the shouts all the way from our house. He almost killed her, you know, which is why she left for Delaware. The wagging tongues said it was because she had affairs with women, but she was one of the reasons I got interested in literature. She gave some spectacular readings in the bookshop …"

At this point, Sadie cleared her throat a little and raised an eyebrow at her husband, as Benjamin was prone to divagation. He could meander on a stray path that caught his mind's fancy for a long time if not reined back in. I was just happy to see some of her old fire back, replacing the emptiness that had set in her eyes after Rose died.

"But I digress," Benjamin said. "The point is that you will never know if you don't try. The *Monthly Review* is a good place to start. That's where she got her debut. When she was just twenty!"

I shook my head no and held my ground. But their words kept echoing in my mind over the next months.

Chapter Twenty-Nine

Meeting Maggie

Sarah

As I stepped into Deborah the hypnotherapist's office, the words "oasis of peace" popped into my mind. I'd been half-expecting strings of crystal beads and gaudy velvet curtains. Instead, there were lush standing plants in all four corners of the room. On a side table, a fountain with a bamboo spout gurgled soothingly over a bed of stones. My body immediately relaxed, and my lungs expanded to fill the newfound space.

Deborah pointed to a recliner chair with a midnight-blue, plush blanket draped over it. I settled into it in the upright position so I could better take in my surroundings and turned my attention to the hypnotherapist.

She was perhaps in her late sixties or early seventies. Long, silvery hair cascaded in waves down her back. Her face was weathered and kind, with wrinkles that accentuated her smile. She made me think of an older Galadriel, had the Elven queen been human and capable of aging. I almost wanted to peek behind her hair to see if she had pointed ears. Her amber eyes watched me patiently as I observed her.

Smiling, she finally asked, "So, Sarah, what can I help you with today?" Her voice was both low and lilting, resounding inside of me like the vibrations of a Tibetan bowl.

I told her about the recurrent nightmares and the automatic writing which had led me to know a little more about Maggie.

"After that first time, I think I might have shut down access to her, except in my dreams. That initial sense of sexual assault was overwhelming, and I was afraid I wouldn't be able to go back to work if I left myself open to what was coming through. But my worst fears happened anyway, and now I think it might be *because* I was avoiding exploring her too closely."

I described what I'd dreamt the night before the assessment and the sense I'd had that I was too late for something.

"I don't really know how hypnotherapy works, and maybe you can describe the process a little more, but it now feels imperative to my healing that I try to 'meet' Maggie, this dream self, in a setting where I'm awake and can interact with her. I need to know more about her life, understand better what she wants of me, or what she's trying to tell me …"

"In general, I find it's better for you to experience it than for me to try to explain how it works, as that is only going to activate the cognitive mind, which tends to be a skeptic. But I'm happy to answer any questions you have."

I found I had few questions, and even my nemesis was quiet. The humility of defeat had silenced my snark, it seemed. I was ready to let go of control and listen to my subconscious. Or so I told myself.

Deborah smiled slightly and began, "Okay, let's get started then. But remember, Sarah, this is your session, and you're in charge. If you feel a little uncomfortable, know that you are safe and guided. It's okay to stay on the edge of your discomfort and explore what that's like. But if that's too much, you can come out at any time, for any reason."

I nodded and pushed the recliner back until the footrest popped up. I accepted the offer of a blanket and eye cover, which plunged the room into pitch darkness. For a second, my breath caught in my throat. I reminded myself where I was and counted from zero to twenty and back down until my heartbeat had evened.

"Leaning back into the support of the chair, take a few nice, deep breaths. As you exhale, say to yourself, 'calm and relaxed.' Take full, deep, abdominal breaths." Deborah intoned.

"Feeling your nervous system starting to regulate, creating a sense of inner peace and relaxation. You can exhale the contents of the day, week, months … Feel yourself sinking deeper and deeper into relaxation, which is your natural state."

Yeah, right, she hasn't met you! My inner nemesis piped up for the first time in days. I felt a little disappointed. It had clearly just been dormant.

Hush, you're not welcome here, I responded as I attempted to push the voice away.

"Feel the relaxation all the way through your forehead and temples, down into your cheek and jaw muscles, allowing the tongue to drop down in your mouth …"

I was stunned to feel my jaw and tongue slacken of their own accord, but I could feel my mind fight the gravitational pull of relaxation, scrambling to stay above ground as it lobbed random fearful thoughts at me to keep me from going under.

You'll never go back to work if you relax.

You messed up.

Think of all the things you need to do when you get home.

A second later, I felt my whole body shudder as gravity won over will. I surrendered as Deborah guided me to soften every part of my body, all the way down to the tips of my toes, which tingled with pleasure.

"As I count you even deeper down, imagine you're going to a safe place where there might be a guide and a path that can take you down the river of consciousness to meet with Maggie, so you can communicate with her spirit and understand her more deeply."

At the words "safe place" and "guide," my nemesis perked up and made a last-ditch effort to sideswipe the process.

See, this is just a load of new-age BS.

But Deborah's voice penetrated through the words and nestled deep into my subconscious, so my nemesis had nothing to hold onto and dissolved like wisps of smoke.

"As I count you down from ten to nine, going twice as deep; eight and seven, feeling very peaceful; six, going deeper, time is unimportant as you drift and float down to a safe place; five and four, going deeper with every exhalation; three and two, breathing all the way down to one."

Before she got to one, I was already seeing myself in the Old Church grove of redwoods, looking up at the sacred geometry of branches and pine leaves. A sunbeam shone down on me and refracted out in front, as though shining a light on where to go.

I tried to speak, but my jaw muscles were so loose I wasn't sure I still knew how. After a few throat-clears, I found my voice again, but it sounded distant and underwater.

"I'm seeing myself in the middle of redwood trees. I see a sunbeam, which I think is both the guide and the path."

"Beautiful. Allow yourself to follow the sunbeam all the way down to a river where a boat and a boatman or -woman awaits you."

"It leads me to what looks more like an alpine lake than a river. There's a boat but no person there. I think the sun is going to navigate us to where we need to go."

As I said that, a raven swooped down and landed on the boat, and I told Deborah about the newcomer to the scene.

"Wonderful. Ask the raven if it's going to help you find Maggie."

"It says yes." My nemesis didn't even object to or question any of this. At this point, it had given up all hopes of pulling me out of there.

I got out of the boat and followed the raven down a path to a forest. That's where I saw Maggie. Or rather, I felt her.

"I'm sensing Maggie in me. It's as though we are one. We're in the forest, but it's not the same as where I usually see her. I feel light, safe. Even though I'm hungry and worried about surviving, I'm content. I like being in the wild …" I slipped into the first person naturally, almost without conscious awareness of it.

"What are you wearing on your feet?"

My vision self looked down and I saw I was barefoot.

"I don't know what happened to my shoes—if I ever had any—but I sense I like the feeling of the earth kissing my feet. Even when it hurts, the imprint feels like love bites …" I said, although I had no idea where the words were coming from. And at that point, I didn't care.

"What are you seeing now, Sarah?" Deborah asked. Hearing my name startled me. I took a few breaths and returned to the vision.

"The raven leads me to a brook, and I drink from it, greedily. I'm so thirsty. When I look up, I see a deer. A doe. She's looking at me." I paused, letting myself dive deeper into her eyes.

"A doe?" Deborah prompted. I must have been silent for longer than I thought.

"Yes. 'Trust your heart,' she seems to be saying. I don't know, it's fading away. I can't see it as clearly."

"As I count you even deeper, imagine that you're moving a little forward in time, with the guidance of the raven, and maybe the deer. Noticing what happens next."

"It's all moving really fast now, like I'm a book, and someone is flipping the pages … I see a railroad, the one I saw in my vision, but clear now, and I seem to be working on it. My chest is really tight—like it's bound or something. Now, I'm at the end of the track, in New York, it looks like. A young girl is sitting in my lap … The page has flipped again, and I'm in a room. Maybe a library. There are men talking. One of them is asking me if I have heard of Ida B. Wells." I stopped. Something was catching in my throat, and I started coughing.

"Take nice, slow deep breaths, Sarah. Remember, you can always come back any time you want. Would you like some water?"

I shook my head no, feeling the cough subside and my breath normalize. I noticed I was gripping the sides of the recliner, so I let go and extended my fingers in an effort to relax them.

"I want to continue. I see myself on my wedding day. I'm happy. My mother is there, maybe? Somebody who really matters to me, in any case … The page has flipped again, and I'm in another house … another city, I think. I see myself going up the stairs of a library. I feel a mounting sense of dread like I somehow don't belong. Now I'm inside, staring at a blank piece of paper. I sense that I should be happy to have the honor of being here. I'm living my dream. But I'm not. I feel like I've lost something …"

"What have you lost?" Deborah asked, in what I assumed was an attempt to slow things down, but everything was moving so fast, and I felt mounting agitation in my body.

"I don't know. My voice, maybe. Maggie is leaving. She's no longer inside of me. I see her walking away. She's saying she doesn't want to have to choose anymore." I said as panic rose in my chest.

I'm going to be abandoned again, my inner child wailed inside of me.

"Choose what? Don't go, Maggie!" I found myself shouting out loud into the void. My breathing shallowed as I fought against the familiar feeling of emptiness.

"Sarah, breathe. I know that was a lot, but you're safe. I'm going to put my hand on your knee, if I may?" Deborah said, her voice as soft and steady as ever. But now her tone had no calming effect on me. I was too far gone in this unpredictable world where I was being left once more. I could barely feel the hypnotherapist's hand touching me after I'd given her permission.

"Follow the path back to the boat, where the sunbeam will take you back to the redwoods. I'm going to count you back from one to ten, and when we get to ten, you'll be safely back in the room and your body."

When she got to ten, I opened my eyes, my body a modicum more relaxed, although I could still feel the residue of agitation and panic. Emotionally, however, I felt completely bereft. As though I'd found something fundamental to my survival and it had slipped through my fingers.

"What was that?! Was it normal that it ended like that? I thought the goal was to get some kind of resolution?" I asked Deborah in a daze, still adjusting to being back in her quiet oasis, back in 2011.

"Everyone's experience is different. But it's not unusual to need more than one encounter to find completion. There seemed to be a lot happening for you and Maggie. How are you feeling?"

"Completely disjointed. Unseamed. Like someone yanked the thread that was holding me together. Who do you think Maggie is? I could really feel her inside of me. It seemed natural during the session, but remembering it now, I feel unsettled."

"Honestly, from my perspective, the who of the matter is more of an intellectual question than anything else and isn't really that important. Depending on your worldview, there are many ways to conceptualize who she might be. Since she came in a dream, she could represent a part of you needing healing. She might be part of the collective unconscious that you're tapping into. She could represent ancestral energy …"

She paused and scanned my face, as though considering whether to say more and deciding against it. And I didn't have the bandwidth to ask.

"As I said, to me the question of who she is isn't so relevant—at least compared to listening, honoring, and healing. And, in this moment, helping you feel less disoriented."

Deborah led me in a few stretches and a meditation to ground me and get back in my body.

"I feel better, thanks," I said afterward as I reached for my wallet to pay her. To be honest, I wasn't any more grounded or in my body than I had been five minutes earlier, but I felt an urgent need to get out of there and was worried she'd keep trying to help me if I told her the truth.

When I got outside, the sun seemed too bright despite the low-hanging clouds that muted it. I found a tree to lean against and took slow breaths to try to orient myself. I walked around the block a few times before my legs felt ready to pedal home.

Once back in my room, I found I couldn't stay in place. It felt as though my skin no longer fit right, and I kept pawing at my body as though I could somehow rip my outer layer off. Frightened by my own reaction, I grabbed my phone and texted Patrick's emergency phone.

"Do you have any slots tomorrow? Just had the hypnotherapy session. Not doing well." I exhaled loudly as I pressed send.

I considered contacting my mother, but I knew she was in surgery all day and her phone would be off. We had planned to go for a walk the next day, so I could always tell her then if I felt the need. Truth be told, for all the progress we'd made, part of me still believed I had to hide my fears and vulnerabilities from her to be safe.

On a whim, I texted Phoebe instead. We hadn't been in touch since the day at the beach, but I figured if I was going to be here another six months, I could use a friend, and I hoped she might welcome an outside distraction during the long daytime hours with her girls.

"In the end, I didn't leave. Long story. Feeling low. Let me know if you have time to talk or meet up this week or next."

Not having the patience to wait for a response from either of them, I changed into my running clothes and hopped back on my bike. I locked it at the entrance of Cesar Chavez Park, next to the Berkeley Marina. I began to run as fast as I could, as though my feet could slam me back into myself and obliterate the trauma of all my losses from cellular memory. Between my fierce gallop and the fury of the waves crashing against the shore, my inner turmoil felt mirrored enough to begin to subside.

When I'd run out of breath and my calves were throbbing, I clambered down some rocks to get as close to the water as I could. I untied my ponytail, opened my jacket, and let the wind whip through me, willing it to wash me clean of every last trace of my past. Looking behind me to make sure nobody was close by, I let out a shrill scream that was drowned out by the surround sound of water and wind.

Does anybody hear me? Will I always be lost? Am I ever going to feel whole? I wondered silently against the roar of the Bay.

Chapter Thirty
May to June 1919

Old Scars

Maggie

Frank and I got to know another layer of each other's past through the scarring on our bodies. First with our hands and lips. My body memorized Frank's map of pain and resilience and the secret places that unlocked his heart.

And then with words, as we told the story of how each came to be. In sharing our wounds, we were allowing the most tender parts of ourselves to be seen. And to be held by the other with care.

I showed him the notch in my chin from when I was five years old. I was helping Mama mop the floor in the big house, and I loved to slide on its glossy surface when it was still wet. But then one day I slipped and banged my chin. Mama was angry with me and sent me home to get cleaned up by my brothers. It stung for weeks and turned into an itchy scab I liked to pick at. What Frank loved the most was the imprint of the forest on the soles of my feet. A little spider web of scars that looked like tiny twigs had embedded themselves there.

I traced the shadow of a welt on his backside.

"That's the only time my pop ever laid a hand on me. I

was maybe nine or ten, I'd stolen some candy from the corner shop. The owner, a friend of Pop's, came to our home and reported me. I'm not sure how he knew—I guess he saw me. When the man was gone, Pop considered me for a moment before taking out his belt. He hit me once, hard. I thought I saw tears in his eyes as he did it. 'We don't steal.' He said after, looking at me intently, to make sure I understood. 'They can take everything else from us. But not our dignity.' I'll never forget that," Frank said, his voice heavy with emotion. I stroked the area lovingly, as though I could erase the pain of our legacy.

"He was a good man, my pop. Decent and kind. But when I was young, I confused that with meekness. I couldn't wait to get out. Make my own way. Be a big man. They had their hands full with me, I realize that now."

His parents had owned a plot of land that had been given to them by his mother's family. They worked hard on the land, and his two brothers were farmers. His three sisters had married farmers.

"Not me. I was going to leave if I had to fight my way out." He took my hand and traced it over the nip in the crevice of his left cheek.

"I got that when I was fourteen. One of the boys at school said something mean about my father. Because he was a farmer and not a merchant like his. I jumped on him, and then he pulled a knife from his pocket and jabbed my cheek." He had a small smile when he said that.

"It probably saved my life. Father Giovanni was my teacher at the missionary school, and after that, he had a serious talk with me. He was a tall fellow from Italy and generally pretty jovial, especially for a Catholic priest. But he had a somber look in his eyes as he said to me: 'Franco, son, you are a smart boy. And an angry one, which can be a dangerous combination. I know, because I was smart and angry once too.

There are many things you don't like. I understand that. But you have a choice to make. You can continue on this road of fighting all who get in your way, which is most likely going to get you killed before you are eighteen.'"

Frank paused to let the import of that statement sink in. I shuddered at what could have been and snuggled closer to him to hear the other choice.

"Then he said: 'Or, you can use your intelligence to study, to leave here. To make a difference in another way. You could go to college if you really want to. But you will need to work hard. If you want things to be different, your mind will serve you better than your fists. There are ways to change unfair laws, you know, and many better men than you fighting for that.' I thought long and hard about what he said. I started putting all of my fight into my studies. Eventually, I did decide to study law. So, I could beat them at their own game."

The months until summer were quiet ones, and we settled into our rhythm. Me at school, this time with much younger children. And Frank with Senator Dyer. The NAACP had agreed to endorse the bill, and he hoped this would help them gain momentum. In addition, in March, the Republicans regained control of both the House and the Senate, which gave them renewed hope for the bill.

On the evenings I didn't have my class, I sometimes rode the streetcar to meet Frank after work, so we could stroll the streets, or go out to dinner. Despite what I knew of what the Capitol represented for my people, I couldn't help but be a little in awe of the grandeur of the building itself. Frank teased me that I should write a poem entitled, "Ode to the Capitol."

I laughed. "I think I might just do that."

Ode to the Capitol

You gleam,
You majestic,
Symbol of man
And his capacity to create
And to destroy.

Can your hallowed halls
Penetrate the ears
Of those deafened
By power and greed?

The seeds of discord
Have been sown.

Can I place my faith in you
To help us reap the justice
We've been robbed of
Without turning our hearts
To stone?

I fear if we
Take up the weapons
Of the oppressor
We shall remain
Shackled
To him through hatred.

When will we be free
To love and be?

In May, racial tensions started escalating. Ever since we'd arrived, I'd taken a back seat in the anti-lynching movement. To

Frank's disappointment, I knew, although he tried not to show it.

"It's just something that brought us together, and I miss that," he once said.

I sometimes went with him to the NAACP meetings, but I was realizing more and more that it was his passion, not mine. That I'd fallen into it because of somebody else's need for my help. While my past gave me an intimate understanding of the importance of the work, it also prevented me from having any distance from it. When I was too closely involved I couldn't breathe, and old ghosts I'd tried to put to rest became nightly visitors.

Thanks to my poetry and literature class, a piece of me that had been dormant for a long time was starting to awaken. The part of myself that had my own dreams and wants, separate from anyone else, that had allowed me as a young girl to love school. To change my speech because I wanted to be more like my teacher. And as I reconnected to my own voice, the one telling me I wanted too much was weakening a little, and I was beginning to loosen the ties of my bargain with the world ever so slightly. To believe that I could do something I loved doing, rather than just one I was good at. That perhaps, I didn't have to relive the horrors of my past on a daily basis.

One night, I came home from class—Paul Laurence Dunbar's "Sympathy" still ringing in my ears, lost in the thought that my caged bird's song was my writing—I found Frank in the bedroom, packing a bag.

"What happened? Where are you going?" I asked.

"I'm going to Charleston, South Carolina, first thing in the morning. We don't have all the details yet, but it sounds like whites attacking Colored folks. What else is new? Representative Hyde is sending me down to investigate the incident. We're hoping to get more leverage for the bill, and what we've heard from the press down there is confusing and contradictory."

*

When Frank came back from his trip a few days later, I felt a shift in him I couldn't quite put my finger on.

"What will it take for this to stop, Maggie?" he asked, not waiting for a response. "Five men were killed and at least eighteen were injured, mostly at the hands of sailors. Of course, it all started with a rumor. A Colored man supposedly pushed a white navy man, and after that, all hell broke loose. The papers said that the white navy man was shot dead, and so mobs descended on the streets. Of course, it turned out the navy man wasn't killed, but by that time, it was too late."

"What happened?"

"It's nothing we haven't seen before, Maggie, but the thing is, this time, we took up guns and fought back. Folks are tired! One of the men I talked to who was being held for firing into the crowds told me he had come back from fighting in the war. He was angry and fed up. He said the president was happy to make pretty promises to get them to fight, and then dropped them like dogs as soon as they returned. That was the general spirit of those I talked to. They're no longer willing to be blamed for all the ills. No longer willing to just take it."

"It's about time," I said. And I meant it, although I had a queasy, unsettled feeling in the back of my throat I couldn't quite put my finger on.

In early July, there were a couple of violent racial incidents—one in Arizona, and one in Texas, each time started by whites—that barely made the papers.

And then, the violence was at our doorstep. There had been rumors for more than a week of an escaped rapist. "Negro Fiend Sought Anew," and "Posses Keep Up Hunt for Negro," the headlines read. The NAACP was worried, and Frank was going to meetings there almost every day.

"We sent the newspapers a letter," Frank told me days

earlier. "We told them, and I quote, that they were 'sowing the seeds of a race riot by their inflammatory headlines.' Do you think it has helped? Not an iota! Today's paper asks people to 'Hunt Colored Assailant!' This can't end well," he predicted.

He was right.

Chapter Thirty-One

Pretty Pale Ghost

Sarah

"Thanks for making the time to meet with me, Phoebe. It's hard for me to admit it, but I don't know what I'm doing right now. I feel really lost," I said, staring at a sparrow pecking at crumbs on the ground because I wasn't quite ready to meet Phoebe's eyes.

It was a warm and sunny day, typical for early September in the Bay. We'd agreed to meet at Café Leila in North Berkeley, which had one of the rare outdoor gardens in the area. My session with Deborah had been almost a week ago, and I was still struggling to tease meaning out of my days.

"Of course! Reach out any time. I'm happy to have an old friend to talk to as well. Being the stay-at-home parent can get lonely. And it worked out perfectly since the girls are with their grandparents today." Phoebe smiled as she spoke. I could feel the truth of her words.

"I know it's not exactly the same, Sarah, but I can relate to some of what you told me on the phone. After Madison was born, I went into a deep depression. Not working, having my whole life revolve around this little being who was still very much a mystery to me … I had no idea who I was anymore.

Eventually, it got so bad I had to reach out for support. Therapy and anti-depressants helped, but it took me a long time to get out of the slump."

"Oh, Phoebe, I'm so sorry you had to go through that. I had no idea," I said, reaching out to squeeze her hand. She put her other hand over mine, and my heart stirred at the warmth of the contact. I hadn't even known how much I'd been missing touch.

"I appreciate you sharing that with me. I know it's not easy to open up about these things. But I feel closer to you, and I'm really happy we've reconnected. Besides therapy and medication, did anything else help you get back to yourself?"

Phoebe was silent, considering my question.

"My therapist suggested I write down what I was grateful for at the end of every day. Such a simple thing, but I'd been spending so much energy dwelling on what I didn't have, what I'd lost, what I wasn't doing with my life, that I'd forgotten how lucky I was."

"Wow, I love that! How long did you do that, Phoebe?"

"Oh, I still do it. I find it grounds me in the present, so I don't obsess about the past or worry about the future as much."

"That's really helpful, thanks. I've been focusing on affirmations and trying to shift my 'negative thought patterns.' A gratitude practice would be a nice complement to what I'm already doing. I think my therapist suggested something like that once, but I was in a totally different headspace then."

Just then, the sparrow jumped on our table, probably drawn to the bread from my avocado, tomato, and pesto sandwich. We shooed it away, laughing as it flew off, only to circle back and land a foot away from our table.

"Don't get your hopes up. I've got my eye on you!" Phoebe warned the sparrow, who stared her down with its black eyes.

"Hey, Phoebe, on a different topic, I was wondering if you've heard of Ida B. Wells?"

"Yeah, why?"

"Remember when I described my hypnotherapy session over the phone?"

"Yes! And I've been wanting to say that I'm so impressed that you're trying all these alternative therapies! Hypnotherapy, and last time you were describing that rapid-eye thingy—EMDR? The Sarah I knew in college would never have been open to anything so new-agey," she said as she nudged me, her tone mocking me in a loving way. I felt a little embarrassed but also able to take her ribbing without getting too defensive.

Yay, progress! My inner cheerleader exclaimed encouragingly.

"Shhh … Don't tell anyone, Phoebe, it might ruin my reputation!" I joked back.

"Your secret is safe with me." She smiled, and I laughed before returning to the topic at hand.

"Well, while I was Maggie, I heard a man mention Ida B. Wells' name. The next day, I went to the library to return some books and found her autobiography. I'm halfway through the book, and I'm floored by her life! Why didn't I ever hear about her in school?"

"I know, right? I learned about her in a Women and the Law class I took in law school. We studied many women who were instrumental in the introduction or passing of groundbreaking laws but never got any mention or credit. Ida B. Wells was incredible."

"Yeah, really! I think reading about her has made me feel even more lost and like I'm not doing enough with my life. You know? Keeping her siblings together when her parents died. At sixteen! And she was just thirty when she was forced to flee Memphis because of her activism."

"And that was in the 1890s! Way before the civil rights movement!" Phoebe added. We were like excited teenagers who'd discovered we both liked the same obscure band.

"But what law did she contribute to? Maybe I haven't gotten to that part yet ..."

"She wasn't directly involved in the actual legislation, so it's probably not in her book, but her work was pivotal to the anti-lynching bill first introduced in 1918."

"I've never even heard of it," I said, realizing that at this point I should probably stop being surprised by how much I didn't know.

"It was passed by the House in 1922, but then it kept on being filibustered in the Senate, and it never passed." As she spoke, I had the strange sensation of something niggling at my brain.

"It sounds oddly familiar, but I don't know why," I said.

"Did you know that lynching is still not illegal in this country?"

"Wow, that's unbelievable," I scoffed, shaking my head.

"Sarah, I know what it's like to feel like you aren't doing enough—or aren't living out your purpose—but being hard on ourselves doesn't help us or anyone else," she said. She paused, looking at me pensively.

"What?" I asked after she'd scrutinized my face for over a minute. My skin had begun to crawl.

"I don't know if I should tell you this, but I think you might be open to hearing it. In college, before you went to Tanzania, you seemed *really* lost. Not like now, when you're going through a rough patch and you're working through it. But like a pretty, pale ghost who had no idea who she was. You put on a good face and partied hard with the rest of us, but I worried about you."

I felt tears welling up in my eyes. Tears of shame for my twenty-year-old self, but also of relief at knowing that I'd been seen. I'd felt *so* invisible. I nodded in agreement.

"Yeah, that computes. Thanks for telling me that, even

though it's a little hard to hear."

"When you came back from Tanzania, you were very different. Laser-focused and passionate. But also closed off. You stopped hanging out or doing anything for you, and I almost never saw you smile anymore. Although I was happy you'd found your vocation, it seemed so all-consuming. Like you'd found a valid and socially acceptable reason to lose yourself, but you were still not totally all there. I don't know how to put what I felt in words … I'm probably not making any sense."

I shook my head. "You're making a lot of sense. And that reflection is helpful. I think you're right. My therapist suggests that I might have chosen this path as much to run away from my life as to run towards something."

"Sarah, I don't want to dismiss how lost you feel now, but to me, you seem more *you* than I've ever seen you. I know it's been over a decade, but maybe that gives me a perspective you don't have."

I nodded in agreement. "Yeah, I think it does too. In my defense, though, I don't think I'm *only* running away or addicted to the work. Probably more so than I'd like to admit, but I also really do value being of service to others. That's part of why I'm so upset about being put on leave for another six months—my life feels pretty meaningless right now."

"You know, I'm sure I don't need to tell you, but there's plenty of need here too. You don't have to go overseas to be of service. An activist friend of mine in New York says there's been a lot of talk in his circles about the one percent. They're planning some kind of big 'Occupy Wall Street' event soon, though I don't know the details."

As she talked, I felt part of me bristle at her words. There was something about activist rhetoric that had always turned me off.

"Or maybe you could apply for nursing jobs working with underserved communities in the Bay Area," she suggested, perhaps sensing my skepticism. I relaxed a little now that the conversation had moved away from activism and considered her second suggestion more carefully.

"You know, it's not a bad idea. I don't think I'm ready to apply for actual jobs here yet. It would feel like admitting defeat. I'm lucky that I have savings from my past work, and that—since I'm living at home with few expenses besides therapy—I don't *have* to work. But I could volunteer somewhere using my nursing skills. And who knows? I might even surprise both of us and check out those Occupy folks." I winked as I said that, enjoying having a friendship where there was enough history that we could joke about our idiosyncrasies.

"I'm grateful for all this focus on me. It's been so helpful! But now I want to know more about you and how you're feeling nowadays. Is there any way I can support you while I'm here?"

"That's really sweet of you to ask, and if there's anything I'll definitely let you know. Overall, I've been doing well these past few years," Phoebe said. She glanced at her watch, then jumped up. "Whoa, I had no idea we'd been here so long! I've got to pick up the girls, but I'll give it some thought, and we can pick this back up next time we talk." This time, when we hugged goodbye, I knew in my bones that I would see her again. We clung to each other a moment longer than needed, our bodies communicating wordless gratitude.

A few days later, as I was walking back from a yoga class, I noticed a flyer tacked onto an electric pole: "Occupy planning meeting to take back our streets! All welcome!" it said, with a date and place to meet. Had Phoebe not mentioned her activist friend, I probably wouldn't even have seen the flyer.

I wondered if this was a sign to get involved. Try something new? I jotted down the address and decided to give the group (and myself) a chance.

Chapter Thirty-Two
July 1919

The Red Summer

Maggie

July 19. A hot, steamy Saturday.

Growing up working in the cotton fields, I knew about heat. Dry, prickly heat. At times, it felt like the cotton had gotten stuck in my throat, and if I didn't drink water, I would choke. Heat surrounded our skin like a halo, though we definitely weren't in heaven.

But here, the heat dripped with moisture that beaded down our eyes, our backs, our legs. It collected in little puddles in the nooks and crannies of our clothes. Clammy. Humid. Moist. Muggy. So many adjectives for it, but so few ways to escape it. I longed for a stream to dunk myself in—if I was going to be drenched, I'd rather bathe in water.

I spent the day with Sadie and Thomas. First, we tended to the wilting roses in the garden. The crow had long since healed and flown away, although every so often I heard cawing and imagined he was back for a visit. Next, we rode the streetcar into town and ate iced strawberry cones. To finish the day, we splashed in the fire hydrants (almost as good as a stream!) and chased pigeons at the Mall. I was asleep before

Frank came home and was only vaguely aware of him mopping my sweaty face with a wet rag before joining me in bed.

I was roused by the sound of loud pounding on our door. It was pitch black, and I had no sense of what time it was. "Frank, Frank, you have to come," I heard and felt Frank slip out of the bed.

"What's going on? Where are you going?" I mumbled through sleep.

"I'm not sure, Maggie. I heard some rumor of trouble earlier. Don't worry, I'll be right back," he said, kissing me lightly before hurrying off, donning his clothes as he went. I grabbed my shawl and went to the living room just in time to see him following Douglas, one of the young men he'd befriended at the NAACP.

He didn't come right back, and my worry chased away any possibility of going back to sleep. As soon as I saw a light on at the Brinkmans', I went and knocked on their door.

"Maggie, what's wrong?" Sadie asked. She was standing there in a light paisley nightdress. It couldn't have been later than 6:30 a.m., and I was grateful that they were early risers. After I told her about the middle-of-night visit, we turned on the wireless, which sputtered static like a dying animal. Over the next few hours, the news started trickling in.

"White soldiers, sailors, and marines on leave in the city, said to have been aroused by repeated attacks on white women by Colored men during the last few days, invaded a Colored residential district last night. Two men—Charles Ralls and George Montgomery—were severely beaten by the mob ..." the broadcast droned.

Frank finally came home at about noon. He seemed relieved to find me with the Brinkmans. I could tell he was tense, but there was also a glimmer of excitement in his eyes that frightened me. Images of finding him dead in the streets flashed before my eyes, and I tried not to think of Andre and Papa.

"It's pure madness out there. They are pulling our people from streetcars and beating them to a pulp. We talked to a seventeen-year-old boy who heard women pleading for their lives before he was knocked out. A marine shot and killed another young man as he passed him on a trolley car. This is never going to end!" he sputtered, out of breath. "You should all stay inside. You cannot leave—for any reason. You understand?"

"Frank, if it's too dangerous for us, it's too dangerous for you. You can interview people once the dust has settled. You aren't a journalist, and you won't be much good to Representative Dyer dead!" I pleaded.

"Maggie, I know you're worried, but I have to do this. If I stayed, I would never forgive myself. I'm with other members of the NAACP. We are being careful, staying one step behind the action, and I promise I'll be back before nightfall."

That afternoon and in the days that followed, I learned once more how time played tricks on those who waited. Everything stilled until nothing was left but the unbearable ticking of the clock. Benjamin and Sadie tried to entertain me by playing charades, but our hearts weren't in it, and we were soon all glued to the radio. Seeing the haunted look begin to return in Sadie's eyes—as it did at any hint of death—panic gnawed at my belly. I hoped her fear was not premonitory.

I was somewhat heartened when I heard the chairman of the District Commissioners' appeal later in the day: "The actions of the men who attacked innocent Negroes cannot be too strongly condemned, and it is the duty of every citizen to express his support of law and order by refraining from any inciting conversation or the repetition of inciting rumor and tales." I hoped it would be heeded.

Only Thomas, who was antsy about having to stay in all day and sensed our uneasiness, was able to distract me from my vigil with his requests for stories. Frank came back at dusk, as promised, but it was solely to update us and to reassure me he was fine.

"The police have stood by and let the violence go unabated, so the whites have gotten bolder. Benjamin, did you hear about Carter Woodson?"

Benjamin shook his head, looking worried.

"That's Howard University's new dean," Frank explained to me. He motioned to Sadie to take Thomas away, and she gently shepherded her son to the garden with promises that they could cut his favorite rose.

"Don't worry, Carter's okay, but I ran into him on my way back, and he was badly shaken. He said he was walking home on Penn Ave. when he heard the mob coming. He hid in a storefront and watched as they caught a young man he knew. He said they held him up and shot him, no questions asked."

Benjamin shook his head and exclaimed, "I can't believe this is happening here. In the capital. With President Wilson promising us glory and freedom! All he's done is bring his Southern cronies into office."

"I know. Benjamin, can I talk to you? Maggie, I'll be right back," he said, and the two disappeared into his study. I paced for a minute or two, and then followed them, pressing my ear against the closed door.

"… so tired of it!" I heard Frank say. "The marines who have come in are arresting more of ours than whites. Did you see the *Post* headline—'Mobilization for tonight'? The police are asking for all available servicemen to report to headquarters for a 'clean-up' operation. We all know what that means! Some of us want to fight back. Give the message that enough is enough. We are telling everyone else to stay inside. I know this is asking a lot, but do you have a gun I could use?"

I strained, but I couldn't hear Benjamin's response and guessed his back was to me.

"I would only use it if strictly necessary, and hopefully I won't need to at all. I won't do anything foolish, I promise. But it's a war out there, and if we don't do this, we may not be able to protect our own."

More muffled speech from Benjamin.

"Thank you. You won't regret this. You'll look after Maggie, won't you? After I leave, you can go out back, and I'll meet you ..."

I'd heard enough. When they came out, I was standing guard in front of the door, barring it with every inch of my frame. While my body was quite small, I felt my rage fill the room.

"Frank, you can't do this! Are you willing to risk everything you have? Your job, your reputation, your life, us?"

Frank looked at me warily as he approached, as though he were trapped and looking for an escape. He stopped a few feet away.

"Maggie, don't you want future generations to have something better than what we have? That will never happen if we just sit back. Laws aren't changed because people care. Laws are changed when people have no choice but to pay attention!"

"I'm tired of it too, Frank. You know that. I believe in the fight, and I've always supported you. But like this? Through more violence? Frank, even if you survive this, you are going to lose a part of your soul. Don't you see that?"

I saw a fleeting look of compassion on his face, then his gaze was impenetrable again. He came to stand right in front of me and shook his head.

"Don't fight me on this, Maggie. If I *don't* do this, I will lose a part of myself. Of my dignity. I love you, and I know you love me. I *have* to do this. Don't ask me not to."

I started trembling and couldn't move, so he gently but firmly pushed me aside.

*

Fight back we did. For the first time since any of us could remember, more of them were killed than us, though I didn't know that right away. All that night and the next day, I was too nervous to listen to the radio or to the people who stopped in to talk to the Brinkmans, so I stayed with Thomas. He was happy for a playmate to break the tension he felt but didn't understand.

Frank came back late Monday. Although we were civil, we weren't sure what to say to each other. For the first time since we'd met, we were on opposite sides of our convictions. Our words and our pride hung between us, and neither of us wanted to make the first step toward the other. Frank seemed relieved to focus on Benjamin, who was impatient for fresh news.

"They said Colored folks went out in huge numbers buying guns. That there were snipers on the roofs. That Coloreds were pulling whites off of streetcars! Is that true?"

"Oh, Benjamin, you should have seen them! The soldiers in uniform with their old guns and ordinary people fighting back. The death toll today is ten for them and five for us. Did you ever think you'd see the day? I bet Carrie Minor Johnson is going to become a household name. Did you hear about her? She barricaded herself in the top room of their house, fending off a white mob. And when a police officer broke in, she shot him dead! She's just seventeen! Of course, the news is framing it differently, but it was a clear case of self-defense, from what my sources say."

"I heard about that," Benjamin said. "And is it true that the *Post* headline asking people to mobilize was based on a false report? I went to visit Dean Woodson to see how he was doing, and that's what he said."

"Yes, it's true," Frank responded. "But, of course, they'll

probably never find who was responsible for spreading the rumor. A costly one it was. But mobilize us it did, so perhaps we should be grateful."

I don't know if he used the gun. We tacitly agreed not to mention that day. I think we both feared that talking would only widen the chasm between us, rather than bridge it. In the end, it wasn't the two thousand military servicemen President Wilson called in that squelched the violence or calmed the rift between Frank and me on this matter. No. It was the rain.

On the fourth day of the fighting, it started to pour. And it poured and poured until the last embers of murderous rage had been quelled. It was hard not to believe that God had chosen to intervene when we humans were unable to do so ourselves. There were more protests and fighting after that in cities around the country. In his report in the fall, George Haynes, the director of Negro Economics for the Department of Labor and a friend of Frank's, counted incidents in thirty-eight cities! Politicians wrote it off as the influence of the Bolsheviks and swept the whole thing under the rug. It was easier than looking the truth in the eye. Ever since the Russian Revolution, they'd replaced the Germans as our favorite enemy.

But my people hadn't forgotten—and Frank hadn't forgotten. As for me, in the days that followed, I felt like there was a hole in my heart. While I was proud that we fought back, I was flooded by a deep sense of grief and loss that I couldn't name. And so, as I did when I didn't know what else to do, I put pen to paper and let the words flow from my heart to my hand. When I was done, the hollow feeling had been replaced by a dull ache.

Rain

*The rain pours
On the guns,
On the anger,
On the hatred.*

*The rain dampens
The fires
Of our revolt.*

For now.

But when will it end?

*White men and women
Pull our people
From streetcars.
Use us
As target practice.*

*Do our children
Need to take
Up arms
To stop this?*

*When
Will it end?*

*Perhaps the rain
Who showers us all,
Carries wisdom
In her drops.*

Stop.
Stop.
Stop.
Stop.

What are you doing
To your brethren?
To your children?

What will grow
From these drops
Of blood
You splatter
Down on earth?

What decaying fruit
Will you harvest
In your tomorrows?

    I left this poem on Frank's desk, hoping it would explain what I could not—not adequately, anyway. He came into the bedroom, the poem hanging limply in his left hand. He nodded, indicating he understood even if we didn't agree. With his right hand, he reached for my face. He started kissing me, tentatively at first, and then with a passion I'd missed sorely in the past weeks.

Chapter Thirty-Three

Occupy

Sarah

Sitting in the Occupy meeting a week after my lunch with Phoebe, I wondered if I'd overestimated my own ability to stretch beyond my comfort zone.

"The main Occupy organizers in New York are planning a huge protest in Manhattan on September 17th, marching up and down Wall Street. A group is going to stay in a park north of there for as long as they can. We've been discussing what to do here in Oakland to support them. We've decided to wait and see how things go there on the seventeenth and plan our own action accordingly. We need to be ready, though, and this is where you all come in."

The man speaking was perhaps in his sixties, with dark skin, soft white hair, and big, intense eyes. His voice was gravelly and resolute as he spoke. He nodded to the woman next to him.

"Christine, do you want to take it from here?"

She was a stout woman in her forties or fifties with shoulder-length chestnut hair that was peppered with gray, and a determined, stalwart strength that gave the impression she could move mountains if she wanted to.

"Thanks, Fred. Our current thought is to set up an Occupy

encampment in Frank H. Ogawa Plaza—which we want to rename Oscar Grant Plaza—sometime in October. For that, we need to collect donations of tents, sleeping bags, food … If you write your name and email on the sign-up list when it gets to you, we'll send you the full checklist. Anything you can gather would be helpful."

"What are you doing to prep for police brutality?" The young woman across from me asked. She was young and wiry, with a nose ring and hair shaved on one side of the head, dyed blue on the other. She kept tapping her foot against the floor, as though willing the conversation to get to the action.

Behind them was a poster that looked hand drawn. In the top half, a helicopter hovered above the words "Hella Occupy" and tall buildings marked Greed, War, and Bank. Placards emerging from the bottom half proclaimed, "WE ARE THE 99%" and "THE SYSTEM SUCKS."

"Good question," Fred responded. "Those who stay in the encampment will join solidarity pods, and they'll get more training on what to do. We've also been recruiting health-care workers to be on standby. We are anticipating retaliatory action like pepper spray, tear gas, baton use, and arrests." As he described the possible violence, the unease in my belly turned into full-blown nausea. For a moment, I thought I was going to throw up.

What is wrong with you? If you weren't such a coward, you could be one of those health-care workers! My inner nemesis needled me.

Shush, not now! I retorted internally, taking deep breaths to try to calm myself. I closed my eyes in the hope that would help, but nebulous images of violence crowded my mind.

People being pulled off buses and getting beaten up, maybe? It wasn't clear. Bile rose from my stomach to my throat, but thankfully stopped there. I opened my eyes, frantically scanning for an exit.

I found the nearest door and snuck out as discreetly as I could, gulping in big breaths of air as soon as I was outside. I still had no idea what had happened to me. From the images I'd seen, I sensed they might have something to do with Maggie, although I hadn't dreamt of her in a while. My main concern just then, however, was getting home safely. I waited until the threat of vomiting had passed, then pedaled home slowly, stopping every few blocks to get my bearings.

Once back in the house, I drank some ginger water until I felt a little better. I considered doing some automatic writing to connect with Maggie, but the mere thought sent my insides into convulsions.

I searched "yoga for panic attacks" instead and found a twenty-minute video that looked gentle and relaxing. Following the instruction, I lay down on my back, one hand on my heart, the other on top, thumbs interlocking. The pressure on my chest was soothing, and I could feel my muscles start to soften.

When I was done, my body and nervous system felt much calmer, but my mind wasn't letting me off the hook.

You suck. Your life is meaningless! My nemesis chimed in.

I got up, rolled up my yoga mat, and went to my desk where Patrick's Working with Negative Thoughts worksheet was waiting for this very occasion.

I read the first question: *1) Is what your thoughts are telling you really true?*

I thought of Mariol and Hiba. Of all the patients I'd been able to help. Of Amanda and Phoebe. Patrick and Deborah. I thought of how far I'd come in the last three-plus months. And how much more I could heal in the next six. No, my life wasn't meaningless. It probably wasn't even as hard as I thought it was.

2) What emotion might be behind the thoughts?

I felt into my sense of failure that I couldn't even sit

through a meeting. And the panicky feeling that arose as violent images flashed before my eyes.

"Shame and fear," I said without hesitation.

3) What might be more helpful for those emotions than those thoughts?

Thinking of the inner child work I'd done with Patrick, I put one hand on my abdomen and one on my chest.

"It's okay to be scared. Lots of things are changing right now," I whispered soothingly. "You're not alone. We're in this together. And we're going to be okay. So, we might not be cut out to be an activist. That's all right. There are so many other things that bring us joy. There's no rush." I said, and for perhaps the first time, I actually believed what I was saying.

See, you're doing it! My inner cheerleader piped up, and I let myself smile ever so slightly. Yes, I was.

That night, however, my subconscious had other plans for me. I dreamt of Maggie, her back against a door. "Don't make me choose!" she shouted. Then she opened the door and started walking—one foot on a path to the left, and the other on a path to the right. As the two paths curved farther and farther from each other, she reached a point where she was doing the splits and had to make a choice. "No!" she screamed, before dissolving into thin air.

In the next scene, I was mummified, and someone was unwrapping my bandages, although I couldn't see who it was. "You need to unravel completely before you can be whole again," the voice said.

When I woke up, "Fuck!" was the first word out of my mouth.

It just keeps getting worse, not better, I thought, hopelessness gripping the pit of my stomach.

I remembered the second part of my dream, that I had to unravel completely before I could be whole.

"Maybe so, but nobody said I had to unravel alone," I said

defiantly, feeling slightly better as I did.

I considered contacting Deborah for another hypnotherapy session since there seemed to be a connection between my vision and Maggie.

Not yet. You're not ready, came the thought. Neither my nemesis nor my cheerleader. Something else. Deeper. My inner knowing?

I sent Patrick a text to see if he had an opening sooner than our scheduled session four days later. And I made the decision to be more open with my mother about the darkness I'd been navigating these past few weeks. Somewhere in me, I recognized that my well-being didn't depend on her response or ability to receive me. My sense of safety and worth were only contingent on my willingness to own my experience and not feel like I had to apologize for it.

Chapter Thirty-Four
January 1920

A New Decade

Maggie

Towards the end of 1919, I found myself swept up in the national excitement of welcoming in not only a new year but a new decade. After everything we'd been through—a war, sickness, violence against our people—we were ready to welcome brighter days. Since I'd been born early in January 1900, I would soon be entering my twenties as well.

I looked back in amazement at everything that had transpired in the last five years, and I felt hope for the future—albeit tentative. When I'd worked on the railroad—so many years ago—Pepe had taught me to pause and look back every so often. "If not, all you see is what's left. *Sin fin*. No end. You wanna give up. Look back, you see all you did. And it give you *fuerza* to continue. Strength."

In my mind's eye, I saw those tracks. How many trains had hurtled across their sturdy backs since those days? I imagined the tracks' legacy long outlasting mine. I wondered if that was one of the reasons I wrote. To stamp the page with the imprint of where I'd been. To close out a chapter and make space for a new one while honoring how I got here.

Or perhaps I was just hanging onto pieces of dead skin, hooding my vision.

On December 31, 1919, the Brinkmans organized the biggest New Year's party I had ever been to. Sadie, who'd quit her job at the library earlier in the year, had been busy for weeks giving instructions to the extra help they'd hired for the occasion. Out of old habits, I offered my assistance as well, but Sadie was adamant.

"You're my guest and my friend, and there is no way I'm letting you help. We're hiring people for that. It's enough that you listen to me when I complain and that I know I can rely on you if I need you."

I was just happy to see her face light up. The specter of Rosie's death rarely dimmed her eyes now, although I knew it would never fully vanish. I was learning more about who she was when she wasn't grieving. Lit up by activity and social interactions. *Fire to Edna's earth*, I often thought. But she wasn't just the flame. She was also the hearth. The place where people gathered for warmth and connection.

I spent extra time with Thomas, both so he wouldn't be in her way and because I enjoyed his company. We made snow angels in the garden and rode streetcars at random, just to see where they went. Sometimes I wished I could ride them all the way back to New York to see Edna and Josie. I missed them, although I felt guilty at the thought, as though it meant I wasn't grateful enough for my current life.

The party was a grand affair. Everyone who was anyone was there, and Sadie had hired a local band called the Duke's Serenaders to play. She'd been talking about young Duke Ellington for months.

"You should hear him play, Maggie! This boy is going places. And he grew up right here, in LeDroit Park! His parents are pianists, and his mother was my piano teacher. I remember when he was a little boy—he would be tearing around their house, hollering at the top of his lungs during our lessons. You should see him now!" She exclaimed.

That evening, the house that was starting to feel like a second home was transformed into a magical world of colors, sounds, exotic foods, and the promise of something that sparked joy in our eyes and hearts. I could feel how ready we all were to leave the decade behind. For me, it was another door closing on my old world and the prism of pain it contained.

The alcohol was flowing freely, although I wasn't sure where the Brinkmans procured it. Prohibition had been in effect in Washington, DC since 1917, but they usually didn't bother private citizens. However, now that Prohibition had been voted into law nationally and was going to be enforced this very month, nobody knew what the local impact would be. I heard a number of guests saying, "We should take advantage of this while we can."

Although I didn't have any of the spirits myself—I had never been able to tolerate it—I felt drunk and dizzy from the flurry of activity around me. Sadie and Frank took turns introducing me to their acquaintances until the names and faces were a tangled mess in my brain.

I escaped them and hid in a corner close to the musicians, my eyes transfixed on Duke's fingers. I now understood Sadie's excitement. His hands took to the piano the way mine did to the pen, and he got as lost in that world as I did in mine.

When I felt a hand on my shoulder, I turned, expecting to see Frank or Sadie smirking at finding my hiding place. I had to blink a few times to make sure my startled eyes weren't playing tricks on me.

In their stead were Edna and Josie.

"There you are, Maggie! Heavens, you are a hard one to find. What are you doing tucked away here? We weren't going to miss the biggest party in the decade, were we?" Edna said in response to my gaping mouth. "I thought it would be less trouble than having to plan my own party, and we wanted to surprise you so we could have the pleasure of seeing the look on your face! I think it was worth the trip, don't you, Josie?" Edna asked, and Josie laughed in delight. After we embraced and shed a few tears, we found a relatively quiet corner in a back room where we could catch up.

Josie regaled me with stories of the train ride. She had shot up in the year since I'd seen her, and at almost eleven, she was already as tall as I was. The pale-pink dress she was wearing showed off the curves, starting to push out her chest and hips.

I was suddenly transported back to when my body started changing and the tragedy it wrought on my family. But I shook off the sadness and sent a silent prayer of thanks that Josie wouldn't have to live through that.

Edna was excited because she and Lewis had gotten very involved with Marcus Garvey. "He is organizing the first international convention of the UNIA this summer in Madison Garden, and we are helping him plan it. You haven't heard of them? The Universal Negro Improvement Association. Frank told me you haven't been so active since you moved here ..."

Just then, Benjamin and Sadie turned off all but a few dim lights and started the countdown to midnight. We all shouted, hugged, and sang. I hadn't felt this happy in a long time. Frank, who'd been catching up with Lewis, came and scooped me up in his arms. I kissed him extra long, knowing he was the one to tell the Joneses about the party, who had wanted to surprise me once again.

After everyone was done cheering and hugging, Benjamin clanked his spoon on the side of his glass to get everyone's attention. He had to shout for a few minutes before things calmed down enough for us to hear him.

"We have so much talent in this room. Musicians, writers, poets ... As we welcome in the 1920s, I wanted to invite my friends to come up and recite their work or play something for us."

Sadie broke the ice by replacing Duke at the piano. She'd stopped playing after Rose's death and, according to Benjamin, had only recently picked it up again. That night, I discovered how talented she was. Her fingers transported me to a world of pure shadow and light, tenderness and rage.

"*Beethoven's Ninth*," Edna whispered, delighting in the look of wonderment on my face.

"Maggie," Benjamin, who was sitting next to Frank, said after heartily cheering his wife. "You should really read one of your poems. This is the best audience you are ever likely to have."

My heart skipped a beat and whispered that she longed to share the words that poured from her with others. But the old fear of being seen made me hesitate, staying my yes for a beat. This time, however, my excitement won.

"All right. I think I have them memorized."

As I went to the makeshift stage and saw all the eyes on me, I felt panic clutch at my throat. I'd never read my poems to so many people before. I took sips of water to gain some time, looking intently at the glass while I did. When I looked back at the crowd, I was relieved to see that many people had resumed their conversations and seemed too inebriated to notice much beyond the buzzing in their heads.

I started with "Ode to the Capitol" and ended with "You Cannot Keep Us Down." When I finished, I realized the room had gone quiet before bursting into applause a moment later. I felt weak-kneed and had to sit down. A few people came to talk to me after, and I was grateful to have Frank and Edna on either side of me.

The Unbroken Horizon

Ferreted out of hiding
There is no turning back

I wasn't born to hide

I will unearth my story
From its burial ground
For all to see

Is my story worth telling?

Only Time knows
And she holds fast
To the answer

I stand
At the threshold
Between two decades—
And find peace
In the present

Now
Is the sleeper
That connects
The rails of my past
To the ballast
Of my future

I wasn't born to hide

Chapter Thirty-Five

Lost Fathers

Sarah

As I bit into the grilled chicken, pieces of it caught in my throat, and I started coughing.

"It's so dry!" I exclaimed after gulping down a full glass of water. "I'm really sorry. I don't know how I managed to mess up chicken!"

My mother laughed. "It's not so bad, Sarah. It's better than half of what they serve in the hospital cafeteria, that's for sure. And the cashew stir-fried vegetables are delicious."

About a week had passed since I'd been to the Occupy meeting, and after a couple of emergency sessions with Patrick—one of which included EMDR on Mariol's death—I was feeling much lighter, which was why I'd decided to cook instead of getting takeout for my "tell-all" dinner with my mother. In college, I'd been praised by friends and roommates for my culinary skills, but the bar was pretty low in those days. And I was clearly out of practice.

"Mom, I just wanted to say that I'm happy we've had this chance to get a little closer."

"Me too. Who knew that having you home for so long would turn out to be a blessing in disguise?" she said.

"Yeah, I bet we were both dreading it," I agreed, happy

we could laugh about it. "And I've also been realizing that we could be even closer. I've been holding back, keeping you at arm's length. Trying to protect myself. But for my own healing, I know I can't do that anymore. I need to be open and willing to be vulnerable."

I could feel the temptation to look down or away, but I made myself look into my mother's hazel eyes as I talked. Her expression seemed suspended, as though waiting for what I was going to say to know what to feel.

"Is it okay with you if I share more of what's been going on with me these past few months?" I asked, realizing she might not want me to unload.

"Of course, Sarah. I've been wondering ... but I'm not one to pry."

I chuckled. If prying had an antonym, it would be my mother. I'd always taken her lack of curiosity as a sign she wasn't interested in me, but I was now realizing she might have been trying to give me privacy. For all the unilateral decisions she made when I was younger and her strong opinions about my choices when I was older, she always gave me the space and freedom to live my life.

Taking a deep breath to gather my courage, I told her about my friendship with Mariol, his sudden death, and how rattled I'd been because of it. When I got to the part about the nightmares, migraines, blacking out, and being told to leave early, I saw her jaw clench and unclench and felt my throat tighten in automatic response. I took a sip of water to give myself a chance to breathe and collect myself.

I thought about checking in with her but realized that if I invited her to respond I might lose my nerve, so I launched into a description of how I'd frozen during the external evaluation. She nodded but didn't say anything.

When I told her about the inner child work I'd done over the last few months since being home and the hypnotherapy session where I'd felt Maggie, her shoulders relaxed a little. I hadn't been sure how she'd react to the latter, and I noticed my breath coming in more easily in response. I even shared my conversation with Phoebe and what she'd said about me being a pale ghost—and that I seemed to be more me, although that wasn't my current experience of myself.

When I was done, my mother was silent for a long time, considering what I'd said. I watched subtle waves of emotion ebbing and flowing from her face, though I couldn't interpret what they were.

"That sounds hard," she said at last, each word carefully chosen. She leaned across the table and placed a stiff and heavy hand on my shoulder. Despite the awkwardness of her gesture, I could tell how hard she was trying, and was grateful for the effort. I could only imagine how much she'd rather be anywhere else but here, having to deal with the disorderliness of all these emotions.

"Thanks. I know these aren't your favorite kinds of conversations," I sighed, then smiled so she wouldn't take it as criticism.

"Not usually, but thanks to you, I'm learning the value of them. And I'm sorry you had to teach me, rather than the other way around." Tenderness and relief at her admission welled up in my heart and threatened to spill out of my eyes. And for once, I didn't mind if they did.

"I know I should have said this to you a long time ago, but I'm proud of you," she said, and to my surprise, the words sounded almost natural. As though they'd just been biding their time to come out.

"Sarah, I don't think you know how brave you are. For the work you do, of course … but even more so for all the soul-searching you've embarked on these last months. For being willing to take a hard look at yourself, your life. I've *really* seen a difference in you. I agree with Phoebe—you do seem more like you, somehow. It's inspiring. And at my age, that's a rare gift."

The tears flowed freely down my cheeks now. I hadn't realized how much I needed to hear that from her. She brought her hands to my chin, catching the overflow in her fingers. There was no awkwardness anymore; I could see mirror tears shining in her eyes.

"You have no idea how good it feels to hear that, Mom," I said, the term slipping off my tongue as though I'd never stopped calling her that. "And I can see the change in you too. How much effort you're putting into reacting differently to me. That's pretty amazing!"

She tilted her head, and I could see her immediate impulse to brush my words off. But then she paused and seemed to take them in.

At some point, the awkwardness returned, and we weren't sure where to go from there. She withdrew her hands and cleared her throat. I took a Kleenex from my pocket and wiped my tears.

Seeing the need for us to be on safer, intellectual ground, at least for now, I asked, "Mom, do you remember hearing of the Red Summer of 1919 during all the years you lived in DC?"

She shook her head. "No, that doesn't ring any bells. But then again, I was a science girl from day one. History went in one ear and out the other. I'm sure your father would know."

"He probably would," I agreed wistfully. "I got a book called *The Red Summer* out of the library, and I couldn't believe such a critical period of history was never mentioned when I was in school."

"So, what was it?" she asked, and I tried not to feel jarred by her impatience.

"The short version is that racial violence erupted throughout the country, and it was the first time Black people started fighting back in a concerted way. Many of them had fought in World War I and had expected things to change when they came back."

"Actually, now that you say that, I do remember Saul mentioning something about this. Do you remember ..." She paused and thought for a minute before continuing. "No, of course not. You would've been too young at the time. In 1980, maybe late 1979, a Black motorist in Miami—McDuffie, I think was his name—was beaten to death by white cops during a routine traffic stop. Your father was helping the prosecutor in the case against the police ..."

She stopped again, rubbing her temples in an attempt to remember. Feeling like I was getting a rare glimpse of a forbidden world—I didn't remember my father ever discussing his work with me—I stayed absolutely still.

"The details are murky. I think there were seven or eight officers on trial for various charges, but in the end, they were all acquitted. By an all-white male jury, of course. I've rarely seen your father so defeated. He'd run out of energy to be angry. Riots broke out in Miami following the verdict. I remember Saul saying, 'Sixty years later, but nothing has changed.' I wonder what he'd say now. We have our first Black president, which is incredible, but I'm not sure much else has changed ..." she said, her words trailing off for an instant before she remembered what she'd been talking about. "Anyway, that's when he told me what had happened in 1919." As she spoke, the niggling feeling I'd had with Phoebe intensified.

"Wow, I had no idea. I wish Dad were here so I could pick his brain. Speaking of which, when I was with Phoebe, she mentioned something about an anti-lynching bill first introduced in 1918. It seemed vaguely familiar, but I wasn't sure why ..."

I paused. My mother had paled, and I thought I saw pain flashing through her eyes before she closed them.

"Mom, are you okay?" I asked, concerned.

"You wouldn't remember this either. It was before you were born. Your father was fascinated by that piece of legislation. Why it failed. Why the civil rights movement succeeded. If it was due to timing, strategy, or both." Her voice faded away again, and she looked like she was deep in memory land. Then her eyes landed on me and slowly came back into present focus.

"He wrote several articles about it. A few were published in the '70s, and then in the early '80s in a publication exploring the South and the history of anti-lynching. Saul was invited to give talks all around the country. You probably heard us discussing it then, but you wouldn't have known what it meant."

I stared at my mother, taking all this information in.

WTF? Dad knew about the legislation? And researched it? What if I can find his articles?

My brain hummed with excitement as it started connecting dots that had until then just been distinct fragments and at the possibility of getting to know my father a little better, even after all these years. My body, on the other hand, felt like a jumble of overextended nerve endings. By the jittery feeling in my stomach, I guessed my nervous system was about to max out from all the input and emotions. I inhaled deeply and massaged my thigh muscles in an attempt to relax. I didn't want to interrupt our conversation.

Hang in there! I pleaded with my body.

"What happened to those articles?" I asked, unable to contain my excitement.

"They must be somewhere. There are some boxes of Saul's things in the attic. They probably contain his articles and civil rights cases. Maybe the research? I think there were even some old letters."

"What? Why didn't you tell me before?" I asked before I

could stop myself. I had a moment of regret when I saw her shoulders tense up, but I reminded myself of my intention to be more honest and open with my mother. Without apology. I didn't want to attack her, but maybe I didn't need to hold back so much either.

"I always meant to tell you about them, but it never seemed like the right time. And you know that discussing the past is not my forte," she said, looking tired and contrite.

I shook my head gently, as if trying to shoo away the bite of my words. "That's okay, I understand. I didn't mean that as an accusation. It just really took me by surprise. I'm glad you're telling me now. I can't wait to look through his boxes."

And maybe start filling that gaping Dad hole his death left in my life, I thought but didn't say, not wanting to test the growing but still tentative closeness with my mother.

Sensing that we'd both reached the limits of our capacity for this conversation, I got up to clear the table.

"Leave the dishes to me, Sarah," my mother said, getting up as well. "You cooked. And I imagine you have a lot to process. As do I."

The next morning, I woke up early with a sense of bubbling anticipation. What if I found some of the Dad puzzle pieces that had been missing from my life? I decided to skip my morning meditation, yoga, and run, and tiptoed up the stairs to avoid waking my mother on a Saturday morning.

The attic was big. A few rays of dawn sunlight filtered in through the tiny rooftop window, and along with a weak, naked lightbulb, shed enough light to start exploring. I recognized some furniture from our house in D.C. An old rocking chair that, as I recalled, had been in my mother's family for generations. A sturdy, antique table that was probably worth some money was gathering cobwebs in the far corner.

I had to rummage around before I saw the boxes huddled in a corner, with *"Saul's things"* written on top in my mother's neat, clinical handwriting. There were a few boxes of differing sizes, but one of them had the sub-label of *"articles, research, letters, etc."*

The writing was hard to decipher in this light, so I decided to take the box down to my room, stopping to get a rag to dust off the layer of grime covering it. Settled cross-legged on my area rug, I peeled off the tape that was yellowed with age and barely sticking to the cardboard anymore. It had been twenty-two years, I realized to my astonishment. My mother must have packed his things before we'd left for Paris, right after my father's death and—not one to dwell on the past, as she said—had probably never opened them again.

I hesitated for a second before opening the box, a ripple of fear laced with hope and longing coursing through my body. Even with those retrieved during my therapy sessions with Patrick, my memories of my father were few and far between. Those that remained were a child's memories, frozen in time and stale from having been recycled over and over again. I had never known my father as a man, as a person in his own right. In light of my conversation with my mother, I wondered at all the things I didn't know about him. His interests. His dreams. Who he had been before he became a father. Or a lawyer, for that matter.

Slowly, I reached over to unhook one flap from the other. The cardboard was soft from age. Reverently, I began unpacking its contents. There were several manila envelopes labeled "college essays," which I set aside to peruse later.

Then I found them. Several thick folders labeled "anti-lynching bill." Next to them was a withered shoebox with the label "letters from family et al." My hand wavered between the folders and the box, wondering whether to start with the academic or the personal. Finally, I landed on the folders.

Fingers shaking as though I'd discovered the Dead Sea Scrolls and they might disintegrate in my hands if I made a wrong move, I took the contents out ever so delicately. A single page fluttered down, detached from all the other stapled or paper-clipped pages. Upon closer scrutiny, the page looked like the xeroxed copy of a list of handwritten names. "Men and women who died at Auschwitz" was faintly legible above the names. One name was underlined: "Isaac Baum, b. March 12 1905 d. Aug 1942."

I stopped, stunned, scanning my memory for a record of that name. Nausea threatened to overtake me once more. I slowly sipped my green tea until I'd regained my composure and could look at the paper again.

Isaac. Isaac? I hadn't known many people on my father's side. He had an older sister he was fairly close to, but I hadn't seen my aunt since my father's death. I made a mental note to ask my mother about her. My grandmother had died of cancer when I was five or six. From the little I could recall, she had a thick Polish accent and long, dark hair she pulled back in a bun. Babcia Valda, I called her. I liked her a lot better than Grandma Belle—beneath her strictness was a warm heart, I could tell even at that age. And she made the best apple strudel!

I looked at the date of death. Was Isaac a great uncle? My grandfather? I racked my brain for more information. I knew my father's father had died when my dad was a baby, back in Poland, I thought I remembered my father saying. What else? From a vague distant part of my brain came the recollection that when his wife and kids fled to the United States at the onset of World War II, he'd had to stay behind.

But nobody had ever mentioned anything about Auschwitz! I turned the page over, and in my father's handwriting were the words: "Never forget. This is why you do this work."

Never forget what?? And why was it inserted into his research on the anti-lynching bill? I sighed, noticing that a headache had begun to grip the side of my head with the effort of trying to dredge up fragments of family history from the little I'd ever known in the first place.

Not sure where to go from here, having wrenched every last bit of information I could from my own mind, I opened the various folders, rummaging until I found dad's article: "The Anti-Lynching Bill: Why it Failed and the Civil Rights Act Succeeded," by Saul Baum. Seeing his name in print stirred something in my heart, as though a little part of him had been brought back from the dead and was here with me.

As I started reading, I noticed something wedged inside the pages. Opening it up, I saw a square piece of paper that was stiffer than writing paper. On it was a pencil sketch of a baby girl … Of me! I realized with a gasp. I was maybe six months old, laying on my stomach but propped up on my elbows, looking back at whoever was drawing me. My dark hair fanned out around me like a wild mane. My eyes were big and round. Although the rest was in black and white, the artist had colored my irises a light, emerald green. My mouth was open, sides turned upward, as though I'd been caught in a delightful surprise.

The drawing was so detailed and lifelike, I could almost feel every strand of hair touch the roundness of my cheeks like I was reaching back in time to my baby self. I hadn't even known it was possible to capture someone's likeness so vividly with only pencil and shading. Trying to figure out who'd drawn the picture—and what it was doing inside the article—I turned the square over.

My beautiful baby Sarah, may you always know the depth of your love and power, my father had written. And there was another pencil sketch, this one of a black kitten. The shape of the face and eyes (also colored in) mirrored mine. Upon closer examination, though, I saw it had extensive whiskering most cats don't have and was pretty big for a kitten. A baby panther?

All of a sudden, another memory came to me—of being little and sitting on my father's lap, facing him and running my hands through the prickly hairs of his auburn beard. He laughed as he tickled me, and his blue-gray eyes were warm, happy.

"Sarah Panthera, Sarah Panthera, wild and free," he crooned, pronouncing the first "a" in my name more like the "e" in there, to rhyme with Panthera. A few more memory fragments of him calling me his "baby panther" echoed within my auditory field, without an accompanying visual.

I looked at the picture again, front and back, back and front, not comprehending. It was as if some previously well-functioning brain synapses had misfired, and nothing made sense. My dad had drawn this? My father drew? How had I not known this? Why had I never seen the drawing? How could he just forget it in the pages of an academic article?

Underneath the questions, though, I felt a certainty come through. My father loved me. He *loved* me. He was so enchanted with me in that moment, he'd dropped whatever else he was doing (perhaps having to do with the article) and drawn every last detail of me that could fit on that paper. And my baby self was clearly just as enraptured with him.

Although my dad was warm when we were together—much nicer than my mother's coldness, to be sure—my sense had been that he loved me as an afterthought. After everything else he needed to do was done, which, as a civil rights lawyer, was never.

Due to my parents' demanding careers, I had always felt like their very distant second choice. And my young self had learned to believe that their behavior was somehow my fault, and that I didn't deserve any more than what they were dishing out.

As I touched the depths of pain and misery that had ricocheted from believing I was unlovable—including years of avoiding love altogether or seeking it from unavailable men—waves of sorrow crashed through my being followed by wordless rage. *I've wasted SO much time!* I thought as I flopped belly down on my bed and pounded my head on my pillow until the tears came crashing down on me. I sobbed until there was nothing left.

Getting up, I felt something shift—as though some of my old stories had begun to unravel, and there was more space for new beliefs. New possibilities. I opened my journal and picked up my pen.

I am loved.

The words stared back, looking both foreign and true. Some part of me must have always known this. And yet, there were so many other unknowns …

I thought I was supposed to be finding the missing puzzle pieces, I wrote. *But with everything I do, there seem to be more pieces to find. Dad's, his dad's, Mom's, my inner child's, Maggie's … When will it ever end?*

I picked up my phone to text Patrick, then put it back down, realizing he wasn't the one I needed right now. I sighed, knowing what I had to do. I glanced at my watch. 10:12 a.m. Definitely late enough to knock on my mother's door.

The ball's in your court, Mom. I thought. *Your turn to decide if you're ready to be open and honest.*

Chapter Thirty-Six
Fall 1920

Student Life

Maggie

With the start of this new decade, I finally found the courage to apply to Howard University, making the conscious choice to ignore the voices saying I was wanting too much. Frank was overjoyed.

"Maggie, you've been working your whole life. Now is the time for you to do something you love. People love your writing, and they will respect you more if you've gone to college. That's just the way the world is. We've got to beat the white folks at their game, and you are too talented not to do this." He assured me that his income was enough to cover our needs and tuition. I was so excited at the prospect, I didn't argue.

Mr. Milton—the principal at Josie's school and my former employer—wrote a letter singing my praises and attesting that I had graduated high school while simultaneously being "one of the more inspiring assistant teachers the school has seen."

I teared up when I received it. The letter, along with my application essay and Benjamin's glowing reports from the night class I had attended, landed me a spot among Howard's finest. Once I was accepted, I handed in my notice at my teaching job. I was sad about leaving the students and other teachers, but excited about returning to school for my own learning.

One evening, when we were over at the Brinkmans', Frank picked up Howard's 1919–20 yearbook on display in the hall and started skimming through it. His attention was arrested by the future plans of the female senior students.

"Look at this Maggie. 'Will teach … Will teach …' Oh, here's one getting her master's degree. 'Will teach. Will teach …' This one is entering social service … 'Will teach …' I dare you to be the first one of whom they say 'will be a world-renowned author.' What do you think, Benjamin?"

Benjamin nodded and agreed it would be a first. I hid my embarrassment by focusing on Thomas.

"I'll be happy if I graduate," I said.

There hadn't been a day in my life I hadn't worked, and it felt extravagant to spend my days merely studying. Every time I walked up the white stone steps to the main building, with its peaked roof and shining insignia, I felt my heart quicken. I kept waiting for someone to come from behind, startle me out of this daydream, and send me back into my place as a nanny or teacher's assistant.

I met Mabel on my first day while I was wandering the halls in search of my class. I must have looked as confused and dazed as I felt, for she stopped and asked me where I was going.

"Professor Locke's class? That's where I'm going!" she exclaimed. "Come with me. I have three brothers who went here, and I know this campus almost as well as my own home."

I expected to study and work hard—that's what I was there for. What I hadn't anticipated was the added benefit of making friends my age. As grateful as I was for Edna and Sadie's friendships, our age difference (they were thirteen and eight years my elder, respectively) often put them in an older sister role with me.

In fact, having been the youngest in my family, this was perhaps the first time I found myself being the older and more mature one in a relationship outside of Josie and teaching. While Mabel was eighteen and I was twenty, there was a chasm in our experience. The farthest she'd been from Washington, DC, was New York—once. She lived at home and was doted on by her parents and brothers. She admired me for having seen so much of the country and pestered me endlessly with questions. I found her innocence to the ways of the world endearing.

On the other hand, Mabel played the violin exquisitely and painted the most lifelike portraits I'd ever seen—seemingly effortlessly. I learned so much from her knowledge of art, literature, and music. Her mother was the president of the local chapter of the National Association of Colored Women, and some of her passion for the advancement of women had rubbed off on her daughter.

If Edna was earth and Sadie fire, then Mabel was air, always waiting to take flight. Her tongue flitted from topic to topic, rarely landing on one. And with each lilting word, she seemed to pollinate the listener with joy. She immediately put me at ease. I quickly learned she also had a generous and accepting heart that could easily be overlooked due to her chatty personality.

While our differences could have stood between us, she was a hummingbird to my skylark, and we seemed to balance each other out. I reaped the benefit of her social fluttering as she introduced me to who she thought I'd like. Thanks to her, I was soon acquainted with a number of students on campus. She provided the cover I needed while I tried to find my way in this strange new world, and that buffer was more vital than I could ever have imagined.

Up until now, books had been the key to unlocking my own mind, and they freed me from the future that was foretold by my past. Learning had always been a matter of survival. When the world tried to chain me to the limitations of my birth, knowledge helped me feel boundless.

Here, however, with no external threat to my existence and no demands on my time besides learning, I felt small and of little consequence. Dwarfed by the genius of those I was learning from and of my fellow students. Nothing was at stake besides the measure of my own brilliance, and doubt began to edge out my own knowing.

Imbibing others' ideas and theories, I felt my own voice start to falter. Weaken. Even my poems, which had once been my portal back to myself, were starting to ebb out of me. I feared that the rules of syntax were suffocating my creative flow. That I was becoming pedantic. Earthbound. More duck than skylark. Ironically, the more educated I became, the less space there seemed to be for my unfettered, poetic self. Was this just another shackle in disguise?

Carnegie Library, where I spent hours poring over dense, decaying books, became both my refuge and my prison. The deafening silence amplified doubt's reproof. "Do you really think you can compete with these brilliant minds? Letting you in was a mistake," which echoed unrelentingly through the hallways of my mind. The weighty tomes encircling me jeered at my presumptuous arrogance.

Grappling to find my bearings, I clung to my professors as to a life raft, hoping they'd help me find my way back to my own spirit. One of my most influential teachers was Dr. Alain Locke, my philosophy professor. The students were all in awe of him because he was the first Colored man to receive a Rhodes scholarship to go to Oxford University in England. Mabel, whose three older brothers had all studied at Howard, said we were lucky to have him as a teacher.

"Locke was teaching English when my oldest brother, Charles, was a senior, and he couldn't stop talking about him. Norman was so disappointed when Locke went to Harvard to get his PhD—just like W.E. B. Dubois, you know. When Locke returned two years ago, in time for Norman's junior year, my brother was overjoyed! All he could talk about was the 'New Negro' this, the 'New Negro' that. That's what he calls us, you know. Negroes. I like it a shade better than Colored, don't you?

"Anyhow, Father, who's a mathematician, had all but had enough of what he calls 'fancy talk.' I've heard that other faculty think Locke's a rabble-rouser. I didn't read it, but they say his thesis debunks all theories of classification. He says nothing is absolute. I'm not sure what that means, but it sounds grand, don't you think? Did you know that when he got to England, he couldn't get into the first colleges he tried because of his race? Even though he was a Rhodes Scholar! So, it's not just here … Oh, look at the time, we'll be late to class!"

Professor Lorenzo Turner, the head of the English department, inspired me in a different way. Where Professor Locke challenged me to think for myself and stretch beyond all I'd assumed to be true, Professor Turner taught me to understand and love the subtle nuances of the English language. He had an eagle eye for detail and was the most structured of my teachers. At the same time, he was an enchanting speaker with a soft, mesmerizing voice, and he was one of the most handsome teachers we had.

"You know, he was a star debater when he studied here, in addition to being an amazing baseball player," Mabel informed me. "If it weren't for that dratted Geneva Townes who bewitched him into marrying her last year, I might have been the next Mrs. Turner," she said, tilting her head back, only half joking. She had quick, sparkling eyes and a figure that turned heads wherever she went.

"Norman thought he could woo Geneva, poor boy. He didn't stand a chance! If you weren't already married, I'd have him court you, Maggie. Wouldn't it be fun if you were my sister-in-law?"

I laughed at her enthusiasm as we entered the lecture hall.

In June 1919, Congress had agreed to the Nineteenth Amendment to the Constitution. Women could vote! A year later, we were preparing for the presidential elections. Although I was just shy of being old enough to vote, I still got swept up in the excitement. All the people I knew and respected were ready to kick the ruling party out of power. Dyer supported Harding's candidacy, and Frank was keeping long hours.

"After eight years of President Wilson, we're ready for new blood. When he was elected the first time around, he promised us, and I quote—since I was just reading it today: 'Not more grudging justice but justice executed with liberality and cordial good feeling!' Ha! He's the one who allowed government offices to be segregated—saying it would help ease racial tensions, of course. He did nothing about the Jim Crow laws or lynchings. Enough!" Frank said, one of the rare times in recent months we had sat together to eat dinner.

"Maggie, did you hear the latest charges against Harding? They say his great-grandfather was from the West Indies, and his great-grandmother was Colored. Whether it's true or not, it just makes me like him all the more!"

Mabel and I signed up to volunteer for the elections. During our training, Mary Church Terrell came to talk to us about how we could help women who would be voting for the first time.

"It is an honor to have Mary with us today," the young man who was introducing her beamed. "She is a woman of many firsts. She is one of the first Colored women to go to college, one of the founding members of the National Association for the Advancement of Colored People and the first president of the National Association of Colored Women. She's also the president of the Women's Republican League and has been an important contributor to Harding."

As Mary took to the stage and surveyed the audience, I was struck by how regal and at ease she looked. Her back was straight, and her wavy, silver-streaked hair nestled atop her head in an elegant bun, her head up and face still as she took us in with a gaze both warm and resolute. Her high-collared dress with silver-and-gold embroidery added to her royal demeanor.

Mabel leaned toward me and whispered, "Mother loves her and joined the NACW because she was so inspired by her. She says we should thank Mollie—that's what her close friends and family call her—for the right to vote. She's been campaigning for it for at least a decade."

The matronly woman sitting on Mabel's other side *tsk-tsk*ed us for talking, and we fell silent. I was mesmerized by Mary's rich, honeyed voice. She emphasized the importance of putting women at ease as we walked them through the process. "We want these first-time voters to feel proud of being part of a historic event, rather than awkward and ashamed."

On Election Day, Mabel and I arrived at the polling place, a local high school, in LeDroit Park at 4:00 a.m. to help set up. It was dark out, and the crisp November air was frosty. By the time the polling place was ready to open, the line was so long it snaked around the corner. Although explaining over and over again to first-time voters what to do was at times exhausting, the excitement of this historic moment swept me up.

The women were dressed in their Sunday best, pushing prams and soothing restless children. I didn't fully understand the magnitude of what it meant for us to have the right to vote until this moment, seeing the reverence and seriousness on their faces as they bent over their voting slip and scribbled their name or wrote an X. That night, for the first time in months, a poem slipped in before doubt's guards could intervene.

Hope

The fluttering
In my heart.

The rustling
Of the wind,
Whispering
Of better days
To come.

The part of me
That dares to dream
Of a world
Where my daughters
Stand equal
To my sons.

Where my children
Carry the
Color of their skin
With pride
Rather than
A source of shame.

*The music
Of love,
Of change,
The bright green
Of fresh growth
After a long frost.*

*Hope.
The new friend
That joins me
As I step
Into a novel world
Of possibility.*

The Brinkmans held one of their famous parties in celebration of Warren Harding's landslide victory. I invited Mabel, and she spent the night in the Brinkmans' guest room and joined us for breakfast the next morning.

"Maggie, did you see Geneva in her indigo-blue dress? Didn't she look beautiful? And wasn't Professor Turner dashing? I loved the musicians! I wish I could play the fiddle like that. It makes me wish I wasn't so classically trained … Did you see the *petits-fours* they served? They were divine! Wouldn't you love to go to Paris? Let's go there someday, Maggie!"

I laughed, as I always did when Mabel gushed and I couldn't get a word in edgewise.

Frank was silent. When she left, he looked at me pensively, as though seeing me in a new light.

"She's very young, isn't she?" he mused. "With the life you've lived, it's so easy for me to forget your age until I see you with someone like Mabel."

Although I didn't quite know why, fear reared on its hind legs, writhing unhappily in my chest, but I pushed it away. In that moment, I was too happy to worry.

Chapter Thirty-Seven

Unpacking the Past

Sarah

Of course, after psyching myself up to confront my mother with what I'd found in Dad's things, she wasn't there. As I knocked on her door for the second time, I suddenly remembered she'd said she was going to try a 9:00 a.m. exercise class at the local YMCA—having been inspired by my running and yoga. She must have left while I was still rummaging in the attic.

I decided to tackle the letters in the shoebox while I waited for her to return. They had been thrown in haphazardly, so I started sorting them by name of sender. The biggest stack was letters from Ada … "Aunt Ada!" I finally remembered. A letter postmarked August 2, 1965, to an address in Warsaw (Saul Baum c/o Piotr Krakowski) caught my eye.

I took it out of its envelope, which, like all the others, had the stamp cut out of it (yet another mystery to solve).

Dearest little brother,
  I hope you made it to Warsaw without too much trouble. How was your first time in an airplane? I'm jealous! I can't wait to try. I still remember the boat ride from Poland when I was 9. I was seasick for all three weeks. I

thought it would never end. I'm glad there are other ways to travel now!

Please give my regards to cousin Piotr. We were all so relieved to hear they'd managed to flee to Switzerland during the war. I wonder what he's like now. When I was 7 and he was 12, he was a little rough and wild. Mother had to complain to her brother about the bruises I got from our last visit. But don't tell him that.

I know you're angry with me that I never told you about Father. You said that I chose Mother over you. That our closeness was built on a lie. I understand you feel betrayed. I'm so sorry! Believe me, it broke my heart not to tell you. I knew how hungry you were for stories of him.

The truth is, for years, we didn't know what had happened, whether Father was dead or alive. After Mother lost contact, we hoped it was because he'd escaped without being able to send word and was on his way. That one day, he'd arrive at our doorstep, and we'd tell you who he was.

And then, the letter came, and we found out he'd died in Auschwitz. You were still so young, only four at the time, so Mother made the decision to save you the pain the rest of us had to go through. Because you were the only one with no memories of him, she thought she was giving you a clean slate.

I came close to telling you so many times, especially as you got older. But I wanted to trust that Mother knew what was best. And I wasn't sure how knowing might change you. You always seemed so much more innocent and whole than the rest of us. Untouched by what we'd lived through. Still able to be awed by the beauty of the world. Which comes through so clearly in your art. I wonder if you would still have painted the way you did, had you known.

I'm sorry you had to find out the way you did, but I'm

relieved you know. You might not want to hear this, but keeping the "how" of Father's death a secret has been hard on me. I want you to know that everything else I told you about him was true.

It was brave of you to decide to go to Auschwitz so you can better understand who you are. Where you came from. I know I couldn't ever go. I'm also grateful you were humble enough to accept Mother's gift of the airfare. She felt so guilty when she saw how you reacted. I don't think it had ever occurred to her that not telling you might be a mistake.

I know you have big life decisions ahead of you. I'm so sad you might not want me to be part of them, but know that I'm always here if you need anything.

Your loving sister, Ada

Just as I'd finished reading the letter as if on cue, I heard my mother's car pulling into the driveway. I put the letter down and, deliberately not giving myself the chance to change my mind, went to check in with her about a good time to talk.

She came to my room an hour later, having showered and eaten a late breakfast.

In the meantime, my nemesis and cheerleader had been ping-ponging back and forth in their advice.

Don't mess this up! You know she hates it when you're emotional!

You've got this! Don't worry—just be you!

In the end, I'd landed on an intention to stay grounded and not project my emotions onto my mother, as well as a reminder that I wasn't responsible for how she might react.

"What did you want to show me, Sarah?" my mother asked, and I thought I detected just a hint of nervousness in her voice. Neither of us liked unknowns. At all.

I patted the side of my bed as an invitation for her to sit on it and watched her lower her body gingerly onto my quilted comforter.

"Good exercise class?" I asked with a smile, trying to break the ice a little.

"You could say that. Enough to remind me I'm not thirty-four," she said, making me laugh.

After an awkward moment of neither of us knowing quite what to say, I handed her the portrait of me.

"Do you remember seeing this?" I asked.

She held the drawing for a long time, although after a while she was no longer looking at it. Her eyes instead focused on something beyond my grasp. She looked back at the sketch.

"This is really good. I'd forgotten how good he was …"

"So, you knew he drew?"

"Yes, although it was long before we met. And I'm quite sure he never showed me this drawing of you. I would remember. He really captured you. What you were like then." I could see a shimmer of tears dancing in her eyes.

"From what he told me, he was quite passionate about art as a child and got a lot of recognition for it from his teachers. But his mother was adamant he study something practical. He told me that since he had no interest in accounting or medicine, law seemed like an acceptable choice. He had always been fascinated by history and politics."

"Yeah, I remember how animated he would get when you guys talked politics at the dinner table."

The rare times we ate together, I thought, but didn't say.

"Well, as I recall, when it came to politics, he talked and I listened. But yes, he would."

"That's what he studied in college. Politics?"

"He double majored in political science and history with a minor in art. And I'll have you know he graduated summa cum laude and got a full scholarship for law school. Your father was no slouch, of that you can rest assured."

"That's amazing! Though I'm not surprised. He was so smart. Half the time, I had no idea what he was talking about."

Amanda chuckled, "Yes, sometimes I didn't either."

"Mom …" I said, gathering my courage to ask the one question that was really troubling me. "Why wouldn't he have given me this drawing? Why would he have stuck it in an academic article?" My voice quivered, suspended on a thin line of composure before breaking into a choked sob.

"Oh, honey," The term of endearment slipped out of her mouth like it had always lived there. I scanned my mother's face for a reaction, but she didn't seem to have noticed what she'd said. Or if she had, she wasn't in any way phased.

"I'm afraid I don't. We didn't really share those kinds of things with each other. And by the time I knew him, he had pretty much stopped making art altogether. He made one sketch of me when we were dating—to impress me, he later told me—but the few pieces of his that I saw were from his childhood and student years."

"Do we have them somewhere?"

"No, even at that time, it was your father's oldest sister, Ada, who had them. She showed them to me once when we were visiting her in New York. You were still a baby." I had so many questions, including about my aunt, but decided to stick with the original topic at hand.

"Why did he stop drawing? Did he just get too busy with work?"

"I think he was still drawing throughout law school as a way to relieve some of the pressure from his studies and because he loved it. When he graduated, he was at a crossroads. He had to decide whether to become a lawyer or an artist. He was the kind of person who threw himself completely into whatever he did, and he knew that if he tried to do both, he'd be dissatisfied."

I nodded. I could see that about him. And my mother too.

They were well matched in that way.

"And then, he discovered something about how his father died that he hadn't known …" She stopped, and her cheeks flushed a light pink, probably realizing I didn't know either. Seeing that this was a good segue, I showed her the ledger with Isaac's name.

"Do you mean this?"

My mother nodded, so slowly that the movement was barely perceptible. "Oh, Sarah, I'm so sorry I never told you. Saul always said he would when you were a little older—when the time was right—then he died. And you were so angry with me. I didn't know how to bring it up. And as you know, I've always looked at the past as a hindrance to the future. I guess kind of like your Grandma Valda. I didn't realize what I was depriving you of."

"I do wish I'd known. At least when I was a little older, in my college years. I was so lost."

"I see that now, and I *am* sorry." She looked so contrite I had a sudden insight into how it might have been for her.

"But I know we weren't close then, and I can see why it would've been hard for you without Dad there. It wasn't really your story to tell. And I might not have been ready then, so, really, now's the perfect time."

My mother let out a big sigh of relief. I suddenly saw that she was in mortal fear of making a mistake, that much of her tightness came from the impossibly high standards she set for herself. I patted her hand, and this time, she took mine in hers.

"Thank you. Anyway, to get back to what I was saying, when Saul found out about how Isaac died, he decided to go to Auschwitz. He needed to know who he was."

"Yes, I'm getting that sense," I said, but decided to wait until she was finished to bring up Ada's letters. One thing at a time.

"The whole experience of being in Auschwitz—seeing the train tracks, the gas chambers, the piles of hair, shoes, glasses …" She paused, trying to remember and also scanning my face—probably trying to gauge what was too much for me.

"It was devastating for him. Shook him to the core of his being. On the plane ride back, he picked up a newspaper for the journey. He saw a picture of President Johnson signing the Voting Rights Act into law. And that's when he knew."

"Knew what?"

"That he *had* to be a lawyer, he told me. He said that although they had followed the passage of the Civil Rights Act closely in his classes, it had felt like a distant reality until he knew in his own bones what the price of freedom was. That—I'll always remember him saying this—it was a time for action, not art."

"Wow. That's a lot to take in," I said, my mind reeling from all this information. I took a few breaths to let her words sink in and settle my heart rate before I asked, "Why did his father stay behind?"

"All I know is that he was a doctor and didn't want to leave his patients. At the onset of World War II, as soon as Germany invaded Poland, as I recall, your grandmother had the prescience to contact relatives in the United States. They got a visa very quickly, probably because they were among the first to apply, but your grandfather wouldn't go. He said it would blow over. And that if it didn't, he would join them later. Valda ended up going with her two—no, three—children without him, hoping she could convince him to join them later, I'm guessing."

"So, she had to choose between her husband and saving her kids? That's horrible!"

"Yes, I know."

"Was Dad a baby when they left? He was born in 1940, wasn't he? July 11th?"

"Yes ... from what I know, Valda was just barely pregnant with your father when they left, but she didn't actually realize it until after they'd arrived in the United States." She stopped, seeing my face. I was feeling my grandmother's pain: coming to a new country, having left her husband behind, with three young kids, and realizing she was going to give birth to another who might never know his father.

"Poor Babcia Valda. So much loss. Such tough decisions. I understand a bit better why she didn't tell Dad. I never really thought about having Jewish ancestry before. You and Dad were so anti-religion, and we never celebrated anything," I said, trying to clear my voice of reproach, but unable to keep the emotion out of it.

"I know, Sarah. I'm sorry," she said, choking a little on the word—apologizing did not come easily to her. "We'd both seen how hurtful and rigid religion could be and didn't want any part of it. For ourselves or you. We thought we were protecting you."

"I just wish I could have shared that with him. Something ... Asked him more questions." The words started coming haltingly as tears rolled down my face. My mother held my hand and said nothing until they had subsided.

"Maybe we should take a break, for now, Sarah. This is a lot all at once."

"It is, but I have another question I need to ask," I said, wiping my face and begging my fried nervous system to hold on. "Mom, you mentioned Aunt Ada. What did you know about her?" I asked, showing her the letters and describing the little I could remember from my childhood encounters with her.

"Honestly, I don't know much. When we met, she was the only one of his siblings he was still in touch with. She was nine years older than he was, and because their mother had to work so hard to put food on the table, I think Ada became like a second mother to him."

I shuffled the old, yellowed papers in my hands. "It sounds like he was pretty mad that she didn't tell him about their father."

"Yes, he said they were somewhat estranged for a few years after that, but then he made his peace with it, realizing she'd really just been following his mother's wishes and that the choice had been made in order to protect him."

"Did she have any kids?" I wondered, realizing I might have cousins somewhere.

"One, as I recall. A daughter … Eva? Evie? Something like that. I met her a couple of times when she was around fifteen or sixteen. Then she went to college somewhere on the West Coast—she graduated high school a year early—and I never saw her after that."

"What about Dad's other siblings?"

"I think they both lived in Israel. I don't know anything else. Saul wasn't close to them."

"Do you know what happened to Ada? I remember we just stopped seeing her at some point. Did she die?"

"No, she didn't die, at least not at that time. I don't really know the details. When we met, your dad was in his mid-thirties, and I was just a couple of years younger. We both had our share of baggage. We had a tacit agreement to leave the past where it was and start afresh with each other. We told each other what was strictly necessary. The broad brushstrokes of our past."

Until the past few months, I wouldn't have thought my parents had many skeletons in their respective closets. I'd somehow assumed they'd both been born super driven and wedded to their careers, but I was starting to recognize how much I didn't know about them.

"Did he say *anything*?"

"I remember asking him why we hadn't seen her in a while.

He said they'd had a falling-out. She'd found something out about his past she couldn't abide ..." She paused, scanning me, as though trying to decide how much she should tell me.

"I promise I will tell you what I know another day. But I think this is quite enough for you to chew on for today."

Both my head and my heart felt like they were going to explode, so I had to reluctantly agree.

A few days later, my mother arranged to get a ride to and from work so I could use her car for the day. I needed to clear my mind, which had been spinning on its own axis since my discovery in the attic and the subsequent conversation with Amanda. I had decided not to pester her about what it was Aunt Ada "couldn't abide" in my father's past, but that didn't mean I didn't wonder.

After researching various Bay Area hikes, I picked one in Marin County that had waterfalls and redwoods.

The beginning of the trail was elevated and wide with stunning ocean views. I felt my body settle as my lungs gulped in the crisp air. My head was mercifully free from any thought. When I got to the top of the waterfall, I was delighted to see there was still water flowing down the mossy rocks, even this late in the year.

The falls weren't very wide or deep compared to others in the area, but they meandered in the form of a rushing brook for about a mile. Crossing numerous wooden bridges, I admired the yellow-legged frogs jumping happily in the stiller pools of water, albeit from afar. A sign at the trailhead had warned of the species' endangerment and entreated visitors to keep a respectful distance from their habitat. I followed the now dense forest thicket down to a clearing that housed a grove of large redwoods.

A wide sunbeam lit up the center of the grove, as though

inviting me to step in, so I did, feeling a strange sense of déjà vu even though I knew I'd never been on this trail before. I shook off the feeling and looked around me. The base of the largest tree was huge, but was also hollowed out and charred by past fires.

The sun warmed the top of my head, shoulders, and thighs. I sat cross-legged on the soft bed of pine needles, palms up, and closed my eyes.

"Trust," I heard. Or felt. Or sensed.

"Everything is just as it's meant to be. You are loved. You are part of a much larger reality that is guiding and supporting you. Trust."

The wisdom spread from my sun-drenched crown down through every muscle, bone, and tissue of my body. My cells felt as though they were vibrating with the truth of this message.

A moment later, I was shivering. I opened my eyes and saw that the sun had moved away—as though a portal had opened, downloaded the information, and closed again. I got up, and feeling suddenly hungry, ate my picnic lunch by the side of the stream.

Examining the park map I'd picked up at the entrance, I saw that the trail continued to a lake. Stretching my legs, I decided to keep exploring. As soon as I arrived at the turquoise-green waters lined with thin, tall pines, I remembered. The grove, the path, the lake were exactly the same as what I'd seen in my hypnotherapy vision.

I sat with a thud in the middle of the dirt road.

"What?" I said, holding my head in between my knees. How was this possible? I knew for a fact I'd never been here before. And then I felt/heard/sensed it again.

"Trust. You are guided and supported."

Chapter Thirty-Eight
Spring to Summer 1921

Crossroads

Maggie

The winter frost had thawed and given way to spring. Sadie, Thomas, and I went to see the cherry blossoms that had been a gift from Japan to the city almost a decade earlier. The day was clear and crisp. The beauty of the delicate white and pink florets fanning out against the deep blue of the sky took my breath away. Next to me, Thomas cooed with delight.

My internal landscape, however, didn't match the vivacity of the outer world. Now, in the second semester of my first year at Howard, I was feeling more frozen and desolate than ever. Barren but for the doubt (and its twin, fear) that were spreading to the farthest reaches of my mind and body. Like parasitic plants, they suffocated all other life within me until I could no longer feel the stirrings of my heart.

As I filled my head with others' ideas and words, learned the rules of rhyme and verse, and heard the brilliance of my fellow students as they read their creations to the class, I felt more and more cut off from my own voice. Nothing kills inspiration like comparison, I learned. I was so focused on trying to make up for lost time and cram as much learning into my head as I could, that there was no space for my words to grow. I hadn't written a poem in months, not since election day.

As a child working with my family for the Tanners, and even in New York, school had been my doorway back to myself, a way to know my mind. A key to possibilities that were otherwise closed to me. But now, I felt like I had to choose—between others' knowing and my own.

I started wondering if I'd made a mistake. If I'd aimed too high. The thoughts crossed my mind so often that I considered dropping out. At night, fear reminded me of the bargain I'd made in the wild.

"You promised you wouldn't want too much. It was okay when things were landing in your lap. But this. *You* wanted this. You asked for this. Nothing good can come of it."

Fear and doubt were ripe soil for the guilt and grief I'd been pushing away for so long. One day as I was ascending the library's stairs—my bag laden with books and paper—I felt apprehension clutching at my ribcage, squeezing the breath out of me. With each step, my legs felt heavier and heavier. I stopped at the last one and looked up. The columns loomed tall and forbidding over my comparatively small body. They seemed to be judging me as being unworthy of the precious information they were charged with guarding. Chills ran down my spine.

"It's just a building," I told myself, but I had to coax my feet to climb the last step. As I wrestled the heavy door open, my heart pounded in my chest.

Once inside, I found my way to a table in the furthest corner of the room, back turned to the marble busts lining the wall, in case they, too, disapproved.

I sat for what felt like hours, staring at the words "I come from …" on the blank page in front of me. Professor Locke had assigned us an autobiographical paper starting with those simple but mind-boggling three words. He said it would help him understand who we were as people, and therefore as philosophers, because, as he put it, our history informed our thinking.

I stared until the three words started blurring on the page. My forehead throbbed with the effort of thought. And still, nothing came. I closed my eyes, hoping inspiration might come more easily with no visual distractions. As soon as I did, I saw Andre and Papa's bodies dangling from the tree.

Tears stung my throat, and I had to choke back the cry that threatened to break the deafening silence of the library. I rushed outside, ran down the steps, and fell to the ground, sobbing uncontrollably as my unspent sorrow poured out of me. I coughed, cried, and retched out my pain until I felt like I'd been wrung empty.

Just then, looking up from where I'd been doubled over, I saw a doe standing a few feet away from me, her body outlined against the setting sun. I blinked a few times, thinking my eyes were playing tricks on me, but each time I opened them, she was still there. Ears perked up, forming a V with her oval face. Big, limpid eyes stared at me intently, her body unmoving, though every muscle seemed to be on alert. I wondered what she was doing here, in the middle of the city. I had a sudden memory of the doe I'd seen in the forest and felt a stirring in my heart I hadn't felt for a long time.

And then, in a flash, she turned and bounded away. I stayed for a moment, to see if she would come back. Realizing she wouldn't, I went back inside to gather my belongings. I felt weak and shaky. Spent. Not sure how I'd make it back home.

Somehow, despite feeling dazed, I managed to find my way back. As I turned my key in the lock, I hoped by some miracle Frank would be home. He wasn't. He had been working long hours, trying to push the Dyer anti-lynching bill through, and often came home after I was asleep. And I sensed there was something else.

Although we rarely talked about it, I knew he longed for a child. Every time I had my monthly bleeding, I could feel his disappointment. He started turning toward me less in bed and coming home later. He was still haunted by his first wife's suicide and sometimes called her name out in his sleep. Even though her heartbreak was precipitated by the threat to her father's life and her husband's involvement in the anti-lynching movement, I knew Frank traced the origin of her pain back to the loss of their babies.

Lying in our empty bed that night, his absence felt palpable. I yearned for the warmth of his body. The words that used to flow so freely between us. Nowadays, what wasn't said seemed to hang like an invisible curtain between us.

Needing some comfort, I went to get the stone I'd found so many years before. I could use some of its luck now. Stroking its smooth, polished surface, I finally fell into troubled sleep.

I dreamt that Mr. Tanner was standing in front of me, blocking the door to Carnegie library. "Who do you think you are? I only sent you to school to get you out of the way! Don't forget. You will never be free!"

Then, I was at a fork in the road. On the left side was the deer, who instructed me to follow my heart. On the right side were Mama, Papa, and Andre. Frank. Edna and Josie. Sadie. I chose the path on the right, but then they were all grabbing at me, all wanting something both for and from me that I wasn't sure I could give them. I felt overwhelmed and paralyzed. I sat down in the middle of the road, holding my ears, trying to block out all the noise.

When I woke up, my stomach was churning as though I were ill, and Frank's side of the bed was still cold. Locke's assignment was due that day, and I considered staying home. But judging that as cowardly, I chose to go to class. My head hanging in shame, I turned in a blank page, except for a hastily written "I'm sorry, I couldn't do it."

The day Professor Locke was due to give us our papers back, he asked me to stay back after class. I waited for the last student to file out with growing trepidation, although I also felt relief that it would all be over soon because the wait had been agonizing. I fully expected him to fail me and chastise me for my lack of discipline.

"Maggie, what happened?" he asked instead, his voice kind. Concerned.

Both his care and the question threw me back to that night. Crouching in the tall grass. What happened?

"I shouldn't be here," I said, feeling the tears threatening to spill over again.

"What do you mean?"

"My father and brother were lynched, and I saw it. I had to flee from home because my Mama feared they would come after me. That's the only reason I'm here. If they were still alive, I wouldn't be here. It's not right …" My voice faltered and broke as the tears flowed down my cheeks and chin, pooling at my collarbone.

Professor Locke waited in respectful silence, his usually solemn eyes brimming with compassion.

When he sensed I wasn't going to say more, he said, "Maggie, I'm very sorry to hear about your father and brother. Nobody should live through what you did, although so many of our people do. But it's rare that they end up here. I can understand how you're feeling. But I also think what happened to them makes it so much more important for you to share your story. That perhaps you even owe it to them to describe what happened. Since you were the only one who saw," he suggested, his tone gentle.

His words stayed with me, and this time I decided to take my writing material to the park instead of the library. As I dragged my pen across the page, I felt like I was crawling through a swamp of pain and memories I had blocked out. I didn't know how I could write my story without being frozen by the agony of having to relive it. I closed my eyes, and an image of the deer flashed before me.

"I don't have to start with the pain," came the thought, unbidden. And all of a sudden, I remembered the words I uttered to lull myself to sleep as I worked on the railroad.

"I come from cotton and wheat. From the sweet taste of sugar cane juice dripping down my lips and coating my chin with its sticky residue. I come from love so deep it defies the white man's wrath at every turn. I come from sorrow that knows no bounds until it grows wings and soars above its captors with immeasurable joy …"

As I began to write, the rest soon poured out of me. Mr. Tanner's son, Papa, and Andre. My foray into the forest. All the odd jobs I did as a boy. Pepe and Hank. Finally landing a home with the Joneses and how they'd saved my life and gave me a second chance. Meeting Frank and moving to Washington, DC. So elated was I that my voice had returned—or at the very least that doubt had been momentarily kept at bay—that I was barely aware of the pain that accompanied the memories.

A week later, Professor Locke asked me to stay after class again.

"Maggie, I am rarely speechless. Anyone who knows me can tell you that. But your essay—if I can call it that, as it has the makings of a memoir—astounded me," he said, beaming, and I felt almost shy at the praise.

"First off, it's not often I read such raw prose from one of my students. The voice here is very different from your more academic papers. Second, as I knew it would be from what you told me, your story is heart-wrenching."

*

From the day at the park onward, I felt myself begin to reconnect to my own voice. Although guilt and doubt still crept in at times, I'd quieted the voice telling me that I didn't belong and started believing I had a unique point of view that might be of value to others.

At the end of the semester, Alain Locke asked me if I was interested in joining him and a few other students over the summer to dive deeper into his ideas for advancing what he called "Negro art and culture."

Even though I didn't know exactly what it entailed, I immediately accepted. I knew both the intelligence and the depth of the compassion hiding behind Professor Locke's formidable eyebrows and penetrating gaze, and thought I could only benefit from his mentorship.

Among Howard students, there were generally two camps where Alain was concerned: those who revered his audacity and put him on a pedestal, and those who dismissed him as haughty, standoffish, and overly exacting.

He didn't mince words, had no tolerance for fools, and held everyone to the standards he hoped to convince the world to live up to. Although others withered under his critical pen, I relished getting my essays back, parsed with his small, meticulous script. I was always disappointed when they came back with little comment. I asked him about it once.

"When you write about your life, Maggie, it's unfiltered emotion coursing through you. No frills or pretensions. Stylistic comments on that type of writing would be like clipping a wild bush to mold it to someone else's artistic sensibility. You have something that can't be taught, and which many would envy. Never forget that. If you do, I view it as my job to remind you."

With classes out, Frank agreed to take a weekend off work in early June to celebrate the high note my first year at Howard had ended on and to attempt to reconnect. The Brinkmans had friends with a cabin on Chesapeake Bay we could stay at for a couple of days.

But at the end of May, what was later dubbed the "Tulsa Massacre" occurred. Frank went to Oklahoma to gather testimonials from witnesses, and we canceled our trip.

When he came back three weeks later, he was tense and shut down and gave me few details of what transpired. Though he didn't say much to me, I overheard him talking to Benjamin about it in the garden between our cottage and their house.

"I've never seen anything like it, Benjamin, and I've seen a lot. The entire Greenwood District—have you heard of it? They call it the Negro Wall Street—completely burned to the ground. Over a thousand residences. Some said low-flying planes rained bullets down on people. The official death toll is thirty-nine, but we counted upwards of a hundred dead and eight hundred injured. Over ten thousand people were left homeless. All because a young boy may have bumped into a white elevator girl on the way to the service washroom for Negroes! This bill has to pass, Benjamin, or we have to find other means, but things can't stay like this!"

On June 14, Mabel and I joined a silent march denouncing lynching. I had asked Frank if he wanted to go with us, but he'd said he was too busy organizing things behind the scenes. It was about half the size of the march in New York five years earlier, but no less solemn.

We passed the Capitol before making our way to the White House. One man held a placard with the picture of a man hanging, the question "Is this civilization?" underneath. Next to me, a few women held up a banner with the words: "Congress discusses constitutionality while the smoke of human bodies darkens the heavens."

Mabel nudged me and pointed. I followed her gaze and

saw Mary Church Terrell, who was one of the organizers of the march. I was amazed that one person could have a hand in so many different things.

After spending a couple of weeks in Harlem, Professor Locke returned to his summer study group with fire in his eyes as he described the flourishing of Negro music and literature there. He told us he was doing research into this new Negro movement that was unfolding there and in other parts of the nation, saying he hoped some of us would become part of it. I had felt a little intimidated by the three young men in the group, whose fathers were prominent members of the community. In that moment, however, I felt the power of Locke's passion dissolve any remaining doubt I might have.

In July, when the Senate committee assigned to the Dyer bill gave it a favorable report, Frank was so happy he took me to New York the next weekend.

I had no memory of my first train ride to DC; I had been so nervous and excited. This time, I looked out the window the whole time, not wanting to miss a thing. I watched as the city vanished before my eyes. The trees then morphed into houses, into towns, and back into farmland, as if by the flick of a wand. I sent thanks to the tracks that were but a blur beneath us, and to those who laid them for carrying us to safety. My breasts ached a little as they remembered their hidden days as a boy doing similar work.

Frank and I stayed at a little hotel and we made love for the first time in many months. We visited with the Joneses during the day, reminiscing about the old days. I felt content, and my skylark—who'd been pretty silent these past months—started singing a song of hope that we would overcome the distance between us.

Chapter Thirty-Nine

Finding Solid Ground

Sarah

"You're right, Sarah, that is a lot," Patrick agreed when I'd filled him in on my father's drawing, the letter from my aunt, the talks with my mother, and the message I'd received in the grove of redwoods. "It also sounds like many things are moving and opening up for you. How've you been feeling through all of this?"

"It's hard to say, it's been so variable. Like I'm in quicksand, and every time I try to get up, I get pulled back under. I feel some peace around the knowledge that I was deeply loved. And I felt so serene after my hike. But when I woke the next morning, I felt bowled over with sadness. For my grandmother. My father. Myself. For what could have been."

Patrick nodded. "That's understandable. These things often come in waves. And you've just had a huge information dump—some of it very traumatic, like finding out about your grandfather."

I felt myself start to choke up just thinking about him, so I took slow, deep breaths until the panicky feeling had settled.

"You're really learning how to soothe your nervous system, Sarah. That's a big shift!"

"Yeah, it's good to remember I know how. It's easy to

forget when I'm triggered."

"Very true. And you know, even some of the more positive aspects of your discoveries—like recognizing how much your father really loved you—are still going to take time to fully process." Patrick added gently.

"That's for sure. I've also been realizing that this sense of groundlessness is how I felt most of my childhood. My life kept being upended, and there was no person or place that I could depend on that felt reliable." I stopped, noticing how similar my current emotional state was. I'd been so focused on returning to work. Without a concrete goal to replace the old one, I felt untethered. "That feeling of stillness being deadening, I think that's when it started. I learned to find safety in continual movement and change."

"It was a smart strategy at the time. And I'm glad you're learning ways to stay in one place while still accessing your aliveness."

"Yes, me too. There are some unexpected benefits to staying in place, I have to say! Who would've thought? Like Phoebe—and my mother, of all people!" As I said that, I swayed side to side in my chair, feeling how perfectly my butt molded to the seat.

See, there's solidity right here, my inner cheerleader—or perhaps my knowing?—reminded me.

Patrick nodded in agreement as he made a note to himself.

"But I have been wondering if it ever ends."

"If what ever ends?"

"I mean, I know healing is an ongoing process, but is it always this intense? I feel like I keep on finding more and more mysteries I need to solve before I get to be whole, or me, or … something."

"You certainly have been on the accelerated track these past few months," Patrick said, and I was surprised by how relieved and validated I felt. "In my experience, there are often acute phases or crises that prompt deeper healing, and then it plateaus for a while. Until you get to the next layer of the onion that needs to be peeled. Or the next level of the video game. Whichever metaphor you prefer ..."

"Um, neither? Those are terrible!" I teased. "But seriously, first it was my inner children, and when they felt a little more settled, the nightmares were out of control, and just as I'd started making a little headway with Maggie following the hypnotherapy session and research, the ancestral trauma has hijacked my attention ... One loose thread just leads to another, until I'm just dangling at the seams, with nothing resolved."

"I understand it might feel like you're hopping from one thing to the next. I also think you'll eventually see that many of the threads interconnect or mirror each other."

"What do you mean?"

"For example, we started with the limiting beliefs you developed as a child because that was what was most present and accessible. But many of *those beliefs* you picked up from your parents, so healing their trauma will also help your wounded inner child. And maybe the same is true with Maggie. I sense a common theme might be this feeling of having to choose ..." His voice trailed off as he let me process. I had a sudden memory of standing in the sunbeam, surrounded by redwood trees, and felt something shift within me.

"I'm not sure I understand rationally, but somehow, internally, I feel your words to be true. My brain wants everything to be pat and neat, but I sense that I'm being asked to let go of the need to know. To trust where I'm being guided to and not try to control things as much."

"Exactly! I can feel that the message you received during your hike is already impacting you. And I think you'll get even more from exploring your family tree."

"I hope so, but I don't really know where to start. Without

my father's letters, the ones to him feel very incomplete. I googled 'Ada Baum' but I didn't really get anywhere. I don't know where she lives or if she's even still alive. If she were, she'd be eighty."

"Have you tried any of the genealogical data websites?" he asked, and I shook my head no. "You could get DNA tested through them, which has helped a number of my clients get connected to relatives and even birth parents. Or you could sign up and just use the websites for research," he said as he jotted down a few links for me to start with.

"I'll definitely check them out, thanks."

I noticed a heaviness in my chest while I was thinking of how much I didn't know about my family history. The unknowns kept stretching out in front of me, and I needed something that felt certain, which reminded me of an idea I'd wanted to run by Patrick.

"On a different topic, I was adding to my joy list last night and noticed that one of the common threads was children in general—babies specifically. Everything feels so up in the air right now, and I've been thinking I could volunteer with children in some capacity. To help ground me in something I love and am good at."

"I like the idea, and I trust your judgment. The only thing I'd invite you to investigate is whether the volunteering will connect you more deeply to yourself or whether it's just a way to stay busy and avoid yourself."

"I'll keep that in mind. I've been feeling more in touch with my intuition recently, and I'm starting to trust that I'll know the difference."

"I'm very happy to hear that," Patrick said, the smile on his face highlighting his words.

On my bike ride home, I took a detour to the children's hospital. This time, the distinct hospital smell that hit me as soon as I entered the lobby put me at ease, unlike the day of the evaluation. I could feel my inner nemesis skirting around the edges of my mind, wanting to put me down for what a loser I was, but I pushed the thought away.

We're moving forward, not backward, I told myself instead.

"Hi, I was wondering if you had any information on volunteer opportunities?" I asked the receptionist.

She arched a perfectly tweezed eyebrow at me, as though wondering why I couldn't look online like everyone else but finally pointed at plastic holders on the wall containing various brochures. I took a few different ones but was immediately drawn to the one that read: "Become a volunteer baby cuddler in our NICU."

I mean ... Who doesn't want to cuddle babies? Said my inner cheerleader approvingly.

When I got home and examined the brochure more carefully, I could feel the excitement mounting. Premature and chronically ill babies who were in need of holding, without any of the responsibility of being the one in charge of their care. Heaven.

Thinking about what Patrick had said, I decided to sleep on it and see how I felt in the morning rather than calling them right away.

That night, I had yet another nightmare. An older woman—Grandma Valda, it seemed—was pulling on my left arm. "Don't make me choose!" she pleaded.

Maggie pulled my other arm, shouting, "I can't choose!"

"Stop! You're going to rip me in two!" I screamed at them.

I woke with a gasp, my heart pounding in my chest, still feeling the agony of having to make an impossible choice. I hadn't had a nightmare in a while, and the force of it caught me by surprise. There was only one thing I knew with certainty.

I want to cuddle babies.

A smile broke through my night terror just at the thought

of holding those tiny, precious newborns. That was all the confirmation I needed. I might not be cut out to be an activist, but I did know how to hold a baby!

Chapter Forty
Winter 1922 - Fall 1923

Shipwrecked Souls

Maggie

Marriage was a strange beast. Two shipwrecked souls seeking shelter from our own ghosts, finding temporary refuge in each other's arms. What was left when the passion subsided, and we found ourselves living with this person who was at once the other side of our heart and the mirror of our darkest fears? Since Frank and I got married, sorrow and joy had become so entangled, I wasn't always sure which was which.

After the initial surge of hope over Dyer's bill, Frank's hard work started unraveling before his eyes. On a Friday night in early December 1922, he didn't come home at all. I slept fitfully and dreamt that the two of us were on a ship caught in a storm. Frank jumped into a life raft full of holes. I screamed at him that he should stay on the ship, but my words were lost in the wind.

The next morning, I went to the Brinkmans' in case they'd seen him—and for support if they hadn't.

"I heard something on the radio that the Dyer bill was killed in the Senate. That Senate Minority Leader Underwood had threatened to stall other bills important to the Harding administration if they didn't drop it," Benjamin said.

"Frank must be crushed—that's probably why he didn't come home, Maggie," Sadie tried to reassure me.

Just then, we heard the paper boy calling out. Sadie rushed out and returned a moment later with the newspaper in her hand. There it was on the front page.

"FILIBUSTER KILLS ANTI-LYNCHING BILL," Sadie read. "Republican Senators in Caucus Agree to Abandon the Dyer Measure. Deadlock Lasted a Week."

My heart twisted as I imagined how Frank had felt upon hearing this. I wished he were here for me to comfort him.

He came home late the next night, his breath smelling of stale rum, although we were still under Prohibition. His eyes had a glint I'd never seen in them before. Part of me wanted to pretend not to notice anything, afraid of the answer I might get if I questioned him. But I knew that if I didn't say anything, the chasm between us would only widen. Not quite sure what to say to make things better, I put my hand on his shoulder.

"Frank, I'm so sorry about the bill. You must be devastated. I wish I could have been there to comfort you," I said.

He didn't respond, staring blankly at the ceiling.

"Where did you go …" I started to ask, but before I had a chance to finish my sentence, he rolled over so his back was to me, and my hand slid down to the bed.

On the surface, nothing much changed after that—not immediately anyway, but it felt as though a shadow had joined us to form a threesome. And I wasn't sure which one of us would get crowded out.

Over the next few months, I watched helplessly as the shadow grew between us. It fed off Frank's pride, doubt, and fears, taking up residence in our little cottage. Since my attempts to talk to him only seemed to drive him further into shame and defensiveness, I stopped trying, telling myself that he would come back to me when things got better. Unfortunately, they only got worse.

On June 23, 1923, Marcus Garvey was sentenced to five years in prison for mail fraud. Although I didn't know the details, I knew that since the filibuster this past December, Frank had been following Marcus Garvey's Pan-African movement more closely than ever. I started finding literature for Garvey's Universal Negro Improvement Association (UNIA) strewn around the cottage. He'd underlined passages promoting the idea of developing Liberia as a permanent homeland for Negroes. The day after Marcus's conviction, we had dinner with Benjamin and Sadie.

"I read that there were some irregularities with Garvey's Black Star Line shipping company and that the books were poorly kept. I'm assuming that's just an excuse to get him out of the way," Sadie said when Frank brought it up.

"Yes, exactly. We all know it's politically motivated. He's been stirring up trouble, so they were looking for a reason to deport him back to Jamaica. And now they've found that reason! I'm thinking of helping him appeal the judgment," Frank said.

It was the first I'd heard of his plan.

Frank pinned his remaining hopes for the bill on President Harding, the first president to visit the South and openly condemn lynching while touring Birmingham, Alabama. He'd been a vocal supporter of the Dyer bill.

Over the summer, Harding undertook what he dubbed the "Voyage of Understanding," a two-month trip across the country. He was the first chief executive to visit Canada and Alaska. Toward the end of July, the papers reported that he was ill, presumably from eating shellfish, but that he was on the road to recovery. On August 2, 1923, he collapsed and died at the age of fifty-seven.

The nation was in shock. In the months after his death, various scandals erupted about his extramarital affairs and the corruption of his administration. Frank seemed to take both his death and the allegations as a personal betrayal. I watched, helpless, as he retreated further into a place where I couldn't reach him.

The shadow took over as Frank's lover, rendering me obsolete. Nothing breaks a powerful man faster than feeling useless. Frank needed a legacy, and in the face of perceived failure, something inside of him snapped.

Under Professor Locke's tutelage, I was beginning to find my wings at school. I'd been getting high marks, and Professor Turner was encouraging me to submit my poems to be published, although I wasn't sure I was ready for that type of attention. They both supported me in writing an autobiographical essay as my senior honors project.

My relative success only added salt to Frank's wounds and increased the rift between us. I knew that in his heart, Frank wanted me to succeed, yet I sensed that watching me blossom reinforced the shame, anger, and feelings of worthlessness encroaching on his soul.

In addition to my flourishing at school, my barren womb must have seemed like one more act of divine mockery to Frank. He started coming home later and later—and sleeping on the couch in the living room when he did, saying he didn't want to wake me.

Feeling him slipping away from me even more, I decided to try talking to him again, asking what I could do to help. He just shook his head, too trapped in his shadow to hear me when I said I didn't mind being woken up and that I wanted him to sleep next to me.

Some nights, he didn't come home at all. I learned that

no human can save another from the demons in their heart, no matter how much we love them. We can only hold up a mirror reflecting the beauty of their soul and hope they have the courage to look in and see the truth of it. At times, I blamed myself for being too caught up in my own pain, too distracted by my studies that I didn't do more sooner.

A few months after Harding died, realizing that nothing I did was helping, I left Frank a note on the couch.

> *Beloved Frank,*
>
> *Oh, that I could reach through your pain and show you the beauty of your being. That I could tear down the bars of hatred and free your soul to soar above the pettiness of the world in which we live. Oh, that my love could disarm the demons that have invaded your nights, shake your mind free of its tortured thoughts.*
>
> *But since you are on a path I cannot follow, at least for now, may you be free. May you know the depths of your power, regardless of the outcome of your actions. May you see that the path you are on has divine wisdom, whether you chose it or not. May you know joy, love, and ease.*
>
> *With love, always,*
> *Your Maggie*

That night, I thought I felt his presence in the room, his alcohol-laced breath as he kissed my cheek. But it could have been a dream. His only outward response to my letter was silence.

So, I had to sit back, powerless, as Frank spiraled further down into a cage of pain I could not free him from. He sought solace in drink and activism. I sought mine in poetry. Some days, bitterness gnawed at my heart that he could throw away what we had so easily, and if I'd seen him, I would probably have lashed out in anger. On other days, my love and worry for him shattered my heart and haunted my nights. Prohibition was in full force, and I had visions of Frank being arrested at one of the speakeasies I assumed he frequented.

Sorrow

Is the shadow side
Of my heart,
The remains
Of my dreams.

Is my muse
And my nemesis.
My eternal lover.

Even in times of joy,
I know
She will never
Leave my side—
Patient,
Ever faithful.

Sorrow
Is the stone
In the hollow
Of my stomach
That reminds me
I am alive,
Rooted
To the Earth.

Our cries intertwine
As we stand together,
Helpless witnesses
To the destruction
Of our loved ones.

Sorrow
Gives my pen
Flight.
She is the wind
Behind my fight.

Chapter Forty-One

Cuddling Babies

Sarah

"Welcome to the Neonatal Intensive Care Unit," Juan said with a smile.

He was in his early twenties, and as I learned a little later, was in the final year of his BA in Social Welfare at UC Berkeley.

"Thanks, Juan," I said, feeling immediately at home, both because of his welcoming grin and the setting. The NICU was short on volunteers, and they asked me if I could do the three training sessions they offered in the same week so I could start my shift the following one. Having little else to do with my time besides chasing Ada Baum leads down frustrating dead ends, I readily agreed.

The training basically consisted of shadowing an experienced volunteer on the first day, a nurse on the second, and a secretary on the third to learn how to complete the paperwork. Juan told me he'd been a volunteer baby cuddler for three years.

"This year, I was able to turn it into my internship. It's been wonderful to be able to do something I love for class credit!"

I couldn't help but smile. His enthusiasm was contagious.

He told me he planned to work with foster children once he was a licensed social worker. His family had come to the United States from Colombia when he was five, and he had been in foster care himself for a few years.

"It's so sad that some of these babies are already in the system," he said, looking emotional as he pointed to one in the far corner.

"What do you mean?" I'd almost forgotten how it worked in the United States.

"You know, the addicted babies. The ones whose moms were on drugs when they were in the womb, so they also develop the habit. The hospital has to report them to social services. If there isn't a relative to take them in when they're discharged, they're assigned a social worker and enter the system."

I'd encountered very few addicted babies in my work. There wasn't access to drugs deep in the bush, save maybe for some pot, and the only support system that existed was family. Taking a child to live with a stranger was unheard of. Even in less rural postings, addiction was a rarity among women, although I'd treated a few child soldiers who were so high their pupils had completely invaded their irises. They broke my heart.

I did have a vague memory of an internship I'd done during nursing school, seeing a baby who was hooked on cocaine. He was so amped up, it was nearly impossible to soothe him. He kept scratching his face—probably seeking some relief—until we had to clip his fingernails to the quick so he wouldn't draw blood.

"Yes, it's really sad. For the moms and the babies," I agreed. "I bet you wish you could foster them yourself."

"You have no idea! My boyfriend says it's a good thing we're not allowed to, or I'd probably have ten foster babies already and would have to drop out of school."

"I could see that. You know, the foster care system will be lucky to have someone like you working for them. The world needs more Juans, that's for sure," I said, meaning every word. I didn't usually gush over people I'd just met, but I felt instantaneously at ease with him.

After showing me the intake sheet and how they specified which babies needed the most attention, he gave me a tour of the nursery. Each room could hold up to three babies—two if they both had complex needs. Each nurse was in charge of three to four babies and usually needed to shuffle between two rooms. Once Juan had introduced me to everyone, he had me go on a scavenger hunt, so I could demonstrate my understanding of where everything was and what they were used for.

"Wow, you're so good—you got them all right! You look like you've been doing this your whole life!" Juan cheered. I felt embarrassed at being praised for something that seemed so basic to me and probably blushed. In my world, I was lucky if I got a thank-you for even seemingly Herculean feats of medical magic.

Of course, if I'd told him I was a nurse he probably wouldn't have been so impressed. But I had decided I wouldn't volunteer the information unless asked. I was worried things might get awkward if I did, especially with the nurses.

"Okay, now that we've gotten *that* out of the way, let me tell you the things you *really* need to know to survive here," he said with a smile and proceeded to give me the lowdown on all the nurses. Who to avoid, whose good graces to win, who was easy to work with … I took copious notes.

"Oh, and I recommend taking a weekday shift, either 9:00 a.m. to 12:00 p.m., or 12:00 p.m. to 3:00 p.m. That's when most parents are working or busy. On the weekend and other shifts, more parents are there to do the cuddling, and then you're completely at the nurses' beck and call."

"Well, it sounds like nine to twelve on Tuesdays is the slot they need me to fill, so that works out well."

In the last hour, I got to hold my first baby since I'd left South Sudan.

"This is how the hospital gets the volunteers hooked and makes sure they'll come back, after all the logistical blah blah blah," Juan said. I laughed, loving his sense of humor. He'd been so open and transparent with me that I was getting increasingly uncomfortable withholding information about myself. I was about to tell him I was a nurse when he handed me Grace, and I forgot about everything else.

She was a preterm baby born at thirty-one weeks and had been in the NICU for two weeks, so still wasn't full term. She was so tiny; she fit easily in the crook of my forearm, and I could cup her whole head with my hand. Her eyes were shut tight, and noticing how bright the lights were, I used my other hand to shade them, all the while talking to her in a calm, steady voice. She slowly opened her eyes, blinking a few times. Watching where she seemed to have the best focus, I adjusted the distance I was holding her at.

"You certainly know your way around babies! Do you have any of your own?" Juan asked.

"No, but in my regular life, I'm a nurse," I blurted out, relieved to finally tell him. "I'm just on a leave of absence right now."

"Okay, now I get it! And here I thought you were a baby whisperer!" He laughed. "Don't worry, I won't tell anyone if they don't ask, and I'll treat you as if I didn't know."

My assigned nurse for my second training session was Lorna, an older nurse who looked like she'd been around the block multiple times and was no longer amused by anything. I checked my notes from Juan. "Doesn't like anyone. Stay out of her way and you should be fine." Hopefully, I could do that.

Lorna went over the list of problems preterm infants

and other sick newborns might experience. Although I knew them all, I took notes so she would see I was paying attention. I *definitely* wasn't telling her I was a nurse unless she asked. She struck me as being somewhat territorial, as I would know from having been that way myself at times, and I was determined not to step on her toes if I could help it. I needed one thing in my life to be smooth sailing.

Pointing to the monitors, IV pumps, and pulse oximeters, she showed me what to check for in their blood oxygen levels and how to avoid the wires catching on me or the baby. I had to say, it had been a long time since I'd been around so many machines. I wondered how long it would take to get used to all the whirring and beeping.

Once I showed Lorna I could handle getting the babies in and out of the bassinets without any problem, she seemed satisfied.

"You're comfortable around babies, aren't you?" she said, more as a statement than a question, and I nodded.

"Pam will show you how to properly swaddle a baby. Most volunteers are so afraid of suffocating the newborns, they do it way too loosely. The tighter it is, the safer and calmer the baby feels. You'll see. Pam is the expert at it, so you're lucky she's here today."

After Lorna left, I glanced surreptitiously at what Juan had told me about Pam.

"One of the best nurses. From Nigeria. Doesn't suffer fools. If she likes you … will be your best friend. If she doesn't, you better run!" I swallowed—hoping she'd like me—and went in.

"Hello, I'm Pam," she said, barely looking up. She grabbed a blanket and a baby doll to demonstrate on.

"So, you place the head at the top of the diamond, feet at the bottom, and bring the knees up gently like so." She showed me.

I had a sudden memory of Hiba swaddling a tiny newborn with her gentle, steady hands. We'd had a few more email exchanges, and she'd shared some of the ordeal she and Okot were going through trying to get pregnant. My heart ached for both of them, especially being surrounded by all these babies fighting for their lives.

"Eh, Earth to Sarah!" Pam said, looking at my volunteer tag to remember my name and snapping her finger to get me out of my reverie.

"I'm so sorry, Pam," I said, feeling mortified.

Pull it together, my nemesis chimed in, and I realized I hadn't heard it say *that* in a while.

"Well, I'm not going to show you again," she said, hand on her hip, like a teacher giving a pop quiz to a student who'd been caught daydreaming. "It's your turn now."

But this was a lesson I knew inside and out, and I didn't feel the least bit flustered. I swaddled the baby doll exactly as she had. Maybe even a tiny bit tighter.

Pam looked at me, stunned.

"Shut up!" She exclaimed, the *t* and *p* short and clipped. "Where did you learn to swaddle like an African?!"

I laughed, knowing this to be a high compliment.

"In Sierra Leone. The Ivory Coast. South Sudan. My friend there, Hiba, was the best swaddler I ever met."

"You a nurse?"

"Yes, but don't tell the other nurses unless they ask. I'm on a leave of absence, and I just want to fly under the radar for the time being."

"I got you, girl. You know, a minute ago, you were on my shit list. But now I think I'm going to like you."

"Good, because I know I like you," I said, smiling, feeling the best I had in a very long time.

Chapter Forty-Two
May 1924

Graduation

Maggie

In the end, I got the highest marks on my thesis and graduated with honors as valedictorian of my class. The Brinkmans planned a celebration for me at their house, and Mabel's family was organizing a party for our class the next day. I sent the Joneses an invitation to my graduation.

Frank hadn't been home in weeks. Grief, anger, and fear twisted my insides. I knew he didn't want me to come after him, but I couldn't help but worry.

Not able to contain my fear anymore, I sought out Benjamin.

"How is Frank? Do you know where he is?" I asked, trying not to fret.

Benjamin looked at me uncomfortably. I felt a pang of remorse at putting him in the middle, but I wasn't ready to let go completely, and he was my only connection to Frank.

"He's all right. But I can't tell you where he is. I promised," he said at last.

"I understand. If you see him, can you give him this?" I handed him an envelope with the page from my senior yearbook that had my photo and the inscription "will become a world-renowned author" under it (I had once told Mabel what Frank had said, and unbeknownst to me she'd asked the students involved to write that). I hoped he remembered our conversation those many years prior. "Please come," I scribbled at the bottom, with my graduation date and time.

I was hoping he would surprise me once more, this time with the gift of his presence at my graduation. That somehow all the pain and anger that had come between us would dissolve and we could start anew.

In a moment of distress and sadness, I sent a hastily scribbled note to Edna:

Dearest Edna, things are not good with Frank. I really hope you can come!

Edna wrote back:

Dearest Maggie,
Of course, we are coming. We wouldn't miss it for the world. We are so proud of you! Alain Locke came to see us the last time he was in Harlem, and he couldn't sing your praises enough.

How far you have come since you showed up at our doorstep nine years ago! In case it's not clear, I'm bursting with sisterly love and pride as I write.

Josie is fifteen now! Where did the time go? You wouldn't recognize her. She has blossomed into a beautiful, confident young woman. We are eternally grateful to you for helping her find her way into herself so young.

I'm sorry to hear about Frank. Knowing you, I'm sure there is much that you are not telling me. Thanks for trusting me enough to reach out. We will come with bells on to celebrate you.

Love, your heart sister,
Edna

Her response brought tears to my eyes and made me think of home and family. Which brought Mama to the forefront of my mind.

I wanted nothing more than for her and my brothers to be present, to celebrate with me. And yet, every time I went to post their invitation, I found reasons not to. I told myself I didn't want to put them out. My brothers had to work. The tickets cost money, and the train ride was long. It would wear Mama out. I worried that the passage Professor Locke had encouraged me to read—about witnessing my brother and father's lynching—would be too painful. I also didn't want Mama to be disappointed when she found out the marriage she'd witnessed was collapsing already.

Finally, recognizing I needed help to stop the spinning of my thoughts, I brought up my dilemma to Sadie, who'd become almost as close to me as Edna.

"Why, of course, you need to invite them. Why ever wouldn't you?" she asked, surprised.

"I don't know," I said, as tears started rolling down my cheeks.

Sadie stroked my hand until I could talk again.

"I thought I'd stopped feeling this way after my first year, but I guess I still feel guilty. The only reason I got out and could go to university was because of my brother and father's murders. And they died trying to protect me. It doesn't seem right. I think I'm worried my family will resent me …" My voice broke again as I was choked up by my own shame.

"Oh, honey," Sadie said, her voice gentle and warm. "I get you. I felt that way too after Rose died. That I wasn't allowed to be happy. I even felt bad about having too much fun with Thomas. But in time, I realized that my misery would be a double tragedy. That I owed it to her—not to mention to my son—to live as fully as I could."

Her words landed somewhere deep in my heart, and I

felt my skylark wings flutter. I remembered how delighted I'd been to see her slowly find her way back to the land of the living. I recognized that the same was true for me.

"You're right. Papa and Andre would be happy I've done well. And Mama too."

The next day, I sent my family an invitation and train tickets for all of them. Sadie had asked if I'd let her pay for them as her graduation present to me. Although my pride made me hesitate for a moment, I gratefully accepted.

A week later, I got a brief letter from North Carolina thanking me for the tickets and saying it would be their pleasure to accept my kind invitation. I'd been so careful not to get my hopes up, I had to sit and reread the letter to make sure I understood it. I hadn't felt such joy in a long time.

I explained to Professor Locke why I couldn't read the passage about the lynching and, much to my relief, he agreed immediately. "Of course, Maggie! I'm so pleased your family can come, and I wouldn't want to add to what they have already endured. It will be my honor to meet them."

Sadie and I made arrangements for the Joneses—who were originally going to stay at the Brinkmans'—to stay with Mabel's family instead. Mabel was overjoyed.

"Maggie, I can't believe I get to meet your family *and* the Joneses! You've told me so much about all of them—insofar as you talk about anything!"

Despite my silent prayers, Frank did not come. But he left a letter on the kitchen table for me to find that morning, so I guessed he slipped in while I was sleeping. Tucked inside it was a hundred-dollar bill, which was more money than I had ever seen in my young life.

My dear Maggie songbird,
 This is the day we were both waiting for. And although I've been unable to show you or tell you, I am so

very proud of you. If sorry weren't such a cheap, trivial word when weighed against all I've made you suffer, I would tell you how sorry I am that I couldn't be the husband, the man, you deserve. You are in the prime of your life and your youth. You still have that spirit and fire that made me fall in love with you. Your life lies ahead of you like a book you're writing with that magical pen of yours.

I am a broken man. I have given the world all I had to give, but it has spat it back in wicked mockery and defied me at every turn. I can only say that I am cursed and that everything I touch turns to ash. Even though it has pained me at times to watch you bloom just as I wither, I'm grateful that you have come out unscathed. It is a testament to the strength that drew me to you.

It is I who sets you free. Spread your wings and fly as high as you can. Do not let our story drag you down into the depths of the dungeon in which I fester. And please, do not worry about me. Being responsible for your unhappiness would be yet another burden I cannot bear. For me, and for the love that was, be happy. Find a man who deserves you. Know that I am on my own journey and must find my way, whatever that may be.

Peace be with you,
Frank

As I read it, tears rolled down my cheeks. Through my pain and despair, however, I also felt something akin to hope. Not for the two of us, perhaps, although that was still there despite (or perhaps because of) his words. But at least for me. I kept the letter in the bodice of the dark blue dress Sadie gave me to wear for graduation.

Benjamin went to the train station to meet Mama and my brothers. Mabel came with her brother Norman to get me. We donned our gowns over our dresses and walked to Howard together.

"Oh, Maggie, we did it! Are you excited to see your family?"

"Yes! Also, a little nervous. I haven't seen Mama in five years—and my brothers since I left."

"I can't even imagine! I'm so happy for you. They must be so proud of you, Miss Valedictorian! I'm so proud of you."

"Thanks! You, too! We did it," I said, grinning. "How are the preparations for the class party?"

"Don't ask. Mother is running around frantically, wanting everything to be perfect. My main concern is that Angela brings her older brother, Barnaby. His name is unfortunate, but he's sweet to look at, that's for sure. And kind, too, which Mother says matters more. He blushes every time I say anything to him. Oooh, look at the time. We should hurry!"

The rest of the day was a blur, much like my wedding day. Perhaps it was my misfortune that I couldn't remember the most important days in my life. Or maybe it made the other days more bearable. I heard my name being called. Legs shaking, I made my way to the podium where Alain Locke was waiting to introduce me. He looked almost as proud as my father would have been had he lived.

"It is my honor to present Maggie, a student I've had the pleasure to work with personally. Her story is the story of so many of our brethren, although one that most of the students here have had the fortune to escape.

"It is a reminder of the power of courage and love to overcome hardship and the living proof that writing can alchemize pain into beauty. This student is wise beyond her years, one of the more gifted young writers I've met. I'd also like to recognize her family, without whom she wouldn't be here, and who came from North Carolina to support her. Without further ado, I present Maggie Burke."

I watched Mama and my brothers squirm in their seats as the audience applauded, but I could also see the moisture in their eyes as I stepped forward. I sent Sadie a silent blessing for bringing them here.

"This passage, although it is about a time I worked on the railroad on my way to New York and to a better life, is an invitation to my fellow graduating students to have courage and faith as we step into the unknown." I looked out at a sea of faces. My hands trembled, and my voice quavered. I cleared my throat before continuing to read.

"Working on the railroad, 'Where are you from?' is a question seldom asked. Every man I meet has a story etched on his face. Rumors drift on the wind whenever someone turns his back …" The passage I'd selected was a page long. I would occasionally look up to see Mama beaming at me, her love giving my words an additional lift. At the end of the reading, I looked up at my classmates. My eyes landed on Mabel, who gave me a little wave that lifted my heart.

"So, to all of you. All of us. The future stretches out in front of us, as yet unwritten. The beauty of the unbroken horizon. May we lay our plans in the earth, and may the tracks of our hopes carry us to our dreams and beyond," I concluded.

After some cheering and clapping, my classmates then went up, one by one, to receive their diplomas. And then the festivities began, with music, food, and mutual congratulations. I got swept up in so many embraces, I lost track of my friends and family.

Professor Locke somehow managed to take me aside for a moment to tell me to meet him in his office two weeks later, after he returned from a trip to Harlem.

"I have an offer for you," he said, then excused himself before I could ask anything else.

Later that night, at the small party the Brinkmans had organized for me, I felt my heart surge at being surrounded by all the people I loved in one room, minus Mabel, who was celebrating with her family. The only blemish to my joy was

Frank's absence. I tried not to think of him, for when I did, I felt pulled into the shadow of pain and shame that had consumed him, and my heart ached inconsolably.

Mama had aged since I'd last seen her. Her step was slow and uneven, and all of her movements were slow and deliberate. I often saw her wince when she walked, and I noticed that little Margaret was gentler around her than with her parents.

I offered to have Lewis look at her, but she put her hand on mine and shook her head. "Chile, at my age, there ain't nothin' a docta' can do to change what nature done already. There ain't nothin' to do but wait for God's judgment." She smiled at me, and when she did, I saw a deep peace in her eyes.

We sat in comfortable silence as I stroked her hand, and she caressed my hair like she did when I was little. I told her briefly about the situation with Frank, and she nodded knowingly, with eyes that had seen it all.

"This too shall pass, Maggie, this too shall pass."

I fell into easy banter with Arthur, who was always the most outgoing of my brothers. When we were little, he was always getting into capers, and the head tenant farmer often chased after him in an attempt to keep things running smoothly.

But manhood suited him well, as though he had found a tailor who finally understood what mettle he was made of. His wife, Anna, looked very delicate and didn't say much. "She's very prim, isn't she?" was Mabel's comment about her after she met her. But I watched Anna light up when her daughter spoke to her.

Margaret took to me instantly, and I to her. Although I got along with most children, the kindred connection I felt with her went beyond anything I'd experienced before. "This is your aunt, Maggie. The one you were named after," Arthur said.

She sidled up to me and stared at me with big, curious eyes. As I stared back, I felt warm tingles spread across my chest and into my face. We both broke into a smile at the same time. She climbed onto my lap and wouldn't leave. Our bodies relaxed into each other with an invisible sigh of soul recognition. I felt a dull ache in my empty womb and a sudden flash of pain as my mind drifted to Frank.

"Margaret, you're a big girl now. You're too old for your aunt's lap," Anna admonished her five-year-old daughter.

"Oh, Anna, leave her be. Can't you see they've fallen in love with each other?" Arthur said with a laugh, as he encircled her from behind and planted a kiss on top of her head. She smiled back, as though despite herself.

"Maggie always had a magical way with children. Right, Josie?" Edna said, grinning at her daughter, who nodded in agreement.

Roy had been quiet since he arrived. We were never very close as children, although he was the closest to me in age. He was a sullen child, who didn't say much but was always getting into fights with the other sharecroppers' children. He was furious that I was allowed to go to school, but he wasn't because of all the scrapes he got into. One day when we were fighting and I was seven or eight, he called me Mr. Tanner's bastard child. The comment stung, even though I didn't fully understand its meaning. That was the first time I really took notice of the difference in skin color between myself and the rest of my family. He shared a close bond with Andre, though. His big brother was always protecting him from other children and seemed to understand him in a way the rest of us couldn't.

I wondered now if he blamed me for Andre's death. I sensed him watching me as Margaret was telling me about the kitten she'd found near their house. I noticed his jaw muscles tighten, as though deciding whether to give me a piece of his mind for all the trouble my girl-ness wrought on our family. I saw the anger flash in his eyes, but for the first time, I could also feel the pain and sadness his rage was trying to protect him from.

I smiled at him, trying to convey with my eyes that I understood. That I was sorry. That I hoped he could forgive me. He dropped his gaze and went to get Mama a glass of lemonade. When he came back, he joined his niece and me on the sofa. He still didn't say much to me, but I took his coming closer as a sign that time might eventually heal this too.

I sat back and surveyed the room. Margaret had inched off my lap and was now playing patty-cake with her uncle, who was proving how quick he was with his hands. Arthur was rubbing Mama's calves. Anna sat near them, embroidering small pink flowers on a white dress she was making for Margaret.

Edna, Lewis, Sadie, and Benjamin were deep in a heated conversation. I couldn't hear the content, but I was sure it was of a political nature. Josie, who I'd learned from Edna had developed quite a passion for math, was helping nine-year-old Thomas (who did *not* love math) with some catch-up problems he had to do over the summer. Surrounded by the people I loved, I felt all the places in my body that usually felt tight start to soften.

Chapter Forty-Three

Ancestors and Babies

Sarah

I stared at the screen, not wanting to believe what I was seeing. After two weeks of relentless research, chasing dead ends, and finally cracking the family code, this is where it got me.

Ada Baum Cohen (daughter of Isaac and Valda Baum). B. March 12, 1931. D. November 13, 2010.

Last year. My aunt had died less than a year ago. Un-fucking believable!

Really? It couldn't be ten years ago? Twenty? It had to be last year?

The what-ifs were pounding the door of my brain, clamoring for attention. Taking a deep breath, I held them at bay.

Not now.

I thought of looking for Dad's other siblings whose names and birth dates I'd found in my search, but my intuition told me to keep going with Ada. Okay, fine. But she had already passed. So now what? I closed my eyes, thinking.

Ada wasn't the end of the line. Mom said she had a daughter.

After more clicks, scrolling, chasing one screen to the next, I found her! Evelyn Rosa Cohen. Daughter of Ada and Harold Cohen. Born in 1959. Fifty-two years old. My cousin.

With no date of death.

On a whim, I exited the ancestry site and googled her full name. A white pages listing showed up with an address in Manhattan but no phone number. Feeling mounting excitement, I found a website that sold people's emails.

I had a moment's debate with my morality gatekeeper.

Sells emails? I mean what is that? Is that even ethical?

Okay, it's a little shady. But she's my cousin, *for Pete's sake. It's for a good cause ...*

Fifteen minutes later, I'd sent Evelyn an email explaining who I was, expressing sadness for her loss, and describing how I'd come across her mother's letters to my father that spanned over a decade.

Heart pounding in my chest, crossing my fingers that the email wouldn't land in her junk mailbox, I glanced down at my watch.

"Shit!"

One of the volunteers at the NICU was sick, and I'd agreed to cover for her, but I had completely lost track of time.

I slammed my laptop shut and rushed to get ready. I was relieved to arrive only a few minutes late, but Lorna was not amused. My heart sank. I'd really been hoping Pam would be on duty since we'd gotten along so well the last two times I'd volunteered. Lorna was the last person I wanted to see today.

Although the sheet I'd picked up at reception indicated there were two babies who needed special attention—which could easily take up the whole three hours, especially since one of them was recovering from meth exposure—Lorna went through a litany of tasks she wanted me to do for her.

"The laundry basket is full of shirts to be washed. The breastfeeding machines need to be sanitized. There are six blood and urine samples to be taken to the lab ..." she droned on, looking down at her notes rather than at me as she talked.

When she'd gone, I noticed my heart was still racing from

the events of the morning, the rush to arrive on time, and Lorna's prickliness. Knowing how quickly babies pick up on that, especially when they're already agitated, I took a deep breath in and let it out with three short, rhythmic exhales. One of the babies who'd been fussing a moment earlier quieted down.

"Oh yeah, you like that?" I said softly, walking over and seeing it was Grace—the first baby I'd held on the day Juan had given me the tour.

"I'm sorry to see you're still here," I said. Sensing her readiness for contact by the way her fingers were reaching in my direction, I placed a warmed blanket on my right shoulder and picked her up.

I could feel her body relax immediately, molding to fit into mine, our heart rates starting to sync up. I was surprised by the emotion this evoked in me. I'd held so many babies, but I'd rarely had the time to really feel the connection, I was so busy focusing on their health, vitals, feeding them, an so on.

And there was something else, too.

Thanks to the work with Patrick, I could feel my own baby self within me, who'd been so longing for warmth, touch, holding.

"This is for you, too, baby Sarah. I can re-parent you at the same time as I hold Grace," I whispered, feeling something within me settle into a contented hum.

Just then, the other baby, Adam, started to whimper and fidget restlessly. I gently lowered Grace into an automatic rocker: a semi-upright chair that would rock a baby when there was no adult available to do so. I wish we'd had those in South Sudan! "It will even purr for you. How about that!" I joked, and she smiled back.

Adam was inconsolable, flailing his arms back and forth in frog-like motions. His chart said he'd been in the NICU for less than a week, which meant he'd be having full withdrawal symptoms. I remembered something my internship supervisor had mentioned when we were working with a cocaine-addicted baby.

"He's so overstimulated, he can only handle one sense at a time. If there are bright lights, *and* you are holding him *and* humming—that's just way too much!"

I dimmed the lights and re-wrapped his blanket, so the corner created a dome over his eyes to shield them, being careful not to jostle the feeding cannula from his nose. After he'd recovered from being handled, he seemed to calm a little. Good, one sense out of the way. My voice did not calm him, so I fell silent, gave him some space for transition, and tried containment: one hand cupping his blanketed head, the other at his feet, my pressure firm without being constraining.

Ten minutes later, he'd calmed enough to fall into a fitful slumber. I put Grace back in her bassinet so I could start on Lorna's task list while checking in on the babies regularly. I'd dropped the samples off at the lab and was just finishing folding the shirts when I heard one of the baby monitors blaring.

"Lorna," I called, not sure where she was. In that moment, I had a choice. I could either defer to her and go find her—or I could go take care of it myself. For a split second, my brain froze, caught between the "don't step on toes" volunteer part of me, and the nurse part of me who knew what to do and wanted to take charge. I took a deep breath and checked in with myself.

Take charge, my inner knowing said. So, I did.

Entering the room, I saw that Grace's heart had taken a momentary pause, probably due to post-feeding regurgitation, and the sound of the monitor had roused Adam who had started to flail and cry again.

I picked Grace up, memorizing her vitals so I could tell Lorna, tapping gently on her back until her breath had returned and the monitor had stopped shrieking. Still holding her with one arm, I placed my other hand on the top of Adam's head. Balancing on one leg and maneuvering the other over the edge of the bassinet, I carefully put my knee at his feet—just enough for him to feel the contact.

And the yoga is finally paying off! An inner voice said—half cheerleader, half snark.

Just then, Lorna came in, surveying the scene, one eyebrow raised. My breath caught in my throat, knowing I'd probably get rebuked for not going to get her, and I realized that I didn't mind if I did. I could acknowledge the impact of my actions on her, while still trusting I'd done the right thing.

"I see you have everything under control," she said instead, her face deadpan and hard to read.

I nodded.

"You're a nurse?"

"Yes. I didn't want to say anything because I know at the end of the day, if anything happens it's on you, not me. I didn't want to overstep."

This time, she was the one to nod. "Well, we can certainly use some competent volunteers, so you're welcome any time."

"Thanks, that's really good to hear, Lorna," I said, beaming at her so brightly it earned me a grudging half-smile in response.

And just when I thought the day couldn't get any better, I got to do a discharge at the end of my shift. Since we all worked so hard for the babies to be able to go home, there was always a party atmosphere in the ward when it happened.

The nurses cheered and waved as I pushed Kaya's stroller toward the elevator. Her parents followed close behind, laden down with a month's worth of diapers and other supplies.

"Kaya's first elevator ride," the mother exclaimed, and the father and I both cheered.

When we got to the automatic glass doors that led out, I paused—both for dramatic effect and to unroll the rain cover so she wouldn't be wind-lashed on her first foray out of the hospital.

"Drumroll!" I said. The parents, being good sports, made "pa pa pa pa" sounds as we crossed the threshold.

"Welcome to the world, Kaya," I said.

When I got home, I was still feeling the warm glow from my interaction with Lorna and from Kaya's discharge party. On an impulse, I decided to check my emails. Just in case. And to my astonishment, Evelyn had replied.

Dear Sarah,
You have no idea what a happy surprise it was to receive your email. Your timing couldn't be better!
Thanks for your condolences. And honestly, she was sick for a long time, and her mind was pretty far gone by the end. Truth be told, I'm relieved for her that she's no longer in pain. But that may be TMI for a first contact. Sorry! I'm not sure what's appropriate here.
Anyway, I've been going through Mom's things, and I've been sitting with a box of your father's letters to her and quite a few of his paintings for months. I had no idea what to do with them. I wanted to get in touch with your mother but couldn't remember her maiden name—I think I was fifteen or sixteen the last time I saw her. So, what an amazing stroke of luck to have you contact me!
My cell phone number is at the bottom of the email. Feel free to call me between six and ten p.m. (Eastern time, not sure what time zone you're in) on weekdays, and really any time on the weekend.
Sincerely,
Your cousin, Evelyn

Chapter Forty-Four
Summer - Fall 1924

Unmoored

Maggie

After Mama and my brothers left, the silence in my house was deafening. Without my classes to keep my mind occupied, there was nothing to fill the hollowness in my heart where Frank had been. I had recurrent nightmares of looking for him and stumbling over his dead body. The details of his death varied each time, but each was invariably gruesome. The pain of his absence ricocheted off my earlier losses until my heart was an echoing hall of grief.

I had lost everything. Again. And this time, the voices of doubt in my head told me I had nobody to blame but myself. I had survived. I was safe. I'd managed to bend the terms of my bargain in the forest to finish high school and become a teacher. To have a home and a husband. But that wasn't enough. I had to dream big. Go to college. In wanting too much, they chastised me, I'd lost everything. They posited that if I hadn't gone to Howard, if I'd joined Frank in the movement the way he'd wanted, we might not have drifted as far apart. I might have been able to save him from himself.

Desperate, watching the pieces of my life starting to crumble around me, I tried to convince Benjamin to tell me where

Frank was. He shook his head forlornly.

"I'm sorry, Maggie. I know how much you're hurting, and the last thing I want to do is add to your pain. But he made me promise I wouldn't tell you where he is. He says he doesn't want you to see him like this."

Sadie patted my hand as I wept. The next day, telling myself that as long as he wasn't dead, there was hope, I gave Benjamin a letter where I'd recopied "The Colors of Your Heart." It was the first poem I'd ever written for Frank, and I underlined the last verses:

> *I say yes to now*
> *I say yes to forever*
> *I say yes to never again*
> *Alone.*

More silence. The not knowing was perhaps the hardest part. Not knowing whether he was going to find his way out of the shadow. If there was anything I could have done to save us. If there was still hope for us.

At last, I had to concede that he wasn't coming back. I considered sending a message to Frank that I wanted a divorce. I thought closing the door might be better than leaving it perpetually ajar in the hope he'd return. And because then, maybe, I'd force some response from him.

However, the very thought sent me spiraling into a pit of despair and shame. Living apart was one thing. But I didn't know anyone who was actually divorced. As far as I knew, they were still only granted on the grounds of impotence and adultery, and the few divorcees I'd heard of were shrouded with shame.

Since I couldn't imagine ever wanting to get married again, I decided to let it go. Bear his silence. If he wanted to make the dissolution legal, he could reach out to me. And I could always change my mind if circumstances, or the way divorced women were treated, evolved to make me want to.

Now I had to decide what to do next. Although I'd just spoken at graduation about the beauty of the unbroken horizon, the future that stretched out in front of me felt bleak and uncertain.

A week later, I met Alain (now that I had graduated, he insisted I dispense with formalities) in his office. He started when he saw my demeanor.

"Maggie, you look terrible! Are you okay? You look like you haven't slept a wink since I saw you last!" He said with concern. I told him briefly what had transpired with Frank.

"I'm very sorry to hear. I never had the pleasure to meet him, but I know how much he means to you. Is there any chance you might be able to iron things out?"

I shook my head, and he made a sympathetic noise in response.

"Well, I don't know if my offer will be welcome, then, or too much for you right now." He looked at me from across his desk for a moment before he continued. "Maggie, do you remember that I mentioned meeting with Paul Kellogg, the editor of *Survey Graphic* magazine back in March?" he asked.

I did have a vague recollection of him mentioning that name, so I nodded.

"Yes? Good. I like that you pay attention and remember. Anyway, the magazine is planning to publish a special edition on Harlem as the mecca of the Negro race, and Kellogg asked me to be their guest editor."

"Congratulations! That's such an honor," I said, happy that he was getting some of the attention he deserved.

"It is, and it's also a big task. I sent them an outline of my ideas for the issue, which they've just approved. I'm going to

Europe for the summer, as you know. I'm working with two dozen authors or so and need to have collected all the works by June 10. However, I know there'll still be much to do while I'm gone and when I return. I need someone who has a sharp literary eye and can get things done without fanfare."

I raised an eyebrow at him, and my heart skipped a beat, suddenly wondering where the conversation was going. I didn't need to wait long.

"Will you work with me as my assistant? My current plan is to turn this into a much bigger book project after it is done, so if you're interested, I have enough work to keep you busy for a while. If you accept, of course. Take as much time as you need to think about it."

I took the next few days to mull over his proposal. My heart clenched at the prospect and whispered I could go to North Carolina to be with my family. The doomsday voices reminded me that things went better for me when I used my skills in service to others. When I was a boy and did odd jobs. When I worked for the Joneses. When I was a teacher. When I was involved with Frank and the anti-lynching efforts. That if I listened to my heart, I might once again lose everything I had.

I accepted the offer. I was happy to have some income coming in and hoped that having a project to focus on would distract me from thinking about Frank.

And as I immersed myself in the words of the creative giants whose works Locke had collected—some of whom (such as Jean Toomer, Countee Cullen, Langston Hughes) I'd read in my classes—I was indeed grateful to have something to hold on to especially as the different people in my life started frittering away.

I moved into Sadie and Benjamin's guest room so they could rent the cottage out, though I knew living with them could only be temporary. Sadie had found out she was pregnant, and the baby was due in February. I agreed to stay until then to help out but knew that after that, I would need to leave.

It was a solace to have their company during this transition, but witnessing the looks and stolen caresses between her and Benjamin brought my own loneliness into intense focus.

A young couple moved into the cottage where Frank and I had lived. The wife was also pregnant, and she was a month away from giving birth. It was hard having daily reminders of what could have been. If only …

One day, when Thomas and I were in the garden, picking ripe tomatoes for dinner, I heard peals of laughter coming from the cottage's open door. I looked up to see the man reaching from behind his wife, wrapping his arms halfway around her round belly, and kissing the nape of her neck. She looked up with adoring eyes and let out another ripple of laughter.

My heart spasmed in pain and loss. Something must've shown on my face, because Thomas reached over and squeezed my hand. We gathered our baskets and went inside.

Without the common element of school and classes, the differences between Mabel and I became more evident, and I felt us starting to drift apart, despite our best intentions. We met up a few times after graduation, but my mood was as dark as hers was joyful, and I worried about bringing her down. She was devastated for me about the dissolution of my marriage, but I also knew she couldn't fully understand my grief, never having experienced any profound loss of her own. When she and Barnaby got engaged, she hesitated to tell me for fear that the news would further highlight my pain. I assured her I was overjoyed for her. And I was, although I was getting some insight into how Frank must have felt when things were going well for me and everything was falling apart for him.

However, when Mabel asked me to be one of her bridesmaids, I immediately said yes. Both because I wanted to be there on her big day and in the hopes of preserving some of the closeness we'd once had.

A month and a half after Alain had hired me, I received a letter he'd written weeks earlier from Paris.

> *Dear Maggie,*
>
> *Thank you for all your hard work! Kellogg says you have followed my instructions to a tee, and that things are going smoothly despite my absence. I just met with Langston Hughes in Paris, and he is every bit the sensitive artist one would expect from his poetry. We are off to Italy now. What do you think of his writing? And the others you're helping me ready for publication? This generation of Negro artists is incredible!*
>
> *And I count you among them, Maggie, never forget that. Have you been writing? Our agreement included that you would send me a poem or prose every few weeks, but so far, I haven't received anything. Is everything okay?*
>
> *Your concerned mentor,*
> *Alain Locke*

In truth, my writing felt dry and crusted, like drops I was trying to wring out of a parched riverbed. Although the work on the *Survey Graphic* edition was the one thing I could cling to, I was intimidated by the brilliance of the contributors, and doubt in my own ability crept back in, cramping my pen. I felt transported back to my first year at Howard.

At night, after Thomas went to bed and Sadie and Benjamin retired to their private world, I felt myself unraveling at the seams. Unmoored. Alone and without purpose. I tried to eke out a few words to describe what I was feeling, although the resulting poem felt as limp as my brain.

Unhinged

This door
Of hope and despair
Has swung open
And slammed shut
So many times,
It hangs limply
On crooked hinges,
Banging aimlessly
At life,
Neither open
Nor closed,
Neither tree
Nor door
Anymore.

Lost.

That I could return
To my natural state—
Run naked
In a forest of trees,
Stripped
Of the tall buildings
That strangle
The sky
And suck the life
Out of its residents.

Or that a carpenter
Would coax my hinges
Back into place
And set me
On track
Once again.

Alain returned in September. I was dreading seeing him when I felt so low, but I was also relieved to have someone solid I could hold on to.

I had barely entered Alain's office when he waved a piece of paper under my nose. I saw it was my "Unhinged" poem, and I cringed. I'd sent it to him in a desperate moment because I didn't have anything else to show for the months that had passed. He had circled the word "carpenter" and put a big *X* through the rest.

He was the shortest man I knew (student gossip had it that he had a bout of rheumatic fever as a child which stunted his growth and weakened his heart), which meant his famous stare was level with my eyes, all the more intimidating.

"All right, Maggie, I'll be your carpenter, though my hammer may bang a little more than it coaxes. You look like a shadow of the Maggie who stood in front of her class in May and read proudly from her memoir, and I'm worried. I don't want to lose you, and I have every intention of setting you back on track. Are you ready?"

I couldn't trust myself to speak, so I nodded.

"You have a good mind, Maggie, and it can be your salvation, especially if you use it to unlock your gifts. But your thoughts *will* be your undoing if you let them pull you into their vortex of despair. It's your choice which path you go down."

The word "choice" echoed in my head as I tried to grapple

with how it applied to my circumstance. Just then, nothing felt like a choice.

"I know how hard it is to be without a compass or direction. But don't let fear paralyze you or break you down. Instead of drowning in your pain, drink from its source. Let your sorrow nourish your art until your words and the ancient wisdom that fuels them carry you to the other side. Do you understand?"

I shook my head no. My brain felt frozen, and I was struggling to make heads or tails of his words.

"Looking into your eyes, I sense that it feels like something inside of you is dying."

I nodded, yes. Finally, something that made sense to me.

"Well, it is. Everything you thought you knew about the world—and your old ways of surviving and getting by—are dying. You can cling to what was and lose little pieces of yourself in the process. Or you can let go. Again, it's your choice. Nobody can save you but you. I learned this the hard way, though I do keep trying to save some of my friends."

A vein in his temple was pulsing visibly, and his eyes bulged out at me with even fiercer intensity than usual—willing me to choose life. To simultaneously surrender my resistance and fight my way back.

"I know all too well that we can't save those we love," I said, having finally regained the use of my tongue. "I tried and failed with Frank. I know only I can save myself. I'm just not sure how right now."

"Of course not. You're young. And even though it might feel like your life is over, the truth is it's just beginning. For now, just open yourself to the awe and depth of your grief, and you will come out on the other side with more clarity. I promise."

*

Over the next few days, I felt the word "choice" bouncing around my mind, looking for a place to roost. After circling round and round, it finally landed in my heart. What would I do if I truly had a choice?

Sensing there was a bigger decision to be made around the corner, I decided to start writing again. In the past, that had been a way to free the muffled longing of my being, so why not try to rekindle that feeling?

At first, I spent hours glaring at the blank page, daring the paper to talk back. To whisper wisdom into my indurated ears. To blow life into my world-weary fingers. I started trawling the pen across the paper, hoping to fish a few clear thoughts from the swamp of despair in my brain. A part of me resisted, wanting to fly out the window and vanish into the void. It took all my remaining strength to keep that part tethered to my words.

But then, slowly, painstakingly, writing got easier. A little life began trickling back into my pen. My body felt somehow weightier. More here. The shadows my lantern made on the walls came into focus. My wooden desk felt warmer and more alive.

One day, I realized I was back. And in that moment, that was a victory. Even if I had no idea what was next.

Chapter Forty-Five
October 2011

New York Moment

Sarah

"I think the time has come for me to tell you more about your father like I promised. You know, before our trip," my mother said as we finished dinner that evening. We were now eating together as often as we could.

During my call with Evelyn, she'd invited me to come visit, rather than just sending me a box of things, so that we could meet and talk. I'd immediately agreed. Much to my surprise, my mother had asked if she could join me.

As she'd said, "I have so many accrued vacation days. And someone is turning thirty-five soon, so if you let me, I'd love for the trip to be my treat."

I'd grinned, pleased she'd remembered my birthday and genuinely excited at the idea of us learning more about my father together.

We'd checked that it was okay with Evelyn to have an extra visitor, saying we'd stay at a hotel to be less of an imposition, and had cleared it with Mom's hospital. Then we made plans to go from a Thursday to Monday, between my NICU shifts.

"Oh, wow, okay," I said as my belly flopped over in both

anticipation and fear, and I felt myself bracing for what was to come.

"As I said, we didn't share that much with each other."

"Yeah, I know. Broad brushstrokes," I said, and she smiled that I'd remembered.

"What I know is that after his trip to Auschwitz, he got a job working with the NAACP Legal Defense Fund. I think his mother had connections there." She paused, and I watched her chest rise and fall with the deep breath she took.

"I've gone through the few letters your father and I exchanged when we first got together, but there were no references to his past. What I remember is that he got involved with a group called CORE while working for the LDF."

"Do you know what CORE stands for?" I asked. She shook her head, so I quickly looked it up on my phone. Congress of Racial Equality. "He was living in Brooklyn at the time?"

My mother nodded. "He described doing school sit-ins, neighborhood cleanups, and calling for boycotts of discriminatory businesses, but from what he told me, by the time he joined, it wasn't as active as it once had been. A few of the volunteers, including Saul, felt like the group wasn't doing enough, so they joined a Black militant group."

"What, like the Black Panthers?"

"Similar, but not that one, I don't think." She paused and took another breath. "Your father was pretty vague about it, but from what I understood, he played a role in supplying them with weapons."

"You mean he was their gun dealer?!" I exclaimed.

"I think so." She nodded hesitantly.

"Holy shit, Mom!" was all I could say, and she couldn't help but smile a little.

"I know. It was even hard for me to wrap my head around it. I don't think it lasted very long. Martin Luther King Jr.'s assassination was a wake-up call. I think Saul was also involved with a woman in the group and a bad breakup might have been part of his motivation for wanting a fresh start. In any case, he got a job with a civil rights advocacy group in DC, and that's when he left New York and the movement."

"Wow. Okay. Wow," I said, trying to process. My warm, lawyer/artist, "save the world" dad a gun dealer for a Black power group. And maybe more than guns, for all I knew. Shit. I closed my eyes to get my bearings, and a snippet of a conversation I'd had in the occupied Palestinian territories came to mind.

"It's a lot to wrap my mind around. But I remember an ambulance driver in Gaza saying that the first intifada was largely nonviolent, and nobody paid attention. According to him, it wasn't until the second intifada, when they took up arms, that people started taking notice. He said nonviolence only worked if the stakes for killing an activist were relatively high. I don't condone it, but I realize it's hard to know what we might do until we're in that situation."

"I agree. That's part of why I never judged or asked your father too many questions about it."

"Is that when you met Dad? When he moved to DC?" I asked, feeling suddenly drained, and wanting to steer the conversation to safer ground, at least for now.

"It was several years later. I'm sure I told you how we met, right? I don't think I was that derelict of a mother."

"Yeah, but tell me again. I think I need a happy story right now."

"I was an interning surgeon at the hospital where your father went to have his gallbladder removed. He grabbed my hand before going in for the surgery and looked so vulnerable, my heart melted—no mean feat, as you know. And two years later, you were born." I smiled, enjoying the thought of both of them so young, at least relatively speaking. In love.

"So, you think that's why Aunt Ada stopped talking to Dad?" I asked, bringing it back to the thread that tied the story to the present and our upcoming trip to meet Evelyn.

"That was my sense. Your aunt was very committed to nonviolence after everything she'd experienced as a child in Poland and because of how her father had died. If my memory serves, I think she spent a few years with her family on a kibbutz in Israel in the early '60s."

"Really? You mean with her husband and Evelyn?" My mother nodded. "Evelyn would've been so little back then."

"That's true. From what Saul told me, Ada couldn't stand what was happening in the Palestinian territories. Her husband wanted to stay—he didn't share her principles. I imagine there were other differences too. In any case, she left him and came back with her daughter."

"She sounds like one determined woman."

"Yes, but also incredibly bighearted."

"So, what happened with Dad? She found out about the Black power organization and his role in it?"

"Yes. After your grandmother died, Ada found Valda's journals. I guess somebody had told your grandmother about what Saul was doing, and she'd written about it in an attempt to understand."

"That's how Ada found out?! Yikes. Did Dad even know Grandma knew?"

"No, I don't think so. Anyway, Ada couldn't tolerate being in the presence of anyone who engaged in violence or harm to others in any way, so she completely severed ties with your father. I don't think they ever spoke again."

"That's so sad. Dad must have been devastated."

"Probably. He seemed to take it in stride. Just worked harder."

I nodded. All three of us knew about that.

"I wonder what Evelyn knows about all this," I pondered out loud.

"I don't know. If I were to guess, I'd say a lot more than you do. Your aunt was pretty open about things." Unlike your father and I, she implied but didn't say. "After the fallout with your dad over their father's death, I think she didn't want to make the same mistake with her daughter."

"I hope you're right. If so, it's a good sign she wants to meet us."

Two days later, we were on our way to New York. I'd made relative peace with what I'd learned about my father's past. Although I'd decided to pause the hypnotherapy sessions for the time being, I'd continued with my research on Black history at the turn of the twentieth century. Reading more about the Red Summer helped me understand a little more clearly why violence might at times seem like the only effective means to resist systemic oppression.

One piece of the Dad mystery solved, at least as much as it was going to be. I felt ready for the next step in solving the ancestral puzzle. I'd discovered that both my mother and I took perverse pleasure in buying overpriced junk food in airports. We munched loudly on our Doritos and potato chips while watching bad movies on our little chair-screens, our respective reading materials (*The Biography of Alain Locke* for me, sudoku puzzles for her) having been unceremoniously dumped on our laps.

I felt like surprisingly little time had elapsed when we landed at JFK International Airport. As we made our way through the line of passengers, luggage, waiting family members, and taxi drivers, we spotted Evelyn.

Even if she hadn't been waving at us (we'd sent photos at the last minute so she would recognize us), there would have been no mistaking her. She looked just like my father. I stopped in my tracks as soon as I saw her. I glanced over at my mother and saw her looking at me.

"Sorry, I should have warned you, but I'd forgotten ... Or maybe she looks more like him now."

We made our way to her, and after a warm exchange of greetings, I explained why I'd stopped and stared, not wanting to seem rude.

"Yes, Mom *always* said that." She laughed. I liked her immediately, with her thick auburn hair and inquisitive gray eyes. "When I was a teenager and he visited once, somebody thought he was my older brother. He was in his early thirties, but he looked much younger." My mother nodded. That would have been just a few years before they met, I thought.

"Did you know him pretty well, then?" I asked when we were seated in her car. I realized with a twinge of envy that she'd had more years with him than I had.

"Uncle Saul? When we came back from Israel and Mom was trying to find her way as a single parent, I was only three or four, but I remember he was very helpful. He was a senior in college, and we stayed in his tiny student apartment for a week while we looked for a place of our own. Your dad was great!"

"Yeah, I wish I'd known him better," I said, unable to keep the longing out of my voice.

"I can only imagine. He died so young. And I'm happy to answer any questions you might have while you're here. I've taken tomorrow and Monday off work, so I'm all yours," she announced as she pulled into our hotel's circular entrance.

"We're here. I'll let the two of you rest. Ping me when you wake up. Since you conveniently found a hotel so close to me, you can walk over, and we can have breakfast together." We nodded and thanked her profusely for her kindness.

The next morning, we got up later than planned, still being on West Coast time. I texted Evelyn while my mother got first dibs on the shower.

When we arrived at Evelyn's place forty minutes later, she greeted us with bagels and cream cheese.

"This has got to be the best bagel I've ever had," I exclaimed, biting into the warm, chewy everything bagel. "Why aren't they so good anywhere else?" I asked.

Evelyn laughed. "That's the million-dollar question. When was the last time either of you was in New York?"

"I come pretty often for conferences," my mother replied.

"I have no idea. Not since I was little, when we lived in DC," I said, looking at my mother for confirmation.

"If you haven't been as an adult, then the last time you came was for your grandma's funeral." She looked at Evelyn as though debating whether to say more. "After your mother stopped talking to Saul, we had fewer reasons to come."

Evelyn nodded. "I know. I'm not sure if it's the right time to say this, but since we're jumping right in … Mom didn't learn until a few months after the fact, from a relative, that Uncle Saul had died. When she did, she really regretted not having spoken to him all those years. She thought she'd just been stubborn. I remember her crying to me over the phone that he'd forgiven her, but she couldn't do the same for him!" As she spoke, Evelyn had tears in her eyes.

"She did write to you," she told my mother. "But you must have already left for Paris. It came back with 'return to sender.'"

"Oh, Evelyn, I'm so sorry. I wish I'd known. I should have reached out, too, but they hadn't talked in so long—six years, at that point—I didn't think your mother would want to hear from me," my mother said.

"How could you have known? Mom was pretty far gone at the end, but she kept on talking about Saul this, Saul that. Her childhood memories were so much more vivid to her than the present. His name was the last word out of her mouth when she died."

Evelyn stopped, and we all fell silent. I couldn't help but ponder what could have been if Ada had reached out before he died. Or if the letter had found us.

"It makes me feel sad for them. All that lost time." I moaned.

Evelyn and Mom nodded in agreement.

"Did you ever meet Uncle Samuel and Aunt Rachel?" I asked. I'd found their names during my genealogical research. As an only child, I couldn't imagine what might lead to losing touch with one's siblings.

"Once or twice when we were in Israel, though I don't remember them very well. They had joined a community of Israeli settlers, and Mom just couldn't bear to see how intent they were on chasing their Palestinian neighbors off their land. I believe your dad stopped talking to them too, around that time."

I thought about what Patrick said about wounds and patterns being passed on.

"It's as though Valda's trauma of having to choose between her husband and saving her children was transmitted to the next generation—where they then felt forced to choose between their loved ones and their own convictions. Dad with Ada withholding about their father. Ada with Dad. Both of them with their siblings."

"I'd never thought of it that way, but it makes sense," Evelyn said. "So, I guess we're the generation that gets to break the trend, huh, kiddo?" I smiled in agreement. I couldn't remember the last time I'd been called kiddo, but it sounded warm and inviting coming out of her mouth.

We were quiet while we finished our bagels and drank the rest of our morning drinks—tea for me and coffee for the other two.

"Okay, onto serious matters," Evelyn said after we'd cleaned up, winking at us so we'd know she was being facetious. After all, we'd been discussing nothing *but* serious matters. I smiled. Both her openness and her humor were such a breath of fresh air compared to the uptightness of my upbringing.

"You have three days in New York, and it sounds like this young woman might need to do some sightseeing. What would you like to do? Do you want to tour the city, or do you want to start with your dad's things?"

"No sightseeing—not for my benefit, anyway. It doesn't feel like it's that kind of trip. Unless, Mom, you want to? I know you're usually working the whole time you're here."

"No, I agree. It's not that kind of trip. Although, as we discussed, I would like to take you out to a fancy restaurant tomorrow night for your birthday. And, Evelyn, I'd love for you to join if you'd like. I already made a reservation for three just in case, figuring it was easier to change the number down than up."

"Oh, Sarah, I didn't know it's your birthday! How wonderful. How old are you going to be?"

"Thirty-five."

"Ah, what a great age! I'd love to join," Evelyn said, and I smiled, happy Mom's plan had worked.

"And I don't mind what order we do it in, but if you know where Dad and Aunt Ada grew up, or anything about their neighborhood at all, I'd love to go there."

"I'm so glad you said that! I actually made a little map of the area in Brooklyn in case you were interested. Everything is different now, of course, but Mom was a big nostalgist and as such a bit of a hoarder. I have lots of old black-and-white photos to show you how it used to be. Do you want to go now?"

I nodded enthusiastically.

An hour and a half later, having navigated the subway maze from Manhattan to Brooklyn, Evelyn pointed to a credit union building kitty-corner from the Flatbush Avenue-Brooklyn College exit.

"This is where Ebinger's Bakery used to be," she said proudly, although the name meant nothing to me.

I looked at my mother for clarification, but she shook her head.

"You're clearly not a New Yorker!" Evelyn teased when she saw my face. "They were famous for their blackout cake. It was basically chocolate cake with gooey chocolate filling and ridiculously sweet chocolate frosting. If you look up 'sinfully delicious' in the dictionary, I think you'll find a photo of that cake." Mom and I laughed. I could almost taste the cake from her description. "When Saul started volunteering for CORE, he forbade our grandmother from buying from them, because of their discriminatory practices towards Black people, he said. But she snuck them in when he was away. She couldn't help it—they were that good."

As we continued our walk, Evelyn showed us where their high school (now a big Safeway) had been; the old post office (now a small neighborhood gym); the corner store (now a laundromat). The only thing that was somewhat intact was a little park. I saw a mottled oak tree that looked like it had seen better days and wondered if it had known my father.

Finally, we arrived at the location where they had lived. As I stood in front of the tall building that looked *nothing* like the small block house in the old photo I held in my hands, I started bawling. My mother took one hand, and Evelyn took the other.

Sixty-plus years ago, my father and her mother had lived here. Allowing my tears to flow freely down my cheeks, I closed my eyes and let my imagination take over.

Saul, four years old. Everyone else in the family now knows that Isaac isn't coming back. Nobody is telling him anything, but he's picking up on the grief thicker than the smoke from the glue factory. Six years old, trying to teach himself to ride on his brother's bicycle, which is much too big for him. He skins his knee but tries to hide it, so he won't get in trouble. As a preteen, he gets a paper route to try to help out. Ada has already gone, and he feels he has to pull his weight—he gets serious very young. Art is his one escape. That and collecting stamps.

I stopped in my reverie, remembering the stamp collection I'd found among Dad's things Evelyn was storing for us—which had solved the mystery of the cutout envelopes. My tears had now cleared, and when I opened my eyes, I felt more present than I had in quite a while. Perhaps ever. As though some of my missing puzzle pieces had returned.

More fell into place as I read the Dad-half of the letter exchanges with his sister (I'd given Evelyn the Ada-half) and pored over his paintings. The one I liked the most was a self-portrait he'd done when he was twelve. His big, intense gray eyes stared at me from the page as though they could look into my soul. He was the age I'd been when he died, and somehow, that meant something, like he was reaching across the page to let me know that time was circular, not linear. That I'd be all right. That he was still with me.

My lungs sighed with pleasure as I took a deep, full breath in both my belly and my chest. Who knew there could be so much space in those bronchioles?

The birthday dinner was lovely, especially since I couldn't remember the last time I'd celebrated with my mother—and Evelyn was truly the cousin-sister I'd never had. But really, it was just the metaphoric icing on an already delicious and wonderfully gooey cake.

On the day before our return home, there was only one thing I still needed to do, although I didn't quite know why.

Chapter Forty-Six

January – July 1925

A Quarter of a Century

Maggie

The year 1925 started with a bang that shook me out of the residue of my despondency. The Brinkmans threw a big party to mark my twenty-five years in this world. A quarter of a century! I was beginning to feel old, although I received no sympathy from my friends, most of whom had been around much longer than I had.

On February 14, Valentine's Day, Angeline Rose Brinkman was born at home with the help of Eliza, the midwife who also brought Thomas and Rose into the world. One of the few fights I'd ever witnessed between Sadie and Benjamin was over whether to have a doctor or midwife assist with the birth. Still mourning his daughter's death, Benjamin hadn't wanted to take any chances and had pleaded with Sadie to have a doctor instead, but Sadie had been adamant.

As it was, the birth was an easy one, and from the minute she was born, Angeline captured our hearts, prompting her parents to spontaneously change her name from their original plan of Rosaline. We all agreed that her birthday was no accident, for she was indeed our love child. Angeline was born with soft black hair covering her head, deep grooves under her eyes that gave her the look of a tiny sage, and the smallest hands and feet I'd ever seen.

From the moment his parents brought her home, Thomas was besotted with his sister. He was almost more protective of her than his parents were, and we suspected he remembered what had happened to Rose, even though he'd been so young.

Thankfully, Sadie had a parade of people coming to help her, so she didn't need my support, as I had my hands full with my work and helping Mabel prepare for her wedding. Despite a number of delays, the *Survey Graphic's Harlem Number* was finally published on March 1 and was well received in academic and intellectual circles.

Within weeks, Locke told me they had ordered a press run of twelve thousand copies, and *The Nation* gave it a glowing review. But Alain (and I, by extension) hardly noticed, as we were hard at work getting his *New Negro* anthology ready for publication. This was an even bigger affair, as the book had thirty-four contributors to the magazine's twenty-four, with more graphics, and, as Locke explained to me:

"Boni wants the focus to be on the cultural renaissance as a whole, not just Harlem. And to be honest, that piques my interest too, although it means my article on Harlem won't be in it."

My main role was to go through each article with my "eagle editorial eye" as Alain put it and stay on top of the artists and contributors. Even when I was teaching, there hadn't been so many pieces to hold on to all at once, and most mornings, I woke with my stomach clenched in a ball of nerves.

In the midst of all of that, Mabel got married on April 17. As happy as I was for her, I was flooded with memories of my own wedding and struggled to make myself useful. I felt out of place as everyone around me bustled about. Her mother was busy directing the flowers as the groom's brother greeted the guests with a charming smile. Even the flower girls seemed to know what to do, as they helped the florists set their bouquets. When Mabel and Barnaby exchanged "I dos," however, I felt only joy seeing my college friend so happy.

My wedding card to Mabel was also a goodbye letter, as I sensed we might not see each other again.

Dear Mabel,

My heart gladdens so to see you begin this journey into love with Barnaby. So much joy awaits you, I know, because gaiety is what you create everywhere you go. For the past four years, I've seen how tidepools of happiness follow in your wake. I'm so blessed you chose to share this special gift with me.

Thank you for being the air to my water. The hummingbird to my skylark. For showing me that our people can take flight from the sheer power of our own delight. For reminding me, even in my darkest hour, even when I can't quite hear you, that there is always hope. Remember, also, to take time to land, time for yourself, because air scatters under too much pressure.

With love,
Maggie

In the meantime, I'd fallen behind in the writing schedule I'd set myself. Alain himself was preoccupied both with getting the book ready and with managing mounting tensions with the administration at Howard. Although I tried not to listen to university gossip, from the snippets that reached my ears, I learned that Locke and President Durkee had been locking horns over issues ranging from teacher salaries to curriculum changes. The fight to hire a Negro president was ongoing.

On June 15, Durkee announced he was firing Dr. Locke and three other professors, citing financial difficulties. Alain was furious, especially after all of his years of service. He wrote an angry letter to the board of trustees, who eventually agreed to pay him a year's salary and call it a leave of absence.

"I talked to a lawyer, but he said that Durkee had the right to dismiss me!" Locke fumed to me a few days later as he paced the floor of his office. He'd already been dividing his time between Washington and New York to complete his anthology, and had begun renting the top floor of a house on 139th Street in Harlem. When the news of his dismissal broke, he decided to make it his base and urged me to move back to New York.

"Maggie, what are your next plans?"

I shrugged, thankful I could at least be honest with him. "I'm not sure. We've been so busy, I haven't really thought about it. The only thing I know is I can't stay where I am living. I've considered going to North Carolina to be with my family."

"Have you thought of returning to New York? You used to live there, right? With the doctor and his wife?"

"I did, and I have. But last I heard, Frank was there, representing Marcus Garvey …" I said, my voice trailing off. If we were both in the same city, I feared I'd want to look for him, and I didn't think I could face being turned away again.

"Definitely something to consider. If you decided to move back there, you could help me finish the anthology and focus on your writing. Harlem is the place to be right now, and I can introduce you to some important writers and artists if you want."

Over the next week, I pondered what to do next.

"It's my choice," I reminded myself. "What do I want?" The very question still elicited fear. The voice of doom had lost some of its power since I'd started writing again, but I could still feel the residue of its chant: "You will lose everything if you want too much."

I decided to write Edna, to tell her I was considering moving back and to inquire about Frank's whereabouts. Her response was emphatic:

Dearest Maggie,

I'd be so happy if you moved back! New York has not been the same since you left.

I haven't wanted to tell you about Frank, as I know it's such a tender topic for you. But when Marcus Garvey was sent to the Atlanta Federal Penitentiary in February, Frank decided to move there with him.

Josie is quite the young lady now—you won't believe how tall she's gotten—and between her studies and her friends, she has little time for her old Mama. Lewis is busier than ever with his practice and is training a young doctor to take over for him when he retires. Which means that right now, he is working night and day. So, you see, your old friend is lonely, and in much need of companionship. Your room is ready and waiting for you.

Please hurry back to us.
Your loving friend,
Edna

I ignored the small voice compelling me to go to North Carolina and decided to return to New York. That seemed like a safer choice than following my heart, considering how things had turned out the last time I did. I told myself that Harlem might be the font of inspiration for me that it was for so many artists—and that it was the perfect place for me to turn my autobiographical senior thesis into a memoir, the only thing I knew for sure I wanted to do.

And so it was that amid teary goodbyes, I packed a suitcase with the belongings I had acquired during my years in Washington, DC—many books, my journals, the stone, and a few dresses I'd bought or gotten as hand-me-downs from Sadie. I donated the couple Frank had gotten me.

I slipped a letter to Sadie under their door before I left.

Dear Sadie,

Thank you for sharing the brightness of your fire with me. I have been inspired by the passion with which you throw yourself into life. Your care for Thomas and Benjamin (and now baby Angeline). Your love of books, music, and art. The incredible parties that allow folks who might not otherwise have met to gather and share their talents with each other. Your incredible piano playing (I hope you never again stop, for I believe the angels sing when you play).

I was heartbroken to stand by and watch as your spark was temporarily snuffed out by grief. And heartened to witness you slowly start smoldering back to life, using the sheer force of your will as kindling.

Thank you for mirroring back our potential for resilience after seemingly unendurable loss. You have helped me transcend my own.

I am forever indebted to you for helping me bring my family here for graduation. I hope someday to pay you back in kind, in whatever way I can.

Love, Maggie

As I waited for the train to arrive, I had a sudden memory of standing on the platform with Frank. He was elated because the Senate had given Dyer's bill a favorable report. As the train approached, he bent over and kissed me. It was the last time I remembered us being happy together.

My heart doubled over in pain as grief roiled in my entrails. Just then, a crow landed on my suitcase and started pecking wildly at the handle. I was startled out of my turmoil and began to laugh. The crow stared at me for a second, with eyes that rivaled Locke's for intensity, before taking off in a flurry of feathers and cawing.

The Riddle of the Crow

Messenger of night,
What omen do you bring?
I hear your call
But my mind cannot
Fathom its meaning.

Perhaps
Only my heart
Can heed it.

Do you foretell death
Or rebirth?
Will I return
From the cinders
Of my dreams?
Is there a way
Out of the darkness?

Scanning bottomless eyes
For an answer,
I see my question
Mirrored in their depth.

Chapter Forty-Seven

Homecoming

Sarah

On the day before our departure, my feet led me to Central Park. Although my brain kept asking me what we were doing there, I was learning to trust my intuition, no questions asked. At my request, Mom stayed back with Evelyn. This was something I needed to do alone, and in any case, they were both happy to have more time together, completing the missing pieces of fragmented memories and encounters.

I walked past the joggers, the scooters, the skateboarders, and the throngs of tourists with cameras. Past fountains and floral arrangements. Past a sprawling lawn filled with dogs, lovers, families, and friends playing games. To a worn bench by a little stream.

Closing my eyes, I felt the October sun bathing my face. As I took deep breaths and sank deeper into the wooden surface of the bench, I felt a subtle shift in my perception, as though my eyesight had gone fuzzy. I rubbed my eyes, hoping my vision would return to normal, but the feeling remained. I knew I'd felt something similar a while ago, but when …?

The hypnotherapy session with Deborah!

I was sensing Maggie. Or, rather, myself as her. I took a few breaths to steady myself and keep the fear that had crept in at bay.

As I got re-accustomed to this strange feeling of not being quite myself, I had the impression that I, as Maggie, wasn't alone. A man was sitting next to her/me. I felt love and excitement. As well as overpowering grief and mutual relief at being able to share the pain with someone else.

And then, the feeling was gone. As though a door had closed.

I got up, and my body guided me further into the park to a grove of oak trees. I sat down against one of them.

"This is where I knew." I heard/sensed/felt. "It was time to go home."

A flash of white caught my eye. Leaning down, I saw a cream-colored stone, polished smooth by the elements with glints of gold and silver. On the other side was a thin streak of cobalt blue. Loving the feel in my hand, I slipped it into the pocket of my jeans.

When I left the park, I could tell—from the way my vision was crisper and the way my legs felt more firmly planted on the ground as I walked—that I'd just gotten another puzzle piece back.

On the flight home, Mom decided she was ready to open up to me about her own secrets.

"You know, Sarah, this trip really got me thinking about how precious time is. I've felt inspired, witnessing how much learning about your father has impacted you. And seeing you and Evelyn speak so easily and freely about things, even though you just met."

"Thanks, Mom," I said, feeling touched both by her noticing and her desire to share with me. "I felt the same way watching the two of you together. I'm glad we're getting a second chance with each other."

"Me too. And that's why I want to share with you a few things about *my* past that I'm not proud of …" She paused, and I nodded, waiting to see where this was headed. I definitely hadn't been expecting her to say *that*.

"As you might imagine, my mother was not an easy woman to live with," she started without further preamble. "She was so critical and demanding. It only got worse after my father left—I was ten at the time. It turned out he'd been cheating on her with her best friend, although I didn't find out until years later."

"I had no idea. What did she tell you at the time?"

"Nothing. She was pretty tight-lipped, and it was the philosophy back then that children needed to be protected from adult truths."

I nodded, thinking of my father and how they'd tried to protect him from the truth of his father's death.

"When I was seventeen, it was the beginning of the 1960s. One of my friends introduced me to her older brother, Chuck. He had his own studio apartment and rode a Harley Davidson. I felt so alive when I was with him, and I thought I was in love. I wrote my mother a hateful letter describing all the ways she'd wronged me and told her that I was going to live with my boyfriend. I instructed her not to come after me." She paused, a pained look on her face as she remembered.

"Suffice it to say, things didn't end very well with Chuck. I was a senior in high school, and I stopped going to classes. I'd always been top of my class—that had been my way of getting attention and validation." I nodded, knowing that side of my mother well.

"But then I found another way, at least temporarily." She stopped and looked at me. "I've never told anybody what I'm about to tell you. I alluded to it with your father, but omitted the details. I've been so ashamed, and it's been easier to pretend it didn't happen. To tell myself it was water under the bridge."

"I appreciate that you want to share this with me, and it's okay if you change your mind. I can see this is difficult, and there's no reason I have to know," I said, my heart aching for her.

"No, I *want* you to know." She inhaled deeply before letting the breath out with an audible sigh, as if to say, "Here goes nothing."

"Chuck and I did a lot of drugs together. One day I woke up with bruises on my thighs and bleeding. I had no idea what had happened. To this day, I don't know for sure, although from what I was able to glean, he invited someone to have sex with me for money, and I fought him off despite being high on cocaine."

The last words came out in the faintest whisper, so I had to strain to understand, and my mother couldn't look at me as she uttered them. I felt a swelling of tenderness and sorrow gripping my throat for what she'd gone through, and I had to fight back my own tears.

"I'm so sorry, Mom! That sounds really scary and incredibly brave."

"I don't know about that. Incredibly reckless, if you ask me now," she said, her voice dripping with disdain for her seventeen-year-old self.

"I didn't want to go back to Mother after what I'd written in that letter. I felt so embarrassed. Luckily, a friend of mine knew of an organization that worked with troubled teens. By that time, I was eighteen. They helped me get off drugs, finish high school, and apply for colleges. I promised myself I would never be that out of control again and certainly not let a boy take advantage of me." I nodded. I could relate to some of that, at least in terms of vowing to be in control.

"What happened then? You must have had some reconciliation with Grandma. I know you were never close, but she was still a part of your life …"

"I reached out to her when I was graduating from college with honors. To her credit, she came, and we never talked about that period in my life." She let out a sigh of relief at having gotten to the end of her story. "And that's the most shameful part of my history."

"I'm so glad you told me, Mom. I know it took a lot of courage and trust. I really appreciate both."

She nodded, but didn't look at me.

"Can I share something that I've learned in therapy, and you can take it if it's useful or leave it if it's not?"

"Sure," she said, finally glancing over at me.

"You just wanted to know you were loved, and you mattered. And there's nothing shameful in that. As traumatic as the situation you were in was, there was—there is—nothing wrong with *you*. You did the best you could at the time."

"You really believe that?" she asked, her voice sounding tentative and young. I'd never heard her so unsure of herself. Part of me wanted to hug her, and part of me couldn't bear seeing her so vulnerable.

"I didn't used to, but now I *know* it to be true."

"I don't know if I can, but it's a nice thought to mull over."

At that point, I gave her an awkward, seated half-hug and thanked her again for opening up to me.

"Hearing your story does help me understand you better."

After we'd taken a break to eat the lunches Evelyn had packed for us, I decided to make a confession of my own.

"Can I share my own embarrassing secret with you, since we're on the topic?"

"Of course, Sarah."

"I slept with a married doctor when I worked in the Palestinian occupied territories." I said, not quite making eye contact with my mother.

"Really?" Mom said, sounding surprised, though I wasn't sure if it was because of what I told her or because I was sharing relationship information with her. That was something she'd never been privy to in the past.

So I told her about Dr. Zahari. I had been assigned to work in the main hospital in Tulkarem, in the West Bank. It wasn't long before I realized that I was needed as much (probably more) for the protection my nationality provided as for my nursing skills.

Every morning, the ambulance driver picked me up first, then proceeded to pick up the Palestinian doctors and nurses. Dr. Zahari was the last and would be waiting in a navy-blue suit and tie, with his neatly ironed white scrubs over it. Every morning, we were stopped and searched. It pained me that I was treated with much more respect than my Palestinian counterparts, who were by far my seniors in age and experience. But still, at the end of every day, Dr. Zahari never failed to thank me.

"I never heard him raise his voice. Not with his staff, not with the soldiers who *never* failed to taunt him. Not after he'd been stopped at a checkpoint for six hours and had missed a critical shift at the hospital. And certainly not with his patients. When he was with them, he always made them feel like they were the only ones who mattered, no matter how busy he was."

"Those kinds of doctors are rare gems. He sounds special," my mother said, and I nodded.

"He was. And married with kids. A devout Muslim. I knew I couldn't let anything happen, but of course, that didn't stop me from falling in love with him. And then …" I stopped, remembering.

Two days before the end of the fasting month of Ramadan, undercover Israeli Special Forces posing as Palestinians raided a building in search of two men. When they found out the men were not there, the Special Forces started shooting rubber bullets, which could still be lethal at close range, into the crowd.

Thirteen people were seriously injured, and a twenty-year-old bystander was killed. The body of the young man was still warm when he was loaded into the ambulance, along with a young woman who had been hit in the stomach by a stray bullet. She was still alive, but moaning in pain. A soldier shouted something over a megaphone before another round of rubber bullets was fired.

"This is for the children on their way home," Farid, the ambulance driver, had translated for me.

"Anyway, I'll spare you the details, but the days that followed were terrible. The day before Eid al-Fitr—the three-day Muslim festival following Ramadan—when everyone was out shopping for food and gifts, the Israeli military declared a curfew."

"Wow, that sounds dangerous, especially since I imagine you were in the thick of it. I'm almost glad I didn't know about that at the time," she said, and I was moved by her look of retroactive concern. So much for all my assumptions that she didn't really care about my well-being. "Did all hell break loose after that, Sarah?"

"That's putting it mildly. The soldiers raided the town, shooting rubber bullets into the crowd and tear-gassing people as they tried to get home. Over fifty people were hospitalized. An old man with a pulmonary embolism was made to walk between roadblocks. He collapsed from the effort and died in my arms."

"Oh, Sarah, I'm so sorry."

"Yes, it was pretty awful. But that's what drew Dr. Zahari and me together. We spent two straight days and nights caring for people and were so exhausted by the end, I guess we kind of fell into each other's arms." I stopped, feeling the pain of what happened after. "It lasted a week. Maybe two. I don't really remember. And then one night, he stopped coming. He started avoiding me and had me transferred to another wing."

"Do you know what happened?"

"No, he wouldn't talk to me. He didn't even come to the goodbye party when I left nine months later. My guess is that either someone saw us together or his conscience got the best of him. But I felt so …" I said, struggling to find the word.

"Worthless?" my mother guessed.

"Yeah. It's funny, though. I thought I'd feel distraught telling you. I haven't even shared the details with my therapist, we've been so focused on other topics. But the truth is, I don't feel much of anything. It was so long ago, and I'm such a different person now."

"Yes, you are."

By the time our plane landed, we probably both felt a little vulnerability whiplash. But I, at least, also felt so much lighter. We'd ferreted our darkest secrets from their shadowy corners and found that in the light of day, they lost their power over our hearts.

Chapter Forty-Eight
August 1925 - April 1926

The Harlem Daze

Maggie

As I approached the Joneses' house, I stopped. Images of the first time I walked up those steps—more than ten years earlier—came flooding back. I remembered the rustle of the yellow dress I was wearing and how foreign it felt after months of dressing like a boy. My confusion when Edna opened the door. Those first days and my constant fear that I would make a mistake and they would fire me.

I'd come full circle (or so I thought). Retraced the maze of time back to the beginning. I could still feel that young girl inside of me. Fierce. Wild. Scared. Broken. Innocent. I'd acquired so much knowledge since then, but she knew things I'd forgotten. About love. About freedom. Now, I was lost in a different way. The dissolution of my marriage had shaken my faith in my own heart. The voice of the forest had dimmed. I hadn't heard her call or guidance in years. I'd emerged from the narrow focus on survival to find that my struggle was now internal. How to forge my path and find my way back to myself within the fray of "civilized" life.

While at first, I had to adjust to living with the Joneses again without being their employee, Edna made it clear that

I was there as their guest, and we soon fell into a comfortable rhythm. Every morning, I woke to the smell of fresh coffee. We sipped it together, sometimes in companionable silence, sometimes discussing the latest news or gossip. I could tell by the longing look I sometimes caught her giving her daughter and husband that she was indeed lonely, making it easier to accept their hospitality.

Josie, now sixteen, was busy with her studies and friends much of the time, although our special bond seemed to have endured the separation. Josie knew I was often up late writing. Their neighborhood finally got electricity, and even though Lewis complained about the number of patients he saw coming in with burns from faulty lines, it allowed Josie and me to work into the night without straining our eyes.

If Josie saw the light on in my room when she got home, she knocked on my door ever so softly. Once I let her in, she sat on the edge of my bed with her long legs pulled up under her chin and poured out her heart. Her eyes dark and liquid in the flickering light of the bulb, she told me about her dreams of becoming the first Negro woman to get a PhD in mathematics and her doubts that she could even get to the master's level.

I just sat and listened. Sometimes she asked me to stroke her hair the way I had when she was a girl. Other times, I'd lie back and close my eyes, nodding every once in a while to let her know I was still listening, letting the sound of her voice wash over the cluttered activities of my day.

In September, I traveled to North Carolina to visit Mama. Being around Edna and Josie nourished me and reminded me that my life could have taken a very different turn if I hadn't met them. However, it also made me more aware of how much I missed my own family and what was taken away from me when I fled from the Tanners. I also wanted to collect stories of my family's past for my memoir.

Mama told me of her mother, who she said was dark and tall, with a lilting voice. She was the daughter of former slaves, born shortly after the Emancipation Proclamation. Mama hadn't known her father and never pressed her mother for details, but assumed he was light-skinned since she was several shades lighter than her mother—just as I was. She also told me what she knew of my father's parents, who came from Jamaica at the invitation of a cousin, only to find they had been brought over to pay off a debt.

I got my family's permission to tell our tale, promising to change names, locations, and some details to make it less identifiable. The last thing I wanted was the Tanners finding us, although I seemed more worried than anyone else.

"The white man thinks his story's the only one worth telling, while ours rots in the red earth. Chile, I be happy you tell our story. Thas' God's gift to you. And 'twas yo' father and brother's gift to you that you escaped. Never feel like you shouldn't use it because you got away. That would be a waste of ever'thing!"

Mama's lungs weren't working so well, and I kept trying to shush her as she wheezed through her entreaty, but she batted my protests away like flies on a hot day.

Although I'd intended the visit as a work trip, the slow pace of my family's life, Margaret's sweet affection for me, and the love they all shared freely with each other—without a thought that it might be otherwise—imprinted deeply on my heart.

Back in New York, I felt restless, crowded out of myself by the sheer number of people and houses. By the constant noise and bustle. My heart whispered her longing to return to North

Carolina. That she didn't want to live in someone else's home anymore, no matter how welcoming.

I pleaded with her to just let me finish the memoir. I thought that once it was complete, I'd have more clarity on what I wanted to do next. I wrote into the wee hours of the morning since the dead of the night was the only time there was enough stillness to hear my own voice.

I finished my first draft in November. The edits took more time than I thought they would. I had considered a number of possible titles for the memoir, before landing on *The Way Home*. Alain had already commented on an earlier version, and when I showed him the final draft in February, he beamed with pleasure.

"Maggie, do you remember Charles Boni, who is publishing my anthology?"

"Yes, why?"

"Well, his brothers, Albert and Horace Liveright, started Boni & Liveright a few years ago. Liveright's the one who published Jean Toomer's *Cane*. He's innovative and open to Negro writers but also known amongst whites. If he agrees to publish your memoir, you'd have a broader audience. Would you like me to share your manuscript with him?"

I felt uneasy as he spoke, but I dismissed the feeling. I'd worked so hard to complete this. Why wouldn't I want to publish my memoir so my words could reach more people? I nodded yes.

Without the writing to keep me as busy, my restlessness started to mount, but I still didn't feel ready to leave. I threw myself into helping Alain put the finishing touches on *The New Negro* before it went to print. When the final rush was behind us, he introduced me to many of the authors featured in the anthology.

I had already met Langston Hughes upon his return from Paris while he was caring for his mother in Washington, DC. He was two years younger than me, with lively eyes and a groomed mustache that framed his infectious smile. As intimidated as I was to meet the author of "The Negro Speaks of Rivers," a poem that had taken root in my soul, I took to him immediately.

I enjoyed the company of Countee Cullen, Jean Toomer, Zora Neale Hurston, and many of the other authors Locke introduced me to, but it always took me a few meetings to emerge from my initial defensive shyness and participate in the conversations. Much to my disappointment, because I'd really hoped to find my inspiration here, I felt more drained than enlivened by the Harlem culture and grateful to be able to retreat to the safety of the Joneses' house, where I could harness my feelings to the page.

The Harlem Daze

You lure me in
With promises
Of glory,
Glimpses
Of hidden jewels
Beneath gilded words and
Lilting notes that enthrall,
Leaving me gasping for more.

Bewitched,
I find myself helpless
In your charming arms.
I exit your dazzling rooms
Empty
And wrung dry.

*In the pale light of day
My life looks
Limp and gray,
A white sheet washed
Too many times.*

*My soul
Knows that you are
Arsenic to my heart,
Just as you captivate
My mind.*

*I long for green,
For air
That cleanses my lungs
And clears the way
For my thoughts
To flow through.*

It was around this time that I started dreaming of the wild again. Although the details varied, I always felt the same sense of joy and freedom. Of not needing to answer to anyone.

One night, I dreamt I was sitting by a stream, gulping water. When I looked up, Mama was standing in front of me. Beckoning me forward.

I woke up with a start, my heart racing and dread in my stomach. The feeling was still with me when I arrived at Alain's apartment a few hours later to discuss *The New Negro*'s success. I was shaking off the March rain from my pink rain jacket when I noticed Locke grinning from ear to ear.

"Alain, you look like a cat who just caught a mouse. What're you so happy about?"

"Mr. Liveright thinks you are as talented as I do, Maggie. He wants to publish your memoir!" he burst out, his eyes bulging with pride.

I sat down on the edge of his wooden work chair, unsure of why I was feeling so jarred by the news.

"Maggie, you look like you saw a ghost! This is happy news!" Alain said, surprised by my lack of enthusiasm.

"That's wonderful, Alain. Thanks so much for your help," I said, excitement starting to thaw some of the sense of foreboding I'd woken up with.

"Come on, between the sales for *The New Negro* and the publication of your memoir, we need to go celebrate. My treat. No work today, and I'll talk your ear off until that cat you were mentioning gives you your tongue back!"

Back at the Joneses' home, I broke the news to Edna.

"I'm so happy for you, Maggie. But why don't you look happier?"

"Honestly, I don't know. I want it to be published, of course. But I keep on feeling like I'm pushing against a wall here. Nothing feels natural. I've been having dreams of the wild and of home. I'm grateful to be back, but it somehow doesn't feel quite right. Like I'm wearing clothes that no longer fit."

Edna nodded as I spoke. "I've sensed there was something weighing on you. Maggie, is there a reason why you wouldn't go home if that's what you want?" she asked softly. Her gentleness prompted a few tears to flow down my cheeks.

"You're going to think it's silly ..." I hesitated.

"That's not possible."

"Well, when I was in the forest, I bargained with God, or someone, that if I survived and found a safe home, I wouldn't want anything else. When I got here, I told myself that as long as others wanted things on my behalf, like for me to teach, or Frank wanting to marry me, that was okay. But then I decided to go to Howard because *I* wanted to, and I lost Frank. I lost everything," I said, my voice breaking.

I lay my head against Edna's shoulder and sobbed. I had never spoken my bargain aloud to another person. Doing so not only unleashed the emotions I'd been holding in for so long, but also gave me a tiny bit more distance from the belief.

"Oh, Maggie," she said when my tears had subsided. "That's not silly at all. Lord knows how I pleaded with Him when Josie retreated inside herself. That's what we do when we feel powerless." A feeling of relief washed over me as she said this.

"But you must know it's not because of your bargain that you survived. And it's not because you broke it and went to Howard that your marriage fell apart. Nobody and nothing could have saved Frank from himself."

I raised an eyebrow, a little unsure about this. But I could feel some part of me relaxing.

"It's hard for me to trust that, Edna. When I follow what others want of me, nothing bad happens. But when I follow my heart, everything unravels. I feel like tragedy follows me." My voice trembled again. Edna put both hands on my shoulders and looked deep into my eyes.

"Maggie, what happened to Frank wasn't your fault. What happened to your father and brother wasn't your fault. You deserve to be happy." And while doubt still had a foothold in my mind, I felt her words landing in a deep place in my heart that already knew them to be true.

The next morning, I woke up early, Edna's words still echoing throughout my chest. With a heavy heart, I remembered I had a meeting with Locke and Charlotte Mason. She was a wealthy white widow he'd met a few months back. He called her the Godmother and had thought a meeting with me would be beneficial.

"I think you'll like her, Maggie. Langston and Zora have

already met her. She can be a little meddling, but she is a connoisseur of art and literature. More than that, she's a rich patron interested in supporting Negro artists, which is a rare find," he had said.

I was still feeling unsettled when it was time for me to leave, so I slid my cream-colored stone into my satchel for good luck. As I approached 399 Park Avenue, I felt the foreboding feeling intensify. If I'd had a way of getting word to Alain, I would probably have turned around. Instead, I rang the bell, looking up at the most opulent residence I'd ever seen.

An attendant led me down a maze of rooms to an elevator that took me up to her spacious living room, where Alain was already seated, sipping tea. A long window stretching across most of the far wall revealed Manhattan buzzing below us. The thought suddenly occurred to me that it was the first time I'd been inside a white person's home since I had run away from the Tanners'.

In fact, I realized suddenly, I'd had precious few interactions with whites—other than the occasional transactional ones—since I'd arrived in New York. The president of Howard University was the one I saw with the most consistency, but I'd never had any need or reason to talk to him. And although Frank had told me all about Representative Dyer, I'd never met him. With gratitude for the relative peace running in primarily Negro circles had afforded me over the past decade, I turned my attention back to the conversation at hand.

"What is the news about your return to Howard, Alain?" she asked, pronouncing his name the French way. "I would think that Mordecai being the first Negro president would help."

"I hear it's in process. But did I tell you that Fisk University has asked me to be an exchange professor for the 1927–28 school year? I was a little hesitant to spend a year in the South, but I think it will be eye-opening for me. I've traveled the world and faced both their hostility and their curiosity, so why not in my own country?" he responded.

The Godmother had the whitest hair I'd ever seen, pulled back in a bun, and round, wire-framed glasses, from behind which her sharp blue eyes peered out at me. While she spoke with a veneer of kindness and interest, I also sensed something hard and determined in her.

And when she turned her attention from Alain to me, there was something very subtle in the way she looked me over that reminded me of the Tanners. The hint of ownership and domination. It was all I could do not to run out of the room.

"I have read your memoir, Maggie," she said, patting the manuscript resting on her lavender dress as though it were a lapdog. "It shows some promise, at least for one so young. In some places, the language is a little flowery, and in others, it's very raw. Crude, almost. But if I'm your patron, we can work on that for your next work, I'm sure. Give it a little more polish," she said, with the haughty air of a woman used to getting her way.

All of a sudden, I was overcome with a wave of nausea. The restlessness that had been building for months felt like a tempest about to erupt. I knew I had to get away.

I ran out of the room and almost knocked over the maid bringing us more tea. "Water closet?" I managed to ask. She pointed down the hall, and I made it just in time to lose my lunch and dinner from the previous night.

I knew I couldn't go back in and found a staircase that led back down, ignoring the worried voice of an attendant behind me asking me where I was going, if I was all right. The doorman saw me rushing towards him and opened the heavy door as quickly as he could. Once outside, I caught my breath as carriages and motorcars rushed past me. I needed to be near trees.

I somehow found my way to Central Park and scurried until I found a secluded spot with a grove of oak trees. I sat on the ground with my back against one of them. Before I knew what I was doing, I started screaming, trusting that the wind, street noise, and distance from other humans would drown out the sound.

I screamed out all the voices that had ever told me what to do. The Tanners. My teachers. Frank. The philosophers and writers I'd read in college. Even Edna and Sadie's. When I was done, I collapsed against the trunk of the tree, feeling spent. Wrung out. I closed my eyes and had a sudden vision of myself at fourteen, in the forest, making that bargain so I would feel less scared. Less overwhelmed. So I could put one foot in front of the other.

"But that's not *why* I survived," I said out loud, suddenly feeling the truth of these words.

"It wasn't my fault," I whispered. And then repeated the words, over and over, gaining more volume each time, until I was laughing. Feeling a little giddy, I turned my head and saw a dandelion. Plucking it carefully from the earth, I held it a moment in my hand before blowing the white tufts into the wind. As I did, I imagined I was releasing that desperate promise I'd made back into the wild.

"I deserve to be happy," I whispered. This was my new wish for myself.

Without quite knowing why, I took my stone out of my satchel and placed it where the dandelion had been—perhaps to mark the end of a chapter. Or to plant the seeds for the next.

Walking home, I felt light. I knew exactly what I needed to do.

I stayed up late writing goodbye letters. A long one to Josie, filled with all the memories of our special time together and reflecting her blossoming into womanhood. Ending with "Josie + her brilliance = first Negro woman with a PhD in mathematics."

After a few crumpled attempts at writing to Alain Locke, I decided I'd have more time to find the right words on the train ride South. Although I was clear about the things I wanted to thank him for (there were many), I kept stumbling over the part of me that wanted to explain—maybe even apologize for—the events of the previous day. For running out on him. My heart, on the other hand, was telling me in no uncertain terms that I had nothing to be sorry for.

My last letter, I could probably have written in my sleep.

Dear Edna, my heart sister,
  Thank you (although those pallid words couldn't possibly express the depth of my gratitude) for being my rock. My mountain. My safe place to land. Showing me the steadfastness of love. Your care gives life to those blessed enough to receive it. I hope you know that.
  I've seen your earth quake with the tremors of life and return to firm ground just as quickly. I don't know where I'd be if I hadn't met you when I first arrived in New York. You single-handedly changed the course of my life. Of that, I have no doubt.
  With love, always
  Your Maggie

The next morning, I said my emotional goodbyes to Edna, Lewis, and Josie and wired my family to let them know of my arrival. I was just finishing packing when the doorbell rang. The postman handed me a telegram from North Carolina.

Mama sick. Come now.

Chapter Forty-Nine

Dancing with the Loose Ends

Sarah

After I finished unpacking, I checked my emails and opened my Facebook page to have something to occupy my mind. Although my body thought it was 11:00 p.m. and time for bed, it was only 8:00 p.m. in California. I wanted to stay awake a little longer to try to beat jet lag at its own game.

And there, flashing like a sideways lightning bolt, was a message from Fatou. It had been months since I'd messaged my childhood friend, and I'd almost forgotten I had. Phoebe and I were now texting and talking on a regular basis, and my forays into social media had gotten less frequent.

Fatou apologized for not having responded sooner. She was the regional director for UNICEF in West and Central Africa and had spent the past three months traveling all over the region assessing their programs.

"But I'm so happy to be in touch after all these years! We've got so much to catch up on, and I've got big news. Let's set up a Skype chat soon," she'd written in French. Just reading her words made me smile.

Two days later, we were grinning at each other from twin sides of our screens.

"Sarapine!" Fatou exclaimed. I'd completely forgotten the

nickname she'd had for me—a combination of my name and *copine*, a French slang term for friend.

"Fatou! *Tu n'as pas changée*," I said. It was true, she looked exactly the same, with her broad, infectious smile and beautiful, unlined skin. I felt the years melt away as we fell into easy banter in our Fren-glish pidgin. We marveled that we'd both chosen similar careers and found out we'd both worked on the Ivory Coast within months of each other.

"If only ..." we both said simultaneously and laughed.

"So, Fatou, don't keep me waiting! What's your big news?"

"I'm getting married in a month!" She grinned, and I felt her joy in my own body.

"Wow, congratulations! Who's the lucky man?"

"His name is Ibrahim. He's a pediatrician. We met a few years ago when he was doing some consulting for UNICEF. We wanted to make recommendations on neonatal care in the region and needed a specialist's opinion. And I got much more than that!" she said, winking.

"That's wonderful. I'm so happy for you."

"Me too! It's such perfect timing that you contacted me now."

"I agree. I've had more than my fair share of serendipity recently," I said, remembering how Evelyn had also commented on the timing of my reaching out. "It's been pretty amazing."

"That's great. And I want you to come to my wedding ... if you can. It's in Southern Senegal where my mother's family is from, so it will be warm and dry," she said, as if I needed any coaxing.

"I'd love to! I'm on indefinite leave right now, so my time is flexible."

"Fabulous, then maybe you can stay even longer and help me with a project," she said, her face lighting up at the idea.

"What's the project?"

"Well, it's a long story. If you give me your email, I'll send you the concept paper. We're still working out the details, and of course, we will need to do a lot of fundraising." I learned she had both a master's in business administration and a master's in public health and had been the main fundraiser for a local NGO before joining UNICEF.

I was amazed by her accomplishments and told her so repeatedly. I also noticed that my nemesis remained silent throughout, allowing me so much more space to appreciate her success since I wasn't beating myself up over my failures.

"But in short, I'm tired of having my hands tied by UN bureaucracy, and Ibrahim is tired of the red tape and political infighting at the hospital where he works. We want to start our own neonatal clinic in rural Senegal. Through the work we've both done, we've found a number of places where there's inadequate support for babies born early or with complications who need long-term care."

"Wow, that sounds incredible!" I said, describing the NICU where I was volunteering.

"See, I knew you'd be perfect," Fatou grinned. "I'm quitting my job before the wedding. When we come back from our honeymoon, I want to spend all my time on setting up the clinic. Ibrahim will work until we're up and running, so we have some regular income."

"I'll definitely mull it over. Your project might just be the exact thing I'm looking for right now," I said, although, in my body, I was already getting a resounding yes. No mulling needed.

Sitting in Patrick's office the next week, I felt some bittersweetness, sensing it would be one of my last sessions, at least for a while.

"So that's the plan. Go to Senegal for the wedding and

then stay to help her get the clinic off the ground. I read their concept paper, and it's incredible. Our three skill sets seem very complementary, and I can already tell I will learn so much from Fatou and her husband."

"That sounds really perfect," Patrick said, beaming at me. "I hope you're very proud of yourself, Sarah. You've come such a long way since you left South Sudan."

"Honestly, I am. I'm surprised by how different I feel. So much more grounded within myself. I think I've managed to gather most of the missing puzzle pieces. At least for now. I'm sure there will be more along the way."

"I agree. Your whole demeanor is so much more settled. In the beginning, you were often fidgeting through the sessions, and you seemed poised to get up at a moment's notice."

"I probably was," I admitted, feeling a little embarrassed at how transparent I'd been.

"Sarah, what's something you've learned through this process?" he asked, and I smiled at the question. *Ever the teacher*, I thought. Letting the student find the lesson.

"I remember how my mantra those first three months was 'Pull it together.' Like my job was to find every single loose end and tie it in a tight, neat knot. It was so exhausting. Not to mention impossible," I said, and Patrick nodded in agreement.

"Looking back, I'm kind of flummoxed that I didn't know that then."

"Well, don't forget that both your parents heavily modeled the 'pushing through' strategy for you, which was then reinforced by the 'life or death' environments you chose to work in. Not to mention bosses like Jean-Claude." At the mention of my ex-supervisor's name, I felt my throat go dry. I swallowed, reminding myself that he no longer had any bearing on my life. And what a relief that was!

"That's true. Thankfully, I've discovered it's so much more

fun just to dance with the loose ends and trust that everything will work out."

"I like that. Dancing with the loose ends. That would make a great Hallmark card," he said with a grin. "Yes, it's much easier to follow our intuition and the flow of life than to try to control everything."

"That's for sure."

Back home, I emailed Deborah. I was finally ready for another hypnotherapy session.

Chapter Fifty
1926 - 27

Coming Home

Maggie

Arthur and Anna had prepared a feast to welcome me home.

"Mama insisted. Says nothing'd make 'er feel bettah," my brother explained.

Margaret, now almost eight, grabbed my hand and pulled me toward her room.

"I wanna show you my toys," she said, excited.

"I'd love that, but let me see if I can help your mother first."

Anna shook her head and shooed us out of the way. Once in her room, Margaret proudly showed me Polly, a doll her mother had made her from leftover material and yarn. Polly's body was made from a rich brown fabric that matched the curtains in the living room, the eyes and mouth were sewn in with black and red thread, and her hair was made of thick, black yarn. Her dress was the same deep blue as the one her owner was wearing.

"Do all of Polly's dresses match yours?"

Margaret grinned and nodded, proceeding to show me each pair.

"What a clever thing for your mother to do with the leftover fabric!" I exclaimed, impressed with my sister-in-law's ingenuity and talent and with how she provided her daughter with a Negro doll to play with. I'd never seen one in a store before.

When we all sat at the dinner table an hour later, I felt my whole body settle into the warmth of home. As I bit into a piece of perfectly crisp fried chicken, I looked at each one in turn. Roy, who was still tense around me but was beginning to soften a little. Arthur, Anna, and Margaret, and the tight love triangle they'd created. And Mama. Her body looked so small and frail, I wanted to weep. But the glow in her eyes as she looked at me told me she was still strong of spirit.

Home. The skylark hummed happily in my heart. At last. I'd spent the past decade trying to recapture that feeling. In the tracks we'd laid in the freshly turned earth. In Frank's arms. In the hearts of all the new friends I'd encountered along the way. Searching, always outside of myself. I wondered if it had been within me this whole time or if I'd needed to come home to find the feeling again. Either way, I was grateful it was back. That *I* was back.

New York hadn't been my full circle. This was.

Over the next months until her passing, I spent every moment I could by Mama's bedside. Arthur and I set up a cot in her room for me to sleep on. During this time, I considered bringing up the issue of who had fathered me in order to put that question to rest once and for all while I still could. But as I thought of how to raise the question, I realized I didn't need to know. My memories of Papa were enough. There was no sense in dredging up agonizing history that could not be changed.

One day near the end, as I gently stroked her hair, Mama looked into my eyes and said with a smile, "You done found yourself out dere, Maggie. Jus' like I said. Nobody lordin' over you now!"

"Thank you, Mama," I whispered back, as my eyes filled with tears, amazed she remembered after all these years. Of course, she'd been right all along. She knew long before I did.

We were all there when she released her last shuddering breath. I thought I felt the moment her spirit lifted—like a breeze brushing my cheek before returning to stillness. And then she was gone, leaving behind the shell of her body. Her last gift to us, perhaps, was to show us that death, when left to take its own course, could be peaceful.

In the time that followed her passing, I felt closer than ever to my family—united as we were in mourning Mama's death. My restless feet finally felt ready to root.

My memoir was published in May 1926. With the advance I'd gotten for it, the money I'd saved working with Alain Locke, and what I had left of Frank's parting gift to me, I bought a small house a few miles from Arthur's. It was in the woods, away from the town. A brook ran in back of it, and I could hear it gurgle from my kitchen window.

The first time I went to visit the house, I saw a deer drinking from the brook. She looked up at me briefly before bounding away. I took her presence as confirmation I was in the right place.

Following the relative success of my memoir, Shaw University, the Negro University in Raleigh, invited me to join the faculty as a professor of literature. I accepted, both to be able to pay my bills and to keep a toe in the human world.

I spent all my spare time in my house, fully embracing the aloneness I had once feared. I had tried to please others while still trying to honor my heart, and in so doing had split my heart down the middle.

Now was the time to choose myself. And that only seemed possible if I was somewhat removed from the world. I'd learned that as a water being, I ran dry if I followed others' currents. Only the ebbs and flows of my own heart could carry me to the full, oceanic thrumming of my soul.

Although my time in New York had discouraged me from trying to get any more of my work published—not wanting someone else to own my words—I wrote whenever I could. For myself. For the trees and the messages I decoded in the rustling of their leaves. For the raven and its omen of change. Having chosen my heart, my voice returned to me.

Freedom

I, the sky,
Claim ownership
Over the land below

I, the skylark,
Let the wind lift me
Wherever it will

I, the stone,
Polished so smooth
I shimmer in the sun

I, the stream,
Eddy around the rocks
Life has placed in my way

I, the crow,
King of the mystery
Unfolding before me

I, the acorn,
Burrow so deep into the earth
I begin to root here

I, the doe,
Allow my heart
To guide me home

I, freedom

One night, I dreamt that I was sitting by the brook, watching the deer lap the water with her graceful tongue. On the other side were my father and oldest brother. Andre was lying in the grass, letting the sun warm his face. Papa was looking at me, smiling.

Chapter Fifty-One

Wholeness

Sarah

Deborah hugged me like we were long-lost friends. I allowed myself to enjoy every second of the embrace, and to give it back in kind.

"How's Maggie?" she asked.

"Well, I'm not sure. That's what I wanted to find out. To be honest, the first session kind of freaked me out. I have been doing some reading and research to understand her better, but other than that my attention's been pretty much hijacked by family mysteries."

"Ah, yes, that can happen! And in the end, it's all connected."

"That's what my therapist says."

"Patrick? I remember him. Smart guy. Unusually open to the esoteric, at least for his profession." I agreed with her.

"I did just have an experience in Central Park where I felt her on the bench with me. Or rather, it felt like I was her, sitting on the bench. There was a man next to me. I can't even explain it, but it felt very similar to how it was during our first session when I first encountered her."

"Wow, that's amazing. I can't wait to explore more with you, Sarah."

"Oh, and I found this stone in the park, too, which also felt somehow connected to her."

"It's beautiful!" She exclaimed. Her eyes grew big as she turned it over and saw the streak of cobalt. She gave it back to me saying that holding it during the session might help me connect more deeply to Maggie.

"Shall we get the party started then, so we can see if there's a message for you?" she asked with a smile as I settled into the recliner chair.

This time, I felt no resistance to the relaxation. By now, every cell in my body was primed for going deep. As Deborah counted me down, I had the vision long before she got to ten.

"I'm Maggie … I'm in the forest again … But it's not the same one. I see a house, my house, it seems. There's a stream nearby. I see a deer."

"Does the deer have a message for you?"

"I'm not sure, hold on … 'Welcome home,' is what I'm getting."

"Wonderful," Deborah's voice floated in. "And what are you, as Maggie, feeling?"

"It's a little mixed. On the one hand, I feel relieved. I've had one foot in one world and the other foot in another for so long—I was really feeling torn inside."

"What are the two worlds?"

"I think one is the world of people and achievements. Of trying to please others and losing myself in the process. The other is … honoring my heart, maybe? My inner world. Finding my true voice. I only seem to be able to access that in nature, surrounded by animals, away from people."

"And what is the other thing you're feeling, besides relief?" Deborah asked, guiding me back to the beginning of the thread.

"On the other hand, I feel sad. Alone. Not wanting to have to choose."

"To choose between what?" I pondered her question, trying to find words for what I was sensing.

"Between being true to myself and having deep connections with others, I think."

"Is there anything else Maggie wants you to know?" As Deborah asked the question, I felt Maggie separate from me so that we were two but sharing one heart.

"She wants me to know that *I* don't have to choose between myself and others. She says it doesn't have to be an either/or. That if I heal this for myself, I'm also healing it for her, since we are one soul … And that the stone will help me remember, in case I forget."

As I said the words, I felt waves of tingling, vibrant energy ripple throughout my being. I miraculously felt no compunction to dissect the meaning of the message.

After the session, as I got ready to bike home, I remembered a community hot tub Phoebe had told me about.

"It's in this lady's backyard, and only women can have the code to get in. Although it's 'clothing optional,' really everybody goes naked. The water is super hot, but you get used to it. I recommend going during the day on a weekday when there are only a few people. You'll see, it's pretty magical," she'd said.

Twenty minutes later, I entered a wooden archway trellised with vines and walked down a narrow passageway to a gate. I punched in the code Phoebe had given me and exhaled deeply when a green light and whirring sound informed me it had worked.

The gate opened upon a huge redwood tree, in which a large iridescent shell was nestled, and I felt like I'd entered Narnia. An uneven stone path led me to the hot tub. Steaming water poured from a spigot into what looked like a giant wooden barrel. To the left was a little cabin to change and shower in. Thankfully, nobody else was there. I quickly divested myself of my clothes, rinsed off, and gingerly dipped a toe in. Phoebe was right; it was scalding hot! I grabbed my towel and decided to explore the garden first.

A bronze mermaid guarded the entrance to the covered hot tub area. She arched her back ecstatically as she emerged from the ocean. Her nose, shoulders, and breasts were polished gold green by human touch. I stepped onto a wooden yoga platform, then down onto wood chips that lined the garden floor. A pair of flamingos were courting next to a trio of young redwoods. A small ceramic unicorn peeked into a potted plant.

After sitting on a wooden bench for a few minutes, contemplating a smiling Buddha with his arms outstretched to the sky, I decided to brave the hot water once more. Rinsing the wood chips off my feet, I went in cold turkey. Or boiling turkey, as the case may be. I gasped as the steaming water submerged my body. I felt my muscles brace, shudder, and then let go.

As I immersed myself completely underwater, I thought of my father and his father. Valda, Ada, and Evelyn. My mother and her mother. Maggie. All my wounded inner children. When I emerged a moment later, gasping for air, I felt a wholeness I'd never experienced. A profound sense of peace. I was going to be okay; I knew without a shadow of a doubt. My heart was humming, elated to be free from the cage I'd kept it in for so long.

A crow cawed and swooped down. It landed a few feet from me and stared. I smiled back.

Just then, a few drops started pelting the ground. I hadn't even noticed the dark cloud that had rolled in. I got out, and—without any hesitation—began dancing, naked, in the rain.

An image of Mariol twirling his sister in the first downpour of the season flashed before my eyes. I felt the familiar twinge of pain but also something else. A lightness. I could almost feel his presence with me—if only in my own heart.

"See Mariol, I did get more loose," I said, laughing.

Chapter Fifty-Two
1975

Beckonings

Maggie

My body slows and grows heavy, just as my soul lightens and readies itself to depart. My senses have already begun their transition. The sharp contours of my vision have dimmed into shapes and shadows. Sounds are muted, and I am starting to hear the voices of my loved ones waiting on the other side.

I think I discern Papa's deep timbre ringing out, and my heart aches. Words—the portal through which I once drew others into my soul—have become slippery eels that slither just out of reach when I need them the most. As I prepare myself for my next adventure, I have learned to surrender and let the words come to me when they choose to.

The Other Side

Silence beckons to me
From the other side.

Words
Slip away,
Beyond my grasp,

Calling me
To follow them.

A veil drapes
Over this life.
The vibrant blues
Of the brook
Have muted to gray.

My niece's laughter
Is a muffled footstep
To my ears.

Instead, I hear
The long-departed
Chiming my summons
Like church bells
Calling parishioners
Home.

My aching fingers
Let go
Of the struggle
And prepare
For the journey.

This last poem will have to stay on the tip of my tongue because my gnarled fingers can no longer wield a pen, and I will have forgotten it by the time I write it down anyway.

The past few decades of my life have flown by. Oh, how time speeds up when you age. I remember when a year felt like a lifetime. This year, they threw a party for me to celebrate my seventy-fifth birthday.

"You're three-quarters of a century old!" my great-nephews and nieces said in amazement. I saw the century in, and I almost saw it out, though the next twenty-five years will have to proceed without me.

My nieces and nephews and all their children were there. Arthur has been gone for six years now, and Roy for three, but their wives were there with me—the women holding the candle for our generation. Their children made poster boards showing some of the highlights of what I've lived through. Jim Crow, two world wars, the Great Depression, the civil rights movement. The first man on the moon. Everyone fussed all around me as I basked in stillness.

Ah, stillness. A great luxury, granted by my age, that I delight in whenever I can. A young one sat in my lap, and I sank into the feeling of his small body nestled into mine until he squirmed off me and onto more interesting adventures.

Yes, what a time it has been. I watched every one of Dr. King's speeches on my black-and-white TV in my house in the woods and cried for days after the Civil Rights Act passed. Tears of joy and sorrow. The what-ifs threatened to crowd me with regret (what if Frank and I had lived forty years later?), but I kept them at bay.

Frank and I never did officially divorce. He died in 1941. He called me—via Edna and Lewis—to his deathbed, and I came. I hadn't seen him since he left me, and I admit it was a shock to see his emaciated body. Face sunken, eyes tinged with yellow. Liver cirrhosis, I was told by a kind doctor. Frank's eyes looked at me, proud and pleading at the same time. I nodded. I knew. I understood. All was forgiven, if not forgotten. I held his hand, and he heaved a few jagged breaths before his heartbeat flatlined on the hospital monitor. I never remarried nor had children of my own, though a few men—and some women—warmed their way into my bed, if not into my heart.

A few years after I moved to North Carolina, the country was hit by the Great Depression. Those were lean years, but between my teaching, Arthur's carpentry skills, Roy's blacksmithing, and Anna's green thumb, we fared better than most. We shared what we could with our neighbors. Roy married his employer's daughter, and they had one son named Andrew, after his dead uncle, who reminded me so much of Andre he could bring tears to my eyes with one tilt of his eyebrows.

The Second World War ravaged our community. Edna's brother—the one who survived World War I—lost both his sons twenty-five years later. Several young men in our community were killed, and many others came back missing pieces of themselves—both literally and figuratively.

I'd had enough of human folly and decided I preferred the fantasy of my own imagination. I retired after twenty years of teaching and retreated even more completely into myself. I had someone bring me groceries, cook, and clean. I emerged occasionally for family gatherings. Margaret and her children were the only ones who visited on a regular basis.

I never published another word. My memoir eventually went out of print—not helped by the fact that I refused to give talks or interviews. I kept writing, however. For myself and for the natural world that surrounded me.

Being a hermit gave me a mystical allure for some. People from town would seek me out, as though I were an oracle who would tell them their fortune. Occasionally, I did hear the wind whispering some wisdom in my ear, but I found that if I shared those messages with the eagerly awaiting faces, more people came. And more after them. Fearing that I would lose myself again in the presence of others wanting something from me, I began to keep the communications to myself. Until, eventually, I stopped hearing them, and I was left alone.

In the late 1960s—inspired by an article Margaret shared

with me about Buddhist monks who spent months making what they called mandalas only to erase them when they were done—I decided to do something similar. That night, I made a big bonfire in the woods and burned every one of my notebooks in a solemn ceremony.

As I near my death, I sometimes wish I hadn't. To have a legacy for the next generation, something to be remembered by.

Josie, I am proud to say, became the first African American woman to earn a PhD in mathematics in 1939, and came to visit me as often as she could. She never married, and on one of her later visits, she told me she liked women and not men, though she never told her parents.

Edna was diagnosed with cancer in the late 1940s, and I temporarily came out of seclusion to help Josie care for her in the last few months of her life. A few years later, I heard from Josie that Lewis had remarried a schoolteacher and moved with her to Florida, where his youngest sister lived.

Although Alain Locke and I lost touch after I left, I reached out to him during my stay with Edna and Josie, and we continued a sporadic correspondence for the next few years. He retired from Howard in 1953 and died the following year. On June 9, 1954, to be exact. The obituary I read made a point of the fact that it was three weeks after the Supreme Court's decision in favor of the plaintiffs in Brown v. Board of Education.

I would like to think that this ruling enabled him to find peace in the last weeks of his life when his heart disease finally got the best of him. I did not go to the memorial service, not wanting to face all my old acquaintances.

Mabel and I exchanged annual greeting cards for about a decade. Last I heard, she and Barnaby had four children, and she had begun painting in earnest. Years after our correspondence had petered out, I saw an article about one of her exhibits that had gotten considerable acclaim.

Sadie divorced Benjamin after she discovered he had had an affair with one of his students. When she visited me with Angeline (Thomas was apprenticing with a French sculptor in Paris) a few years later, she had opened her own line of clothing in their neighborhood and was thriving. Angeline was a shy and chubby fifteen-year-old, and Sadie told me she had taken their divorce very hard. They ended up moving to Paris to be with Thomas, and I lost touch with them too, although I heard Sadie's line did very well there.

And so here we are. I have meandered my way back to a present that feels less real than the times I am recounting. The wisdom I have to impart to the world has run its course. I am an empty vessel waiting patiently for my time to be carried away. I am ready.

My main regret, besides the dissolution of my marriage, is that I didn't get to share more of my inner life with the world. That I felt I had to disconnect from humans completely in order to choose my own heart. Perhaps, if there's a next time, I can have both.

Chapter Fifty-Three

The Letter

Jean-Claude

Jean-Claude Perrin sipped his coffee, staring at the pigeons out the window of his Brussels apartment. He never knew what to do with himself in this time between missions. He should be resting, or so he'd been told, but he didn't even really know what that meant anymore. Go for long walks? Get an overpriced massage? Write a travel memoir?

He moved his attention to the photo of his father that hung above his kitchen table. It showed him in his late thirties in full military garb, mustache arched up, looking as stern and smug as ever five years or so before he died a decorated war hero.

Jean-Claude wondered idly, not for the first time, why he hadn't taken the picture down. In the beginning, he'd probably kept it up as a reminder of some kind, a warning not to become like his old man—cruel and abusive. Narcissistic. He told himself that while he might have inherited his father's apartment, that was all he'd ever take of him. Later, it was more in defiance. To show Major Perrin that *he* was saving lives, not taking them.

Now? Who knew? In the end, was he really that different? The thought edged around the corners of his mind, but he quickly pushed it away.

He heard the creak and thud of the mail being pushed through his front door's thin metal slot. As he sorted through the various envelopes and junk mail, he noticed a letter that had been forwarded by his organization's headquarters. He looked at the sender's name. Sarah Baum. Berkeley, California. He frowned. His mind struggled to connect the name—decontextualized—to a face … or a place.

Then it came back to him. The American nurse in South Sudan. Thin. Pretty. Opinionated. She'd reminded him a lot of himself in the beginning, although he would never have told her that—until she'd gone soft on that boy who died, and she'd fallen apart. That boy's face still haunted his nights sometimes, he had to admit. One of his many failures to save a life…

What could she possibly have to say to him? If she'd wanted to file a complaint, she would have done it through the organization.

He opened the letter with mild curiosity and a slight bracing of his shoulders.

> *Cher Jean-Claude,*
>
> *If you're reading this, it means that by some miracle this letter has reached you. I'm sure you're surprised to hear from me.*
>
> *To be honest, I'm a little surprised to be writing to you. I didn't think I'd ever want to be in contact with you after South Sudan.*
>
> *But I wanted to express my gratitude. If you hadn't sent me home and then recommended a second psych evaluation for me, I'd be doing the same thing I always did: escaping my life through work.*
>
> *Thanks to you, I've had six months to do some pretty deep soul-searching. I'll spare you the details, but I think*

one of the things I learned might be of benefit to you too.

Caring is not a liability, as you and my upbringing had me believe. It's not a deficiency or a weakness to hide or overcome. It's a superpower. It's my superpower. I mean, without caring, what's the point? Why would we even do what we do?

And being hard, cynical, and guarded is not the same as being strong. Sometimes those feel necessary for survival, especially when we're young. But in the end, they just become prisons for our own hearts.

In any case, I wish you well on your path, and I hope that this letter may provide some food for thought. And if not, at least you know that in this moment, someone halfway around the globe is thinking of you with gratitude.

Sincerely,
Sarah

Chapter Fifty-Four
Rural Senegal, 2014

Denouement

Sarah

Diop and I were crouching by the creek, looking for frogs. Behind us, a tall palm tree swayed in the breeze. One of my hands hovered near his two-year-old body to make sure he didn't fall in, although the water here was quite shallow. He squealed as he spotted one—a running frog with brown stripes down its back—and I laughed at his delight.

"Sarah! Diop! Where are you?" Fatou called in French.

"Over here," I responded in English. We'd been doing our best to raise him trilingual (his father spoke to him in Wolof whenever possible), and we'd all been amazed by his developing brain's ability to sort through and compartmentalize all three. But truth be told, we almost liked it better when he mixed them up—the result adorable and often hilarious.

"I knew I'd find you together," Fatou said, laughing as she picked her son up. He whined that he wanted to stay with me.

"You love your Auntie Sarah, don't you?" she asked, and I beamed. The feeling was mutual. "Good thing I made her your godmother, huh? That way she can never leave us!"

Diop gurgled his approval.

I laughed. "There's no chance of that! Unfortunately for

you, you can never get rid of me," I teased back.

"Good. That means she'll still be here when you wake up from your nap," she said, kissing her son's eyelids, drooping despite his protests that he wasn't tired.

Once they were gone, I lay down on the grass and closed my eyes. After three years of almost nonstop work, we finally had enough help to each get a day off a week, and today was my day. The free time was both welcome and a little bewildering.

An image floated before my eyes of the very first moment I saw Diop twenty-six months and three days before, which simultaneously felt like yesterday and a lifetime ago.

Fatou had been in labor for thirteen hours and was exhausted. Ibrahim and I were playing tag team to keep her spirits up. And then, after a final, desperate push and yell on his mother's part, his head crowned. I saw the black fuzz of his hair matted down with the liquid he'd been bathing in for nine months. Ibrahim and I cheered and proceeded to coax the rest of his beautiful round face and perfect little body into our arms.

Although I'd attended more births than I could count, this time felt like the first, only infinitely better because I had full permission to fall in love with him. And fall in love I did. In the beginning, I tried to maintain some distance to allow Ibrahim and Fatou some space, but they insisted on me being part of the parental team.

"More love—and free babysitting! Who wouldn't want that?" Ibrahim teased. From the start, his ease and grace helped me feel like a welcomed member of the team and then the family.

"I was raised by an army of women, and I want the same for my children," Fatou said, adding that she planned on having as many babies as time and her body allowed. She was an only child like me and, because of that, felt like she was expected to be a mini adult from a young age. She didn't want that for Diop.

The buzz and sting of a mosquito on my cheek pulled me out of memory land. I took the mosquito repellent from my bag, sprayed my hand, and slathered some onto the exposed parts of my skin, hoping that the extra coating would keep them away this time.

I looked around, surveying the fruits of our labor. My heart swelled with pride and gratitude at having been given a second chance at doing something meaningful, this time in the community.

I really *didn't* have to choose.

"We did it," I said aloud, knowing the weight those words carried.

In reality, that first year, we weren't sure we would. There were so many unexpected obstacles, not least of all getting the administrative go-ahead. Without the help of our mothers, our project probably would have tanked before it had the chance to get off its feet. But Fatou's mother, Amina, used her considerable political leverage (she worked in the Ministry of Agriculture, and her ex-husband was a diplomat) to help cut through the bureaucratic red tape. Mine called in favors from every hospital she'd worked with to collect some essential medical supplies and equipment. Not to mention that they both made sizeable donations. In the process, the two women became good friends—much to Fatou's and my delight (and surprise, since we'd originally thought they might be more like oil and water).

For the last year and a half, my mother, now retired, had been coming every few months, staying for a couple of weeks. At her suggestion, we scheduled non-emergency surgeries during her stay. She was a different person when she worked—she really came to life—and seeing her in her element further deepened my understanding of her. In my last conversation with her, she casually mentioned she'd be bringing a "gentleman friend" on her next visit, which was the subject of much speculation and titillation between Fatou, Amina, and me.

In the last year, our reputation spread. Thankfully, volunteers started showing up out of nowhere to meet the increased need. And five months prior, Pam joined our team. I couldn't believe our luck. I'd stayed in touch with her after I left the United States. When things were starting to take off, she decided to join us (following the many hints I'd dropped), so she could be "closer to home, but not actually home," as she put it. From what I'd gleaned, she didn't exactly get along with her family in Nigeria.

Hiba and Okot were also talking about joining us, at least for a little while. Their three IVF attempts were unsuccessful, and they said they needed something meaningful to pour their energy into. I tried not to be too pushy, but I really hoped they came to complete our team. Even Hiba's joke that she could "see if Jean-Claude wants to join too" didn't dampen my excitement at the possibility.

At last, tired of reminiscing about the past and daydreaming of the future, I decided to go to the clinic to see if they could use my help, even though I knew Pam and Ibrahim were likely to shoo me away and tell me to go rest.

As I entered the airy, thatched-roof building, with its surround sound of bird calls, I thought:

Here we are, following our dreams.

Each of us dancing with the loose ends in our own way.

Chapter Fifty-Five
Liminal Space, 1976

On Soul's Door

I am so weary. I am not ready to go back. I have been through this too many times.

Just let me rest here a little longer, I plead. I am weightless, floating. Without a physical body, the hungry ghosts have no power over me. I relish this state between lives. All is space—expansive. There is no form to tie me down to my needs, no ego to defend or protect.

I ask why I can't remember this when I go back except as fleeting moments of peace. They say it is my task to remember. That I must return to put my hungry ghosts to rest. If only it were so simple.

Every time I return, they only seem to grow stronger and multiply with new mistakes and grievances. There is no end to their hunger. I can hear them now, waiting for me.

But my guides say it is time. There is a white family, they tell me, with a baby girl in the forming named Sarah. The parents are affluent and liberal. The father is a Jewish lawyer who has spent his life defending civil rights.

A residue of my last life balks at their whiteness. "That's all I need!" I can hear Maggie saying.

But from where I am now, I know it makes no difference. I have been all colors of the rainbow, all manner of beings. As a salamander, I slithered in water, flexible and spineless. As a skylark, I rode the waves of the wind. As a human, I have been the victim and the oppressor. And each time, I must return to heal the wounds that scar my soul, and to right any wrongs I may have committed.

Affluent. White. I like the idea of not having to struggle so hard this time. All right. I guess I'm as ready as I'll ever be. If I had a body, I would heave a big sigh as I prepare for the descent.

It's time.

Author's Note

The birth of *The Unbroken Horizon* came in 2011, during a healing workshop. Suddenly, I had the sense of being in a forest. I saw flashes of white hoods and torches. I felt dizzy and nauseated. The images and feelings followed me for days until I finally sat down at my computer and started writing what ended up being the outline of Maggie's life. Throughout the process of bringing the novel to life, I used meditation and automatic writing to access more of her story.

Intensive research fleshed out the details of what was happening during that time period, and I wove that into what I had sensed about her. I became fascinated by the anti-lynching legislation, and the fact that after four years of promising debate Congress had effectively filibustered it. I was outraged that—at the time I started the novel—lynching was still not illegal in the United States. Maggie's story is set in the context of Reconstruction and the backlash of Jim Crow laws, and she was part of the Great Migration of six million Black people between 1910 and 1970 who left rural Southern towns for urban Northern cities. World War I and the promises made and broken to Black soldiers was important to understanding what was dubbed the Red Summer of 1919.

Scouring Howard University yearbook photos and captions from the 1920s gave me a sense of what the campus might have been like and who was teaching at the time. Alain Locke immediately captivated my imagination through his writings and biography, and I knew that had they met, he and Maggie would have gotten along famously. I tried to be faithful to the dates and events of his life and what I sensed of his personality.

Even though all the dialogue and the main characters (except for Alain Locke) are fictional, newspaper headlines, descriptions of the pamphlets and placards at the 1917 march, and other quotes from speeches all came from archival footage. Real historical figures featured in the novel include Mary Church Terrell, Marcus Garvey, Duke Ellington, Charlotte Mason, and the Harlem Renaissance writers featured in the New Negro Anthology. I should note that Martha Euphemia Lofton Haynes (not Josie, who is a fictional character) was the first Black woman to earn a PhD in mathematics in 1943.

The novel, the world around us, and I have evolved quite a bit in the decade or so of writing and rewriting it. I experienced the start of the Black Lives Matter movement in the context of the research I was doing, recognizing how little the basic inequities and racism deeply embedded in the fabric of our society have changed. When the COVID-19 pandemic started in 2020, I was startled to find the number of similarities with the Spanish influenza epidemic a century before.

I wrote the first draft of the novel mostly in a bubble of research and deep meditative conversations with the Maggie voice that was coming to me. I had a sense of Sarah's story from the beginning, but I soon found I had to write Maggie's story first and add in the nurse's chapters later.

Knowing I was not qualified to write some of the speech patterns in Maggie's chapters (in particular for Mama), being white and not having grown up in the United States, I reached out to specialists in African American Vernacular English (AAVE) early on. The few who responded didn't feel equipped to help with the language used in that time period. My sensitivity reader and Black editor helped me make it as authentic as possible, with the understanding that none of us are experts or were alive at that time.

Although not autobiographical by any means, the broad strokes of my life informed Sarah's story. My parents were nothing like Sarah's. Mine were artistic, literary, very loving, and financially struggling. They met in (and never left) Paris, and that is where my sister and I were born and raised. My father died of a sudden heart attack when I was eight, the day after my mother had gone on a trip, and my sister and I found him. After my mother's sudden death seventeen years later, we discovered a box of his journal and writings. Since we never knew anyone in our father's lineage of Latvian Jews (they had all died before we were born, or when we were very young), I spent years doing ancestral research and healing some of those wounds of displacement and persecution.

The first decade of my professional career was focused on international humanitarian work in Nepal, Indonesia, the Middle East (West Bank, Lebanon, Syria), as well as short missions later on to Pakistan and Somalia. On a Fulbright Scholarship, I researched a system of bonded labor prevalent in Nepal at the time. After my scholarship ended, I got involved in the movement that led to the system's abolition. When I returned five years later, I discovered that while the system had changed in name, since the conditions that led to the inequities hadn't, their lives weren't much better, and in some ways were more precarious. While the era and cultural contexts are very different, I believe that experience helped me better understand what Maggie and her family might be living through. Sarah's description of her time in the West Bank (minus the affair with the doctor) were taken straight from the journal I kept when I was there. My sister did similar work, and spent a year directing a project in South Sudan. Her photos and accounts helped bring those chapters to life.

Burnout and health issues led me to decide to make a

change in careers. In 2010, I moved to the Bay Area in California to study holistic healing modalities and establish a private practice there. My healing journey and that of my clients informed some of Sarah's evolution towards wholeness. The nature here (and in particular the waterfalls and redwoods) have been an integral part of my healing, and some of the passages in the novel are meant as a love letter to my adopted home.

When I emerged from my bubble with my first draft in hand in 2019 (having had no formal training in writing), I discovered the OwnVoices literary movement, and the controversy surrounding white writers writing nonwhite voices. In my internal inquiry of whether I had the right to tell this story and my debate over whether to publish the novel or not, what I kept hearing was "what gives you the right *not* to." More than the writer, I feel like I've been granted guardianship over this precious story, and I hope to have done it justice. I appreciate all the support I received to make the voice, the story, and the language as authentic and sensitive as possible. Any content that isn't is entirely my responsibility. I'm open to questions, feedback and dialogue about the novel.

I hope Sarah and Maggie's journeys have inspired and/or touched you in some way.

Further Reading

This is not an exhaustive list by any means, but is a starting point for further reading.

For Maggie's Story:

- *A Colored Woman in a White World*, by Mary Church Terrell
- *Crusade for Justice*, by Ida B. Wells
- *Red Summer: The Summer of 1919 and the Awakening of Black America*, by Cameron McWhirter
- *The New Negro: Voices of the Harlem Renaissance*, edited by Alain Locke
- *Alain L. Locke: The Biography of a Philosopher*, by Leonard Harris and Charles Molesworth
- *Harlem Renaissance: Five Novels of the 1920s*, Edited by Rafia Zafar
- http://www.naacp.org/pages/naacp-history-anti-lynching-bill

For Sarah's Story:

- *The Body Keeps the Score: Brain, Mind, and Body in the Healing of Trauma*, by Bessel Van Der Kolk, M.D.
- *It Didn't Start with You: How Inherited Family Trauma Shapes Who We Are and How to End The Cycle*, by Mark Wolynn

- *My Grandmother's Hands: Racialized Trauma and the Pathway to Mending Our Hearts and Bodies* by Resmaa Menakem
- *Many Lives, Many Masters,* by Brian Weiss

Other Resources:

- *Post Traumatic Slave Syndrome: America's Legacy of Enduring Injury and Healing,* by Joy DeGry, Ph.D.
- *How to Be an Antiracist,* by Ibram X. Kendi

Questions for Discussion

1) What do you think the title *The Unbroken Horizon* refers to? Is it the same or different for Maggie and Sarah?

2) In the first chapter, Mariol says to Sarah: "You need to get more loose." In what way does his death precipitate her healing journey? Do you agree with Sarah's assessment at the end that she did, indeed, get "more loose"? If so, how?

3) In chapter four, Mama says to Maggie: "I think you gon' find yo'self out there, who you be when nobody lordin' over you." Do you agree with Mama's statement towards the end that: "You done found yourself out dere, Maggie. Jus' like I said"? If so, in what ways did she find herself? Were there ways she lost herself along the way?

4) Sarah begins her healing journey by connecting with her wounded inner child. Did any of the wounds and/or limiting beliefs she uncovered resonate with you? If so, in what way? If not, what wounds and beliefs do you think you carry? What would you want to say to your inner child as reassurance?

5) Maggie makes a bargain to herself in the wild: "Just let me survive and get to safety. And I promise I won't ask for anything more." While this mantra gives her strength to keep moving forward, later on—once she's safe and her circumstances have changed—she needs to let go of her

bargain to be free to follow her own path. Do you have survival strategies that once served you, but are now holding you back? Did the book give you any ideas on how you might release those?

6) After Sarah "fails" the mental health assessment, she starts exploring her inner nemesis with Patrick. Do you have an inner critic who holds you back? If so, what are some of the things that voice says to you? What is the voice's intention for you (such as keeping you safe or motivating you to do better)? Are there other ways to meet that intention that might be more nourishing?

7) It is implied that Maggie's biological father is not the same as the siblings'. What impact does this have on her?

8) In what ways (either explicit or implicit) do you think Sarah and Maggie were impacted by their respective parents' and ancestors' trauma? What are the wounds of your lineage, if any, that you think might still be affecting you today?

9) Chapter fifty-three is written from Jean-Claude's point of view. Did that change your opinion of him at all? What did you think of Sarah getting the last word with him?

10) In her letter to Jean-Claude, Sarah wrote: "Caring is not a liability, as you and my upbringing had me believe. It's not a deficiency or a weakness to hide or overcome. It's a superpower. It's my superpower." Do you agree that caring is one of her superpowers? If so, in what way did she evolve into this realization throughout the novel? What do you think are Maggie's superpowers?

11) In what ways do you think Maggie and Sarah also carry the resilience and strengths of their ancestors with them?

What gifts of your ancestors do you think you might have inherited?

12) The final Sarah chapter is titled "Denouement,' which in French literally means "the untying." Which jumbled threads (if any) does the chapter untangle, and which loose ends are left for the reader to dance with?

13) Did any of the historical events described in *The Unbroken Horizon* strike a cord with you in some way? If so, which ones, and how?

14) What do you think about the connection between Maggie and Sarah as revealed in the last chapter? Had you guessed beforehand? Did it color how you viewed the rest of the novel, in hindsight? Is this something you believe in or are skeptical of?

Acknowledgments

First and foremost, I'd like to thank Laura, sister extraordinaire. For the photos and descriptions of the bush hospital in South Sudan. For reading every single permutation of the novel from beginning to end. For encouraging me to continue even when I wanted to give up.

A heartfelt thanks to Selene and Elana for being Maggie's Godmothers, and for reading every chapter in our writing group, once a month, out of order, one character at a time. I would never have finished that first draft without you. Maggie thanks you too, since our encounters pulled her out of the fifteen-month freeze she'd been in when I'd decided to give up. To Elana, for sharing so openly your experiences visiting Auschwitz and with CORE. To all my amazing friends (you know who you are) who read the various versions of my novel and gave me invaluable feedback. To Sue Moon, for the great prompts that inspired some of my favorite paragraphs of the novel.

To Tara Creel, my wonderful editor, for helping me understand about character arc and development and finding the perfect place to start Sarah's story. For lifting me up every time I felt discouraged. To Dan Ross and Surja Jessup, for the deep hypnotherapy sessions that helped release some of my writer's blocks and connect on another level to Sarah and Maggie. I'm grateful to Carol for all the information on being a baby cuddler in a NICU, and to Charlie for the EMDR expertise.

To D. Ann Williams of Tessera Editorial, thank you for providing such a thorough and thoughtful sensitivity read both before and after the major rewrite. Thank you for your historical knowledge, feedback, and help with Mama's speech patterns. To Ashley Elizabeth, poet extraordinaire and beautiful human, thanks for helping with Maggie's voice as a poet and for the thoughtful overall edit of the manuscript.

I'm grateful to the whole team at Atmosphere Press for your support in every step of the process (editing, incredible cover design, sensitivity consultation, design process, marketing and more). Without your expert advice, my book would never have seen the light of day. To Malcolm and the fabulous group of writers you've gathered around you. To the #WritingCommunity of the Twitterverse, thanks for showing me how supportive and helpful the platform can be when used well. And to Jessica Bonin, my amazing virtual assistant, for giving me so much behind-the-scenes support from A-to-Z.

I'm grateful to my parents, whose love of words and travel led to my bicultural upbringing in Paris, surrounded by books, art, and culture. Both the gifts you imparted to me, and the pain of your early loss and my healing journey permeate the novel.

To the healers who helped me on my personal growth journey (you are too numerous to name). And a special thanks to all of my clients who have trusted me with your healing. A part of each of you is represented in Sarah, and I feel so blessed I get to do this work every day.

About Atmosphere Press

Atmosphere Press is an independent, full-service publisher for excellent books in all genres and for all audiences. Learn more about what we do at atmospherepress.com.

We encourage you to check out some of Atmosphere's latest releases, which are available at Amazon.com and via order from your local bookstore:

Icarus Never Flew 'Round Here, by Matt Edwards
COMFREY, WYOMING: Maiden Voyage, by Daphne Birkmeyer
The Chimera Wolf, by P.A. Power
Umbilical, by Jane Kay
The Two-Blood Lion, by Nick Westfield
Shogun of the Heavens: The Fall of Immortals, by I.D.G. Curry
Hot Air Rising, by Matthew Taylor
30 Summers, by A.S. Randall
Delilah Recovered, by Amelia Estelle Dellos
A Prophecy in Ash, by Julie Zantopoulos
The Killer Half, by JB Blake
Ocean Lessons, by Karen Lethlean
Unrealized Fantasies, by Marilyn Whitehorse
The Mayari Chronicles: Initium, by Karen McClain
Squeeze Plays, by Jeffrey Marshall
JADA: Just Another Dead Animal, by James Morris
Hart Street and Main: Metamorphosis, by Tabitha Sprunger
Karma One, by Colleen Hollis
Ndalla's World, by Beth Franz

About the Author

JENNY BRAV was born and raised in Paris, France, to American parents who instilled in her a love of words, a sensitivity to the human condition, and a passion for travel. She did humanitarian work in Asia and the Middle East before settling in Oakland, California, where she practices holistic healing. In her spare time, she writes poetry, dabbles in vegan cooking, chases waterfalls, and caters to her calico cat's whims. *The Unbroken Horizon* is her first novel. It brings together the themes that are close to her heart, especially how we find wholeness within our wounding.

www.jennybrav.com
Twitter: @brav_jenny
Instagram: @jennybravwriter

Milton Keynes UK
Ingram Content Group UK Ltd.
UKHW010013180823
427072UK00014B/175/J